HE

SAID

HE

WOULD

BE

LATE

HE
SAID
HE
WOULD
BE
LATE

JUSTINE SULLIVAN

HENRY HOLT AND COMPANY

NEW YORK

Henry Holt and Company
Publishers since 1866
120 Broadway
New York, New York 10271
www.henryholt.com

Library of Congress Cataloging-in-Publication Data

Names: Sullivan, Justine, author.
Title: He said he would be late / Justine Sullivan.
Description: First edition. | New York : Henry Holt and Company, 2023.
Identifiers: LCCN 2022052732 (print) | LCCN 2022052733 (ebook) |
    ISBN 9781250842855 (hardcover) | ISBN 9781250842862 (ebook)
Subjects: LCSH: Marriage—Fiction. | Spouses—Fiction. | LCGFT: Psychological
    fiction. | Thrillers (Fiction) | Novels.
Classification: LCC PS3619.U4344 H4 2023 (print) | LCC PS3619.U4344
    (ebook) | DDC 813/.6—dc23/eng/20221121
LC record available at https://lccn.loc.gov/2022052732
LC ebook record available at https://lccn.loc.gov/2022052733

Our books may be purchased in bulk for promotional, educational, or business use. Please
contact your local bookseller or the Macmillan Corporate and Premium Sales Department at
(800) 221-7945, extension 5442, or by e-mail at MacmillanSpecialMarkets@macmillan.com.

First Edition 2023

Designed by Kelly S. Too

Printed in the United States of America

1   3   5   7   9   10   8   6   4   2

HE
SAID
HE
WOULD
BE
LATE

Liz lies motionless, her head in her arms, her face in the pillow.

She feels bone-tired, though she never left the house today.

Each time she hears the light crunch of tires on gravel, she lifts her head, listening.

Out the bedroom window, a dog barks a greeting to its owner.

It isn't him.

Head returns to pillow. His pillow. She uses it when he isn't there.

It's starting to smell like her hair: eucalyptus and lemon. All wrong.

"What time will you be home?"

She says it to herself to hear a human voice. An adult. Someone reasonable.

Crickets chirp in return.

"Well, he did say he'd be late."

Liz lifts a pale arm in the dark. Turns it this way and that, making shapes on the wall.

The night grows long. Sideways. The shapes become monstrous.

If only she could fall asleep . . .

CHAPTER 1

Our kitchen, like everything else in our house, is white. White Shaker cabinets, quartz countertops, ceramic backsplash, stainless-steel appliances.

"They look striking against the dark wood floors," my husband said when we toured the house a few years ago.

It still doesn't seem like my home, though I search for the feeling like a child who's lost her toy.

"Is it here?" I wonder, as I roll out dough for cinnamon buns on the white marble island, my daughter blessedly asleep in her crib.

"What about there?" I think, planting zinnias in the flower beds beside our stone walkway in a late-afternoon glow that turns my bare shoulders pink.

Sometimes, I catch a glimmer of it when it's just before dawn and I'm alone in our backyard, holding a steaming cup of coffee, listening to the chirping chorus in the cedar and maple trees, but it usually fizzles out by the time I've padded back indoors. One day, it will stick. I'm sure of it.

Affection, like familiarity, requires time.

I hear the screech of the shower's faucet being turned off, the bathroom fan turned on. Arno getting ready for another day at the office. There's the familiar buzz of his electric shaver, keeping his facial hair at its most desirable length, between one and three millimeters.

He needs to catch the train today, and the next one leaves at 6:45 a.m., so I work quickly to prepare his lunch, moving between the refrigerator and the island like a ballerina: chin up, back straight as a ruler. I compose a taco bowl of ground beef and lettuce, whole-grain rice, black beans, charred corn, and salsa, everything prepped last night after the baby was put down to sleep.

I scoop the salsa, the cheese, and a dollop of sour cream into separate small Tupperware containers so that they won't make the rest of the meal wet. A presliced wedge of lime goes on top. It looks like it could have come from Rosita, Arno's favorite local Mexican restaurant, and I smile with a tinge of satisfaction before carefully placing all the clear containers into his portable cooler.

I catch a glimpse of myself in the window of the microwave: thirty-three years old and I've already got dark purplish circles beneath my eyes, wan skin, a faint line creasing my forehead even while at ease.

Am I still beautiful?

I half smile, tuck an errant blond hair behind my ear. It feels drier with each passing year, more strawlike. Frizzy. Who cares? It's just protein, I remind myself. Vanity is for boring people.

I imagine the confident woman Arno met half a decade ago.

"Morning, sweetie," Arno says, breaking my reverie.

"Morning," I reply, leaning in to meet his kiss, a quick peck on the forehead that leaves a slight damp spot between my temples.

"You look nice," I offer, because he does.

Arno turns back and forth in fake modesty, admiring the pale blue oxford shirt I got him for Christmas. It matches his Paul Newman eyes perfectly.

"Wow, I guess I do," he says, grinning. "I must have really good taste."

I wrap my arms around him and hold him close, enjoying the pressure of his taut stomach and strong arms against my body. He squeezes me back, nuzzling his nose into the crook of my neck like a kitten, and I fight the urge to squeal, it tickles so much.

"So tonight will be another late one, huh?" I murmur, trying to sound as though it doesn't matter to me one way or the other.

Arno sighs, turning away from me to fill his thermos from the Chemex. The nutty smell of coffee envelopes us, and the conversation pauses as we enjoy the scent of a chocolatey Guatemalan roast.

"Yeah, unfortunately," Arno says in a tone that mocks defeat, to give off the impression that he doesn't love every aspect of his job, including the late nights.

"We have an IPO bake-off Thursday, and I need to review the pitch."

I pretend I care what this means, nodding with a semblance of concern.

"Okay, I understand."

I busy myself with a vase of tulips, which Arno bought for me three days ago. They're starting to open their cupped heads, creamy yellow and smooth as butter. They don't look quite real, I think, as I pour a cup of tap water into the vase, nourishing them.

"I know you do," Arno says behind me. "And that's just one of the many reasons I love you."

I ignore his pale attempt at flattery and, to my surprise, Arno doesn't press it.

"I should say goodbye to Emma," Arno says, setting his thermos down. "Then I'll head out."

The soft slaps of his rubber soles on the hardwood floors—creeping, so as not to wake the baby. I am relieved he makes this effort.

Maybe I'll go to the Arnold Arboretum today. Emma's never been, and according to Alexa, the day will be dazzling: 70 degrees and mostly sunny. Warm for early May.

I imagine myself showering, blow-drying my hair till it's smooth and straight, and putting on makeup, maybe even a pop of red lipstick. Perhaps I'll wear that Reformation sundress I bought before I found out I was pregnant and never got the chance to wear. It's off-the-shoulder and red, dotted with small white daisies with sky-blue pistils. I hope it fits, conforms to my new body, softer and more supple than I ever imagined it could be. I picture taking a selfie of me with Emma, her downy hair tickling my chin, and sending the image to Arno around lunchtime. He'd show his coworkers, and they'd coo over our angelic beauty.

"You're a lucky man, Arno," one of the bankers or senior analysts would say, groaning over their tragic singleness.

A sudden buzz fills the room, as if from a mechanical fly.

Arno's phone skitters across the island, coming to a tedious halt at its edge.

I lunge, grabbing the device before it falls, and then compulsively look down at its screen.

> **Viv**
> If we don't win this fucking beauty contest, Brian's gonna send me up the river. Thx for helping me with the presentation last night, Arnie.

Two seconds later.

> **Viv**
>

I drop the phone as if it contains nuclear waste, and it clatters to the floor, tumbling over itself till it comes to rest by our potted yucca plant. Thank god for that hideous OtterBox; I've poked fun at it for years by calling it just that.

"Everything okay?" Arno asks, emerging from the hallway, eyebrows raised. "Don't worry, she's still asleep," he says, gesturing toward Emma's half-open door.

"Um, yeah." I point to his phone. "It fell off the counter. You got a message."

My cheeks are burning, but Arno doesn't seem to notice. He stoops to retrieve the phone and looks at the message. I stare at his face, wanting and not wanting to witness a betrayal of emotion.

Nothing.

He pockets the phone without responding to whoever "Viv" is and grabs his gym bag, slinging it over his shoulder.

"Good thing I got this hideous OtterBox, huh?" he says, his eyes meeting my own. My face relaxes, and I realize I've been clenching my jaw.

"It's still terribly uncool," I say, smiling. "But yes, I'm glad you got it."

Arno picks up his coffee thermos, lunch bag, and leather briefcase and, laden down like a donkey in Greece, ambles over to my side of the island, offering up one last kiss, this time on my lips.

He smells like Arno—that is, slightly sweet, like a juicy fig, but also spicy. A bite of cinnamon. That Harry's bodywash I ordered for him online because Dove makes him break out. I kiss him back, breathing in. Mine. I exhale, letting him go.

The tide recedes.

Mine.

"Have a great day," he says, squeezing my arm.

He has no idea how impossible that will be.

CHAPTER 2

The baby is crying.

Wet, thick sobs that are reminiscent of a screeching cat, or a fire engine. How can something so small be so loud?

I pull my robe a little tighter, feeling bolstered by the squeeze of the belt encircling my rib cage. I'm okay. I'm fine.

We're fine, my mind reprimands, so quick is my heart to think of me and me alone.

I wait a beat, wondering if she'll be tricked into thinking she's truly alone and soothe herself, but no, that's silly. It's 7:00 a.m. She's been out for twelve hours and is starving.

I tiptoe into her bedroom, and Emma immediately quiets.

"Ma-ma?" she asks suspiciously.

"Yes, it's me, sweetheart," I say, sweeping her out of her crib and kissing the top of her soft, golden head. She looks like a small rabbit in her white cotton pajamas with tiny orange carrots stitched onto the edges, one of a hundred similar sets she's received from Arno's parents.

She's wriggly today—all squirming legs and pinching hands—and I try to squelch the familiar panic that I've given birth to an alien that wants nothing from me but sustenance.

"Okay, okay, Miss Squirmy," I scold her. "Let's sit down."

I sit in the balsam-green velvet lounge chair by Emma's window, which looks out on our laughably idyllic Wellesley neighborhood. The majority of the homes surrounding us were built in a colonial style prior to 1940, so they lack the "cookie-cutter" suburban look Arno so detests.

"It's just so depressing," he'd said once, as we drove by a new housing development in Needham, "to ruin a town with so much history with these sanitized boxes. What's next, a Walmart next to Town Hall?"

No, every family in Wellesley boasts a carefully crafted estate with plenty of surrounding greenery and privacy, not to mention a two-car garage, a minimum of two college degrees, and the knowledge that they live in one of the most expensive ZIP codes in Massachusetts.

"The country, actually," Arno corrected me, faux sheepishly, the last time I mentioned this fact.

I settle myself deeper in the chair, savoring the luxurious tickle of velvet beneath my thighs, one of the main reasons I ordered this ridiculous piece for nearly two thousand dollars two years ago. One of the first purchases I made from joint checking with Arno. I'd felt dizzy with anxiety at the black, inky numbers on our bank statement, but he barely blinked when I showed him the receipt. I open my robe and wait for Emma to nuzzle her head against my chest, but I stop and tremble, remembering the sensation of her latching on to my breasts with her grabbing, purposeful lips.

Nursing never ceased to feel like some kind of robbery. I weaned her as quickly as I could, around eight months, but some days I didn't have the energy to resist her pressing need. Nothing about breastfeeding made me feel closer to Emma, only resentful.

Still, I love her. More than anything, I suspect.

I just never realized how much my daughter could disorient me. Frighten me.

A small voice in my head laughs. *Now, you know that's not true! Just look at your relationship with your own mother.* I shudder involuntarily again, and Emma looks up at me with wide, unblinking eyes.

"It's okay," I reassure her. "I'm not my mother. I'm my own person."

She looks skeptical.

I trace circles around her small, sturdy back as she sucks warm milk from a plastic bottle and gaze out the window, trying to focus on anything other than the text I read on Arno's phone just a half hour ago.

The view is of the usual suspects: Tracy Kaplan, my neurotic next-door neighbor who lives in the 1.75 million–dollar twelve-room Cape to our right, power walking through the neighborhood with hot-pink wrist weights affixed to her arms, jabbing and punching the air in a way that makes her look mentally deranged. And Chesley Preston, the sixty-five-year-old widower with jet-black hair and a fondness for pinching the asses of other men's wives, hosing down his Mercedes-Benz so lethargically, he might as well be pissing on it. His home looms behind him, a comically large brick-front colonial with two acres of manicured gardens and an infinity pool that I've only swum in once. Because, well, the ass-pinching.

To my left, Doreen Edwards kneels in a flower bed, deadheading some Shasta daisies and bleeding hearts. Her movements are graceful and efficient, belying the type of surgeon I imagine her to be. She often works weekends, so Thursday must be her day off this week. Her thick black hair gleams in the sun, shocking against the creamy, pale skin of her neck and arms.

Since Arno and I moved into this neighborhood, Doreen and I have had a total of three conversations, all of which were initiated by me: Once, when my pregnant brain accidentally locked myself out of our house in a snowstorm and I desperately needed to pee. Once more when I approached her at a block party thrown by Tracy and Terry Kaplan. I'd sensed an ally in Doreen—someone as levelheaded and practical as myself, perhaps even witty—but she took no interest in me, or anyone else at the party for that matter.

She gave off the impression of an island unto herself, someone for whom idle chitchat was neither enjoyable nor necessary to reinforce her stature in the community. I recall saying something to the effect of, "So, where do you work out around here?" and she'd stared at me with a blankness that sent goose pimples down my forearms. "I don't work out. Just walk," she'd said.

"Ahhh, yes, very nice community for walking!" I'd blurted out stupidly, hating myself for feeling withered by this complete stranger who'd already revealed herself to be an icy bitch.

Or perhaps Doreen wasn't a bitch at all, she just saw through our neighbors' facades. The gaudy diamond jewelry, the at-home spray tans.

Faces Botoxed into smooth submission. All of the luxurious ostenta-
tion designed to shock the viewer, then cow them into subservience.

All designed to hide what was rotting beneath the surface.

Yes, everything in Wellesley is best viewed from a distance. Through
a carefully trimmed boxwood hedge, for example. Though I'd never seen
anyone on our street knee-deep in a dirty flower bed except Doreen.

The third time Doreen Edwards and I spoke was a week ago. Her
husband, William, had carefully affixed a cluster of pink and white balloons to their mailbox. I craned my neck out the window to read what
was scribbled on them in gold italics: *It's a Girl!*

So Doreen Edwards was having a baby girl. I'd noticed her growing
stomach only in the last month. She was such a petite woman and carried the baby the way every pregnant woman hopes they will: high in
the center of her stomach, like a cute basketball, while the rest of her
remained lithe and ballerina-like.

It was a cooler, breezy day, and rain threatened every hour. The balloons jittered like a team of nervy colts, itching to cut loose from their
stable. Partygoers made their way to the Edwardses' residence, a carload
or two per hour over the course of the morning and early afternoon. Most
people I guessed were family members, except for a couple pairs of Prius-
driving thirtysomethings I immediately identified as fellow surgeons.
Their nondescript clothing and prim mannerisms always gave them away.

The baby shower attendees trickled out as they'd trickled in—slowly,
then all at once—and by the time they were all gone, Doreen sauntered
down her driveway to where William had affixed the balloons. She
drew a pair of scissors from a hidden pocket in her skirt and slashed
the balloons, one after the other, before removing them from the brick
mailbox entirely.

Something in her expression—was it despair?—prompted me out
our front door, down our stone walkway, and thirty feet to the left,
where Doreen stood by the mailbox, holding the pink and white rubber
in her hands like entrails.

"Hey, Doreen," I said, feigning casualness. "Just thought I'd pop over
and say congratulations! A baby girl, how exciting!"

I rubbed my arms against the nip in the air, but also in preparation
for Doreen's chilliness. It never came.

"Thank you," Doreen said without affect. Her eyes were cast downward to the balloons in her hands.

"You okay?" I asked.

Doreen looked up. Her eyes met mine. In this gray, pre-evening hour, you could make out the varying shades of brown: amber, honey, warm cinnamon. She was a very striking woman—sharp cheekbones and small rosebud lips.

"No," she said. "I'm not sure I want a baby."

"Oh," I said, unsure of where to go from there. We both looked up at the clouds, as if awaiting divine intervention.

Finally, I sighed.

"Honestly, I didn't want Emma at first, either," I whispered, conscious of Arno somewhere in the neighborhood, jogging to stay in perfect form. "But eventually, you realize it's the best decision ever," I said, questioning the words even as they flowed from my mouth.

"You'll realize being a mom is why you were put on this earth."

Doreen looked at me quizzically, then laughed: a sharp, clipped sound that reminded me of a tree branch breaking in the wind. "You don't believe that," she said.

I stood stock-still as if I'd been slapped, feeling the warmth spread from my cheeks down my neck and chest.

"I . . . I do," I said. "I mean, every woman is different. That was just my experience . . ." I was stammering.

Doreen's eyes narrowed. "Well, my purpose is to be a good surgeon. To be the *best* cardiothoracic surgeon," she added.

"Can't you—can't you be both?" I asked. "A mother and a great surgeon?"

"I'm afraid not," Doreen said. It was clear she'd given the matter a lot of thought. "I don't see how I could spread myself so thin and still be good at either. Surgery is my life."

I nodded, sensing the conversation, which had taken such an unpredictable and terrible turn, was over. I turned to go, leaving Doreen to her balloon massacre.

"Hey, Liz?"

I spun around, surprised. I honestly wasn't sure Doreen even knew my name. It sounded strange in her mouth, like an unfamiliar language I'd never heard spoken out loud.

"Yeah?"

"What did you want for yourself, before"—Doreen gestured at my manicured lawn, the bright white colonial behind me, our spacious two-car garage—"all this?"

"This *is* what I wanted," I snapped, shocking myself. "My family is what I want. Arno and Emma are all that matter."

Doreen nodded slowly, just once. Her eyes never wavered from my own as pools of pity oozed from them.

In that moment, I vowed to never talk to Doreen again. So what if she too was having a girl? Toxic, that's what Doreen Edwards was. A miserable, uppity bitch.

"Too bad you won't be able to have a little friend soon," I coo into Emma's hair, breathing in her baby powder scent. "I don't think Mrs. Edwards will let you play with her baby girl. She'll be much too busy for us . . . surgeoning."

Emma looks up at me blankly, stretching her arms overhead, warm and full of milk. Soon enough, she'll be fidgeting once more, struggling to get out of my grasp and onto the floor, where she will crawl about ceaselessly in pursuit of dangerous objects to cram into her mouth.

I set about the tasks that fill every morning so fully it's shocking I ever thought I'd have time to make lavender scones, or do yoga, or take a walk with Emma in her stroller before the sun ascended to its highest peak in the clear blue sky.

I change Emma's diaper. I dress Emma in fresh clothes: today, a russet-colored romper, 100 percent cotton, with white lacy frills on the shoulders. I prepare Emma's breakfast: sweet potato pancakes, blueberries, and bits of sausage that she grasps with her tiny fists and chucks onto the floor. Emma regurgitates half of her pancake, orange mush spilling onto her terry-cloth bib and dripping onto her chunky thighs and beautiful frock. I change Emma into a new outfit—this time, a pink onesie and floral bubble shorts that Arno adores. I snap a photo of Emma, send it to Arno.

I sit Emma on the floor of her tropical-paradise activity gym and soother that Arno's parents bought her for three hundred dollars. It's a mess of soft, pillowlike objects to grab and pull: fuzzy sloths and cheetahs, koalas with detachable arms that Emma likes to shove in her mouth and try to choke herself on. I set all of her favorites within arm's reach: a banana teether toy, a crinkly monkey, and a toucan chime. At thirteen months, she's outgrown them, but I try anyway, desperate for a moment's reprieve.

"Here, play with these, sweetheart," I plead. I still haven't changed out of my bathrobe.

I vacuum all of the room-sized rugs on the first floor of the house: family room, living room, dining room, foyer, Emma's bedroom, my office, and our master bedroom. By the time I'm finished, my armpits are drenched, and I can feel sweat seeping from the top of my head. I don't have the energy to even attempt to clean our second floor, which houses three extra bedrooms, two bathrooms, and a second office we never set foot in.

I shower with Emma on the floor outside of the glass door so I can see her. I encourage her to play with a stack of wooden blocks, but soon enough she's reaching her hands into the small wicker trash bin, rooting around like a stray dog. She picks up a used tampon and draws it toward her mouth.

"Emma, no!" I shout, louder than I intend to.

"No!" she yells back, and immediately begins weeping.

I exit the shower with soapy hair and unshaved legs and gather Emma into my arms. I cocoon her into my favorite blue towel and sing about twinkling stars and diamonds in the sky. She stops crying but still eyes me suspiciously, like she's an elderly spinster I'm grooming for her banking information.

For the second time that day, I think about what it would feel like to put Emma down for a nap and drive away.

I remember that morning, cupping my steaming mug of coffee on our back patio, listening to the din of robins and thrushes ushering in a new day. Hadn't I made a plan? What became of it?

I check the clock on the wall: almost noon. I think about that sundress again, hanging in my walk-in closet, tags still on. I want to laugh, or cry, or cry-laugh. Such a silly dream, the two of us in dresses, strolling through the arboretum and snapping selfies for Arno to coo over at lunch. I still have conditioner in my hair. There is dried sweet potato vomit under my fingernails.

I peer out the window, Emma clutched tight to my chest, and see Doreen step into her gleaming green Range Rover. Her baby bump is vague, a trick of the light. She looks like she could be going to a trendy brunch or even a business meeting in her pink, flowy midi skirt, expensive white T-shirt, brown leather jacket, and minimalist kitten heels. Her hair is flawless, an asymmetrical bob I hadn't noticed since our troubling conversation last week. Is it new? I wonder what her friends are like, or whether she has friends at all.

A stab of guilt, straight to my gut, travels up my chest like acid reflux.

I should be getting out of the house, going to the public library or the arboretum, or at least the grocery store. Nothing is keeping me trapped in this house.

Our house, I correct myself.

The text.

It flashes before my closed eyes like an aura before a migraine: *Thx for helping me with the presentation last night, Arnie.* Followed by a kissing-face emoji.

I've never called Arno "Arnie." That's what his parents and siblings call him. No one else.

But there was no heart emoji, and this clue seems significant. Surely if Arno was having some sort of, I don't know, *tryst,* this Viv person would have sent the kissing face emoji *with* a heart.

"Ma-ma," Emma says, and I realize I've been mumbling to myself.

"Nothing, sweetie," I say. "Do you want to go to the library?"

Emma scrunches up her nose like she's smelled something horrid. She can't possibly know what a library is, but somehow, she's decided she hates it.

"Fine, no library, then," I agree, bouncing her up and down on my knee.

Emma pouts, crocodile tears welling up in her big blue eyes, so much bluer than my own.

Arno's eyes. That's what our daughter has.

"No, no," I reprimand her. "None of that today. We're going to go have some fun, Em."

I smile down at my child so blindingly, so forcefully, she begins to wail once more.

CHAPTER 3

I'm wearing the red sundress.

I feel a little like—what did my mother used to call them? "Sausage casings." Her cruel description for women who stuff themselves into too-tight dresses and dare to wear them out in the world.

Not that I'm overweight. But the baby weight, twenty-five pounds over the course of nine months, has been tougher to eliminate than I'd anticipated. I feel it clinging to my ass, softening my thighs, filling out my breasts, and fattening the chipmunk cheeks Arno playfully squeezes, saying how cute I am.

I've stepped onto the scale religiously since about a month after giving birth to Emma, and I still have more than a few pounds to lose in order to get back to my prebaby weight. I feel awkward in the dress, my newly plump breasts bulging over the neckline. But do I look lascivious? Vulgar?

I'm not sure because I have no one to ask. Emma eyes me over the lid of her yellow sippy cup, hesitantly meeting my gaze in the rearview mirror. We're going to the arboretum, just like I planned, and I feel a buzz of excitement at the thought of being out in the world, among people, among strangers!

When was the last time I went somewhere other than the grocery store? I'm sure there's been *some* sort of fun family outing in the last thirteen months, but I can't seem to think of any. Is it possible I've become a hermit? Do I even *remember* how to talk to strangers?

The afternoon is slightly warmer than I anticipated—70 degrees seems generous, Alexa—and I can feel the crotch of my underpants sticking to my vagina. I pray that their dark, sweaty outline can't be seen through the dress, which is, regrettably, made of rayon.

We park beneath a glorious maple tree that must be hundreds of years old. I tell Emma this fact, and she blinks warily in the harsh glare of the sun.

"It's hot," I observe, as I strap her into her stroller. It looks like a Transformer: gleaming black edges, large removable wheels, and a three-position recline function that I have no idea how to adjust. Arno's parents gave it to me at our baby shower, calling it the "Mima Xari" stroller, like I'd have any idea what that meant.

"All the rage these days," Arno's father, George, had said confidently. I looked it up on Pottery Barn Kids when they left. It cost fifteen hundred dollars, more than my monthly rent when I first moved to Boston years ago, and its primary material is plastic.

"Okay, Emma, we're going to take a nice long stroll around the arboretum and look at all the pretty flowers blooming," I tell her.

Emma points a chubby finger aimlessly ahead.

"Yes, sweetie! So many flowers."

I rattle off names as if I'm preparing for an exam: "That's an orchid tree. That's lily of the Nile. Those are lilacs. These are irises. That shrub over there? That's eucalyptus. See that vine? Wisteria, one of my favorites."

It feels good to be sure of something, and I'm impressed by how much knowledge I've subconsciously retained from a college botany course. Emma doesn't babble much, but she seems to be enjoying the new scenery. When I peek down at her small face, shielded by a wide-brimmed white hat, her eyes are wide and curious. She barks, "Woof! Woof!" when we pass dogs, and the dog walkers beam at the two of us.

I feel a bit silly in the red dress, which is terribly fancy for a midweek, midafternoon stroll through a public garden. There's a slit up its right side that reveals most of my pale thigh, something I become acutely aware of when we pass an elderly man who openly stares at my flesh.

Most of the fellow parkgoers are wearing athletic gear: Lululemon leggings with cropped white T-shirts; running shorts and visors; biking shorts with sports bras. Their outfit choices only heighten my embarrassment over the dress, but I press on, determined to take Emma to the top of Peters Hill for a couple of photos to send to Arno.

I briefly read about the gardens on the arboretum's website in the car before we left. It sounded beyond idyllic: "A serene landscape of temperate woody plants, gentle walking paths, and shaded benches." About an hour into our stroll, the "shaded" part of the description seems crucial. I drip with sweat, and when I wipe my forehead with the back of my hand, my skin comes back orangey and sparkled: the color of my bronzer.

Online, it said that Peters Hill was the highest point of the park, providing an impressive view of the Boston skyline. I scan the distance for some sort of map, but see none. I must have missed one at the entrance on our way in, too preoccupied with how I looked.

I pause beneath a white trellis covered in pink climbing roses and peek at Emma.

"Ma-ma," she confirms.

Her little face is pink and sweaty. She squirms with discomfort.

"Yeah, I know," I reply, irritated. "I'm working on finding a nice little outcropping for us to relax by."

Emma kicks her legs against the seat and screeches.

Fuck.

"Calm down, sweetie. We're on our way to a cooler spot."

Emma's face begins to scrunch up into her familiar pre-wail expression, so I duck behind her stroller and root around in the lidded storage basket where I threw some snacks for exactly this situation. I find a ziplock bag of Cheerios and whip it out, victorious.

"Want some cereal, sweetie?"

Emma nods furiously, opening and closing her hands like a Venus flytrap.

I sprinkle a few onto the tray before her and she snatches at the cereal messily, scattering most of the Cheerios onto the ground, where I expect they will become some animal's lunch soon enough. I look around to make sure no one is witnessing the mess we're making. Emma shoves a small handful into her mouth and chews laboriously, masticated grain dribbling down her chin and pink shirt.

"Wa-wa," Emma says suddenly, her hands empty.

"One sec," I reply, rooting around in yet another hidden stroller compartment for the yellow sippy cup filled with ice water I'm sure I packed.

Nothing. Just a bag of cubed cheddar cheese, a pacifier, and an empty container of wipes.

"What the—"

I must have left it in the car.

"Wa-wa!" Emma shrieks.

"Shhhh. Mommy forgot to pack water. I'm sorry. We'll head back to the car now and get some fresh water at home or on the way."

"WA-WAAA!"

I look at Emma in surprise. Public tantrums aren't usually her thing, but here we are. I flip the top of the stroller down so that more of her body is shielded from the sun and hustle down the gravel path that I'm hoping leads to the entrance of the park.

We pass elderly couples holding hands, college-aged joggers in spandex, stay-at-home moms on lunch walks. They look at me and my wailing baby with a mixture of sympathy and open distaste. Screaming isn't what they signed up for when they left their homes on this stupidly gorgeous day.

Azaleas. Bonsai trees. Crabapples. Rhododendrons. Large swaths of moss and rocks.

Everything looks the same, and I have no idea whether we've passed this particular hemlock tree before or not. Sweat drips down my legs and into my white leather sneakers, which begin to make a squelching sound with each step. I no longer care whether anyone can see my underwear.

A buzzing sounds in my purse.

I pull out my phone and hit "Answer" without looking at the screen.

"Well, hello, Elizabeth."

Shit shit shit.

"Hi, Freja."

"You've been MIA lately. What's going on?"

Freja Jensen, my literary agent, is *this close* to dropping me. She's said as much in the last twenty emails, fifteen phone calls, and sporadic texts she's sent over the last year. I staved her off for a while by claiming migraines (true), exhaustion (also true), and various Emma-related issues, but she's getting antsy. Irritated. I promised her a finished manuscript at least six months ago.

"Well, Freja, as you know, this novel involves a lot of . . . research. A mysterious illness that causes severe memory loss isn't an easy thing to conjure into existence. I just need a little more time to get it right."

Freja is quiet.

"Liz, I'll give you a few more months, but I want you to be more communicative with me. When you block my calls, I have no idea whether you've fallen off the face of the earth."

Freja doesn't mince words.

"I haven't been 'blocking your calls,' Freja. Don't be ridic—"

"I'll check in next week." Freja cuts me off. "Goodbye, Liz."

Click.

Suddenly, silence.

The heavy quiet feels as loud as Emma's cries, and I peer around the side of the stroller, wary of ceasing movement and risking another tantrum. She is fast asleep, her head lolled to one side like a drunk's, her cheeks bright pink. She is far too hot, I think guiltily. We need to get the fuck out of here.

Out of desperation, I approach a couple who appear to be in their late twenties. No rings. No kids. Matching orthopedic sneakers that look as hideous as they do comfortable.

"Excuse me," I say, too loudly for the open space, the sun-drenched pastoral scene encroaching on us. I'm sure I look frantic, crazy even, with my face dripping foundation and my sunburnt toddler.

The couple, deep in conversation about Boston real estate prices, slows. They eye me warily, as one would a raccoon that gets too close while diving for trash.

"Hi, I'm so sorry, but I think I'm a bit turned around," I explain. "I missed the map when I first started walking and I'd really like to get back to the entrance. Do you know which way that might be?"

The couple exchanges a quick glance, deciding who will be the one to deal with me.

The guy finally speaks up. "The arboretum is two hundred eighty-one acres. It's no surprise you got lost."

He says it gently, but there it is, the slightest hint of reprimand for this scandalous-dress-wearing mother who dared enter the arboretum with her baby and no map, no plan, not even a sippy cup of water. I fight back tears.

"I didn't realize it was so large," I say defensively. "I've never been here before."

The couple nods knowingly, in unison.

"A lot of people get lost here," the woman says. "It's important to do your research beforehand."

I nod in agreement, words failing me. Determined not to let this stupid Barbie and Ken fitness duo see me lose my shit.

"The entrance is that way." The guy points over my shoulder, toward the way I just came from. "About two miles away."

"Really?" I say, confused. "But I just came from that direction."

"She probably didn't make a left at the Blackwell Footpath," the woman says to her partner.

The man smirks. "Probably not. Did you see the Blackwell Footpath?"

"The—the Blackfoot what?" I stammer. "I'm not sure. Was it marked?"

I draw a hand across my brow, but my hands are as sweaty as my forehead, so I just wipe sweat onto more sweat.

"Yes," the woman says tightly. "It's marked. With a sign." She tugs her partner's arm, and they quickly move around me, disappearing down yet another gravel path, two sloshing canteens thumping at their sides with each step.

"All right, Emma, well, at least we know the way home," I say to the air, pushing her back up a steep hill. I pause to tie my wet hair into a messy bun, all efforts at appearing well groomed and demure long dead.

I trudge in silence, thinking about something Arno mentioned earlier in the week.

"Why don't we hire a nanny?" he'd said over mouthfuls of Thai take-out. I'd tried to make the spontaneous Postmates delivery sound like a fun date night at home, but really, I just needed a night off from cooking. It was one of the few days in our entire marriage in which Arno arrived home before I had time to "freshen up," otherwise known as

waiting till 6:00 p.m. to shower, get dressed, and put on makeup so as to appear like a fully functioning adult woman.

I used to take pride in my appearance, derived real enjoyment from my ability to style my clothing in a way that felt authentically *me*. But after Emma arrived, the pleasure I had once taken in getting dressed and doing my makeup simply evaporated. Poof. Both tasks were just another thing to *do* in order to keep up appearances, and for whom?

Arno. Just Arno.

"Drinks with the team were canceled," he'd said sheepishly, stepping through the front door as if he wasn't quite sure if this was where he lived. I was still wearing my pajamas from the night before but hoped he assumed I'd changed into them a bit early. I tried to sound chipper as I unpacked green curry with beef and eggplant, tom kha soup, chicken satay, fried rice noodles, and mango salad. I'd ordered enough food to feed three families.

"Why would we need a nanny?"

"Well," Arno began, clearing his throat. "A lot of people have nannies. It would give you time to get back to work on your novel, or freelance . . . or just get out of the house and do the things you love."

"The things I love," I echoed, grabbing Arno a cold beer from the fridge.

"Yeah, you know." Arno rushed to explain himself. "Like yoga, running, hiking, reading, writing . . ." He trailed off, looking for me to fill the void. "All the stuff you did before Emma was born."

"I love being Emma's mom," I'd said quietly.

"I know you do! No one is questioning that. I just think a nanny would make life even better. You could finally finish your second book!"

I nodded, trying to seem amenable, but seethed inside. Arno had no idea how exhausting days alone with Emma were; he'd only been home for the first month after her birth. Besides, Arno's mother had stayed in our guest room the entire time, rushing to his assistance for diaper changes and rocking Emma well into the night while both of us slept peacefully in our king-sized bed.

And now, just because he'd witnessed me in a moment of weakness, he assumed I needed a nanny. I'd been raised to think nannies were something lazy rich women needed—women who spent their days shopping and doing Pilates and sneaking in episodes of *The Real Housewives* at 11:00 a.m. Women like Tracy Kaplan, who trounced around the neighborhood with a gin and soda in her hot-pink thermos, her perfectly manicured nails always tapping away at her iPhone as if maybe *she* was the one writing a novel.

"I'll think about it," I said, and the relief on Arno's face made me question my own sanity. Maybe I really was losing myself. I tried to remember the last time I'd taken a yoga class, gone on a spontaneous hike, or worked on my novel. Maybe eighteen months ago? When I was pregnant but not, like, grossly pregnant?

The problem is, Arno works late so often—even some weekends— and I feel like I need to be available whenever he's home. I mean, what kind of wife would wait for her hardworking husband to get in after a sixty-hour workweek just to saddle him with their baby and drive off for some vinyasas? There simply isn't any time to do all of the activities I used to love.

Emma sucks up all of my daylight hours, and Arno owns my nights.

Now, as I trod down Blackwell Footpath—which does, apparently, exist—I wonder if perhaps Arno is right. How nice would it be to drive to New Hampshire on a random Wednesday and hike the White Mountains? Wouldn't it be luxurious to get my nails done, or indulge in a massage? Maybe I'd finally make some friends besides Tracy Kaplan, whose idea of a wild Friday night consisted of a bottle of French rosé and *10 Things I Hate About You* streamed on the big screen in her and Terry's completely absurd basement movie theater.

Perhaps being the best version of myself means giving myself some time back, I think, turning the stroller down the final bend in the footpath, the parking lot now visible ahead.

And it's not like I'd be the only one with a nanny, I reason. In fact, the majority of the partners at Arno's firm use nannies, sometimes more than one. The nannies go on vacations with their employers, celebrate major holidays with families that aren't their own, sometimes even live in the house of the children they help care for.

But I wouldn't rely on my nanny like *that*, I think. She'd just be helpful and always available, like a rideshare app. Maybe we'd even become friends.

As I strap a sleeping Emma into her car seat, I imagine myself sharing a cold glass of wine on my back patio with a middle-aged French woman. Someone just beautiful enough to be cool, but old enough not to be a threat. Someone who speaks English fluently but still enjoys teaching me about her heritage.

Maybe we'd even visit France together, explore her hometown on the Seine!

I picture Emma and me wearing matching berets, eating chocolate croissants as a Parisian sunset splashes the sky orange and pink, the Eiffel Tower looming in the distance.

That wouldn't be so bad, I think, as I turn on the radio and Stevie Nicks croons "Landslide."

I blast the AC and roll the windows down, chiming in.

Emma starts to wail.

I turn the music up.

CHAPTER 4

Arno said he would be late, so why am I so anxious?

It's 10:00 p.m., and Emma has been asleep for three hours. I've showered, blow-dried my hair, and applied a tinted moisturizer that evens out my complexion and hides the now-perpetual dark bags under my eyes. I've changed into a nightgown that Arno's described as "impossibly sexy" a few times, which always makes me cringe. It's like an oversized button-down shirt that gives off *Risky Business* vibes. It's pretty itchy and uncomfortable, actually. Kind of like wearing a starched oxford shirt to bed. But Arno likes it, so it's worth it, and I've unbuttoned the first few buttons so that my black lace push-up bra is fully visible underneath.

I nurse a cup of chamomile tea, seated on the loveseat that's tucked into the corner of our living room, my legs arranged beneath me. I've tried to read the intro of this novel, *The Water Cure*, five times, but every time I get to the end of the first page, I realize I have no idea what the words mean. They're like skipped rocks that never land.

Instead, my mind is a Ferris wheel, cycling past the same scenery over and over.

Viv
If we don't win this fucking beauty contest, Brian's gonna send me up the river. Thx for helping me with the presentation last night, Arnie.

What's the meaning behind it? Where's the context?

I turn the words over, hold them up to the light. Try them on like garments in a store I was never meant to enter.

I'm assuming "beauty contest" is just another expression for the "IPO bake-off" Arno mentioned this morning, something to do with investment banks competing for the same business. I don't know what deal they're vying for, but it must be something big. As for Brian, I'm well familiar with that asshole. He's Arno's boss, a director at Stonebridge Partners, also known as a "rainmaker in training"—as well as a royal douchebag.

I met Brian at a Stonebridge holiday party my first year dating Arno.

First impression: red-faced and shiny, like the surface of a balloon, biting the head off a cocktail shrimp, chewing with his mouth slightly open. As though he had a sinus infection and couldn't breathe through his nose.

His wife, a sedated-looking redhead of indeterminable age, wore an over-the-top, floor-length goldenrod velvet dress. It was belted, and the neckline cut a deep "v" down her alabaster chest, two pert boobs close to revealing themselves with her every movement.

"She must have some really good tape," I'd murmured.

"What?" Arno asked, confused as all men are about the lengths women go to in order to look effortless.

"Nothing."

"Let me introduce you."

I guzzled what remained in my champagne glass and grimaced, pleasantly buzzed but out of my depth in the world of investment banking, money old and new. My parents were a couple of the burgeoning middle class: a history professor and a grocery store manager. Divorced by the time I was eight. As far as I knew, they'd never saved a dime.

Every time Arno had to pee, I also excused myself to the bathroom, just to avoid small talk with strangers. With Arno, I felt unstoppable. But the second he left my side, I faltered. Did I belong here?

"Arno!" the man I would soon know as Brian bellowed across the parquet floor.

In response, Arno beamed, flashing the smile that had felled me a few months prior at a basement punk rock concert in Cambridge.

"Brian! Cynthia!" Arno called, pulling me by the arm to follow him through small groups of partygoers in different iterations of evening wear: silver sequined minidresses for the girlfriends still in their twenties, chic black midis for the newly minted wives pushing thirty-five, and for any woman beyond fifty, shapeless taffeta gowns in shades of midnight blue and emerald that conjured about as much sex appeal as a great-aunt in mourning garb.

For me, a violet Marchesa cocktail dress in sequined ombré tulle with ruffled trim, a dainty ribbon tied at my waist like a promise. The garment, which had an estimated retail value of four thousand dollars, made me a fairy among robot women who thought they could only wear jewel tones to a holiday party. *It's 2015!* I wanted to shout at the lot of them. *Live a little!* I'd rented the entire ensemble, complete with a beaded silver purse and moonlight-colored heels, off Rent the Runway for a hundred dollars. When Arno's eyes lit up upon seeing me, I'd never felt more beautiful. Or smug.

"Nice to meet you," I said, carelessly holding out my hand like a party favor. Cynthia looked me up and down, then smiled.

"She's cute, Arno. Where'd you find her?"

Like I was a lost puppy left beneath a dilapidated porch. I withdrew my hand. Her mouth was the color of strawberries.

"At a concert!" Arno shouted above the music, Mariah Carey's somehow never tired version of "All I Want for Christmas Is You" booming from unseen speakers. An acclaimed jazz band was set to go on shortly.

Brian's eyebrows lifted in a manner that suggested he thought attending concerts was for young people. I stifled a laugh and, despite Cynthia's cool greeting, felt a fizzle of warmth in my stomach. Arno really *was* all I wanted for Christmas this year.

"Well, well, well," Brian said, turning from Arno, finally, to me.

Like his wife, Brian appraised me with the seriousness of a county fair judge eyeing a lineup of Holstein cows.

"She's lovely, Arno. Just lovely. What's her name?"

"Elizabeth," I said, unwilling to give them my nickname, which was an earned epithet reserved for close friends and family.

"Elizabeth," Brian said slowly, as if my name was a riddle he could decipher. "And what do you do, Elizabeth?"

Somehow I had known this was coming, but I still resented how Brian asked it, like I was applying for a job at the firm.

"I'm a writer," I said, willing my chin to remain high.

"A writer!" Cynthia said, as if I'd admitted to being a rodeo clown, or a part-time professional wrestler. "A writer of what?"

"Fiction, mostly," I said.

"She's being modest," Arno cut in. "She's not just a writer, she's a *published author*. At twenty-eight, no less."

It's true. After finishing graduate school, I'd sold the book that came out of my thesis project—a novel about two best friends who realize they've fallen in love with the same man—for a not-entirely-insignificant sum of money that I'd been living off ever since. It didn't win me any Pulitzer Prizes, but it did marginally well in independent bookshops and won some "Under 30" prize at a local book festival, and I was proud of what I'd accomplished. None of my other friends from BU had published anything yet.

Arno beamed, his white teeth nearly fluorescent beneath the purple and blue lights. He loved my trade, thought writing was the most romantic thing any person could do to make a living. When he first brought me home to his parents' historic mansion in Newburyport, they all made a big deal of showing *the author* their collection of rare first editions, which included the works of Dickens, Hemingway, and Fitzgerald. It seemed so sweet at the time.

"Well, that's brilliant," Brian said, leaning in conspiratorially. His breath was awash with the cloying, sweet scent of Magners on ice. "Our Arno, he's a numbers guy. Bit perfect for him to end up with an artist of sorts, no? What's that they say about opposites attracting?"

He nudged my rib with his elbow. The ribbon at my waist threatened to come undone.

My eyes met Arno's over Cynthia's glass of wine, and his pupils undressed me while Brian shared a story about one of the directors' teenage daughters crashing his brand-new Porsche.

"Arno, let's go dance!" I cut in, desperate to get away from the unnerving duo. As we walked toward the throng of moving people, hips swaying and heads bobbing in and out of sync with the latest number-one song on the pop charts, I could feel Brian's and Cynthia's eyes on our backs as if we wore bull's-eyes.

One year later, Brian secured his seat as one of the managing directors of Arno's branch at Stonebridge. This was no shocker, as everyone knew that Cynthia's father was a Stonebridge founder. In addition to a company car, a six-figure raise, and a private office overlooking Boston Harbor, Brian got the satisfaction of "owning" Arno, a man twice as smart but with the misfortune of not being married to a founder's daughter. As a VP, Arno would have to grind his way to the top through countless late nights at the office, dinner parties at Del Frisco's Double Eagle Steakhouse, and meetings conducted over the course of eighteen holes.

"Vice president" might sound like an impressive title, but through Arno, I knew it was the most junior title for senior bankers. While Brian pulled in millions via delegation, Arno worked his ass off crunching numbers and schmoozing clients for bonuses that would earn him a fraction of Brian's income.

Arno still made *stupid* money. I understood that. But to Arno, he was just skimming the surface, doing time till he got what he wanted: real power. Brian's job.

And as for me? By then, I was beyond smitten; I was entrenched. As it turns out, 365 days is plenty of time to cement yourself into someone's inner circle, not to mention his body and mind.

I slept at Arno's apartment so often we decided to sublet mine. We took vacations to Ireland, Martha's Vineyard, and Bar Harbor in Maine. We tried pizza from all of the top pizza spots listed in *Boston* magazine, ranking our favorites against the publication's. We ran a half marathon with other Stonebridge couples, raising thirty thousand dollars for breast cancer research. We hiked to the top of Mount Washington and shared a sleeping bag in a bunk bed through a subzero night. We bought a couch together. We went to a Halloween horror movie marathon at Coolidge Corner Theatre. I introduced Arno to the Oreo cannolis at Mike's Pastry in the North End, and he took me to a hole-in-the-wall ramen shop in the belly of a Dedham strip mall.

We slurped, sipped, walked, and fucked all over the East Coast. We shared our favorite baby names. Mine, nearly all literary: Emma, Jane, Viola, Oliver. His, old-fashioned, with a heavy-handed dose of Anglophilia: Imogen, Briony, Edmund, Colin. I won that battle. We were married by the time I was thirty, and we were pregnant with Emma one year later.

The point is, Arno and I built a life together. I might not have understood some of the friendships in his inner circle, or even his passion for investment banking, but I understood him, his heart and his mind, and maybe even that ineffable stuff we call the soul. And at the end of the day, what else really matters? We became best friends. We still *are* best friends.

Right?

My head rests on the wall behind me, stiff as a board. I get up and crack open a window so I can hear the crickets begin their nightly chorus from our lawn, pitch-black in the moonless evening. I sit back down and close my eyes.

> **Viv**
> If we don't win this fucking beauty contest, Brian's gonna send me up the river. Thx for helping me with the presentation last night, Arnie.

> **Viv**
>

I open my eyes.

Well, it's no surprise that Brian's riding Arno's entire floor into the ground. Maybe this "Viv" is just a new analyst, a grunt, who's found an empath in my kindly husband. He has always struck me as a sort of mentor figure to some of the younger guys at Stonebridge. How sexist of me to think any differently just because he's being helpful to a young woman.

I mosey from my seat by the window to the kitchen, where I open the cupboard to retrieve a wineglass, which I fill three quarters of the way with ice-cold sauvignon blanc from the Loire Valley.

I need something to still my nerves, my jittery hands that are like beached fish, still wriggling. Something numbing to eliminate Brian's elastic—probably facelifted—appearance from my mind. His frigid spouse, an evil queen from a Disney movie—Maleficent from *Sleeping Beauty* or, even worse, the evil queen from *Snow White*.

I really need to stop letting Emma watch so many movies.

The text.

Silly. I'm being silly.

I lean against the counter, feeling idle. Maybe I could watch a movie? Easier than concentrating on words. Louder. Deafening, even.

My gaze lands on my laptop, peeking out of the top of my leather messenger bag. I haven't used the computer in god knows how long. Perhaps I could . . .

No.

I am not Google stalking Viv, I chasten myself. How would I even go about doing that? I don't have an age or even a last name.

LinkedIn, my brain immediately suggests. Or even just the local Stonebridge website. Surely they have a "Meet Our Team" page, like every other company in the country.

No.

You're being so boring, I tell myself. *Like a desperate housewife. You're not a "kept" woman; you're in a loving marriage based on partnership and equality.*

But if Viv is super ugly or overweight or old, you'll feel better immediately, my mind reasons. Why not rip the Band-Aid off, you pussy?

I shuffle over to the messenger bag, my starched nightshirt itching my armpits with each step. Maybe I should take this thing off, put on some boxers and a T-shirt. I look weird, like a video vixen. *I don't need to dress like a high-end prostitute in order for my husband to want to sleep with me, okay*, I tell an imaginary Viv, who just happens to have a thick, dark unibrow above tragically close-set eyes.

I pull out my MacBook.

I sit down on one of the barstools by the island, an uncomfortably trendy thing I ordered from a well-targeted Instagram ad, and crack open my laptop. The background is a photo of Arno and me at Lonesome Lake in New Hampshire, tanned and sweaty after a grueling summer hike to one of the huts along the Appalachian Trail. That night, we'd listened to the mournful call of loons tracing circles around the lake's perimeter, our arms wrapped around one another as we lay on a flannel blanket beneath the stars, sipping instant hot chocolate from a single orange thermos. That trip was when I first realized, with a thrilling jolt, that Arno would one day ask me to be his wife. I was as sure of it as the sun rising at 5:38 a.m. over the Franconia Range before us. And that was a big deal for me, as I had always harbored the suspicion that I would end up alone. Why? I wasn't entirely sure, but the therapist I had started seeing in college said it was rooted in my relationships with my parents: their divorce; my mother's chaotic dating habits post-divorce; my father moving literal *states* away from my brother and me, in Virginia, to a woodsy town in Vermont with poor cell-phone service. My mom's further retreat from motherhood into her new relationships after my dad was long gone.

I click on the Google Chrome icon and fire up the search engine, my fingers feeling taut and unpracticed above the keyboard I've been ignoring for so long. I wonder what it says about me that I've not bothered to update my screensaver to a photo that includes Emma.

I type in "Stonebridge Partners + Boston" and click on the investment firm's local page. I read about the background and history of Stonebridge Partners, how it was formed in the 1980s with the goal of investing in "high-growth companies" and working closely with their management teams to "realize their full potential." I force my brain to cut through all the marketing talk to learn about the 150 private-equity investments they've made across consumer products and retail, technology, industrials, health care, and communications, starting with a 1982 investment in a popular packaged food brand. The "Background and History" page goes on to tout some of the firm's most impressive investments, notably, its efforts in building a privatized railroad system throughout the United Kingdom, as well as one of the United States' leading brands in organic skin care and makeup.

This is the most time I've ever spent trying to understand what Arno does, I realize, thinking of all the times he's tried to get me excited about a new wireless tower in Wales or a "fascinating" health tech company that's bringing telemedicine to remote parts of Alaska.

I feel guilty and a bit nauseous.

How many times has he tried to explain his role in the company to me, while my eyes glazed over like the top of a freshly tossed donut? On the other hand, how many hours has he spent listening to me in earnest as I rattled off potential plot twists for my latest short story, or described how reading the poetry of Ocean Vuong was like being punched in the stomach, over and over, till you couldn't breathe and vowed never to put pen to paper again because nothing could ever be as beautiful as his words?

Deep breaths, I remind myself. No use ruminating on past mistakes.

"Be a better listener," I scribble down on an errant Post-it Note stuck to the inside of my messenger bag. I press down on the small yellow square, sealing it to the space beside my keyboard. There. No more excuses.

My cursor hovers over the page I'm really here for: "Our Team."

"Our investment team is a synergistic union of professionals with a wide range of backgrounds including general managers, analysts, consultants, investment and commercial bankers, and entrepreneurs. Though our team has grown since our humble 1980s origins, we've retained our core values of collaboration, trust, and tenacity here at Stonebridge. We also note, quite proudly, that with the exception of three retirements, no partner has left the firm in the last three decades."

I snort-laugh on "synergistic" and the fatalistic last line about no one ever leaving, picturing a boardroom of dried-out skeletons belonging to old white men.

I'm at the bottom of my wineglass. I get up, quickly refill it, then resume my seat at the island.

My eyes scroll through the sixty-five or so names listed for the local office. They aren't in alphabetical order but rather are lumped under job titles: "Capital Markets," "Associates," "Senior Advisors," "Portfolio Support," "Administration," "Principals," "Vice Presidents," etc. I've no idea what most of them mean, but I understand that "managing director" is what they're all after anyway.

I land on "Arno Bennett" in the "Vice Presidents" category and feel a surge of pride. He's so close to getting what he wants; I can feel it. Like when I intuited that Arno would propose to me by an old schoolhouse on Nantucket as we shared a chicken salad sandwich and played cards, and then it happened, just as I'd imagined.

I close my eyes: Arno setting his half-eaten bag of kettle-cooked chips down on the picnic blanket and rolling over to face me, his auburn curls falling into his eyes because he hadn't had time to get a haircut before our summer vacation. The way his irises matched the Atlantic Ocean behind him. His sunburnt nose. The smell of sunscreen, synthetic coconuts, and baby powder. My seersucker dress, slightly tight from the soft-serve ice cream and buttery lobster rolls I devoured every day for a week. Purple hydrangea, my favorite. The blue box in his hand, velvet and heavy looking, so out of place for our beachy getaway. The two-carat solitaire inside, sparkling so hard it looked battery operated. I'd never seen jewelry so imposing. We'd only been together for a year and a half, but I knew he was my person, and that he had changed me forever—transformed the chronically anxious, self-doubting book-worm into a confident *author* who took spontaneous day trips, ate lobster rolls with reckless abandon, and felt both beautiful and seen in his gaze.

I'm so busy imagining the celebratory party we'll host when he's promoted to director that I'm taken by surprise when I find the myste-rious Viv just two names away from my husband.

Vivienne Wood, vice president.

Relax, I think, as I click on her name. *She's probably a wool-suit-wearing, briefcase-carrying troll. Someone who wouldn't know fun if it slapped her right upside the head, and—*

A sharp intake of breath.

The feeling at the top of a roller coaster, stomach lurching, head swimming. The crowds below so small they might be made out of plas-tic. Then, the drop.

She's gorgeous.

Vivienne Wood joined Stonebridge Partners in 2015 as an associate and returned in 2019 after graduating from business school. She is a member of the health care industrial team. Prior to joining Stone-bridge, Vivienne was an analyst at J.P. Morgan.

EDUCATION
Harvard College, AB
Harvard Business School, MBA

And she's brilliant.

I take a swig of wine that no longer tastes like wine, just sugary syrup that will make me feel like garbage tomorrow—a mommy with puffy hands and diarrhea and a sippy cup full of nonorganic milk that may or may not cause developmental problems or obesity in my child, according to the Internet.

Back to Vivienne.

We are a study in opposites: dark hair where mine is gold. Honey eyes where mine are blue. Olive skin where mine is fair. A smattering of freckles cresting the bridge of her nose. "Ethnically ambiguous," my mom would say.

But "exotic" is the word that hovers on the periphery of her head-shot, sandwiched as it is between the faces of youngish white men bearing Goldman Sachs names like "Blair" and "Whittaker" and "Preston" and "Yates." Her face doesn't seem to fit.

"Vivienne" conjures images of the female version of Blair and Whittaker: a blazer-wearing, boarding-school-attending pale blond waif who's overcome bulimia to realize her dreams as daddy's little princess, queen of the trust fund.

This Vivenne, however, looks like she's in on the secrets of the universe while the rest of us dumb fucks wallow in the trenches. Amused—that's what her expression implies. Amused that she's figured out how to use her intellect and beauty to make obscene sums of money and transcend the mundanity of a middle-class life. Or amused that she's even found a seat at the table at all, like a kid who's snuck through the back door of a Regal Cinemas and watched four back-to-back R-rated films. That's what her smirk conveys.

I immediately envy her. Regardless of whether my husband is sleeping with her, I want some of her shine to rub off on my skin. Want to ask, like I'm staring at the *Mona Lisa* in her gold frame at the Louvre, "What are you laughing at?"

I scroll to the bottom of the page, but there's no further information on Vivienne.

A quick scan of the rest of Stonebridge's site reveals no further photos of her, either. She's somehow escaped the painfully awkward roundtable shots of middle-aged white men hovering over slightly outdated laptops (the subtext being that Stonebridge employees are always hard at work); the shaking-hands, "I've just made a ridiculous deal" photos—middle-aged Stonebridge guys with gleeful-looking young entrepreneurs, many still wearing their MIT or Harvard insignia. I move on to the Facebook page of one of the partners' wives and peruse shots capturing drunken holiday bacchanalia: towers of prawns and oysters on ice; men with no ties on, shirts unbuttoned to reveal either perfectly hairless or dark, furry chests, nothing in between; Jell-O shots in shades of toxic green and candy-apple red; a Stonebridge wife dressed up as a slutty Mrs. Claus. Kind of surprised that one made it into the queue, to be honest.

Vivienne is nowhere to be found.

I spy myself and Arno in the background of no fewer than four pictures: at the annual Make-A-Wish charity ball, downing prosecco and laughing on the dance floor; patiently waiting to zip line through Costa Rica, supposedly for team building; playing cornhole at a summer barbecue hosted by Brian and Cynthia; at a Red Sox game deep in the middle of my pregnancy with Emma, my pale ankles swollen to twice their normal size in the clawing humidity. The last one is just Arno and me in profile, but I can still remember how miserable I felt. How fat I was in my gray jersey dress that refused to hide sweat. How tired I was, like I'd just run four marathons back-to-back. How bored, how incredibly *disinterested* I was to be having the same conversations with the same people over and over. Cynthia whispering in my ear about how dumb the new secretary was, how tacky her knockoff hot-pink Tory Burch flip-flops were, and mimicking her Quincy accent. Brian pinching a novel layer of fat on my underarm, leering at my newly endowed chest with something like approval.

I slam my laptop shut, too loudly, and then hold my breath, waiting for Emma's screams.

One. Two.

Nothing. I exhale.

This is utter nonsense; I'm spiraling because of an attractive headshot. A single text!

I go to our bedroom—extra quiet like an exaggerated drunk—undress, and crawl under the duvet with newfound weariness. My eyes feel like porridge, so I close them to the world.

I try to remember if Emma's been fed. Of course she has, right?

The problem is, when every day bleeds into the next, sometimes I find myself forgetting. Maybe I should start making a daily checklist. But what if Arno found it? Would he think I can't remember the basics of childcare?

I turn over.

I'm sure I fed my daughter.

I fall asleep thinking, *I know my husband.*

CHAPTER 5

A key in the keyhole. A fumbling, rattling sound, like an overloaded washing machine full of coins.

Click.

Arno's feet on the hardwood floors of the parlor, mismatched steps like a newborn colt getting its footing. He's drunk.

I lie as still as a corpse, tracking his movements in the dark. In the kitchen, the sucking sound of the refrigerator door opening, then shutting. A cabinet door creaks. The sound of glass on marble, too loud. The grind of the ice machine, a mechanical beast, irritated from having been woken up so late.

I roll over to check the time, and the alarm clock flashes 3:30 a.m. in bright, bleeding red, the numbers swimming in and out of order.

The unmistakable glug of Arno's Adam's apple rising and falling as he chugs water. Responsible, even while inebriated. Keys clattering to the kitchen table, where my laptop sits forgotten.

A bloated pause, and then, Arno's shoes kicked off, one after the other, and I imagine him holding on to one of the bar stools for balance, threatening to pull the furniture over. I pray for his dexterity.

Finally, finally, Arno begins to walk down the hallway to our bedroom, and I remember that we are both drunk. He pauses around halfway, probably to peer in on Emma's sleeping form, and I feel a surge of affection toward him, viscerally sweet, like sucking on rock candy. I vaguely wish I had stayed in the black push-up bra, the starchy button-down shirt he likes so much, but the idea fades as quickly as it appeared; I am much too intoxicated for sex.

Arno appears in the doorframe, clutching its edges with hands like claws.

He is a shadow. A boogeyman from a shitty horror film.

"Arno?" I ask. "Is that you?"

I know it's him.

"Shhhhh," he replies in a voice far louder than my own. "Emma's sleeping."

Arno stumbles forward a few steps, spins around to face the door, and sits down heavily onto the edge of the bed, causing me to list toward its center like I'm being sucked into quicksand.

"Arno . . ." I reprimand, but the heat's not there.

He doesn't hear me, just fusses with the buttons of his shirt, flinging the garment to the floor, where I will find it in the morning like a scorned lover. His belt ends up coiled next to it, a black leather snake. Down to his Swiss boxer briefs—they have a cultlike following among the men of Stonebridge—Arno stands, for a moment, before falling face-first into memory foam.

His snores vibrate the pillow cover his face presses into, fluttering its edges with a steady breeze. The sound is as annoying and constant and nasal as the drone of cicadas, contracting their tymbal muscles all summer long.

I lie there for a while until my mind is no longer fuddled and sloshed; I feel alert as an owl, my vision and hearing improving with each nocturnal hour. I turn to face Arno in repose and evaluate.

Does he look different?

One of his eyelids twitches involuntarily, reminding me of my childhood dog, Honey, who was eventually diagnosed with epilepsy. Drool dots the corners of his open mouth, rendering his expression aghast at some unseen horror. His breath is pure Grey Goose vodka, each exhale the slightly sour stench of winter wheat. The brine of olives. An afterthought.

And yet, he is still handsome.

His sandy reddish curls that recall a Heath Ledger character in any one of his movies from the early 2000s, his nose cleaved from a Roman statue at the Museum of Fine Arts. The bristle of gold flecks on his jawline. The effortlessly lithe body from decades of competitive swimming, little concavities in his honey flesh outlining muscles most men will never see on their own bodies. Eyelashes as fine as thread and girlishly long.

Why did he ever choose me?

But, according to Arno, *he* is the lucky one. When we first started dating, I had to tell him to stop gushing about me at dinner parties and family barbecues. It was too embarrassing; I always inevitably felt like I'd set the whole thing up, coerced him into describing my writing as "brilliant," my success, "unavoidable."

Sometimes, I felt like he jinxed me. All that adulation before I'd become an established author, produced a second book. His love ballooned my promise, and then carried me to the stars with no return ticket.

What point was there in trying when you'd already won the lottery?

Beyond the whiff of too many dirty martinis and Arno's signature cologne, I try to suss out whether any other scents linger on his frame. The jasmine scent of a woman's perfume. Lingering sweat from a raunchy tussle in a bar bathroom. That unmistakable latex fragrance that accompanies any American condom.

Nope. Nothing.

There is no bronze glitter on his cheeks, nor the creamy nude shade of concealer I've smeared on one too many of his favorite shirts. No lipstick stains. No long dark hairs on his stark white briefs. He is the same man I met in a basement bar four years ago, eyes closed to the crowds around him, listening to the live music with a stillness that only those utterly comfortable in their own skin can access. I'd noticed him immediately and pretended to bump into him on my way to the ladies' room. It was Mariana's idea.

I sigh with something like relief, but my innards are still wound up. Too much sun today, too much wine this evening. Not enough sleep; never enough sleep. I should really rest.

Hours later, I dream that Arno and I give birth to a second screaming baby girl, but as I lie on the hard hospital bed and look down at what just came out of me, I see a stranger's infant: tanned and wet, with a full head of black hair like a yarmulke. She opens her pink, crusted eyes and, still screeching, grabs at my face in realization and fury.

Even as the nightmare presses on my temples, logic pulls through: I haven't cheated on Arno, so my baby could only look like some iteration of Arno and me. This is an imposter's child, thrown atop my chest to send me into delusion.

Well, it won't work.

I pick up the tiny fiend and, with the casualness of a moviegoer tossing out an empty paper popcorn bucket, heave the baby at my husband.

Surprised and horrified, Arno barely catches the infant before it hits the ground, clutching the wailing beast to his chest.

"There," I say. "Are you happy now?"

CHAPTER 6

Mommy and Me classes, a definition: "activities hosted by child-centric businesses that include music, art, movement, and other classes that encourage creative self-expression."

It's the "other classes" part that causes my eyebrows to lift, tucked in among all the other more descriptive words like a trapdoor. What could it possibly mean? Prayer? Chanting? Would Emma be forced to learn the foxtrot? I scroll through the synopsis of "Sing-alongs with Sam" a second time, searching for clues.

"These classes are designed to initiate parent-child bonding via enriching, instructional learning."

Well, that sounds nice, I guess. I'd like to bond with my daughter, teach her the ways of the world.

I glance at the rearview mirror, which reveals Emma with a right pointer finger crammed up her nasal cavity, fist deep.

"Stop that," I say lightly, like I'm reprimanding a very cute puppy that's not supposed to jump on strangers although clearly no one cares that much. I remind myself that I don't want to ruin her mood before we've even gone inside.

Emma ignores me, eyes cast firmly out the window. Roots around a little deeper. Extracts a thick, yellowish booger.

"Emma, don't—"

It's too late. My daughter plunges the mucus into her tiny mouth and swallows.

"Emma."

Her finger emerges wet and clean. She finally looks at me in the mirror, cocks her head, and smiles.

The building before us is squat and tan, emitting about the same frequency of hospitality as a police officers' recreational facility. Small windows that face the street have their blinds drawn tight. The only hint of children: a half-dozen colorful pinwheels, stuck into a dry patch of dirt out front, lolling backward and forward in a stale breeze. I double-check the address, thinking perhaps I've got it wrong, but nope, this is the Natick Kids Tumbling Center.

Arno found the class online, forwarded it to me in a text yesterday morning.

"Looks fun!!!!!" he'd said, followed by a beaming-smile emoji and the one of a mother and child. "Maybe you and Em can make some friends."

My knee-jerk reaction was one of distaste. Everything I knew about Mommy and Me classes was from movies or TV sitcoms: a bunch of exhausted mothers in sweats clutching their spit-up towels as they sang along to "Twinkle, Twinkle, Little Star" and cast judgmental looks at one another, trying to gauge which among the babies was furthest along on their developmental journey.

But what had I gained from being judgmental thus far?

Nothing, that's what. I spent most of my waking hours alone, babbling at my daughter and contemplating whether the shade of her bowel movements fell under the spectrum of "normal." I judged all of the mothers at our local all-organic grocery store as they stared at their phones, as pointedly averse to making new adult friends as I was. I hadn't read a book, or a news article, or really anything that wasn't a nutritional label on a jar of baby food, in months. I hadn't spoken to another adult outside of Arno in weeks, and what about Emma? Shouldn't she be exposed to fellow toddlers, who would teach her how to play and share, and maybe even make her feel less alone?

I would go to Mommy and Me for Emma. And perhaps just a little bit for me.

Maybe Arno was right. Maybe there would be another mom who reminded me of myself, only a little bit happier, and she'd ask me out to lunch and we wouldn't talk about our kids at all. Maybe we'd talk about movies and literature and current events and food. Our children could be friends, and influence each other for the better, and perhaps I'd remember that being a mom could be fun.

Also, it was an excuse to wear pants and leave the house.

I'd registered for "Sing-alongs with Sam" that morning, and now, here we were. Just two girls with no expectations and nothing to lose.

I reassure Emma in the rearview mirror: "This will be *fun*."

"Fuh," Emma echoes, testing it out.

The inside of the building is surprisingly colorful, as if the owners saved all their energy for decorating the interior and then just really *went for it*. The walls are painted lime green, the exact color of the slime from the iconic Nickelodeon show *Slime Time Live*. The floors, some sort of sticky rubber material in a checkered pattern of primary yellows and blues. On the walls, posters of smiling, diverse groups of children engaged in various activities: tumbling, holding hands and singing, painting, and playing musical instruments, their tiny mitts clutching maracas and tambourines and even miniature bongos.

"Wow, Emma!" I coo. "Look how neat!"

A small, pleasant-looking woman with chin-length jet-black hair sits behind a metal desk wearing a crisp white oxford shirt and a name tag that says *Constance*. She smiles widely at Emma and me, waving us closer to the desk.

"I'm guessing you're here for 'Sing-alongs with Sam'?" she asks. "Starts in just a few minutes. If you don't mind signing in here . . ."

She pushes forward a heavy-looking white binder, stuffed with thousands of yellowed pages representing the legacy of, I'd imagine, generations of Mommy and Me classes. Emma and I are a part of history. I bend down to sign.

A sharp intake of air from down below.

"Ma-ma."

Emma points to a doorway just off to the right. Through it, I can see a large, colorful playscape with slides and tunnels and ladders, like the kind you'd see at—

"CHEEEE," Emma says confidently.

I know that she's referencing Chuck E. Cheese and momentarily feel pleased with how advanced my thirteen-month-old is.

"Not quite, Emma, but just as fun."

Emma seems not to hear me. She begins bouncing up and down on her chubby, unsteady legs and emitting a high-pitched squeal, sounding akin to a pig that's about to get butchered. I honestly can't remember ever taking her to Chuck E. Cheese—she's way too young for it—but I guess we have at some point. Must have been a special father-daughter trip between her and Arno.

"This happens a lot," Constance offers. "You can go on in."

Emma surges forward on unsteady legs, and I have to run to keep up with her. I grab her under the armpits before she can either fall or catapult herself into the nearest ball pit. She kicks her legs and screws up her face in preparation for a good scream.

"Not yet, my love!" I whisper in her ear, covertly shoving a small handful of Cheez-Its into her pink, gummy fist. "Soon enough, but not yet."

There are about eight other mommy-and-baby duos, including one brave father who looks sickly and wan beneath the harsh fluorescent overheads.

"I'm Fred," he says to no one in particular.

We all look around at one another, eyeing each other's outfits and haircuts just as I feared we would, shuffling from one foot to the other while all of the babies and toddlers ogle the playscape hungrily. I feel my heart start to race and remember that adults are just grown-up children, desperate for structure and instruction. Throw us all together with no rules in a knockoff Chuck E. Cheese, and we might as well be cast adrift on the open sea.

I'm just about to feign a phone call and leave with Emma when a tall, broad-shouldered man in a red polo shirt and a jester's hat strides purposefully through the entryway, notable in his childlessness.

"HI, FRIENDS! I'M SAM!"

We all turn to attention: Sam, the sun, and we his planetary orbits.

"Hi, Sam!" we reply in unison, as though programmed to do so.

Sam is *hot*. He sort of looks like Tom Brady, with pectoral muscles that bulge right through his flimsy polo and a jaw that could have been cut from glass. That's why the floppy jester's hat with its jangly little golden bells is so disconcerting; it's incongruous with Sam's face, his body. My brain does backflips to right itself, and I can see all the women around me stand up straighter, tuck their phones into their purses. Even Fred looks like he's doing a little better.

"Thank you all for joining me today," Sam says, taking a moment to turn and flash a megawatt smile in each individual's direction, even the babies, who look flabbergasted. Sam explains that the purpose of his sing-alongs is to unite mothers—"or fathers," he says, winking at Fred—with their children in creative purpose.

Sam pauses to hand out "news articles" about babies' brain development and the importance of sensory experiences that he encourages us all to read on our own time. In the top left-hand corner, it says *Wikipedia*.

"This is about so much more than making music," Sam continues, his brow furrowed in seriousness. "This is about healthy development and creating *lasting* bonding experiences with your little one. We're going to explore everything from rhythm and beat"—Sam does a little fancy footwork and slides across the floor like a cat; the kids stare, transfixed—"to movement and dance." Sam claps his hands above his right shoulder like a flamenco dancer.

"But first, a sing-along!"

Sam asks us to retrieve brightly colored and fringed serapes from a cupboard in one corner of the room and lay them in a circle facing one another on the floor. We oblige in silence, struck dumb in the face of Sam's splendor.

I sit between Fred and a woman who looks to be about my age or a few years older, with the curliest blond hair I've ever seen, like the wigs my cousin used to wear to Irish dancing competitions growing up. I compliment her on her poncho, which is covered in mustangs and wolves running somewhere.

"Thanks," she says wearily.

Sam passes around a large canister of hand sanitizer that we squirt into our hands, rubbing them together so that the air is filled with quiet squelching. Seems a little late for this, I think, since we're already sitting on these old blankets, but I try to tamp down any judgment as it arises, like snuffing out a candle's flame with a lid.

"So," Sam says, holding a huge stuffed dog that looks like a deflated Snoopy. "Follow my lead.

"*Here we are at Sam's house, at Sam's house, at Sam's house. Heeere we are at Sam's house, at Sam's house, we sing!*"

Sam pauses, expectant. The air frizzles with electricity.

Like obedient schoolchildren or well-trained farm animals, we adults repeat Sam's made-up song back to him in perfect unison, swaying slightly back and forth as Sam did. The children look from their parents to Sam to each other with wide eyes, mouths open and drooling.

They do not sing and they do not sway. Most are far too young to form complete sentences.

Sam leads us through three more verses before waving his spirit fingers in the sky and screaming, "WHO'S READY FOR SOME FUN?!"

Finally, the children are aroused from their stupor. They stumble up from their parents' laps or their serapes and begin playing in earnest, crawling around in circles or bouncing up and down and screaming, waving their arms over their heads like their hair is on fire. A couple of slightly older toddlers head for the ball pit and do cannonballs. Fred starts giggling awkwardly. His kid is the only one left in the circle, seeming fixated on a loose string in their serape.

Well. This wasn't so bad, I think, watching Emma and a little girl with glasses that look like goggles crawl beside each other around the playscape, pointing at the slides and tugging on each other's arms. Emma's already made a friend! Arno will be so pleased. My insides feel all mushy, like warm goop, just thinking about it.

I pull out my phone to take a photo of her. Click.

"NO PHOTOS!" Sam roars, losing his flawless veneer of enthusiasm for the first time in the last hour. His blue eyes are wide, deranged. "Didn't you read the sign-in sheet?! We have to protect the babies' identities!"

My cheeks flush, hot and red. "Oh, of course," I stammer. "I'm so sorry."

But it's too late. All of the parents are glaring at me as though I've just asked for their children's Social Security numbers. Like I'm trying to sell their babies' images on the dark web to molesters and pedophiles.

"Deleting now!"

I make a big show of pressing the red trash can icon, turn on the volume so they can hear the gobble-gobble sound of deletion.

"See? All gone!"

They turn away from me, a blanket of collective scorn. Even Fred.

Maybe Emma and I won't be coming back after all.

CHAPTER 7

We hired a nanny. Someone Arno found through a recommendation from a friend at work.

She is not the well-traveled, middle-aged-verging-on-old French woman I'd envisioned, but she is still competent, sweet, and, most importantly, nonthreatening. To be honest, the entire transaction of telling Arno to ask around for a good nanny, him getting a referral, and then hiring her was unnervingly fast. Almost like the time it takes to select a new blouse and check out from a store, but I guess that's par for the course in our on-demand world.

Her name is Kyle, which confuses approximately everyone but me.

"Wait—you hired a *male* nanny, Elizabeth?" Arno's mother all but hisses into the phone when I deliver the news. "What on earth prompted you to—"

"She's a woman, Adrienne." I don't have the energy to scold his mother's sexism.

"Oh," Adrienne says, chagrined. "Well, what kind of a name is that?"

Kyle is a full-time nanny, part-time doula, and graduate of Wellesley College. I think she's twenty-four years old, but I'm not entirely certain because she mentioned something about age discrimination during her interview and it felt weird to ask after that.

She has closely cropped white-blond hair and unnervingly large blue eyes, pale as ice and made to look even bigger behind a pair of clear, boxlike Warby Parker glasses that remind me of something a senile grandmother would wear, but I get the sense Kyle is entirely unironic.

Kyle is fluent in Spanish and French, has a tattoo of women's breasts on the inner side of her wrist, and exclusively wears oversized men's button-down shirts with fun patterns like tiny sailboats and pineapples.

What sold me on Kyle was her immediate ease around Emma. During her interview, she made goofy faces and blew kisses till Emma dissolved into a pool of giggles on the floor. She picked Emma up like she weighed no more than a stuffed animal and carried her to the kitchen for a snack and, later, to her bedroom for a long nap.

I know that toddlers can't understand the concept of respect, but still, I saw Emma gaze up at Kyle as if she was god on earth, or maybe even Barney, and in return, Kyle spoke to Emma with the patience and tranquility of a Buddhist monk. She was kind but firm, silly but serious. I liked her immediately.

We decided that she would come over every morning at 9:00 a.m. and stay till 5:00 p.m., like a typical office worker, with some exceptions; namely, when Arno and I have to attend dinner parties or want to go on the occasional date night. Then, Kyle will work late and receive overtime—and at a pretty generous rate, at that. She will probably come on family vacations, but we didn't set anything in stone. Like I said, I don't want to be one of those crazy Stonebridge wives who only spends two hours per day actually interacting with their kid. We set up an individual coverage health reimbursement arrangement and committed to two weeks of PTO and unlimited sick days.

When Kyle signed the forms Arno printed out, I was giddy with elation. If not for gravity, I feared I would lift right off the kitchen floor.

"So, when do you want me to start?" Kyle asked, smiling politely.

"Tomorrow?" I heard myself say, feeling like a bank robber getting away with a double murder.

"Sure," Kyle said, smiling widely to reveal extremely white buck teeth and the slightest hint of an overbite. "Tomorrow sounds great."

The only awkward moment in the entire transaction was when Kyle asked me with utter earnestness, "So, what do you do, Mrs. Bennett?"

The question caught me off guard, that's all, but I was still ashamed to hear the bite in my voice when I replied, "I'm an author, Kyle."

"Oh!" Kyle said, her cheeks flushing crimson as she realized she'd caused offense. The silence that followed enveloped us both like a tossed sheet.

"Sorry," I rushed to explain myself, filling the void, "I'm just . . . I'm trying to finish my second book, and it's been really hard. Ever since I had Emma, there just never seems to be a good time to work . . ."

Kyle nodded emphatically, as if she totally understood.

"Of course, Mrs. Bennett."

"Please—call me Liz."

"Okay."

"To be honest," I said, shaking my head, "I'm really nervous. I haven't written—really written—in over two years. I just couldn't focus while I was pregnant, and since having Emma, my head is all fuddled all the time . . ."

"You don't have to explain yourself, Liz," Kyle assured me, reaching out to pat my arm. "I can't imagine getting anything productive done while growing and then caring for a tiny human!" She squeezed my hand like a kindly priest, and I remembered that she went to one of the most liberal schools on the East Coast.

"Can you tell that to my agent?" I joked.

"Child-rearing was never meant to be done alone," she countered.

She must think Arno is an asshole, I realized, wanting to laugh out loud, but I did nothing to dispel her presumption. Instead, I nodded tragically and looked down at my limp hands.

"You're right, Kyle. No one should do it alone."

CHAPTER 8

Driving through Brookline, a section of greater Boston I haven't visited since before Emma was born, brings back blurry memories of grad school I haven't accessed in years: late-night sushi at Genki Ya with a South African poet who said he loved me, twice, before saying it was a joke; greasy bagel sandwiches from Kupel's Bakery with my friend Mariana as we relived the night before, hungover and crusty-eyed. Getting stoned with Mariana and our friend Rose on Rose's dilapidated porch before traipsing around the Brookline Farmers' Market, picking up turquoise rings and hammered gold bracelets and heirloom tomatoes as big as our faces, holding them up to the light, but never buying anything because we were too broke. Spending an entire Sunday on Mariana's saggy brown couch, supposedly writing but mostly napping while murder mysteries like *The Fall* played on a ceaseless loop before us on the TV.

What became of Mariana, I wonder, as I turn onto Brookline Avenue, tree-lined and dewy and cluttered with students who only move around in tight packs.

She'd been my first and closest friend at Boston University.

We were both in the fiction program, but Mariana always gave off the distinct impression that she wasn't really sure why she was there—both in the program and in Boston in general. She was Colombian, born and raised in Miami, and had gone to Florida State University for undergrad, where she'd earned a degree in communications, a baccalaureate she said was as useless as the paper it was printed on.

She liked writing short stories about her home state, Florida: sinister, twisting vignettes that left classmates wringing their hands and wondering what her childhood was like. Those tales were the darkest thing about her; Mariana wore bright, popping colors that accentuated her perpetually bronzed skin, fuchsia and teal and geranium red. She was incredibly short, just over five feet tall, but I always forgot because her presence crackled.

She was a live wire, couldn't sit still to save her life. That's why she smoked so much weed, she explained, while rolling the tidiest joint I'd ever laid eyes on.

My favorite thing about Mariana, though—other than her laugh, which was like the cackle of a disturbed crow—was that she chose me.

Sitting in the front row of our writing workshop, the very core of the curriculum that was supposed to separate the writers from the capital "w" Writers, I could feel anxiety emanating off my classmates like the smell of decay.

The class was small, maybe twelve people total. Like many MFA programs in creative writing, BU's was designed to make us feel special. Chosen. We relished the small class size and the rickety old desks that we crouched over, far too big for the metal seats. We'd heard Junot Díaz might be teaching a seminar in the spring. This was exactly what we had all come for.

I tapped my mechanical pencil across the spine of my planner, something glittery and pink and unserious that I regretted purchasing immediately, and scanned the room. Most of the other students looked like me—that is, white, nervous, middle- to upper-middle class, slightly neurotic, still on the shiny side of thirty. Lots of dark jeans and tweed blazers, beanie hats and symbolic tattoos.

There were a handful of older classmates, mostly prematurely bald men in tortoiseshell glasses who were either in their midthirties or late fifties—it was difficult to tell. We all felt bad for them, thinking they'd wasted their youths and realized their calling too late. Far too late. They instinctually sat at the back of every classroom, as if they knew their presence was embarrassing and felt ashamed.

There were a couple of attractive girls who I immediately eyed as potential friends. (A secret: I find the biggest threats in any room and neutralize them through intense friendship. I've done this since kindergarten, when I invited shiny-haired Ruby Rosedale—her real name—over to play a Nancy Drew computer game because I somehow knew her mom didn't let her use their computer, and she agreed immediately, that sucker.) One was a redhead with green cat-eye glasses and an Alabama Shakes T-shirt reading the latest Zadie Smith novel, a walking caricature of my aesthetic. The other was a focused-looking Black girl with the most stunning gold eyes I'd ever seen, like tiger marbles. She typed on her laptop with a pen clenched between her teeth, and I imagined she was already working on her memoir in between classes.

Then, a flutter of color and movement.

In the doorway, chatting animatedly with Mariana, stood the professor, a notoriously cruel East Coast success story with one National Book Award under her belt and rumors of another on its way. She'd just been recognized as one of the "5 Under 35" by the National Book Foundation, and here she was, teaching wannabes who were more or less the same age as her.

They looked like old friends, reunited after months apart, picking up where they left off. Mariana even *touched her arm* before glancing around the room for a seat. I believe everyone in the class had the distinct feeling that we'd interrupted them.

Someone coughed loudly from the back of the room as if to remind the professor why we were all there.

Mariana, unperturbed, made shocking and prolonged eye contact with me before whisking herself into the desk beside mine.

"Hola!" she said ironically, as out of place among the mostly drab student body as a flamingo among pigeons.

"Hey," I said, noting her pineapple-yellow peasant dress and leopard-spotted sneakers. Red heart-shaped sunglasses perched atop her head. She unwrapped a stick of tropical-flavored Trident gum and popped it into her mouth, chewing somewhat loudly, I thought, for the small space.

But beneath the papaya and guava, I detected something skunkier. Had she just gotten high? I wondered if she'd stumbled into the wrong room and was looking for the art students, or maybe the fashion design cohort.

"You're in the fiction program?" I asked, trying to keep the judgment from my voice.

"Mm-hmm!" she murmured. Then she turned to me, her face clouded with seriousness.

"Do you want to get a burger after this? I'm fucking starving."

I was so surprised I laughed out loud, then hastily covered my mouth, as if *I* was the one chewing like a cow.

"Sure, I'll get a burger."

"I'm Mariana, by the way."

"Liz. Nice to meet you."

I shake the memory from my periphery like a dog dispelling water after a bath and cruise into a metered parking space in front of Trader Joe's.

I'm not here to shop.

I turn off the engine and feed a handful of dusty quarters into the meter, marveling at how old-fashioned so many aspects of greater Boston are: parking, transportation, the public parks. The fact that there are no happy hours.

Brookline itself, one of the largest towns in New England, and, according to its website, a "residential community with urban characteristics," feels dated, antiquated: The John Fitzgerald Kennedy National Historic Site. The Larz Anderson Auto Museum. The Coolidge Corner Theatre, circa 1933.

Visitors get the feeling Brookline is a town anxiously trying to revive its past.

You'd think having such a concentrated student population would provide Brookline with at least an aura of hipness and modernity, but no. Though there are quite a few vegan food chains and artisanal donut shops sticking off the main artery like thumbs, Brookline is mostly home to middle-aged and older white-collar professionals, mainly in the fields of medicine and education, who have no trouble handling some of the highest property taxes in the entire country.

Therapists. There's a bunch of those, too, and that's why I drove the twenty-five minutes northeast from Wellesley today—to see Dr. Sharon

Abelson, on account of my insomnia. I've had it before, early in my relationship with Arno, when I fluctuated between feeling 100 percent sure he was in love with me and 100 percent sure he was too good for me.

The sleeplessness hasn't been terrible, exactly, just bad enough that each day I feel hungover and a little bit slow, as if my thoughts are traveling through molasses and the viscosity isn't allowing them to connect in any meaningful way. Makes it quite difficult to focus on my writing, which is the whole reason we hired Kyle in the first place, so I'm hoping Dr. Abelson can offer some advice.

Her office is tucked away on Pleasant Street, and the irony is not lost on me. I wonder if she chose this location for connotation alone.

A large redbrick building, probably from the early 1900s, with slightly lopsided Victorian staircases and an elevator that's perpetually out of order. Multicolored candies in cellophane wrappers in a dusty glass bowl. A rocking chair at the end of a long, carpeted hallway that leads nowhere. A smell of must and, more faintly, cat.

She shares the space with a dentist, a chiropractor, and a grief counselor. I feel so terrible for anyone who's been to all four establishments.

I knock on her heavy wooden door and feel as if I'm standing at the entrance of a mausoleum. Maybe it's not too late to turn aroun—

Dr. Abelson swings the door wide open before my knuckle can complete its second rap, causing me to stumble forward a couple steps. Dr. Abelson steadies me, gripping my arm firmly, and looks at me with wide, concerned eyes. I've already made a terrible impression.

"Sorry about that," I sputter, gathering myself.

Dr. Abelson continues holding my biceps.

"Are you all right, dear?"

"Yes, completely. Just tripped a little. This rug's tricky . . ." I say, scuffing at the maroon carpeting for emphasis.

"All right, dear, well, why don't you have a seat over there."

Dr. Abelson gestures toward a brown leather couch with her free hand before releasing me slowly, like one of those exotic-animal veterinarians you see on Animal Planet, stepping away from a drugged tiger they've just performed surgery on.

"Sure."

My voice, even to my own subjective ears, sounds brittle and frayed. A crack somewhere in the vowels.

We go way back, Dr. Abelson and I, but I haven't visited her since before Emma was born. Actually, come to think of it, I've not been since I officially moved in with Arno. I slept more soundly when he was perpetually by my side.

Tempus fugit. Time flies.

"So, Elizabeth," Dr. Abelson says, "it's been quite a long time since I've last seen you. A few years, at least. You'll have to fill me in on your life."

I nod. I'd been expecting this but somehow hoping to avoid it. I know a therapist's job is to help people deal with mental and physical issues, sans judgment, but on some level, I've wanted to make Dr. Abelson proud of me. I fear that when she hears how little I've done professionally since graduate school, how I'm still struggling with the same sleep problems, the same anxiety and insecurities, she'll think me a failure.

I first started seeing therapists after I started having panic attacks in college. There had been a brief fling, a bad breakup. It wasn't anything serious. With the guy, I mean. But his abandonment brought up old feelings I thought I'd crammed away.

My childhood was anything but rosy. My parents hated each other, fought constantly, and finally got divorced when I was in elementary school and Jack was just a tiny thing. My mom started dating immediately, juggling a fellow professor with a gold tooth, an auditor who was nearly twice her age and clinically depressed, and someone she claimed worked for the FBI.

My dad picked up and moved to the woods of Vermont. He built a log cabin "tiny home" there and lived as though he were a hermit. He spent his days managing the local organic food store, woodworking, taking long walks in the forest with his rescue mutt, Helga, and preparing for winter.

We saw him every couple years, when he felt guilty enough to appear at one of our birthdays, always looking skinnier and more wild somehow. He'd usually take us out for pizza and spend the evening talking about different canning methods and railing against politicians who were destroying the ozone layer. At some point, we stopped inviting him.

My mom was a more consistent presence, though neither Jack nor I was sure whether this was a good or terrible thing.

She never seemed interested in anything we did, much less proud of us, and was much more wrapped up in the politics and scandals of academia, which were legion. She was always throwing fancy dinner parties at our modest two-story Victorian home and taking three-week vacations to Lake of the Ozarks and Montreal with the auditor or the professor or the guy who probably didn't work for the FBI. By the time I was in middle school, Jack and I were left home alone a fair amount, and even though we were old enough to handle it and could have even made some fun of the situation, we always ended up retreating to our bedrooms with pints of ice cream and heavy novels, grieving our splintered family in solitude.

If there was an extended family worth mentioning, Jack and I never heard about them.

Holidays passed with little fanfare. Sometimes, my mom would invite us to a Christmas dinner at the auditor's house, but Jack and I hated meeting his sniveling little children who could potentially become our stepbrothers or stepsisters; hated the expectation of perfect manners and small talk and entertaining the random senile grandmother that was always present and unattended on these occasions and whom we somehow became responsible for.

We stopped going, started spending the holiday together, just the two of us. My mom still got us presents, of course—she wasn't a complete monster—but Jack and I would open them before she got back from wherever she'd gone Christmas Eve night. Jack would ride his new red bicycle or scooter in long loops around the neighborhood, while I'd bag up all of the wrapping paper and throw it away, carefully folding any gift bags that could be reused the following year.

As a result, Jack and I were different from other kids and, now, other adults. We were more solitary, self-contained. We enjoyed having friends, but we never relied on them. We doled out our love carefully and were always prepared for retreat.

It also made us paranoid.

"Right, of course, of course," I murmur, looking down at my black leather Chloé boots. A lot has happened since 2015.

"But I'd also like to know why you've come back," she says, reading my mind. I smile at her gratefully. "It's important to address any immediate or dire concerns, too."

"Right. Yes. Thank you."

I run my hands through my hair, which is blown dry and straightened, thanks to Kyle's fresh presence in our household.

"I can't sleep."

"Ah, this again," Dr. Abelson says, nodding deeply, reminding me of an ancient sage. "And why do you think that is, Liz?"

"Ummmm . . ."

It's human nature to want to deliver information to others in a manner that presents ourselves in the best possible light.

"Well, I have a baby now. Emma. She's just over a year old."

"Oh, that's so wonderful, Liz. Congratulations." Dr. Abelson smiles at me, genuinely, over the rim of a cup of tea. It's steaming, and the tang of chai hits me in the hippocampus, bringing me back to when I last sat on this leather couch, three months into dating Arno, weeping into my palms. Convinced he'd see through my charade of a cool, normal girlfriend.

"Yes, thank you. It's wonderful. She's wonderful."

"But she keeps you up at night?"

"Yes."

The lie comes out easily, but I immediately feel guilty. Why come to therapy if you aren't telling the truth?

Dr. Abelson's seated behind a sleek glass desk, where she takes notes on a yellow legal notepad in purple pen. She looks older than I remembered, and I wonder if she's physically aged drastically or if my memory was just incorrect. Her hair is a wild mess of curls, some black, some gray, and tied back from her face with a silk paisley scarf. She must have poor eyesight; her thick-rimmed glasses magnify her pupils, giving her a bug-like quality that feels all-seeing, all-knowing. Or maybe they're just there for effect, like the purple chaise lounge to my right that I imagine no one's ever laid on.

"Wait. That's not it."

"I'm sorry?"

"Emma. She isn't keeping me up at night. To be honest, she sleeps for like eleven hours straight. Bit ridiculous, actually."

I trail off, looking at a small metal gong atop Dr. Abelson's desk. Once, when I was spiraling toward a forest of despair, the gnarled arms of witch elms clawing at my equilibrium, she'd struck it with a tiny metal hammer. The reverberating noise had shocked me so completely, I'd forgotten what I was catastrophizing about and laughed out loud.

Dr. Abelson offered her clients an expensive assortment of talk, sound, and cognitive behavioral therapy. I required all three.

"Then what is it?"

"I think Arno's cheating on me. We're married now. He's Emma's father."

Dr. Abelson is silent for a moment. Her eyebrows lift slightly.

"Okay. Let's start there."

Over the course of the next fifty minutes, I tell Dr. Abelson about the text I saw on Arno's phone a couple of weeks ago from a mysterious coworker named Viv, who I'd never heard him mention previously, even though they're both VPs at the same branch and, evidently, quite close.

I walk her through the wine-stained night of my research, in which I figured out who Viv was and passed out in bed feeling stupid and jealous. How Arno came home late, very late, and completely hammered. So full of vodka and god knows what else he could barely remove his clothes. How I'd felt on the precipice of unnamed doom ever since. How I couldn't sleep through a three-hour stretch, let alone a full night, without waking up with my heart racing and our sheets soaked through with my sweat. The nightmares of a dark-haired baby with an alien face, mutant screams. How I couldn't focus on anything: not my daughter, not my writing, not even the road. (I'd hit a mailbox the week prior, and Emma had screamed from her car seat for an hour straight.)

I just wanted to sleep. That's all.

Dr. Abelson peers at me through her Coke-bottle glasses in silence, her long fingers pressed together at the tips. Silver rings wrapped around each digit. I wonder if she takes them all off every time she showers. Seems like a lot of trouble.

"Liz." Dr. Abelson cuts through my thoughts like she's fileting a fish.

"Yes?"

"Why don't you just ask Arno about the text?"

"Because . . . I . . . well, I . . ."

Why haven't I?

I pause, looking at my hands, and a small voice answers: *Because if it's true, you will have to leave Arno, and if you leave Arno, you will have nothing.*

Dr. Abelson clears her throat, cutting through my mind chatter.

"Do you remember when you visited me after you and Arno first got together, when you were convinced he would eventually tire of you?"

"Um . . . kind of?"

"And you were sure that if you ever did get married to him, you'd just sabotage the relationship, as your mother did?"

"Well, I—"

"And that your ex-boyfriend from college didn't really love you?"

"Well, he didn't, but—"

"And that you weren't a talented writer, so why even bother?"

"Okay, I think I get the picture of what you're trying to—"

"And that you were destined to die alone?"

I fiddle with my engagement ring and wedding band, twirling them in circles around my ring finger. They'd gotten so tight while I was pregnant that I used butter to slide them on and off before bed. It never occurred to me that it wouldn't be a big deal if I didn't wear them for a while, till the swelling went down.

"Yes, I vaguely remember saying all those things. I was a bit of a basket case for a while there. Till I moved in with Arno, I guess . . ."

"Do you remember what I told you when you had all of those fears, Liz?"

"You said there was a difference between my thoughts and what was real. What *is* real."

Dr. Abelson sighs and leans back in her chair like she's just closed a multimillion-dollar deal.

"Well?" she asks. "Do you think maybe this is another instance of catastrophizing?"

"I . . . I'm not sure . . ."

I think about Arno's behavior over the last few days. Facts: He bought me a bouquet of pink tulips—my second favorite flower after hydrangeas—Saturday morning, along with a bag of hot, buttery croissants and pastries from a fantastic bakery in Wellesley.

On Sunday, when I mentioned I was having trouble sleeping, he'd immediately ordered a thick eye mask from Amazon, along with a somewhat ridiculous sound soother machine that plays ocean sounds, gently falling rain, and even simulated thunderstorms from a small black box he plugged in beside our bed.

We'd had sex twice in the last week; once when he surprised me in the shower while Emma was sleeping and I'd just gotten back from a long, sweaty run. I blush recalling it and resume fidgeting with my rings.

"You might be right," I admit.

Dr. Abelson nods vigorously, as though she's relieved I've decided to join her down on planet Earth.

"Do you remember some of the techniques we used before, Liz? Techniques to help replace irrational thoughts with rational ones?"

"Ummm . . ."

I try to recall the flurry of self-help books I bought when I first started seeing Dr. Abelson. Something about your secret love language and how to find a partner who makes you feel secure. There was also the yoga mat I ordered. A book about understanding your chakras. A journal made of hemp and bamboo that I wrote approximately one entry in. Endless boxes of chamomile tea, straight from India. A crystal or two that cost more than my heating bill for the month of February. The small metal gong from a third-party seller that never arrived. Some CBD oils from a pet store in Somerville that definitely didn't sell pets. And weed. Lots and lots of weed. Mostly from Mariana, but she stopped supplying me when I never paid her, so I eventually relied on my next-door neighbor, who I think was once a Harvard med student but maybe dropped out. I never bothered to check.

"Meditation?" I ask tentatively. It's been so long.

"Exactly!" Dr. Abelson shouts, clapping her hands together. The silver metal rings clack in approval. I exhale in relief. "Meditation and mindfulness are crucial for breaking your downward spirals."

"Mm-hmm," I mumble, imagining another sleepless night filled

with nightmares of evil, alien stranger babies with black hair. Screaming, wailing, shrieking cries from the bottomless pits of hell.

"Have you considered seeing a psychiatrist?" Dr. Abelson asks, as
though reading my mind. She pushes her glasses up the bridge of her
nose.

I bristle immediately, even though I know plenty of people who have
felt immeasurably better after taking antidepressants and antianxiety
medication. "No," I reply, too quickly. "I don't want to take anything."

Dr. Abelson's eyes narrow.

"There's nothing shameful about needing medication to assist you
in managing life, Liz. Many of my patients take them and feel immediate relief from their anxiety. Many report sleeping better at night."

I rush to reassure her that I'm interested in "doing the work" holisti-
cally, as she's so fond of describing my mental health journey.

"Liz . . ." Dr. Abelson says softly.

"Yeah?"

"Think about it."

Of course I have. And I'm not going on pills.

I imagine myself like my mom's ex-boyfriend Greg, the auditor, who
could typically be found completely zonked out on some combination
of Lexapro, Prozac, and Ativan, wandering the empty halls of our house
like a clone of his former self. A mechanical puppet happy to just sit
in one place and stare out the window into nothingness until he died.
I'm sure he was taking a bad combination as well as too high a dose,
but still.

I shiver, a full-body chill that sends goose pimples up and down my
arms and legs. Arno would never want me like that. And who would
blame him?

"I don't need medication. I've just been feeling really desperate in
the evenings, that's all. I just want to be able to sleep through the night
beside my husband."

"Well, Liz, have you been doing the work?"

I think about the last few months: a blur of changing diapers, grocery shopping, preparing baby food, cooking adult food, cleaning our
overly spacious home, and trying desperately to sleep.

"No."

Dr. Abelson nods so deeply her chin nearly touches her concave chest. She reminds me of a stork, or some type of long-legged shorebird. All pointy limbs and piercing eyes.

"Perhaps some yoga tonight? Maybe some guided meditation through an app you have on your phone?"

Used to have.

"I suppose I could . . ."

Dr. Abelson offers up these options like they're the evening specials at a Michelin-starred restaurant, her eyebrows raised with forced enticement. Suddenly, she frowns.

"And you're quite sure your anxiety and insomnia have to do with that text message, and not the transition to motherhood? We didn't spend much time talking about Emma."

"Yes," I snap, feeling attacked and unsure why.

Dr. Abelson's lips press together, and I'm not sure she believes me.

"All right, dear. Then we can meet again, same time next week, and see how much progress you've made."

"Sounds lovely."

CHAPTER 9

Chicken Milanese.

Juicy chicken breast, butterflied, so it's thin and tender, before dipping the cutlets into salt-and-peppered flour, then an egg-and-milk mixture, and, finally, a bath of panko breadcrumbs, with extra Italian seasoning. Cook in a skillet laden with butter and olive oil till the breading is golden brown and crisp. Top generously with peppery arugula, salty Parmesan shavings, and a squeeze of lemon for a tangy bite. Maybe a drizzle of balsamic vinegar, but that's unnecessary.

My mouth waters as I pull into an open parking space at Whole Foods in Wellesley.

For reasons unknown, my meeting with Dr. Abelson has rendered me ravenous, as well as a bit embarrassed. How very like me to see a shoelace and assume it's a snake.

I hop out of my SUV and check my reflection in the window. Hair, smooth and blow-dried. Cream, crepey blouse tucked in. Lipstick, shade "Berry Kiss," unsmudged.

You'd never know I was a woman who'd just been reminded of her lingering generalized anxiety disorder.

I shoot off a text to Kyle, letting her know I have one more stop to make before I get home and relieve her of Emma. A twinge of guilt, brief and hot, like touching a teakettle with the tip of my finger. It's been quite nice spending the day by myself.

That morning, I'd told Kyle I had some important errands to run, vague descriptions of "car stuff," as well as an allusion to a literary workshop I might take through a local writing nonprofit I really have been meaning to check out for years.

Instead, I took a spin class themed to Shakira's and J. Lo's early 2000s hits.

The instructor could not have been more than twenty-two. Her name was Kandy, and she wore a one-piece spandex unitard that looked incredible. I sweated and sang and felt my ass muscles burn with purpose for fifty minutes, and it was fucking glorious. At the end of the class, I gave Kandy a high five and called her "my inspiration." She looked surprised and said she thought I was a new student. My cheeks began to burn, but luckily for me, it was pitch-black in there. The only light emanated from strobing disco balls.

The point is, for one beautiful hour, I forgot who I was.

(And that my husband may or may not be cheating on me and that I hadn't slept in the two weeks since reading the mysterious text message.)

After spin, I had a couple hours to kill before my appointment, so I walked around the Boston seaport like a tourist, admiring the new clothing boutiques and outdoor beer gardens that had popped up. I probably hadn't visited the area since some date with Arno in the early throes of our courtship. Maybe that time we went to the Barking Crab and got so drunk off blueberry beer that neither of us has touched the stuff since. I smile at the memory, grabbing a forest-green shopping cart without a baby seat, and the choice happens so easily, so automatically, I feel guilty once more.

As I'd wandered around the seaport, high off endorphins and Shakira, I felt lighter, more hopeful than I'd felt since long before Emma was born. Knowing that Kyle was taking care of things at home made me feel giddier than Kevin in *Home Alone*.

I hummed "Hips Don't Lie" as I spontaneously bought some new lipstick from a Sephora store clerk who said it brought out my "peachy undertones." I bought an oatmeal-raisin cookie the size of my face from Flour Bakery and ate it without hesitation while sipping a whole-milk vanilla latte with extra cinnamon on top. I ignored two calls from my literary agent, but I did think about my manuscript, unaltered and unopened on my laptop for over a year now, and instead of feeling stressed out, I felt excitement. With Kyle around, look how much time there was in a day. Look how the minutes stretch like elastic when you get to be alone.

Truth be told, I rode the spin high until I knocked on the door of Dr. Abelson's office. Something about being back in the dark halls of that dingy old brick building sucked me backward into a far more troubling period of my life. Just seeing the *Out of Order* sign still hanging on the gold elevator doors made me feel hopeless. In disrepair.

But in talking with Dr. Abelson, something astonishing happened: I believed her.

Maybe we'd always disagree about the efficacy of daily meditation and mindfulness, but Dr. Abelson and I could agree on something far more important: Arno wasn't cheating on me. I was simply spinning through my old cycles of catastrophe, like a ballerina in a broken musical jewelry box. Assuming the worst of everyone for no reason other than a chemical imbalance in my brain. Same tune, different verse.

I grab a hunk of Italian Parmesan and chuck it into the cart, where it thunks with the pleasing thud of a ripe watermelon. I struggle to remember whether there's anything else Arno and I need from the grocery store because I'm so excited about my recent self-discovery. Thank god for Dr. Abelson and her psychology degree from Barnard, her weird metal gongs and shitty bank candies.

My good fortune shimmers off me and collides with passersby: I smile benignly at a pregnant woman carrying a large fern. Wait patiently behind an elderly couple who definitely cut me in line at the deli and are hemming and hawing over the price of pepper Jack cheese. Laugh at the hijinks of a little boy, maybe three or four, who picks up a banana and, without warning, cracks it in half before shoving the gooey banana flesh into his face.

Chicken Milanese is a special dish—the first meal I ever cooked for Arno.

During the third week of our relationship, he'd mentioned craving a home-cooked meal; we'd been eating out so often. I blurted out that

I'd cook him dinner at my place, without thinking anything through. I lived in a studio apartment in Back Bay, by Kenmore Square. I didn't have a dining room table or chairs, and my kitchen was so small only one person could stand in it at a time.

I'd picked the apartment for romanticism alone. It had refurbished hardwood floors, a defunct fireplace, and a sweeping bay window that overlooked the Charles River and Cambridge in the distance. At the viewing, I imagined myself setting up a desk in front of the large window and writing a novel as the crisp air turned the maple trees brilliant orange and fire-engine red, and tiny little Harvard rowers guided their rowboats on the breast of the river. Rent was fifteen hundred dollars per month, and I paid it with a credit card that I would max out within a year.

But back to the Milanese. It was something I remembered my mother making whenever she had guests over, which, as a tenured history professor, was pretty often. She'd boasted to me in private that it was an elegant dish that was also deceptively simple. And guys loved it.

"I mean, who doesn't like crispy chicken?" she'd whispered to me conspiratorially over a glass of sauvignon blanc, wildly flipping the crackling chicken breasts in a frying pan with her other hand like some kind of New Age chef.

So, I'd done what lots of young women looking for advice do: I called my mother. That was new for me. New for us, I mean. We just weren't that kind of mother-daughter duo.

Case in point: "Are you okay???" she'd shouted into the phone, fully alarmed.

"I'm fine, Mom."

"Is your brother okay?"

"Yeah, he's fine, too. I think."

"Well, then, what do you need?"

"What do you need?" was a favorite question of my mom's. As if we, her children, were constantly trying to pry something away from her, whether it be attention or just general assistance. I guess in this instance she wasn't completely wrong.

"Do you have the recipe for that chicken Milanese you used to make sometimes?"

I could almost hear her smile through the phone.

"Why are you asking?"

My mom knew I didn't cook proper meals for myself. In grad school and the year since graduating, I had subsisted on frozen Trader Joe's pot stickers and dark-chocolate-covered raisins.

"I'm cooking dinner for a guest, and I want it to taste good."

"A guest? What guest?"

"A guy I'm seeing."

A pregnant pause.

"Don't get excited. It's new."

"Well, he must be pretty special if you're cooking him dinner, Elizabeth." And then, because she can't help herself: "It's quite unlike you to go to that much trouble for someone else."

"Can you just send me the recipe? Like, via email, or copy the link into a text?"

"I don't know how to 'text' recipes," my mom said disdainfully, as if I'd asked her to send it via telepathy or carrier pigeon. "But I suppose I can try to find the recipe online and email it to you."

"Thanks."

"You know, I make the recipe by muscle memory at this point. Just a flick of the wrist. All intuition."

"That's great, Mom. I gotta go."

"Tell your new friend I said hello, will you?"

"I probably won't. Bye, Mom."

"Elizabeth—wait." That tone: a mosquito's bite on the flesh, drawing blood. I hear it in my sleep.

"Yes?"

"I'm assuming this fellow has a name."

"What makes you so sure my suitor is a 'he'?" I asked, hoping to rattle her.

"Don't be silly, Liz. You're as heterosexual as they come. To pretend otherwise is an insult to lesbians everywhere."

"His name is Arno."

"Arno. That's an interesting name. German?"

"I'm not really sure."

"And I'm assuming his parents bequeathed him with a surname?"

"Bennett," I said, cringing inwardly as I imagined her Googling the name the moment we hung up. Instead, she laughed.

"What?"

"Well, I assume you've already done the math on this one, sweetheart," my mom said, relishing the moment. "If you two get married, you'll be Elizabeth Bennett. A modern-day heroine! I'm sure you love that."

She knew *Pride and Prejudice* was my favorite novel of all time, but she was poking fun at me; she remembered how I obsessively read it as a child, till the pages were yellowed and thin. How I dreamed of being swept away from my family by a handsome stranger.

"Uh, I guess so. Hadn't thought about it, really."

Of course I'd thought about it. That's how I *knew* we were destined to be together. I hung up before she could say anything else to ruin my mood.

I smile, running my fingers over some imported dark chocolates before tossing those in the cart as well.

At this point, I can make the Milanese by muscle memory alone, too. It's one of Arno's favorite dishes, but I try to save it for anniversaries, special occasions, and that sort of thing, to keep the significance of the meal intact for us.

I toss the final ingredient, a box of cherry tomatoes, into the cart and head for the checkout line. I'm still ebullient from my visit with Dr. Abelson. By the cash register I almost purchase a small bound book with the title *Giving Thanks*. On the jacket, it advises the consumer to write one thing they're grateful for every single day, for 365 days, and then reflect on how lucky they are. But then I see the teenage cashier eyeing me and the book skeptically, like I *would* be the kind of schmuck to subscribe to such silliness, and I drop it back on the rack in distaste.

"What a joke, right?" I say, smiling at the pimple-faced girl with a black nose ring.

"Total bullshit," she agrees.

The drive home passes in a haze of warm fuzziness, like the feeling after drinking a half glass of wine and knowing you've still got a whole bottle and entire evening before you. I listen to weepy indie songs that remind me of the year I met Arno, hoping to cast an aura of nostalgia

on the evening: Father John Misty's "Holy Shit" and "Chateau Lobby."
I made him playlists chock-full of Bon Iver, Courtney Barnett, and
Sufjan Stevens, and he pretended to love them for about a year until
we became comfortable enough with each other that he revealed he
actually preferred punk rock. Jazz for cooking. Pop for working out
and closing deals. But never indie. Still, I found his commitment to
try to like what I loved charming and sweet; no boyfriend before him
had ever sat through a three-hour First Aid Kit concert packed to the
gills with hipster college students wearing flannel and openly weeping.

By the time I pull into our driveway, I am twenty-eight again, dewy
and golden and witty and a bit melancholy, but in a sexy way. On the
flip side, Emma is just on the cusp of becoming a fully realized human
adult, someone I can take to poetry readings and art showings. Someone self-possessed and irreverent and shockingly funny, with a touch
of gallows humor. I imagine her at eighteen, with dyed dark hair and
heavy eyeliner, rolling her eyes as Arno and I still kiss one another on
the lips while cooking dinner.

Everything is going to be just fine, I think, and I hold this warmth
inside of me like a marshmallow to a campfire, savoring its toasty glow.

CHAPTER 10

The glow lasts about ten minutes.

Kyle delivers the news with trepidation that emphasizes her wisdom: "Arno called," she says, as soon as I walk through the front door, my arms laden with brown paper bags, still cheerfully humming "Just Like Heaven" by the Cure. I had forgotten we had a landline, and am confused why Arno would use it instead of my cell.

"Oh?"

"Yeah," Kyle says, biting her cuticle, looking at the floor. "He said he might be running late."

"Oh."

"Yeah."

"Did he say how late?" I ask, trying to hide my irritation. It's not like it's Kyle's fault, but her discomfort in relaying his message needles me.

"No. I asked, but he said he didn't want to guess. Just depends on some project he's working on."

"Okay, well, thanks for letting me know," I huff, depositing the bags onto the kitchen counters. I bought a stupid amount of food for one person's dinner, but I'm irritable at the thought of putting it all away for another day.

"He said not to wait up for him," Kyle adds, pouring just one more tablespoon of salt in the open wound that is my heart.

"Okay."

"*Is* that okay?" Kyle asks, her face as open and innocent as a newborn's.

"Is what okay?"

"That he'll be late."

"Yes. Why wouldn't it be?"

I try to hide the unanswered question in my voice, but there it is. The dizzying, ugly fear that coats my throat like cough syrup.

"I just mean, if you need my help a little later, I don't mind staying," Kyle says. She looks pointedly at the overflowing bags on the counter. "Mind if I start unpacking those?"

I laugh, exasperated.

"You're our nanny, Kyle. Not our maid. You don't have to do that."

"I don't mind, Liz."

I smile gratefully and nod, letting Kyle take charge of unpacking my grocery haul when the idea strikes, fully formed: "Hey, would you want to stay for dinner?" I ask, knowing that she will say yes.

"Sure, that sounds really nice," Kyle says, turning from the bags to give me a blinding, bucktoothed grin.

It goes without saying that this meal is "off the books," as it were. Emma is napping, and Kyle and I will be enjoying one another's company as friends. I ask Amazon Alexa to play Leon Bridges and pour each of us massive glasses of rosé because I'm feeling girly. I light a few candles that I purchased last Christmas but haven't gotten around to using. The cloying smell of vanilla and cinnamon and nutmeg mixes with the greasy smell of pan-fried chicken.

Kyle is a lovely dinner guest, and by my second glass of wine, I've dropped all pretense of being her buttoned-up employer, and we enjoy full-on girl talk, something I hadn't quite realized I was missing so much.

I show her how to make my mom's chicken Milanese, and she asks thoughtful questions throughout, as if I'm a Food Network chef with legitimate training: "Which spices do you recommend using on the chicken?" "How thin do you butterfly it?" "Do you have a preferred brand of Parmesan?"

I try to answer all of them honestly: "Parsley, basil, salt, and pepper." "Doesn't matter." "Nah, just something that's from Italy and the size of your head and it's pretty much guaranteed to not have wood pulp in it."

Kyle shares a lot about her life—like the fact that she's one of six children and the only one without dyslexia—and also asks questions that show her social maturity, like, "When did you know you wanted to be a writer?" and, "What books do you hope Emma reads as a young adult?"

She asks a few polite questions about Arno, like where he grew up, where he went to college, and how long he's been at Stonebridge Partners, but I detect a slight hint of disapproval in her tone and guess that she's judged Arno from afar.

Usually, unwarranted judgment of my spouse would infuriate me, but with Kyle, it doesn't. I get the sense that Kyle probably feels low-level hostility toward all men who work in finance and drive Audis and leave their wives home alone like forgotten goldfish. A part of me relishes the completely unearned empathy she bestows upon me.

We eat the chicken Milanese in the backyard on paper plates because the sun hasn't yet set and it's warm, in the mid-70s. Emma remains fast asleep in her crib after a successful day with her new wunderkind nanny.

Kyle oohs and aahs over the golden-brown chicken, giving me a literal chef's kiss while taking the daintiest nibble, and I feel as if the evening hasn't been lost after all. I have two servings and polish off the meal with thick slices of salty Parmesan that I pop into my mouth like after-dinner mints till there's nothing left but rind.

"You should save that for soup," Kyle says, betraying her own chef's wisdom. I raise my eyebrow, and she smiles. "I enjoy cooking the odd soup for friends every now and then." Her button-down shirt today is navy blue, with tiny silver dolphins leaping out of the shirt ocean.

She tactfully drinks only two glasses of wine, declining a third, which only makes me respect her more. I fill my fourth glass to the brim.

"So, Kyle, tell me. Have you ever been in love?" I ask, hoping I don't sound too drunk.

Kyle looks visibly uncomfortable, and I regret asking her but let the question hang in the air, like mist, to see what she'll do with it.

"Honestly, I'm not sure," Kyle says finally, toying with her greasy paper plate. "Hey, I think these are reusable."

I wrinkle my nose.

"I want to save the world, Kyle, but not *that* badly."

Kyle laughs heartily, and the spell seems to have broken: she visibly relaxes in her seat, her shoulders dropping a hair.

"I thought I loved my girlfriend, but I've been having doubts recently."

"Mm-hmm." I nod knowingly. "Doubts about how much you care for her?"

When we first came outside, I turned on the twinkly fairy lights that wrap around the ceiling of our wooden gazebo. The yellow glow plays across Kyle's face, casting shadows in the hollows of her cheeks, making her appear far older and wiser than usual.

"I guess so," Kyle says. "I thought we were pretty perfect for each other when we first got together, but it's been a couple years, and I'm starting to feel like it's run its course." Kyle smiles wryly. "Plus, there've been some trust issues."

I set my wineglass down. Lean forward. Could my nanny and I actually have something in common?

"Tell me more."

Kyle shifts in her seat, unused to the spotlight. "Hailey is a jealous person," she says finally.

Oh. Great. So, Hailey is me.

I top off my wineglass. Take a swig. "Well, why do you think she's jealous?" I ask, trying to hide the defensiveness in my tone. "Do you ever, perhaps, *do things* to make her worry, even without meaning to?"

"She's insecure, of course."

I glance up, stung, but Kyle is looking out at the fast-darkening yard.

"It's sad," Kyle continues. "And at first, I was really empathetic. I would always tell her exactly where I was going, who I was with, what we were doing, et cetera. I even turned on that 'find my location' thing on my phone. But I've come to realize that's toxic behavior, and that if she doesn't learn to trust me, our relationship will never work. Love on its own isn't enough."

I swish wine around my mouth and swallow.

The sun has fully set, and the moon's replaced it in the prime-time slot in the sky, dripping silver onto the black shadows of our manicured backyard. I shiver even though it isn't cold.

"Must be getting late, huh?" I say, trying to keep the anxiety out of my voice.

Like a beloved hunting hound, attuned to my every whim, Kyle looks up, jittery. "Yeah, I suppose I better get going." Kyle stands up, stretching her long arms overhead. "You want to give Arno a ring, see where he's at?" she asks.

"No, Kyle," I snap. "If he said he's working late, he's working late. I don't want to be a nag."

I rise from my seat and gather up the greasy plates in one hand, the empty wineglasses in the other. I'm drunk enough that I stumble ever so slightly up the stone stairs to our sliding glass door that leads to the kitchen.

Kyle looks scared for me.

"Can I help you with those?"

"No, you should get going," I say, trying to even out the edges of my voice. It's not Kyle's fault Arno isn't here. I'm being a bitch. "I don't want you to be on the train *too* late, that's all," I add. "It isn't safe."

"Okay, well I'll head out then. I guess I do have a pretty big day tomorrow," Kyle says, winking at me. "Emma and I have to read *The Very Hungry Caterpillar* for the hundredth time." My annoyance evaporates like smoke, and I return the smile wholeheartedly. I do not deserve Kyle. Kyle could do so much better.

"Thanks for dinner. It was really delicious," she adds, swinging her black JanSport backpack over one shoulder and heading out the front door. There is a rainbow of pins and badges stapled to it that say things like *Flaming Feminist, Brooklyn, Give Bees a Chance*, and *Resist and Persist*.

A little green pin, up near the JanSport logo, catches my eye just as the door slams shut behind Kyle.

Proud Vegetarian, it says.

The realization hits me like a swift punch to the ovaries, and I double over the kitchen table, coughing violently: Kyle, a vegetarian, felt so bad for me she ate chicken Milanese.

CHAPTER 11

The next morning, I studiously avoid Kyle, like a teenager who snuck out, got high, and then was caught by their mother with a roach in their hoodie pocket.

I breeze by her as she unpacks some new toys and reading materials for Emma onto the family room rug. The smell of macadamia-nut milk steams out of the lid of her forest-green thermos that she's set, quite thoughtfully, on top of a hand-knitted coaster *that she brought herself.*

"Morning, Liz," she says calmly.

"Hey," I say awkwardly, wondering if she realizes I put two and two together about the chicken Milanese. I decide to forge ahead.

"So, today is going to be a head-down writing day for me, I think. Is that okay with you?"

"Oh my gosh, totally!" Kyle says, beaming. Like, *actually* beaming. "I'm so glad to hear you'll get some deep work time."

"Erm . . . Mm-hmm." I nod. Is "deep work" what the kids are calling not multitasking for five seconds these days?

"Yeah, so, I'll probably be working in the office upstairs for, like, hours on end, but feel free to knock if you need me."

"Sure thing!"

I hover around her like a beetle, wanting to say something, anything, that will make me feel some semblance of control.

"Arno got in around midnight, poor thing. He's working on a huge deal for the company. Like a multimillion-dollar deal. Huge." I nearly gag, realizing I sound like Donald Trump, and swallow the excess of spit that's welled up in the back of my mouth.

"That's cool," Kyle says without looking up. She carefully stacks a tower of wooden blocks, one on top of the other, on the rug beside some children's books. I lean over to get a better look and see that the blocks have different words on them describing emotions: happy, sad, silly, angry. When you flip over the blocks, the faces match the emotions. I wonder if there's one for "panic."

Kyle looks up, realizing I haven't left the family room.

"You can go write, Liz. I've got it."

She smiles so easily it makes me wonder what it must feel like to be her: self-assured, compassionate—especially to the less deserving—great with kids, smart, and even-tempered. A vegetarian. I want to paraglide into Kyle's head and steal whatever golden dust is sprinkled around in there, bag some up for myself.

I go upstairs to my "office," a room so unused it still has a new-house smell, and sit down at the acetate desk that looks like it belongs in a spaceship. A heavy-looking gold-framed mirror hangs on the opposite wall, and I stare into my hungover, droopy face. Lines crease my forehead and form parentheses around my mouth, which is parched. I use my phone to shoot an email to my dermatologist asking for a reliable Botox artist.

I fire up my laptop—man, it's seeing a lot of action these days!—and find my manuscript among my Google Docs graveyard for underdeveloped ideas. I scan the last chapter I wrote, over a year and a half ago, and realize I've completely forgotten what the whole point of this novel was supposed to be.

A woman falls ill with a mysterious disease and, upon waking up from a coma, remembers nothing of her life. Not her closest friends, nor her parents or her husband. Not even her kids. Most importantly, she can't remember herself: what makes her unique, what she likes and dislikes, what she's scared of. The idea came to me during a dream, around the time Arno and I found out we were expecting, when I'd been particularly anxious. There was a certain untethered feeling coursing through my veins, as if I'd been on the precipice of a cliff, and now I knew for certain I'd be falling over the edge.

I *think* I'd been trying to explore what it would feel like to wake up one day a blank slate: no childhood trauma, no knowledge of preexisting conditions or predilections. Who would my protagonist be then? What would she want?

What would she do?

Isn't there already a book just like this? I wonder. What hole did I think this novel would fill in the memory-loss literature canon?

I chew on a hangnail, disturbed and unfocused. Scroll through the previous chapters (all twenty of them) and try to feel the excitement that must have spurred me to action.

There is nothing. No glimmer of recognition, like seeing the face of an old friend in a crowd, as I read my own words. The tone doesn't even sound like me—too flowery and stilted for my taste, which leans toward wry and economical. I feel like a senile person in a supermarket, wandering the aisles with no list in hand but *sure* I came there for some specific purchase.

I fire off an email to my agent, who somehow hasn't given up on me yet, to let her know I'm getting back in the saddle; we have a nanny now. I tell her I'll have the second book "locked and loaded" in just a few months, probably.

I change the font of the novel from Arial to Cambria, which feels more artistic. Then, I adjust the type size. Maybe making the words bigger will help.

Isn't there such a thing as "mom brain"? Maybe that's my problem.

I close the tab on my manuscript and open another window, where I Google "mom brain." There is an extensive literature on the phenomenon that happens to a woman's mind after giving birth.

Long story short: you become dumber.

One scientific journal claims that women's brains are "resculpted" for two years after their pregnancy, in which time gray matter shrinks in areas related to processing new information and, instead, you become a robot attuned to the singular task of keeping your infant alive. I find another article that talks about how rodent mothers become better at foraging for food after pregnancy.

All of this information disheartens me—but for the wrong reasons. I'm not upset about being able to attach a reason to my forgetfulness and difficulty concentrating; if anything, these articles confirm that how dumb I've felt lately isn't entirely my fault.

What upsets me is the void in new purpose.

Unlike the women interviewed in these articles, I never hear phantom crying when Emma is fast asleep in her crib. My boobs have never leaked milk in a movie theater after hearing another kid whining. I've never been out to dinner with Arno—or anywhere, really—and unable to think about anything other than my child, at home, without me.

Alarmingly, none of the women describe feelings of profound, unnamed, deep-in-your-bones dread. Not one of them says they've irrationally accused their husbands of cheating. No one says they feel uglier after giving birth than when they were pregnant and peeing their pants every time they laughed and vomiting into stray trash cans and thirty pounds heavier. In short: no one regrets their baby.

I close out of all the "mom brain" literature and try to steady my shaky hands. Take a few deep breaths, in through the nostrils and out through the mouth, as Dr. Abelson recommends. Or is it in through the mouth, out through the nostrils? I can't remember, and this makes me again think of "mom brain," which pisses me off.

I reopen my manuscript. Maybe I'll just do some editing and outlining today. Writing can come later. I need to refamiliarize myself with the plot, iron out the character development and whatnot. I read a few pages from chapter 11, in which the woman goes on a date with the man who was her husband before she lost her memory and they get into a blow-out fight because the husband expresses frustration with the woman's slow, reluctant progress, her inability to step back into her old life with enthusiasm. He expects her to be grateful. After all, he stuck by her side while she was comatose for a year. Ultimately, the woman storms out of the restaurant wondering how any version of herself could have loved someone so unempathetic.

Oof. My protagonist is so *annoying*. Doesn't she realize how lucky she is to have this second lease on life, a husband and kids so devoted to her well-being? How could she squander everything just to "find herself"?

My coffee is now room temperature. Tepid, like urine. I check the clock to see how much time has passed and am horrified to find I've only been "working" for an hour. It's too soon to go downstairs for a snack, and Kyle would hear me if I tried to sneak into our bedroom and turn on the television. So, I give in to the thing I was going to do all along: I log on to Facebook and look up Vivienne Wood.

I find her immediately. Her Facebook profile is surprisingly public. Which honestly seems kind of lowbrow to me. I thought only hot college girls, celebrities, and maybe middle schoolers had public profiles.

Profile picture: Vivienne doing a complicated yoga pose at the top of a mountain in Costa Rica, her arms and legs intertwined like cobras while she balances on one leg. I think it's called eagle pose, but I'm not really sure. Her face isn't visible because some kind of jungle mist hangs in the air, but her body is, and *damn*.

Vivienne is all lean muscle and golden colored, like a California surfer girl or a Hawaiian princess. Her dark hair, almost black, is tangled in an effortlessly sexy way that conjures mussed-up sheets and smeared eyeliner. Her black leggings exhibit a perfectly sculpted ass, probably from hours and hours of hot yoga. Despite how thin she is, a white athletic top—more of a bra, really—highlights perky cleavage, her nipples slightly hard in the cool Costa Rican morning air.

I scroll through the rest of Vivienne's images, where it becomes evident that her wanderlust is real: Vivienne on an African safari, a lion stalking the plains behind her; Vivienne petting an elephant at a sanctuary in Thailand; Vivienne snorkeling with sharks in Australia; Vivienne doing more yoga, this time in Peru; Vivienne at an art museum in Brussels; Vivienne looking insanely charming in a field of sheep in the Cotswolds, in England. Is there anywhere on this trampled earth this bitch hasn't been? Sicily. Salzburg. Tokyo. Egypt. The list goes on.

I scroll and scroll and scroll some more till I reach Vivienne's last profile photo: Vivienne and an elderly woman who looks like Vivienne but a hundred years old, embracing on a faded leather couch.

"Love you forever, avó."

A quick Google search tells me *avó* is the Portuguese word for "grandmother." Well, that explains her exotic good looks.

I try to find any mention in her posts of a boyfriend, husband, fiancé, anything, but there's nothing. Mostly just well wishes from dozens of friends on her birthdays and statuses about wherever she was traveling to next. She's liked a few different causes around homelessness in Boston, climate change, feminism, and LGBTQ+ rights, which makes me feel even shittier than her hot yoga photos because she's obviously a conscientious, socially minded person.

How did Arno seem when he got home last night?

It was all a bit fuzzy in my mind, mostly because I was still pretty drunk when he walked through the front door just after midnight. I was sprawled out on the couch in that weird twilight zone in which you're too tired to go to bed, so you just lie on the nearest piece of furniture while a romantic comedy lulls you into a disturbed half-sleep.

Arno had seemed alarmed, pausing in the foyer as if he'd walked in on me masturbating or something.

"Liz? Why aren't you in bed?"

"Hey, honey!" My voice sounded drunk, even to me. "I just wanted to see you when you got home. I miss you."

"Oh. All right. Well, let's get you to bed."

Arno seemed exasperated, as if I was just another client he had to wrangle into submission. He offered me an arm and pecked me on the cheek as he guided me to our bedroom. I mumbled something about cooking chicken Milanese for him but he hadn't been there to enjoy it, and he apologized, slipping off his button-down shirt and pants without looking in my direction. I mentioned Kyle staying over for dinner, in hopes this would assuage any fears he had about my random midweek boozefest, but I sounded unconvincing even to myself.

"That's nice," Arno deadpanned in response.

I'd hoped, foolishly, that maybe he'd want to have sex, but like most people, sober Arno doesn't find drunk people attractive. Two seconds after climbing into bed, he turned over on his side and faced the opposite wall, an island unto himself. He smelled like office furniture and Wite-Out, and I felt horrible for my suspicions. I rubbed his back until I dozed off.

When I woke up in the morning, my mouth was hanging open, spittle dripping onto my cheeks. There was so much gunk in my eyes, I could barely see. My breath was rancid milk, day-old bologna, a tin of tuna fish left out in the sun.

Arno had already left for work. As I brushed my teeth in front of the mirror, swigging Listerine like a sailor, I vowed to stop drinking, at least for a few days.

Now, I feel an ache in my gut to see him. Or, more accurately, for him to see me as my normal, competent, attractive self.

I close my laptop, a plan forming.

CHAPTER 12

Downstairs, Kyle is stuffing her backpack with various supplies: diapers, sunscreen, a first aid kit, Emma's blanket, pacifiers, a changing pad, bibs, and toddler-friendly snacks like cereal, cucumber slices, and cheese cubes. There's even a small yellow rain jacket I didn't know we owned.

"There's a thirty percent chance of isolated T-storms," Kyle explains, as she neatly folds a spare change of clothing for Emma, a pink gingham dress that looks like it was designed for an American Girl doll.

"Where are you going? It looks like you're kidnapping her," I joke.

"To the zoo," Kyle says. "I disagree with its politics, but they have a really great flamingo display."

"Oh, totally," I gush, slightly jealous of Emma for having such a fun nanny. It has never occurred to me to take Emma to the zoo. I didn't even know there was one nearby.

"She's getting really good at identifying animals," Kyle says, ruffling Emma's tufts of blond hair. Emma giggles appreciatively and, as if Kyle had bribed her, points to a stuffed zebra: "Zee-bah," she says confidently.

"Yes, Emma!" Kyle says. They high-five.

Emma has never high-fived me before.

"Wow, impressive," I murmur. I look down at Emma's minuscule hands, which finger the pins on Kyle's JanSport.

"Er . . . do you want me to come?"

Kyle looks up from her packing, surprised. "Oh, no, that's okay, Liz! You've only just started writing for the day." She looks down at her wristwatch. "Don't feel any pressure; just let those creative juices flow."

"Right, right." I nod vigorously. "The writing process doesn't even really begin for the first few hours, you know."

"Totally," Kyle agrees. "You've got to ease into the zone, I'm sure."

"For sure."

I feel like the biggest fraud in the country, but I remain glued to my spot in the kitchen as nanny and child head out the front door into the sunshine. I've given Kyle the keys to my car and insisted she drive it to the zoo, which makes me feel only marginally better about the type of person I am.

Kyle's backpack is so engorged she looks like Quasimodo. Emma does not wave goodbye.

I get to work as soon as they peel out of the driveway: I'm baking cookies.

As I sat in my office upstairs, searching for a reason to see my husband immediately, I remembered something Arno had said over breakfast last week. One of his friends at work, Mark something, or maybe Mack, had lost his dog, Chance—or was it Chaco?—to a drunk driver in Somerville. The asshole had sped through their quiet neighborhood in the early morning hours, going sixty-five in a twenty-five. He'd thought Chance or Chaco was a speed bump.

The only thing I'm certain of is that it was a Pomeranian. I've always hated those fluffy little fuckers.

It only takes me forty-five minutes to whip up a batch of mediocre chocolate-chip cookies using some semisweet chocolate chunks I'm pretty sure I bought last Christmas. Whatever. They look fine, if a little dry and anemic.

I box the cookies up, still warm and slightly gooey, in some random tin Arno's mother gave me, with snowflakes on it. I hope Arno doesn't recognize it.

Luckily, Arno took the train to work, so I'm able to use his car to get downtown.

The neatness of his vehicle never ceases to shock me. The floor mats are recently vacuumed, the carpet raised and fluffy, and his windshield shines with a recent wiping. "Are you a serial killer?" I've asked him once or twice.

Arno likes the smell of those little air fresheners shaped like trees, but he got rid of them when I got pregnant and insisted the smell of Black Ice would cause me to projectile vomit onto his seats. Still, nearly two years later, the musky men's-cologne-type smell sticks to the corners of the car, and I roll all the windows down, letting the breeze whip through my hair.

I feel a little manic as I cruise through the Financial District, catching the reflection of the black SUV as it sails past multistoried glass buildings. Why am I doing this again?

I glance down at the cookie tin and feel momentarily soothed: because I'm a good person. I stop by Walgreens and purchase a card for those grieving the loss of a pet. It's vaguely religious, but it's all they have left. I hurriedly sign my name and Arno's beneath an illustration of a dog sitting beneath a weeping willow tree.

When I arrive at the glass building that's home to Stonebridge Partners, my hands are shaking, and I wish I hadn't thrown away my stash of CBD gummies when Arno and I moved in together. I could really use something to smooth my edges right now.

In the parking garage, a kind-looking valet named Zeke takes my car keys and points me in the direction of the nearest entrance, even though I already know where it is. I've been here dozens of times. It unsettles me that Zeke is new and doesn't know who I am. Then I realize with alarm that perhaps Zeke isn't new, and I just haven't visited in longer than I realized because of Emma.

Cookie tin in one hand, card in the other, I struggle to compose my face into a serene mask as I take the elevator up to eleven, Stonebridge's floor.

Behind the front desk in the reception area sits an unfamiliar secretary. She looks to be in her midthirties, pretty in a bland kind of way, wearing Ann Taylor from last season. A name tag says *Betsy*. I didn't know that was a real name anymore.

"Hi, Betsy!" I say, louder than I mean to, my voice like the screech of a marker on a whiteboard.

"Hello," Betsy says, looking up with suspicion. Her blond curls frame her face in a Shirley Temple–like way that makes her look either far younger, like a toddler, or as old as a Golden Girl. I can't decide which. Someone should teach her how to separate the curls for a more tousled look. She glances down at what appears to be a calendar, as if confirming there are no appointments for noon on this particular Wednesday.

"I don't think we've met before. I'm Liz," I say, sticking out my left hand so she gets a good look at my ring finger. "I'm Arno Bennett's wife."

"Oh!" Betsy says, smiling widely. "We love Arno," she gushes.

I remove my hand. "Yes, he's quite lovable."

Who is this woman?

"Are you two getting lunch together?" Betsy asks. "That's so nice," she says before I can respond.

"Um, yes, we might get lunch," I reply. "But actually, I'm here to show support for a coworker, a close friend of ours, who has suffered a recent loss."

"Oh my goodness!" Betsy coos, a pale hand floating up to cover her mouth. "Who???"

I look around to ensure we're alone. "I'd actually rather not say, Betsy. He's a private person."

"Of course, of course," Betsy says, her cheeks burning a brilliant shade of scarlet. "That was incredibly rude of me."

"No worries," I say, patting the top of her hand. "Do you mind ringing Arno and letting him know I'm here?"

"Sure, Mrs. Bennett," Betsy says, blond curls bobbing.

As Betsy gets to work typing something onto an iPad, I take a look around the lobby. When *was* the last time I was here? I honestly can't remember.

It seems they've done some updating to the place. New black leather couch, all hard angles with geometric throw pillows. A new marble coffee table with gold legs displaying oversize photography books featuring Tuscan vineyards and Swedish architecture and New York City in the 1960s. A high-tech water dispenser that lets you choose seltzer or still, lemon or raspberry. A walk-in coat closet that wasn't there before.

A bronze statue of a goat, the mascot of Stonebridge for reasons that escape me.

"He'll be right out," Betsy says, and I give her an award-winning smile that I feel confident she'll remember.

I sit down on the couch and flip through one of the coffee table books without really looking at the photographs; I just want to seem at ease and normal when Arno—

"Liz?"

Arno pokes his head into the waiting area, looking confused and . . . irritated?

"What are you doing here?"

"Hi, sweetheart," I say, unfazed. I hold up the cookie tin. "Just thought I'd do something nice in honor of your friend's beloved dog, bless his heart."

Arno looks bewildered.

"Are you talking about Mack?"

I knew it!

"Yes, and his Pomeranian."

"Cookie?"

Well, I was close.

"Yes, Cookie. Poor rascal."

"I didn't even know you were listening when I told you about that . . ." Arno trails off, looking perplexed. "Well, come on in, I guess."

Not exactly the reception I was hoping for, but he's just busy, I assure myself.

Arno swings open the wide glass door, and I follow him into the office.

Glass-walled offices stuffed with modern, dark furniture and extra-wide TV screens break up the open floor plan Stonebridge Partners had a decade ago.

"Turns out, people like peace and quiet to get shit done. What a revolutionary idea," Arno had murmured wryly the first time I visited him here.

Sleek wooden benches and crushed-velvet sofas in yellow and blue (Stonebridge's colors) are parked at optimal locations along the hallways

for spontaneous discussion, though Arno once told me no one really works outside of the glass corner offices. Out the floor-to-ceiling windows, I spy magnificent views of the Boston skyline from one direction and Boston Harbor from the other, suddenly understanding how easy it is for partners to feel *above* everyone else.

Besides the wall made of living plants (how? why?), the thing that always surprised me most about the Stonebridge office was how quiet it was, like the eye of a hurricane. I once asked Arno why that was; you'd think with so many men confined in one place in a generally high-stress job, tempers would flare and voices would rise, but I always got the impression I was walking through a college library or hospital waiting room when I was there.

"Oh, there's yelling," Arno had assured me, pointing to yet another glass cubicle, where a tall Asian man was gesticulating wildly. "Sound-proof walls, that's all. We've got to keep up the semblance of quiet control for our clients." At that point, he'd winked at me, and I'd melted into butter in the palm of his hand.

Stonebridge has made considerable efforts to seem cooler and hipper of late: quiet coffee shop music plays from an unseen source, and new sparkling water machines like the one I saw in the lobby abound.

"Want some cucumber sparkling?" Arno asks, turning suddenly. It takes me a full five seconds to register that he isn't joking.

"No, I'm okay. Those things are cool, though."

"We're trying to be more eco-friendly," Arno explains. "These machines are a million times greener than the fifty-pound cases of La Croix we used to destroy in a week." He laughs before turning serious. "Being environmentally conscious is what sets us apart from our competitors."

"Ahh, I see." So even the water is politicized.

As we walk toward Arno's private office, I scan the halls for familiar faces. I wave quietly at Jack Taylor, one of Arno's closest friends, who smiles and gestures that he's waiting for a call. Jack looks like a linebacker, six feet five and 230 pounds, with shoulders so wide you could fit two dachshunds across his back nose-to-nose. I nod empathetically as Arno guides me past a new art installation that looks like a giant clitoris.

"Is that a—"

"Yes," Arno says, without looking backward. "We're also trying to make an effort to be more feminist." These are words I never thought my husband, much less his employer, would ever say, and I cough into my elbow to avoid laughing.

We pass an attractive blonde who seems new and alarmed, her eyes wide as she smiles at me while struggling to balance a tray of Starbucks lattes in both hands. Must be an intern.

As we pass the office kitchen, I see the lanky back of Ryan Simcat, another old friend and colleague of Arno's, but he has his ear glued to his phone and is nodding seriously while juggling hacky sacks. I don't approach him.

"Well, China is *fucked*," we hear him say as one of the hacky sacks finally hits the ground with a satisfying splat.

Somehow I don't see anyone else I recognize over the course of the next few minutes, and as Arno swipes a key card that opens his office door, I feel awash with disappointment. Who would have thought I'd miss these people? I really need to get out more.

Arno closes the door behind me and pulls out one of his mid-century upholstered leather chairs, gesturing for me to sit down. Ever the gentleman.

"Thanks," I say gratefully, aware, suddenly, of how exhausted I am.

"Coffee?" Arno asks, nodding to a chrome Keurig on a side table.

"No, I'm okay, thanks."

Arno clears his throat, looking uncomfortable, and I dive in: "So, where is Mack's office? Maybe I could stop by and drop these cookies off." *And scan every glass cube I pass till I find Vivienne.*

"Liz, stop."

I pause, surprised. "Stop what?"

"Why are you really here?" Arno asks, reaching across the table and taking the cookie tin. He looks at it thoughtfully before setting it aside. "You barely know Mack. Why would you give a rat's ass about Cookie getting hit by a car?"

"I love animals!" I shout, outraged. My heart thumps like a caught hare.

"C'mon, Liz," Arno says, exasperated. He runs his hands through his curls, which are perfectly tousled today. "Why are you really here? Is everything okay with Emma?"

I frown, irritated that all his worry always circles back to our child, like a trick mirror.

"Emma is fine. She and Kyle went to the zoo."

"Well, that sounds like fun. Why didn't you want to go?"

"Because . . . because I was trying to get some writing done, Arno! I can't very well work on my manuscript while I'm sweating in front of a gorilla exhibit, now can I?" I don't understand the turn this conversation has taken.

Arno looks confused. "So, you wanted to spend the day writing, and instead you . . . baked cookies for my coworker's dead dog?"

"They're human cookies, Arno. Human cookies for a human person grieving the death of a beloved dog."

Suddenly, I am crying. Hot, fat tears that seem wrung from my eyeballs by an unseen force drip down my face, where they cascade off my chin and run down my denim shirt, mixing with green snot.

"Oh my," Arno says.

And, because he is Arno, he gets up from behind his desk and strides quickly to my side, where he bends down to my eye level and kisses my forehead tenderly.

"Sweetheart, what is going on? Be honest with me. I'm just trying to help."

I cry so hard I hiccup, his kindness only making matters worse. I shove him away from me, needing some measure of space between us.

"I've just felt a little lonely lately," I admit. I grab a tissue he's procured from one of his million drawers and blow heartily. "You've been working late a lot, and while I obviously respect and appreciate how well you provide for our family, sometimes I just feel really . . . out of the loop."

Arno nods sadly, reminding me of Dr. Abelson and a little bit of Kyle. Another person who feels bad for me.

"That makes total sense, Liz. Really, it does."

Arno's phone rings, and he doesn't answer it. "Do you want to get lunch together?"

"I'd really like that," I say, dissolving into fresh tears.

Arno takes another tissue out of the dispenser and reaches down for me to blow into his hand. He throws away my snotty secretion and then tells me to go take a seat on his velvet couch, put my feet up. I comply.

He orders sushi, which the pretty blond intern delivers thirty minutes later, setting it carefully down on Arno's wooden desk like it's an ice sculpture.

"Thanks, Soph," Arno says, giving the young woman a wink. She smiles widely, revealing Invisalign-perfect teeth. "No problem, Arno."

"Sophie, this is my wife, Liz," Arno says. "Liz, this is our intern, Sophie." I smile weakly from the couch, glad only a temp is seeing me in my degraded, red-eyed state.

"Nice to meet you, Mrs. Bennett," she says so sweetly. I almost expect a curtsy.

"You can call me Liz," I reply. "'Mrs. Bennett' sounds about as old as a Jane Austen novel." Sophie laughs too loudly, and I realize she's probably never even read Jane Austen. The girl gives an awkward little wave before leaving, pulling the door shut tight behind her.

"Jesus, young people look younger every day, don't they?" I say, as I crack open a plastic tray of spicy tuna rolls.

Arno laughs. "Tell me about it! I don't ever recall looking quite so . . . innocent." He smiles at me mischievously, and I reach out and pinch his nose. Arno separates a pair of chopsticks for me and fishes through a desk drawer for napkins.

We split a cold IPA from Arno's mini fridge and talk about everything outside of our daughter for the first time in ages: a storm that toppled an entire town in the Midwest yesterday, leaving ten thousand people without power; that new play we've been hearing so much about, we must get tickets; a French film that's playing at the Coolidge Corner Theatre next week.

I feel nearly giddy by the end of our meal. Full of cold fish, salty edamame, and yeasty beer, I stretch luxuriously before giving Arno a long kiss on the lips. He squeezes my thigh.

"I guess I should be getting back home," I say, hoping very much that Arno will decide to play hooky with me. Flashes of fun activities we could do together flit, mirage-like, across my mind: a spontaneous aquarium trip. A wine tasting. A shopping spree that ends with new lingerie. We could even rent a luxurious penthouse suite for the afternoon.

"Okay, sweetheart, sounds good," Arno says instead, breaking my reverie with a peck on the nose. "Give our girl a kiss for me."

CHAPTER 13

Obviously, I have to see her in the flesh.

As I weave through Stonebridge's matrix of hallways, I tell myself that if anyone asks why I'm there or what I'm looking for, I'll simply say I got turned around on my way to the bathroom. *It's been so long since I've visited, you see.* Or simply: mom brain!

I peer into glass cubes that line an endless hall, each one named after a famous dead musician: Janis Joplin, Jim Morrison, Kurt Cobain, Jimi Hendrix. Super morbid and incongruous for a financial firm if you ask me, but of course no one did.

She's in none of them. Just long glass tables, lots of potted plants, widescreen TVs, and complicated phone systems. Nespresso machines and framed photos of different cities around the world, London and Paris and Havana and Prague. Men in suits. Men in ties. Men in athleisure answering quick client calls before they bust out ten miles on a Peloton.

I'm grateful that the glass is grainy, one-way; they can't see me peering in. Where are all the women employees? Besides Betsy and the intern, it's men as far as the eye can see.

I check the kitchen again, where Ryan Simcat is still on the phone, nodding his head in agreement with an invisible voice as his feet tap a rhythm on the hardwood floors. "Well, you have to spend money to make money, Sid," he says to the air.

I pass more new water fountains, each one displaying a rotating menu board of flavors like "sparkling raspberry" and "coconut dream."

A few office dogs greet me near the Stonebridge gym: an Italian greyhound that looks like it's seen better days and a King Charles spaniel wearing an argyle sweater. Their name tags (Olga and Henry) and vaccination and pet insurance tags tinkle wildly as they jostle for my attention. I give them each a couple pats on the head as they lick the sushi scent off my hands. I peer into the windows of the gym and see about twenty women seated in a circle, the lights dimmed. A projected image on the wall behind them reads, "Women of Stonebridge: an ERG dedicated to empowerment, diversity, and inclusion."

So this is where they've been hiding.

I try to scan the faces of the seated women, but the lights are too dim. A heavyset woman stands and holds a hand outstretched, clicking an unseen button so that the projector switches to a new image, this one of a mother breastfeeding a child. I press my ear to the edges of the window and can barely make out her words: "It's come to our attention . . . discrimination against new mothers . . . adding new maternity leave benefits . . . breastfeeding room . . . flexible schedules . . . yoga . . . taught by our very own Vivienne Wood."

My eyes widen in surprise.

A lithe person in leggings stands as the women on the floor clap in unison.

She nods at the crowd and takes a microphone from the heavyset woman. Turns it on. A crackling as she adjusts the mic.

"Testing, one, two," she jokes. All the women laugh. She clears her throat. Silence.

"As you know, Stonebridge was founded by men in the 1980s. Since then, the firm has seen a slow but steady acceptance of women entering the world of investment banking. Today, we are still far outnumbered, but that's changing. For the first time in history, women outnumber men in obtaining law degrees, medical degrees, and buying homes. Women are about to take the world of finance head-on, but to do so, we need to be supported. We must stand together. As the founder and president of Stonebridge's first women-focused ERG, I'm here to shake things up for our female colleagues. Today, I'm proud to announce a sweeping overhaul of our maternity leave benefits package, a brand-new, state-of-the-art breastfeeding room, flexible work schedules for new mothers, and free yoga classes led by yours truly."

The woman turns from the screen, suddenly illuminated in its harsh white glare: Vivienne Wood. Gleaming white smile. Long dark hair pulled into a high ballerina bun on the top of her head.

The seated women clap wildly, many of them clambering to stand. One woman shouts, "We love you, Viv!"

The excitement is palpable. The dogs at my feet stand on hind legs, claw their little paws at the gym's entrance door. The women embrace Viv as if she is a guru at an ashram; they, her loyal followers. From where I'm standing, it looks like one woman even kisses her hand.

The meeting breaks up. A light is turned on, bathing the gym in an umber glow. Women are dispersing, gathering their belongings—jackets, purses, and laptops—from a wooden cubby in the corner by rows and rows of weights. I need to get out of here.

I turn away from the gym, palm sweaty on my purse strap, as I begin to walk toward the Stonebridge lobby. My feet feel wobbly, my calves distrustful of my body's ability to propel itself forward in space. I put out a hand to hold on to the wall to my left, the taste of yeast climbing the back of my throat.

"Liz? Is that you?"

Fuck.

I turn around, plaster a smile to my face.

Leslie Beauregard. Wife of Dirk Beauregard, an analyst at Stonebridge. I haven't seen her in over a year, since some company fundraising event for colon cancer, the silent killer of a significant number of older Stonebridge partners.

"Hey, Leslie!" I say, fake joviality bubbling from my voice.

"What are you doing here?"

"Oh, you know, just got lunch with the hubs." *Hubs?* What on earth . . .

"Oh, that's so nice! What do you think of the new renos?" Leslie says, gesturing her hands around to encompass some of the new office decor, the flawless gym she just exited, and yet another fucking water dispenser, this one advertising "luscious lemon" and "refreshing mint."

"It's really, really beautiful," I say honestly. "I love the new feminist art display, too."

Leslie nods seriously.

"That installation was all Viv—she's a newer VP here. *Unsung Flower* is the name of the piece."

I cough into my elbow. "How cool."

Leslie stares at me expectantly, and I'm reminded of how vapid I've always found her to be. She worked here before Dirk did, does something on the "people team" that sounds mostly like party planning and making sure new employees are all given enough Stonebridge swag to become walking billboards for the firm: emblazoned Patagonia jackets, North Face windbreakers and backpacks, Nalgene bottles and baseball hats.

Whenever she's drunk enough at office parties, Leslie inevitably tells the story of meeting Dirk. "Well, I was setting up his new work laptop," she'll say, giggling lusciously over a can of peach-flavored White Claw. "And Dirk asked me how long I'd been working in IT." At this point, Leslie always pauses, to let the audience laugh sexistly at the thought of Leslie working in IT. "And then, when I told him I worked in HR, he asked whether it was against company policy for him to take me out to dinner." A chorus of cooing. "Five months later, we were engaged."

Finally, the moment she's been waiting for: Leslie holds her ring finger up to the light and turns her hand ever so slightly till the 2.5-carat princess-cut diamond reaches optimal twinkle.

Barf.

"Oh, congrats, by the way!" I say, remembering that Arno had mentioned recently that Leslie and Dirk were expecting.

"Thank you soooo much," Leslie says, her hand fluttering immediately to her barely-there bump. "We are *so* excited."

I try to remember all the things you're supposed to ask newly pregnant people. "Are you going to find out the sex?" Seems like a safe enough choice.

"No, no, Dirkie and I want to be totally and completely surprised." Leslie smiles serenely, looking off into the distance. I try to see where her gaze lands, but it's just a glass maze of reflections.

"That's fun," I reply. "Most people seem to wait these days."

"I know you and Arnie didn't," Leslie replies, her cobalt blue eyes widening. Glass marbles, all reflection with no depth. "I'm sure you just *couldn't wait.*"

I laugh uncomfortably at her use of *Arnie.* "Yeah, something like that."

Really, I just thought waiting to find out the sex of your child was inefficient. Knowing before the birth allows you to come up with potential names, decorate the baby's room, purchase all of its tiny clothing, and come to terms with the sex so that if it isn't what you wanted, your disappointment is well hidden by the time of your labor.

I'd wanted a boy. Is it taboo to admit that? Whatever. It's the truth. Men move more easily through the world, and I loved the idea of a miniature Arno looking up at me with wide, adoring eyes. Besides, what model of mother-daughter adoration did I have to look forward to? When I thought about my own mom, I felt cold.

"And how is little Miss Emma?" Leslie asks, and I'm honestly surprised she knows my daughter's name. I'm not sure I could recall any of Arno's colleague's children's names if you held a loaded gun to my temple.

"She's . . . she's great," I say, smiling widely, my face a mask of postnatal bliss. "She's very . . . strong. And, and, developed. You know, for her age."

Leslie nods in agreement. "Arnie shows me photos of her all the time. She's really quite beautiful."

"He does?"

"Of course, silly! Who wouldn't?"

I nod, laughing. "Of course. Who wouldn't?!"

Leslie reaches out and squeezes my arm. "It was so nice seeing you, Liz. I've got to get going, though. We've got a new-hire board game night this evening, and I'm somehow stuck with trivia duty again! And I'm so bad at trivia!" Leslie laughs self-deprecatingly, and I wonder what handsome, competent Dirk sees in her.

"Nice seeing you too, Leslie. Take care. And send Dirk my best."

"Don't be a stranger!"

I hustle out of Stonebridge Partners like I'm being chased and I don't stop speed-walking till I've reached the valet, where Zeke stands sentry, white AirPods plugged into each ear.

"Zeke, can you . . . ?"

Zeke nods knowingly and hustles off to retrieve Arno's Audi from somewhere far away.

I don't realize I'm sobbing till I pull out of the parking garage and a homeless man stops begging for change to stare at me through my half-open window at a red light.

"I'm sorry," I apologize.

"Don't be," the man replies. "Find peace in your heart."

As the light turns green, I peel away so quickly, my tires screech like a fork on glass.

⤫

CHAPTER 14

Tracy Kaplan and I are having a "girls' night."

I'm ashamed to say it was my idea, but I needed to get out of the house and distract myself. Arno's working late again. I gave Kyle an extra hundred dollars to watch Emma through the evening, and she took the cash noiselessly. Reason number 550 why I love Kyle: she knows when to not ask questions.

It's 7:25 p.m., and the sun is starting its descent, splashing the Wellesley sky in generous pastel shades of orange and purple; it calls to mind the saltwater taffy I used to eat as a child on vacations in Virginia Beach before my parents split. I pause on my walk over to Tracy's, soaking up the intense quiet of our secluded neighborhood: crickets chirping. A dog barking halfheartedly somewhere in the distance. Wind whispering through a tangle of branches, forcing a pair of lindens to embrace like old lovers. Manicured lawns looking hydrated and effortlessly green in a way that belies the actual maintenance that goes into their verdancy.

The stone walkway up the gentle slope to Tracy's home feels never-ending; the inhabitants get a solid three minutes to watch their visitors approach as they cast judgment. It feels unfair.

I'm wearing leisure wear: an oatmeal-colored cashmere sweatsuit that costs more than most of the fancy dresses hanging in my closet. It was a postpartum present from Arno's mom, who said I'd need comfortable yet tasteful loungewear while I "got my figure back." A hemp bag with two wine bottles inside clinks happily at my side.

I hear her before I see her. "Hey, girl, hey!" Tracy calls in her nasally voice. It's not as bad as, say, Fran Fine from *The Nanny*, but still.

"Hey, Trace," I reply, already questioning my sanity for subjecting myself to this.

Tracy stands in front of her open double doors, beaming. It's been a while. She's also in athleisure: baby-pink Alo leggings and a matching cropped sweatshirt that laces up the front. Highly inappropriate for a woman of her age with young twin boys, but who am I to judge? Her figure is insane, like a twenty-something Instagram model's. Her lips, freshly injected, are smeared with some sort of glittery lip balm that calls to mind Lisa Frank coloring books, circa 1995.

"I am soooo glad we're doing this," Tracy says. "I desperately need some girl time. The boys have been driving me crazy this week!"

"I bet," I say honestly.

Tracy's twin sons, Cooper and Ashton, are eight years old. Spending any amount of time with them serves as the most immediate and effective birth control a woman could ever ask for. At the last barbecue she and Terry threw, Cooper got in trouble for shoving a handful of mulch into a little girl's mouth while Ashton sat on top of her, holding her down. As far as I can tell, they spend most of their time riding around the neighborhood on motorized machines—small cars, bicycles, electric scooters, a golf cart—and raising hell. They have a fondness for catching small animals and doing god knows what with them. I do not let them within ten feet of Emma.

"Where are they right now?" I ask hesitantly, one foot over the threshold.

"A birthday party, thank god," Tracy replies promptly. "Their friend Tom's parents rented out that new arcade in Fenway, can you imagine?" She's not referring to the obscene amount of money this must have cost; I know Tracy well enough to know that what she's actually horrified by is the sheer number of terrible little boys that must be inside the arcade as we speak, running around spilling soda and french fries all over the floor, wreaking havoc.

"That sounds like a nightmare," I reply. Tracy laughs and guides me inside her palatial cape, taking the wine bottles from my grasp with a cluck of approval.

"You know your girl so well—rosé all day!" Tracy hip-bumps me as if we're twenty-one years old. I ignore her and make my way toward her kitchen to get glasses.

Tracy and Terry's kitchen could be in *Architectural Digest*. Seriously. She and Terry recently remodeled it in stainless steel from top to bottom. Hard to clean, I think, but impressive nonetheless. The cabinets are stainless steel, as are the sink and refrigerator and Miele oven, cooktop, and hood. Wooden bowls of real Tuscan lemons brighten the space, their sun-yellow exteriors a welcome contrast against the walls, which have been painted some sort of marble-y charcoal color. Large, handwoven shag rugs with black and navy tribal patterns emphasize the kitchen's hip, modern vibe.

Now, if only they would redesign the outside of their home to match. Their most recent lawn addition? A six-foot, eyeless bronze unicorn statue, straight out of a Guillermo del Toro film.

"Ice?" I ask Tracy, moving deftly around her kitchen as if I were the hostess and she the guest. It's crucial to get glasses of wine into both of our hands as soon as possible, or Tracy will spend an hour standing in her foyer talking about Cooper and Ashton's latest episode of homegrown terrorism.

"Yes, please," Tracy replies, perching on a leather stool at their island.

"So, how are you and Arno? It's been ages since we've had a couples' night," Tracy says.

"We're okay . . ." I reply, filling both stemless glasses three fourths of the way full with pale-pink liquid as the nauseatingly sweet aroma fills the room. The ice cubes rattle around the glasses. I haven't decided how much of my inner turmoil I want to reveal to Tracy. Not because I'm worried she'll gossip with neighbors—Tracy is as friendless as I am in this neighborhood; she wouldn't jeopardize whatever you want to call our relationship. I'm just not sure I want her pity.

"Yeah?" she asks. "And how is Emma?"

The hair stands up on the backs of my arms as if I'm a dog raising its hackles. "Can we . . . not talk about her for one night?"

I am a monster. I don't deserve to have a child.

"Sure, honey," Tracy says easily.

I exhale.

"I'm sure she's all you think about all day long. We all need a break sometimes."

I want to scream, but instead I take a long gulp of wine and enjoy the way it burns my throat and coats my teeth in saccharine.

To buy time and get a little drunk, I let Tracy tell me the latest elementary school gossip from Cooper and Ashton's downtown New Age school, where annual tuition is as expensive as their kitchen renovation. Tracy always has suspicions of teachers popping pills, drinking on the job, and sleeping with one another, but I've never bothered to say, *"Then why are Cooper and Ashton still in attendance?"*

"Never trust a school that doesn't have grades," Arno said once, while I was still pregnant. "Our girl will only go to normal-people schools."

Tracy and I polish off the first bottle of wine and, pleasantly warm and blurry, we tumble downstairs into their home theater. Twelve movie-style leather seats face the largest screen I've ever seen in real life. It looks like they hijacked it from an actual movie theater. The carpet is red and plush.

"Do we want a happy movie or a sad one?" Tracy asks.

"Er . . . can we do something scary?"

"Liz!" Tracy remonstrates in fake disapproval. "You know I can't do scary movies."

"You know, psychologists say that horror films actually help with emotional regulation," I say, but Tracy isn't listening; she's busy flipping through Netflix. "It gives you a false sense of control over the feeling of fear."

"What about something naughty, like *Superbad*?!" Tracy suggests with the giddiness of a teenage boy discovering his first porn site.

"Um, sure. Whatever."

Tracy fires up the movie and crawls into the seat beside mine, which I've already reclined so far back it's nearly physically impossible to see the screen. My fingers mindlessly shovel air-popped kettle corn into my mouth. Tracy would never eat butter, and I file this away under my mental list of reasons why Tracy isn't my real friend.

The movie plays for an indeterminate period of time. I finish my glass of wine. Tracy noiselessly refills it. I tap my nails on the rim. Jiggle my leg up and down. Even though the movie chair is objectively very comfortable, I can't sit still.

"Tracy, can I ask you something?"

"Of course, Liz! You can ask me anything."

"Do you think Arno would ever cheat on me?"

Tracy doesn't reply immediately with gushing reassurances, and somehow, this is the most scared I've felt yet. I press the button on the side of my chair, propelling myself forward with such velocity, wine spills down my shirt.

"Shit!"

"Oh no!" Tracy leaps up from her seat. "I'll go get club soda and a washcloth!"

"No, no, Tracy," I say, exasperated. "It's fine. Don't."

Tracy sits back down hesitantly. I'm a bomb that might detonate. "Are you sure, Liz? Isn't that cashmere?"

"Yeah, I don't give a fuck."

"Oh. Okay."

Tracy looks like a rabbit that's been spotted by a bloodhound; her eyes are wide as golf balls. I stare at her expectantly, willing her to answer my question. To say anything, anything at all.

"What was it you . . . ?" Tracy trails off, staring at her cuticles, which have suddenly become enormously interesting.

"I asked whether you think Arno would ever cheat on me. Jesus!"

Tracy flinches, readjusting in her chair. "Liz," she says finally.

"Yeah?"

"All men cheat."

I look into her face, waiting for a punch line that isn't coming. "What do you mean, *all men cheat*?" I splutter, furiously gulping at what's left of my wine.

"I mean exactly that: All. Men. Cheat." Tracy sighs, as if she's just revealed the secret of the universe.

I gape at her. "Tracy, of course plenty of men cheat. I know that. But we're talking about the father of my thirteen-month-old child, not some stranger or the average guy. We're talking about *Arno*."

"I know!" Tracy squeaks "And Arno is great; he really is. But I think that biologically, it's in every man's nature, at some point or another, to cheat. To be honest, I'm sort of surprised you're only just figuring this out now."

"So you're saying that you think Terry would cheat on you?"

"Terry has cheated on me," Tracy says, shrugging. "A few times, actually. And we get through it every time."

The bottom has fallen out of the room, and I am floating down, down, down. Pitch-black nothingness coats the backs of my eyelids.

"Liz? Liz! Are you okay?"

I open my eyes and find Tracy hovering above me, her edges outlined in black, buzzing like a gnat.

"I think you just fainted or something."

"What's that?" I ask, bleary-eyed. "Sorry about that. I must've blacked out for a second. Didn't eat enough carbs today."

"Um . . . do you want me to go get you a sandwich? Call a doctor? Text Arno?"

"No!" I shout, louder than I intend. Tracy flinches.

I blink a few times, and Tracy's edges become solid again. That's reassuring. I look at my cup holder, and my wineglass is still there. I take a sip.

"So, where were we?"

Tracy looks as though she'd like to sink through the floor to avoid my gaze. Maybe she's scared I'll faint again. "Er . . . we were talking about men and how they, uh, cheat sometimes? And I told you that Terry has cheated on me before—but now we're better than ever!—and then you, I don't know, passed out for a second."

Tracy laughs awkwardly.

"Right," I reply. "Right you are."

Tracy looks around the room, her eyes refusing to meet mine. "Do you want to hear how it happened?" she asks finally.

"Duh, Tracy! Why haven't you told me this before?"

I can't hide my exasperation, or my . . . hurt? I can't believe it, but I'm actually offended that Tracy—Tracy, who never misses an opportunity to gossip about every other neighbor on our street, her children's teachers, even her *priest*, for fuck's sake—has withheld the tastiest morsel of all.

Tracy explains that she first discovered Terry was cheating shortly after they got married, with a secretary at his law firm.

"It was all so . . . typical," Tracy spits. "She was younger than I was, dumb as bricks, and she was basically paid to take phone calls and fetch coffee for the partners. Eye candy, that's all she was."

Tracy had a sinking feeling after a holiday office party and hacked Terry's Gmail account: the proof was in the pudding. Or rather, an emailed receipt from a Holiday Inn Express downtown.

"Ew, an Express?"

"It wasn't anything serious," she assures me. "And neither were the next two women that came after."

This is all too much for me. "Tracy, I can understand taking your husband back after one transgression, but three? How do you trust him at all?"

Tracy laughs. "Now that I know it's one of Terry's weaknesses, it's easier to manage. I can just sort of expect it now and then, like a bad cold."

"A *bad cold*?" I lower my voice in case Tracy and Terry have video cameras installed, which I'm sure they do. I glance around the edges of the theater for small black telescopic eyes, feeling tweaky.

Tracy's face gains some color, high splotches of pink on her cheekbones, getting irritated. "Yes, Liz, and if you can't respect how I've managed my relationship . . ." She shakes her head, voice quavering: "Well, it's not really any of your business, now, is it?"

She's right; what do I really know about Tracy and Terry's relationship? Who am I to judge—me, who can't even spend an entire day alone with her child anymore? Me, who is so paranoid that my husband is cheating on me, I baked cookies for a dead dog? Me, who would share my deepest fears with a therapist I haven't seen in years and a fake best friend but not with my own husband?

"I'm so sorry, Tracy. You're right. I don't know the first thing about what you've been through."

Tracy nods like a wounded bird and mimes brushing dust off her shoulder. "It's okay; that's all in the past now."

"Well," I begin, unable to help myself, "if it keeps happening again and again, is it really in the past?"

Tracy sighs, exhausted from trying to explain the nuances of modern marriage to me, a not-yet-evolved simpleton who thinks her husband is still capable of keeping his dick in his pants. "Infidelity is just one of the many obstacles that Terry and I have to work through if we want to be together and raise Ashton and Cooper as a family unit. It's not perfect, but I accept him for who he is. At least he's not on drugs." And then Tracy fucking smiles, and takes a dainty sip of wine, like her husband *not being on drugs* is reason enough to keep going to couples therapy week in and week out.

Finally, I am rendered incapable of speech.

I try to watch *Superbad*, a movie I know I found hilarious and refreshing at some point in my life. But my mind keeps doing wheelies trying to understand this new reality: Terry—dumpy little Terry, with his neck fat and his armpit sweat and his receding hairline, is cheating on *Tracy*? Instagram-hot MILF of the Year Tracy?

Life is so unfair.

Tracy moseys back upstairs and returns minutes later with another bottle of wine and tiny hummus and vegetable sandwiches on herbed focaccia that do not look homemade. She refills my glass, hands me a sandwich, and settles down beside me, giving my forearm a gentle little squeeze.

"So . . . why do you think Arno is unfaithful?" Tracy finally asks.

"He received a text last week," I murmur in between bites.

"A text? What kind of text?" Her eyebrows lift, and I imagine all the possible horrible texts Tracy's witnessed in her marriage to Terry: dirty verbal foreplay, photos of naked breasts larger than her own, vagina pics with intricate pubic-hair designs, vibrator videos.

I grimace and set down my half-eaten sandwich.

"Nothing crazy, just a text thanking Arno for all his help on some major project and then a stupid kissy-face emoji. From someone named 'Viv' who I've never met before."

Tracy's eyebrows lift even higher. "What else?"

"Huh?"

"I mean, what else?"

"That's it. Nothing else. The text is what made me feel suspicious."

"That's it?"

"Er, yeah."

"No suspicious phone calls late at night? Maybe from an unfamiliar name that sounds fake, or just an initial, like 'F'?"

"No."

"No weird receipts for lingerie that he never gives you, or designer chocolates?"

"Nope."

"No unexplained work trips to Miami that get extended because of 'bad weather'?"

"No."

"No burner phones?"

"What?! Jesus, Tracy, no! What the hell is Terry putting you through?"

Tracy throws her hands up. "Just covering all the bases. These boys of ours, they can get pretty creative!" She winks.

I feel like I'm going to vomit hummus and popcorn and wine all over Tracy and Terry's movie theater–worthy carpet, so I stand, unsteadily.

"Trace, thanks for having me, but I better get home."

"Really? It's only ten p.m.!" Tracy whines.

"Er, yeah, I only paid Kyle till . . ." I pretend to check my phone. "Till now, actually," I lie.

"Ughhh. Okay, well, I guess I'm going to have to finish all this rosé by myself!"

"I guess so. Sorry about that."

I stumble up the stairs and out her front door, barely remembering my purse hanging on the coat rack. Outside, in the cool evening breeze, I gasp for air like a fish that's been tossed onto a dock. Floundering.

Down her stone walkway, I hang a left and careen up our driveway jerkily, my body moving more drunkenly than my mind feels it should. I heave open the front door, which I left unlocked, and am aghast at what I find: Arno and Kyle sitting at the kitchen table, eating spring rolls. They both smile in unison and call, "Hello!" as I kick my shoes off at the entrance and stagger down the hallway.

"I thought you had to work late?" I gasp.

"I thought I did, too," Arno says easily. "Things changed. Spring roll?"

"I . . . no, no thank you," I manage. Beside the spring rolls are four opened cartons of Chinese food. Each one is marked "v" in black marker, I assume for "vegetarian." Even Kyle and my husband have secrets, for Christ's sake.

Kyle looks at my sweatshirt. "You okay, Liz? It looks like you spilled something."

I look down at myself. Pinkish splotches dot my sweatshirt, and one largish one hovers near my crotch.

"Yes, erm, I spilled some wine at Tracy's by accident. That's actually why I came home. This is cashmere . . ." I mumble.

"I'm sure I can get that out with a little soda water," Kyle says, hopping up from her seat to make herself useful.

"Did you two have a fun girls' night?" Arno asks, grinning. "Get into any trouble?"

Did you get into any trouble? "We just watched a movie, caught up. Had some wine."

"That sounds great, sweetheart. I'm so glad you've made another mom friend," Arno replies easily, tearing into some crispy broccoli with his canines.

I open my mouth to respond to him but am overcome with a dire need to expel my stomach's contents immediately. I sprint to the master bathroom in record time (really, someone should have timed me), and violently heave pinkish-brown liquid and tiny bits of vegetable—eggplant chunks and zucchini and crushed-up tomatoes—into our white porcelain toilet bowl.

"Honey?" I hear Arno call from the other room.

"I'm fine!" I shout back, red-faced and manic, wiping vomit from the edges of my mouth. "Everything is fine!"

CHAPTER 15

Memorial Day weekend is here.

I'd nearly forgotten, but on Friday, Kyle asked me if Arno and I had any plans, and I realized I had no idea. A quick text to Arno later, I was informed that we did, in fact, have plans: a Saturday cookout at Cynthia and Brian Roger's beach house in Cohasset.

Normally, this information would have disappointed me.

I have always hated Cynthia and Brian in a way that felt personal. I hate their three-story Victorian home overlooking the Atlantic Ocean, with its private beach, nine-foot ceilings, marble mantels, and quartz counters. The stupid Sub-Zero fridge that never has any practical food in it—a lone cantaloupe going mealy beside green glass bottles of San Pellegrino. I hate Cynthia's faux humility as she shows off their stunning master suite, with its spalike bathroom and walk-in closet that she "had trouble filling" because she's just too busy.

"*With what???*" I've always wanted to ask. "*Waxing your crotch?? Riding your Peloton?*"

The mansion features a walk-out lower level where their au pair stays. Cynthia and Brian actually refer to her as that: their "au pair," like they're French. It has a king-sized bed and a shower with a bench inside of it.

But this time, their invitation left me ecstatic; I actually had to tamp down my enthusiasm lest I raise Arno's suspicion. He knows I'm not their biggest fan.

Cookout @ Brian n Cynthia's, he texted me Friday afternoon. Followed by Sorry for the short notice! and It's OK if you don't want to go. Sad-face emoji.

OK!!!!! I replied initially. Then added, I suppose I'll come . . . to sound more like myself.

We had to "do time," as Arno said—make our requisite appearances on the Stonebridge circuit and hobnob with the worst of them (i.e., Brian and Cynthia). The alternative was Arno never getting the promotion he so desired and deserved.

Arno always apologized profusely to me after these sorts of events, as if I was a toddler who'd sat patiently through Christmas mass, or held back tears while getting a vaccination shot. He'd buy me tulips or roses and give me massages late at night, whispering in my ear about how amazing I'd been, how much everyone loved me. This always made the hours of small talk and stiff drinks and painful heels worth it, but this time, no reward was necessary: I was finally going to meet the illustrious Viv.

"Kyle, can you work a double for us on Saturday?" I'd asked, alarmed at how much work needed to be done. "We'll pay overtime."

"Sure, Liz. You got it."

What did I do to deserve sweet Kyle?

ON THE MORNING of the barbecue, I awake at 5:00 a.m., while Arno snores peacefully beside me, his hair matted into tufts like a Brussels Griffon terrier. I kiss his cheek, enjoying the prickle of facial hair on my chapped lips, and whisper into his ear that I'll be running a few errands before the party. I don't know if he hears me.

I change into some leggings and an old T-shirt and go for a four-mile run around our neighborhood, which is misty and still. The only sound—save for some twittering songbirds—is my tennis shoes slapping evenly on the pavement, like a drumbeat. I haven't run in over a week, and my hips whine in protest, my bunions pulsing against the fabric of my sneakers. But I persevere because I imagine Viv is an early riser who always starts each day with physical activity. She's probably the type of woman who downplays her aerobic activity, saying, "Oh,

I just try to break a sweat every day, nothing crazy," but actually logs eight hours per week of strenuous exercise.

I listen to pump-up music from the *Rocky* films and throw in a few squats and lunges at the end for good measure.

"Looking good, Liz!" Terry calls from over their hedges.

"Thanks, Terry!"

Gross.

Once I get home, slick with sweat and out of breath, I get down to business.

I have quite a few appointments before the cookout: an eyebrow wax and tint at 9:00 a.m. A manicure at 10:00. Haircut and color at 11:00. And a booking with a stylist at a boutique clothing store that claims on its Facebook page to "dress clients perfectly for every occasion under the sun" at 2:15 p.m. The cookout starts at 4:00, so there should be plenty of time for everything, I assure myself—before wondering whether Kyle knows how to make a decent pasta salad.

I booked all of the appointments in a frenzy yesterday afternoon, after making sure I'd secured Kyle for the entire day. I have to look my absolute best for my very first encounter with Viv. I can't seem like some tired, washed-out mom with bad roots and chipped nail polish.

No, this is my shot to make a withering first impression. And by "withering," I mean charming, gorgeous but in an effortless way and, most importantly, fun. Arno's always been proud of my quick wit and disarming manner that helps him cozy up to higher-ups and climb the Stonebridge ladder. I wouldn't be surprised if Viv is completely taken with me—so entirely bewitched by my agreeableness and charisma that she leaves the party with her tail between her legs. Embarrassed that she ever thought she had a chance of winning my husband's affection.

Luckily, all my appointments are in downtown Wellesley, so I don't have very far to go. *Just one of the many perks of living in our uppity little Massachusetts oasis*, I think, as I nearly hit a biker while sliding into a parking spot.

"Sorry!" I shout through my open window.

The biker, clad in some sort of purple spandex getup, flips me the bird as he wobbles onward. I pretend I don't see.

The artistic brow spa is sandwiched between a French bakery and a store that sells all different kinds of olive oil. Across the street is a doggie day care called Paw Luxx and an insurance company that offers coverage for kidnapping and ransom. A tasteful gold sign in the window says in small block letters, *What would you do if someone ran off with your Rembrandt?*

I haven't had my eyebrows done in ages. Truth be told, I'm sort of a baby about bodily pain, but I survived childbirth, didn't I? Still, I've only waxed my nether region just once, before a vacation to Bermuda, and swore never again. But today isn't an everyday occurrence. Today, I'd like to have eyebrows that are Brooke Shields thick, but in a honey-gold shade that calls to mind fields of wheat, undulating in nameless patterns across the American Midwest.

This is exactly what I request when a kind young woman named Nina tilts my head back in a red leather chair and begins vigorously brushing my eyebrow hairs with some sort of tiny little comb. I giggle, because it tickles, and she shushes me.

"Brow lamination, tinting, and extensions, right?" she asks in a vaguely Eastern European accent.

"Um . . ." I hesitate, having no idea what she's talking about. "Those are all . . . eyebrow treatments?"

"Yes," Nina sighs, annoyed at my lack of brow knowledge. "We also offer threading, microblading, and brow lifts." Her pronunciation of "we" like "ve" renders me more than a little scared.

"Okay, I definitely don't want microblading. That sounds . . . painful," I reply, laughing sheepishly. "And no lifting, please. I want to look natural. Can you do that, er, Nina? Just make me look *natural* and *beautiful*." I mouth the last two words slowly, although Nina speaks English perfectly.

In response, Nina rolls her eyes. She's wearing purple contacts and a black collared polo shirt that says, *I am browed of my work.* There's lint stuck to her name tag.

What happens next is a blur of vigorous activity—on Nina's part; I just sit in the leather chair with my thighs glued to the seat in submission. First, she applies some sort of keratin-infused straightening solution to my brows and brushes them straight up, like Oscar the

Grouch's. Then she wraps plastic wrap around and around my head, securing the brows in their surprised expression. I sit in silence while Nina texts away on her phone, her fingers moving so quickly it looks like she's performing magic. I half expect to disappear.

She repeats this process three or four more times—I lose count— each time applying some new solution to my poor, tortured brows, which now feel wet and threadlike. Every so often, she takes the little comb to the hairs and brushes vigorously upward, like she's trying to untangle a particularly stubborn knot from a child's hair.

Finally, Nina applies a tint to my brows, which she says will make them "much, much better."

Well, I think, *I can't argue with that.*

At the end of forty-five minutes, Nina pronounces me "veenished." The entire process costs $250, and I'm so overwhelmed and flustered, I tip her far more than 20 percent. Nina seems surprised and almost guilty; her own reddish eyebrows lift in pure shock.

"Thank you veery much, ma'am."

I start for the door, to scurry to my next appointment, but Nina stops me with her voice: "Don't you vant to see them?"

"Oh, right. Of course."

She walks over to my side and hands me a small handheld plastic mirror, Barbie pink.

I gasp in true horror at the reflection of the woman in the mirror, who cannot possibly be me, but somehow is? Despite having blond hair, my reflection has thick, blackish eyebrows that resemble the banded woolly bear caterpillars I used to catch as a child and let run up and down my arms, tickling me. I run my pointer finger over the fur tentatively, like it might come alive and bite.

"Ohmygod, I loooove your brows!!!!" a woman squeals behind me.

I look up and turn around in horror, expecting mockery, but the stranger's face is open and kind.

"Really?" I ask, my voice squeaky.

"Ohmygod, yes! Are you kidding? You have, like, model eyebrows," she gushes, her wide hands flapping. "Like Cara Delevingne. And you're even blonder than her, so it's superrrr striking."

"Thank you for saying that." *I look nothing like Cara Delevingne.*

After a quick manicure next door, I head to the salon down the street. The moment I open the door, Tori, my pink-haired stylist, shrieks.

"Did you just get those done? They look so fab, girl. Thick brows are all the rage this year. If I could afford lamination, I'd go, like, every month."

If a total stranger hadn't just said the same thing, I would think Tori was trolling me. But she actually likes them; I can tell. And Tori, someone who works in the beauty industry for a living, has to know more about looking good than me, right?

The thought settles my stomach like an antacid. Tori gestures to a stiff leather chair, and I take a seat. Feel my shoulder muscles loosen. I wish I had time for a massage, too.

Tori asks what I want to do with my hair, and because I'm feeling inspired, like I've gone through battle and come out on the other side victorious, I tell her, "Whatever you think looks best."

She asks me if I'm sure about this at least four times before raising her hands in surrender.

"Okay, okay; just checking. People usually only say shit like that when they're, like, going through a breakup or a divorce," Tori says with a laugh, and I nearly choke on my complimentary mint.

Three hours later, I have the pixie 'do of 2019 Emma Watson, but platinum blond. Paired with my new thick, dark brows, I am a sight to behold.

Tori and at least fifteen other hair stylists gather around me and agree that I look like a young Mia Farrow, but hotter. I don't know what to do with this information other than trust the flock of women and trip into the high-end boutique next door for my 2:15 p.m. appointment with their "top stylist." The shop is called Cucci Coo, which reminds me of the noises people made when they first spoke to Emma. Not me, though. I never did the baby-voice schtick.

The exterior of the building is lemon yellow with blue shutters, like Barbie's vacation home, and a bell rings, clean and bright, when I open the front door.

"Bonjour!" a busty redhead cries from beside a faceless mannequin she's trying to attach some sort of glittery sash to.

"Hello," I reply cautiously.

"You must be Elizabeth," she purrs. "I'm Fran."

Fran emerges from behind the mannequin fully, and her long, lacquered red nails shake my hand. She looks to be in her midforties, if I had to guess, with a bouncy red perm and purple eyeshadow that's slightly uneven. She's wearing a two-piece beige pantsuit that doesn't quite inspire my confidence in her as a fashionista, let alone Cucci Coo's top stylist.

"Liz is fine. I made an appointment for 2:15 p.m?"

My butthole clenches at the terrifying prospect that Fran is their top stylist. Maybe I should just run out now while I still have t—

"Ahhh, yes!" Fran says. "That would be with Willow, our very finest fashion guru." Fran beams before leaning in close. "She's styled at *Vogue*, you know," she says conspiratorially, her breath a flurry of nutmeg and dried rose petals.

"Wow, that's quite impressive," I admit.

The scream of a curtain being wrenched aside startles me, and I look toward the back of the store. A young woman, probably in her early- to midtwenties, slouches toward me.

As she gets nearer, weaving through racks of dresses and blouses and sweaters like a wraith, the full image of Willow, Wellesley's very own *Vogue* stylist, comes into perspective. She's stunning, all long limbs and pale whitish hair that falls down her back, grazing the top of her butt. She has pale skin and clear blue eyes and the fullest pink lips I've ever seen.

"Hey," she says, when she gets close enough. Her voice is pure gravel, sandpaper-sexy like Mila Kunis's. "I'm Willow." She sticks out a long, slender hand that's ice-cold to the touch.

Immediately, I know that I would wear anything this girl suggests.

Willow, who's wearing the tightest bell bottoms I've ever seen and a simple black T-shirt that says *I'd Rather Not* with no bra, leads me to the back of the store, where she lights a cigarette. The sheer audacity of this illegal act—in a high-end clothing store in Wellesley, Massachusetts, no less—causes me to laugh hysterically. So hard, I clutch my sides like a giddy teenager.

"I didn't know you could get away with that around here!" I manage, nodding toward her cigarette.

Willow shrugs. "Want one?"

I hesitate, thinking how cool it would be to smoke an illegal ciga-rette with this beautiful, elf-like model—way cooler than anything Viv's done today, I bet—but I stop myself. "No thank you," I reply, imagining the look of disgust that would transform Arno's face if I arrived at Brian and Cynthia's smelling like a dive bar from the eighties.

Willow looks like she couldn't care less either way, then asks me what brings me to Cucci Coo today, as well as a whole host of other shocking questions: what event I'm attending, how I'd describe my personal style, what my favorite brands are, and whether I've ever created something called a "vision board." It's all very thorough and impressive. I find myself opening up to her about Emma, mentioning that I haven't bought any new clothing since my daughter arrived. Then she takes my measure-ments, and I try not to suck my stomach in as Willow wraps a thin yellow tape measure around my hips, then my waist, and, finally, my breasts.

"Wow, and you had a kid just over a year ago?" Willow asks in her affectless monotone, and I nearly die of gratitude.

She works quickly and efficiently over the next twenty minutes, jot-ting a few words down on a scrap of yellowed paper before moving up and down the aisles between metal racks of clothing. She grabs a dress here, a pair of sandals there, a hat, a scarf, sunglasses, and a weathered-looking brown belt. I can't keep track of everything in her lithe arms.

"Come here," she says eventually, pulling open a curtain to reveal a surprisingly spacious dressing room that does not contain a mirror, just a few tasseled satin throw pillows on the floor. She pushes me gen-tly inside before I can say anything.

"Try this stuff on. Together."

I acquiesce to her request, obviously, and emerge from the room minutes later. I'm wearing a blue gingham midi dress with flounce sleeves and delicate pearl buttons going up the front, cinched at the waist with the distressed brown leather belt. A thin red paisley kerchief is knotted at my neck, and oversized cat-eye sunnies hide my eyes. To top it all off, a wide-brimmed western-style hat. I honestly can't tell whether I look like an insane Amish school teacher or someone Willow would invite to an art gallery.

"You look great."

"Seriously?" I ask, not wanting to offend the stylist, but also kind of unsure about the whole look. "I mean, it's great, obviously, but, like, can I pull it off?"

"Yes," Willow deadpans.

"Okay," I relent, swishing side to side so that the dress flutters against my calves. "I guess I do look pretty cool. Like a modern-day home-steader who raises grass-fed cows in Vermont or something."

"Or a jewelry maker in Brooklyn who's married to an artisanal chocolatier."

I look at Willow in surprise and see that she's smiling. "I'm fucking with you, Liz," Willow says. We dissolve into laughter, but then Willow reassures me that I *do* actually look hot and cool. "I know it's trendier than you're used to, but trust me," she says.

I stare into her glacial eyes and nod, knowing that this almost-stranger wouldn't lead me astray.

I pay for all of the clothing and accessories immediately, so that I don't have to take anything off. Willow helps snip off all of the tags and peels the tiny clear stickers off of everything. By this point, I'm running late and won't have time to stop home before the cookout. I fire off a text to Arno, letting him know I'll meet him there and will pick up some premade fruit salad and wine at Whole Foods on my way.

I thank Willow for all her help as Fran watches from a corner of the store where she seems to be dusting a felt hat.

"No problem."

I turn, one hand on the brass knob of the front door, when I feel a cool palm on my arm. I whip around in surprise. It's Willow. She glances from my face down to my wedding band.

"Liz?" she says with some urgency. "Whoever you're doing all of this"—she gestures from my hair to my eyebrows to my dress—"for? He's not worth it, girl. He's just not."

Willow smiles and squeezes my arm, then releases me out into the world.

Clearly, Willow has never been up against a Vivienne.

CHAPTER 16

An hour later, I pull up in Cynthia and Brian's circular stone driveway, where there's already a small army of luxury SUVs parked in formation. I find an open spot behind a forest-green Porsche and look around for Arno's car. I spot the Audi immediately, nestled between a cherry-red Mercedes and an obnoxious mustard-yellow BMW. I wonder if either vehicle is Viv's.

I pause before walking inside in order to gather myself and put my best foot forward, so to speak. I breathe deeply, practicing one of Dr. Abelson's breathing techniques called the "7/11," breathing in for a count of seven and out for a count of eleven.

By eight, I'm hacking into my elbow like a lifetime smoker, unable to catch my breath.

The air smells like saltwater, hydrangea, coconut sunscreen, and, somewhere in the distance, hot dogs and hamburgers sizzling on a grill. Charcoal and melted chocolate ice cream and lemonade and corn on the cob, glistening with butter. My stomach rumbles, and I realize I've had nothing to eat all day. My arms are heavy beneath a large, ice-cold bottle of champagne and a platter of sliced watermelon that cost more than ten whole watermelons. I have no free hand with which to open the front doors.

"Let me get that for you!"

I turn my head to see an exquisite, tanned figure in white jeans and

a Rolling Stones T-shirt bound up the steps behind me, long dark hair swinging in the lusty sea breeze.

It's her.

"It's you," I say, then gasp, once again conscious that I have no hands available to cover my mouth or shield my face. Instead I just stare at her.

"Huh?" Viv says, but not in a weirded-out way, just in an easy, carefree "what'd you mean" way.

"It's so blue!" I cough. "The ocean, I mean."

Viv's brow furrows momentarily, then her whole face cracks open into a smile that looks like sunshine itself. Straight white teeth. Amber-colored eyes like chocolate quartz with ribbons of caramel sauce. A slender, slightly aquiline nose.

"You're Arno's wife, right?"

"I . . . I—yes!" I splutter, nodding like an idiot. "The one and only, ha ha!"

"So nice to meet you. I'm Vivienne, but you can call me Viv. I work at Stonebridge with Arno. I've seen photos of you guys around the office. Your hair was a little different then," she says absentmindedly.

The way she says it all, so earnestly, as though I haven't the slightest clue who she is. It's almost enough to take my breath away.

"And I'm Elizabeth," I manage, as Viv opens the gaping front doors to Cynthia and Brian's seaside estate. "But please, call me Liz."

Viv offers to take the watermelon platter from my arms and hustles it into the kitchen, where a long white table has been set up for the occasion. It is absolutely covered in food, and I spot no fewer than five assorted fruit platters. It crosses my mind that this is why Viv offered to take the fruit—to spare me this small humiliation—but I shake my head, dispelling the thought.

"Everyone's already out back," Viv explains. "I just stepped out front to get a couple pics of the ocean. It's *stunning* today!"

"Indeed. *Stunning*."

I trail her, like an extra from a zombie movie directed by Tommy Hilfiger, through the palatial chef's kitchen—past the Sub-Zero fridge and blond-wood cabinets, the quartz counters and floor-to-ceiling windows—through some sliding glass doors that hardly seem like doors

(they're more like massive clear walls), and out into the backyard, where fifty or possibly a hundred people are schmoozing around an infinity pool.

I search for Arno's auburn curls like a retriever longing for its tossed stick. I am sick with anxiety.

There he is.

Arno is sandwiched between Brian and Cynthia—of course—with his head cocked back in full-belly laugher, clutching at his sides as Brian, red-faced and shiny as usual, bulges his cheeks out and does a little pretend march, clearly impersonating someone he doesn't like. Arno slaps at a khaki'd knee with one hand, the other clutching what looks like a gin fizz.

He could win an Oscar, that husband of mine.

Before he sees me, I make a beeline for one of the waitstaff, a pimple-faced boy with dyed black hair that covers one eye better than any patch could. Wearing a nondescript black polo, he holds a tray in each hand: one covered with salmon crostini, the other nearly folding under a rainbow of various cocktails. Classic Brian and Cynthia, I think with a sneer. Catering a Memorial Day cookout, of all things.

"Can I have one of those?" I ask him, pointing in the general direction of the cocktails.

"Oh, sure, miss," he stutters. "Would you like a, er, watermelon margarita, peach gin fizz, or a white-wine sangria?"

"Gin, please."

Cocktail in hand, I readjust the little red scarf at my neck and roll my shoulders back before crossing the length of the pool and sidling up to Arno, who stops midsentence in surprise at my arrival.

"Liz?" he asks, like I might be an imposter playing the role of his wife.

Ah, yes. The newly shorn hair could be a bit of a surprise.

"That's me," I say loudly, slapping his arm amicably.

"How was Coachella, Liz?" Cynthia cuts in. She swishes her long red hair over one shoulder, green eyes sparkling.

The trio laughs in unison.

"That is quite the getup, sweetheart," Arno says. "You look great, though."

I bare my teeth at Cynthia in what I hope appears to be a good-natured smile, all venom beneath the surface.

"So good to see you, Cynthia," I nod. "And you too, Brian. It must be difficult to plan a party with everything you've both got going on." This is supposed to be a subtle jab at Cynthia, who as far as I can tell only volunteers a few hours per year on the Stonebridge board helping plan charity galas.

"Oh, it's nothing," Cynthia says, swatting the air as though ridding herself of a pesky horsefly. "Anything for the Stonebridge fam."

"Indeed," Brian says, nodding. He leans in closer to me as if examining a hemorrhoid through a microscope. His polo shirt is the exact color of a cocktail shrimp. "Did you cut your hair, Liz?"

My free hand flies self-consciously to my head, which thankfully is mostly hidden beneath my new hat. "I did, Brian. Thanks for noticing. Unlike you boys to take interest in such vanities."

We share a laugh, and Brian says, "Well, it looks quite nice on you, Liz. I normally prefer my women with long hair, but it's actually rather becoming on you. Like a young Mia Farrow."

"Not so young anymore, I'm afraid," I say self-deprecatingly, swigging heartily from my bubbly gin drink.

Cynthia grins, then takes a sip from her glass, which appears to contain vodka on the rocks.

"I think it's brave of you, Liz. So very brave."

I have nothing to say to this, so I compliment her on her outfit, a summer floral embroidered maxi dress with an open back that strikes me as far too formal for a summer cookout. Rather than saying thank you, Cynthia just does a full twirl, arms straight out, so that the dress swishes pleasingly around her feet and everyone can get a good look at her toned back.

"Gorgeous, honey," Brian says, ogling his wife with red-rimmed eyes.

"So, how's Kyle working out?" Cynthia asks when she's finished twirling.

The question catches me off guard. "Sorry?"

"Kyle," Cynthia repeats herself, slower this time. "The nanny?"

"Oh, I hadn't realized . . ." I trail off, thinking. "You were the one that referred her?"

Arno cuts in. "Liz, I mentioned that, sweetie. Remember?"

I don't, but Lord knows I've been distracted lately, so I just nod.

"Of course, right! She's fantastic, Cynthia. Truly a gem."

The thought of poor Kyle dealing with Cynthia and her bratty step-kids each day brings a smirk to my lips. Here Cynthia is thinking she's done us a huge favor, when I'm sure Kyle was ready to jump ship at the first opportunity that came her way. Arno and I basically performed a miracle for the young woman.

Cynthia smiles knowingly. "I miss that Kyle. So smart and sweet, and she knows how to be discreet, you know?"

"Right . . ."

I skim the crowd for Viv, but I've lost sight of her, so I make small talk with the few Stonebridge people I like (Jack Taylor; Ryan Simcat and his new girlfriend, Claire; Dirk and [sigh] Leslie Beauregard). Then I branch out and talk to people I like decidedly less, but whose approval is required for Arno's success: other managing directors like Brian, older white men with simmering alcoholism and prominent potbellies straining the edges of their waistbands. Wives whose faces barely move. Younger models—second and third wives—who are clearly struggling with anorexia as they clutch delicate flutes of champagne they never sip from.

I mingle with associates with names like Blake and Saxon, senior advisors named Wilder and Brooks. We talk about tennis and which private schools are the best and how we absolutely have to throw a Kentucky Derby party next year. Through it all, a steady stream of alcohol washes down the back of my throat: a couple more of those delightful peach gin fizzes, two sangrias, a watermelon margarita . . . who's counting?

Eventually, my go-to topics of conversation start to skew toward less palatable fare: late-stage capitalism, ecological disaster, fake-news bots. I can see concern in the faces of the Stonebridgers, wondering why Arno's cute wife has gone off script, but for some reason, I can't stop. I can't talk about canapés and Cap Ferrat any longer. I'm just about to tell an associate about the record-breaking ocean temperatures this year when I spot my husband, making moves.

Across the pool, I see Arno getting some face time with the man of the hour: Cynthia's ancient father and the cofounder of Stonebridge Partners, Thomas Stone.

The two men lean into each other conspiratorially, Arno's mouth mere centimeters from Thomas's ear. Whatever Arno's said is a hit. Thomas guffaws, clapping one liver-spotted hand to his stomach and the other onto Arno's shoulder. I can practically *see* the hunk of salmon crostini fly out of the old cod's mouth.

Well done, Arno, I think to myself. You'd never know he was strategizing.

Out of the corner of my eye, movement. White pants walking toward the house.

Arno pats Thomas on the back before turning and following close behind.

Like a hawk or owl or some other bird of prey, I abandon my conversation with Macallister Something-or-Other and make a beeline for the sliding doors. The leather straps of my new sandals dig into the tender flesh of my feet, and I become painfully aware that there are multiple blisters forming. Any discomfort is blessedly dulled by the alcohol, however, and I trot up the stone steps to the sprawling patio that overlooks the pool.

Inside, Arno and Viv stand beside a bowl of pineapple chunks. They pick from the bowl absentmindedly, somehow already deep in conversation. Their eyes never leave the other as they reach mechanically—bowl to mouth to bowl—popping smooth yellow chunks into their open mouths like baby birds. It's quite sensual to watch.

Hand on the sliding glass door, I'm about to make my entrance when a voice behind me says, "Liz, a moment?"

I turn.

It's Cynthia. Glass tumbler in one hand, the other twirls her long red locks into corkscrews, as though she's anxious about something.

"Um, sure, okay," I say, glancing quickly back at Viv and Arno before following Cynthia to a quiet end of the patio where no one is sitting.

We sit in wrought iron chairs facing one another, and I can hardly hear the talking and music back by the pool. I realize I've never been this alone with Cynthia before. With nothing but still air between us, Cynthia rattles some ice cubes around in her glass, tipping a few into her lipsticked mouth. She crunches them loudly.

Finally, she takes a deep breath and looks me in the eyes.

"Liz, I know we haven't always been the closest," she starts. "My humor isn't for everyone, that's for sure. But I just want to say a heart-felt thank-you, from the bottom of my heart, for letting Brian take the New York opportunity."

I stare at her, confused and expectant, waiting for her to explain what she's talking about.

When I say nothing, she continues: "Boston has been really great for Brian, but he's ready for the next step, you know? I think he's just sort of *reached the ceiling* at the Boston branch. He needs to spread his wings and fly."

"Cynthia, I—"

Cynthia cuts me off. "When I found out Daddy had offered Arno the position to launch the Stonebridge New York office, I thought he would take it, no hesitation, and you two would move to the city this fall. I mean, it's a huge career opportunity. Who wouldn't want that? But he and Brian are close, you know? And I feel like Arno—and I'm sure you played no small role in this—knew that Brian just . . . deserved it a little more."

My mouth is now open, but no words come out.

"Obviously, there will be other, future opportunities for you two to move to New York as that branch gets its sea legs," Cynthia says absentmindedly, the ice cubes rattling around her glass like dice. "But Arno said you two are just happy as clams here in Boston. And there's nothing wrong with choosing happiness over opportunity, Liz. There really isn't. And furthermore, this opens up a lot of space for Arno to move into upper management at the Boston office. I bet he'll follow in Brian's footsteps in no time. Daddy is quite taken with him, you know . . ."

I'm completely gobsmacked. Arno was offered a new job in a new city and somehow neglected to tell me about it? Turned it down, basically handed it right over, to a man he can't stand?

My stomach roils with all of the different types of alcohol I've consumed on an empty stomach in the last few hours. The tops of my arms and hands are sunburnt, crispy pink. I hadn't noticed till now.

Cynthia stands, as though there's nothing else to say, so I stand, too. She envelopes me in an awkward embrace, smelling of cedarwood and jasmine. Her hard, fake boobs poke against my squishy ones like new tennis balls. When she pulls back, her green eyes glimmer.

"Oh, and I'm sorry I made fun of your outfit," she says, an afterthought. "It really is cute, it's just—well, it's a bit *much* for Boston, isn't it?"

"When do you move to New York?" I manage to ask.

"September first," Cynthia says, smiling widely. "Well, Brian will, at least. The girls are *deep* in their education at Trotterdam Academy, so I can't just *yank* them out. They're learning Mandarin this fall! Thank *god* their mother saw the light and let me enroll them there. She can be so *provincial*, you know? And Poppy finally found a ballet instructor who can keep up with her talent, so we'll stay here, and Brian will travel back and forth on weekends and such. It will be a great excuse for me and the girls to visit the city, too. I've always loved Fifth Avenue . . ."

She cackles and does a little hip sashay, making her way back to the party people milling about in seersucker blazers and Lilly Pulitzer tea dresses. I stumble toward the sliding glass doors, determined to finally speak with my husband alone.

Arno and Viv are still by the pineapple, but a few other Stonebridge people have gathered around them. They're talking about the stock market, and I just can't.

"Hey, Arno," I say, too loudly. "I'm not feeling well. Can we go?"

Arno looks up from the group and seems to take in the entirety of me: my reddish face, thickened and tinted eyebrows, sunburnt arms, swollen feet now visibly bleeding in my new sandals. An empty cocktail glass in each hand.

And there it is—disgust. A quick, hot flash, like a bolt of lightning through a half-opened window. My husband is disgusted with me.

"Yes, Liz. We can go."

Arno is good at keeping the mask on, though. He exchanges goodbyes with everyone in the circle: a handshake here, a fist bump there and, for Viv, a one-armed hug and a kiss on the cheek.

"See you Tuesday," she says, before turning to me. "So nice meeting you, Liz."

I wait for the same zap of disgust, but it isn't there. Viv's face is open and warm, her smile full and easy. Like a mug of tea or a freshly baked chocolate-chip cookie. If I didn't feel like I was going to hurl all over Cynthia's white kitchen table, that combination would actually sound quite lovely right now.

"Nice meeting you as well, Viv."

Arno seems surprised that he missed our introductions. I try to decide whether he looks alarmed at this update, but it's too late; his pleasant mask is back in place.

We walk out the yawning double doors into the most spectacular sunset I've ever seen, the tangerine sky lighting up the ocean's surface with a million glittering diamonds.

I turn toward my husband to comment on the cotton-candy clouds, how I wish I could pull them apart with my hands and taste them, but he's not there. I look around me, frantic, and catch the back of Arno's Audi as it peels out of the circular driveway, into the fast-encroaching night.

CHAPTER 17

"I should not be driving," I say to myself approximately 130 times on the way home from Cynthia and Brian's. If I got pulled over, I would immediately be put under arrest and have a DUI on my record for the rest of my life. I wouldn't be allowed to drive for what—a year?—and it would be all my fault.

But part of me is angry.

Surely, Arno noticed that I had too much to drink. Wasn't that wrapped up in the disgust I saw in his eyes just a few minutes ago? If that's true, then why is he letting the mother of his child behind the wheel?

Part of me wants to crash my car just to spite him, hit a guardrail and splinter the fender into a thousand jagged metal pieces. Have the airbags go off with a bang! Bruising my innards and concussing me for days.

My hands jitter at the thought.

Still, I make it to our house without any fanfare, pulling into our driveway just as the sun disappears from the sky, leaving behind that pale-blue twilight hour in its wake. I step unsteadily from the car, head throbbing and mouth dry as a dust bunny. I crave a large electric blue Gatorade. How I would guzzle its contents with reckless abandon, letting the blue dye my gingham dress and dribble down my hands and arms.

Inside, Arno is seated at the kitchen table. His head in his hands.

The TV hums from the family room, where Kyle must be watching something while Emma sleeps. *Probably a documentary about meat processing plants*, I think. *A film on women's rights in Saudi Arabia.* I bet she's never watched a second of the Kardashians.

I sit across from Arno, wondering, on a scale of 1 to 10, how bad my breath is.

"We need to talk," I hear myself say. Words I have never before spoken in this relationship.

"That we do," Arno says to his hands. He runs his fingers through his bouncy curls, which reflect the overhead light. He looks slightly older than he did yesterday, I think with some satisfaction. *You look tired*, I'd say, if I was a crueler sort of person. Instead, I say nothing and wait him out.

"What the hell is going on with you?" he says finally, so quietly I wonder if I've heard him correctly.

"Excuse me?"

"I said, what the hell is going on with you, Liz?" Arno looks at me pointedly. "First, we hire a nanny so you can spend more time working on your novel, and the next thing I know, you're showing up at my office with a tin of cookies for a stranger's dog who died?"

"I thought you understood where I was coming fr—"

"Next, you disappear at the crack of dawn to run some mysterious errands and show up at Brian and Cynthia's an hour late with all of your hair cut off, dressed like some kind of . . . of . . . teenage hipster! Have you lost your mind?"

"I can expl—"

"And I don't even *know* what's going on here." Arno pauses to point an accusatory finger at my eyebrows. "What even are those?"

"Tori thinks they look good," I say defensively.

"Who the hell is Tori?!" Arno shouts, exasperated. Then he glances in the direction of the family room and lowers his voice. "Today was unacceptable. You can have all the drunk nights you want with Tracy Kaplan, Liz, but getting hammered in front of my colleagues is repugnant. Do you know what that does to my reputation? You looked off your rocker today. And Thomas was there!"

I'd rather he screamed and raged, I think. That sort of punishment I could cope with. But this? His quiet, disappointed tone, his thinly veiled disgust, the way he looked at Viv as he squeezed her arm and said he'd see her Tuesday? This, I cannot handle.

"Can I ask you something?"

Arno scoffs. "What, Liz?"

"Why didn't you tell me you were offered a job in New York?"

Arno nearly chokes on a sip of water, and I pat his back as he coughs.

"Who told you about that?"

"Who do you think?"

Arno looks down at his hands as if they belong to a stranger. "I didn't tell you about New York because we don't want to move there," Arno said. "What would be the point in starting a discussion when the outcome's already been decided?"

I frown. "*You* decided the outcome, Arno. You made that decision without even asking for my opinion. How would you know what I want?"

Arno laughs unkindly. "Liz, my entire family is in Massachusetts. All of my childhood friends are here. All of my friends from work. The branch I've worked so hard to build. This gorgeous home we bought. Kyle, who Emma's grown so close to. Hell, we've had her on the waiting list for the top Montessori preschool in the state since she was in utero." He turns to look at me. "Why would I want to leave any of that behind?"

"Yeah, but what about me?"

"What about you?"

"What do I have here?"

"What do you have in New York, Liz?"

"My brother!" I shout, irate. "My brother lives in New York, Arno. And Mariana, my best friend from grad school. Plenty of other writers I went to school with are there, too. It's *the* place to be if you're a writer. And furthermore, New York is hours closer to my mother!"

"You never see your brother."

"Yeah, because he's in New York!"

"And I haven't heard you mention Mariana in years . . ."

"Well—"

"And you hate your mother."

I'm silent.

Arno sighs wearily. "Liz, moving doesn't just magically make someone who's unhappy happy."

"Don't talk to me like you're a therapist."

"Look, what if we *had* discussed the possibility of moving to New York? Do you actually want to move where the cost of living is even higher? Where the threshold for success is exponentially less attainable? Where you're a tiny little speck"—Arno pinches his thumb and forefinger together like they hold a grain of sand—"in a sea of talented, young authors? Would that make you any happier, Liz?"

The walls are closing in on me, so I slide from my kitchen chair to the cool wood floor.

Arno takes a deep breath, then joins me. He stares at my fresh pixie cut. Runs his fingers through the closely cropped hair like he can't quite believe it. He smirks.

"You know, this haircut does look pretty sexy on you," he says. "You're like an entirely different person."

I glare at him. "You said I looked crazy."

"Maybe I like a little crazy sometimes."

"And my brows?"

"Those might take some getting used to."

I shake my head, wrapping my arms around myself.

"You said I embarrassed you in front of all your coworkers."

"I mean, you were pretty drunk." He pauses, rubs his eyes with his fists. "But it's okay. Everyone has too much now and then. You haven't had many opportunities to cut loose since Emma was born, have you?"

His voice is transformed, gentle, like the tickle of a fleece blanket.

"No, I have not."

Arno pinches my cheeks, and it's impossible not to smile. Acquiesce.

"There's my girl," he murmurs, kissing the edge of my ear.

Arno helps me up and pours me a cold glass of water. Watches me as I drink it down. Then makes me drink another, and another. Once I've finished, and liquid sloshes around my belly like a water balloon, Arno takes me by the hand and leads me to the master bathroom. He draws a warm bath, adds lavender-scented bubbles, then slowly unties the silly little red scarf at my neck. He kisses the insides of my wrists, draws circles on my cheekbones. Undoes the pearl buttons of my gingham dress, which slithers to the ground in a puddle.

CHAPTER 18

The week following the disastrous cookout, Arno works late nearly every night. I can't tell if he's punishing me, or if the work is legitimate and I'm just needy and, well . . . crazy. Perhaps the possibilities aren't mutually exclusive.

Each day feels like Groundhog Day, only I'm expected to feel grateful for my stability. Grateful for the opportunity to live another day in my clean and tidy Wellesley bubble, where the worst thing that can befall you is a bad brow job, or your Rembrandt getting stolen.

In the mornings, I jog circles around our neighborhood with Emma's pram, up and down the little swells in the asphalt, past magnificent estates whose residents would never describe their homes as "mansions"; perfectly landscaped yards that homeowners try to pawn off as their own handiwork; yapping dogs that look better cared for than most children in the United States. Now that it's June, the mornings feel slightly more humid and stuffy, the temperatures already limping into the high 70s.

It feels like I'm running through maple syrup, my limbs tight and painful.

After my runs, I shower and make breakfast for Emma and me. She's going through a phase where she only wants bananas, so every morning I cut one up into bite-sized pieces that leave my hands wet and gloopy. I'm starting to truly despise the smell.

By 9:00 a.m., desperate for Kyle to arrive, Emma and I sit by the front door like military brides awaiting our soldiers after a lengthy deployment. Emma chews on the edge of a pink blanket that looks like it might have once been a stuffed rabbit, while I worry a molar I'm convinced is getting looser with my tongue. My dentist says it's not.

Emma says Kyle's name like a rhythmic chant that could summon the blond, bucktoothed twenty-four-year-old from the ends of the earth. It generally works.

Once Kyle is safely within reach, Emma dissolves into shrieks of joy I've only ever seen her employ for Arno. I can't say it doesn't hurt, but honestly, I feel the same way.

To her credit, Kyle does not give in to all of Emma's whims or indulge her hysterics. "Quiet voice, Emma. I'm only coming inside if you talk like the big girl I know you are." This only makes Emma more obsessed with her.

Child taken care of, I disappear into my office around 10:00 a.m. each day and attempt to write. It isn't going well.

First of all, I no longer feel confident in the novel I passionately lost myself in before I had Emma. I read and reread the outline I created and I can't find a resolution. Should the amnesiac woman go back to her family or start her life anew, alone? When I try to come up with an ending now, nothing seems sufficient for the scale and scope I initially envisioned, so I scrawl "protagonist suddenly dies???" into the margins and hope for the best.

The other mental roadblock is five foot nine, Portuguese, and went to Harvard.

Her social media accounts are ridiculously easy to stalk. So much so that I wonder if these are red-herring accounts for legions of jealous wives around the country and Viv's actual accounts are private, hidden under a middle name or a pseudonym. I spend hours switching among her Facebook, Instagram, and Twitter for any updates or clues about her life. All I've learned this week is that Viv goes to yoga at some place in Cambridge called the Healing Lotus; she hates Harvey Weinstein (well, duh); and she has a rescue cat named Timothy. *Ha!* I think viciously. *Arno hates cats. He's allergic to their hair. I bet that makes hanky-panky time at Viv's apartment pretty tough.*

Then I panic, thinking that this means they have to have sex at fancy downtown hotels, to avoid the cat. I make a mental note to check his suits for cat hair and his eyes for red rims and excessive watering.

His nose *has* seemed particularly itchy of late.

This cycle—stalking Viv, pretending to write, stalking Viv, catapulting down various digital black holes—goes on for a few hours, till it's safe to go to the kitchen for lunch. I spend a ridiculously long time making deli-style turkey sandwiches with fancy breads I pick up from the French bakery in town. Avocado toast with microgreens from our garden. Cacio e pepe with homemade noodles. Anything to avoid my manuscript.

Unfortunately, when Kyle is around, she unfailingly asks me how the book is coming along. After the fourth day of this, I snap, telling her it stresses me out to talk about my progress.

"What does progress even *mean*, anyway?" I huff.

"I'm not sure, I was just wondering . . ." Kyle mumbles, clutching Emma to her side as the toddler taps on the sides of her plastic eyeglasses.

"Why do we feel the need to measure success by our productivity, Kyle? It's so unhealthy. I'm not a machine! This isn't Amazon!!!" I say, gesturing wildly to the house around me. "I'm not a fulfillment center!!!" Emma stops her tapping then, staring at me with the same wide eyes as Kyle.

She stops asking after that.

In the afternoons, when the sun reaches its highest point in the sky, my anxiety peaks. It hits me in waves that are debilitating. Sometimes, I sit on the floor of our bedroom, rocking myself back and forth while practicing Dr. Abelson's breathing techniques. Other times, I strap back into my running shoes and run maniacally around our neighborhood, blasting true crime podcasts through my earbuds till I'm sweaty and defeated.

On days when my anxiety feels particularly unmanageable, I drink.

Not so much as to ring alarm bells, just enough to regulate my racing heart and mind, to blur out the edges of the day a bit. Make the sun shine less brightly through our windows.

My drink of choice is vodka. Or gin; doesn't matter. I mix it with plenty of crushed ice and a twist of lemon or lime or orange peel, whatever we have lying around. One day I try cucumbers and a sprig of basil. It's disgusting, but I drink it anyway.

I hope the Grey Goose in my water bottle looks like water. I'm careful about brushing my teeth before getting too close to Kyle, who I could easily see ratting me out to Arno. She would have the best intentions.

Arno would be appalled, probably send me to some fancy-ass rehabilitation center in Vermont, or one of those wilderness retreats in the Moab desert. Everything would get blown out of proportion, and it would be this whole thing. So, I have to be covert.

Once I'm decently tipsy but not in an obvious way, I call someone.

I never start out with the intention of doing so, but I'll be scrolling through my texts with Arno, looking for any hidden messages or signals that I might've missed, and then I'll feel my hands start to shake and sweat break out on my upper lip. Sometimes the corners of my field of vision turn black, like I'm entering a long tunnel. And in those moments, the only thing I can think to do is call someone who will be able to distract me long enough to gather my bearings.

In the past week, I've called Tracy Kaplan (three times), my brother (twice), and my mother, who didn't answer (once).

The conversations usually start with the receiver asking me if everything's all right, if Emma is all right, if Arno is all right.

"Yes, yes," I'll say, frazzled and twitchy.

Then they'll grow all quiet and concerned-like.

"Are *you* all right, Liz?"

"Yes, yes, of course," I reply indignantly, offended they'd even ask. "I'm just checking in to see how *you're* doing." This conversational pivot usually throws them for a loop. Suddenly they wonder, *Well, shit, am I okay?* This gets the ball rolling, and then I'm able to sit back and relax and suck on my water bottle while someone rambles on about their day and I pretend to listen. It's incredibly therapeutic to listen to other people's small problems.

I should start charging Dr. Abelson *to listen to me*, I think.

These forced phone conversations usually last forty-five minutes to an hour, and by then, the sun is setting. Since Arno invariably isn't home yet, I cook dinner for two—three, if Kyle stays—and we eat in silence in front of the television, which I turn to the loudest setting that doesn't make Emma scream.

I've categorized TV shows in my mind into two buckets: "safe" and "unsafe."

The safe shows are usually fantastical or educational: Pixar movies about cursed princesses or talking trolls. Specials on emperor penguins, monarch butterflies, African lions. Cooking competitions where no one is an actual chef, and instead, all of the entrants are eight-year-old boys who attend a reform school in England's Lake District.

"Unsafe" shows are high-stakes dramas that involve infidelity, high-stress jobs (especially in finance, business, or law), lying, and/or betrayal.

I scroll through Netflix and Hulu and Peacock, flying past *Scandal* and *Suits* and even *Grey's Anatomy*, on which literally every single character has had an affair at some point or another. Once I'm shoveling pad thai into my mouth while Morgan Freeman drones on about the life span of a honeybee, I relax into the cushions of our couch and pretend I'm not Elizabeth Bennett and I don't have a child or a husband or a nanny or even a house or car.

I'm a nothing nobody who no one expects anything from.

I'm a fleck of dust hovering by a windowsill after someone's shaken a blanket. I'm a grain of sand on the largest beach in the world, enjoying the feeling of being suffocated, then released, by ocean waves. I'm a gnat stuck to the side of a windshield, waiting for the wind or an errant wiper blade to slice me into something even smaller.

CHAPTER 19

"How have you been doing since our last visit, Liz?"

Dr. Abelson looks freshly tanned, as if she just got back from a tropical island, and I am shocked to remember that she is a fellow human being who has an entire existence outside our therapy sessions. Her messy curls look lighter, sun-streaked and golden, framing her angular face.

"I've been better," I answer honestly.

Dr. Abelson's eyes narrow, catlike, over the rims of her thick black glasses. "And why is that, Liz?"

I zero in on her wrinkled and sun-spotted hand, hovering above the yellow legal pad where she takes notes. All I can see are purple scribbles from where I'm seated. I pause, gauging how much I want to tell her today. My head is already throbbing, as if an invisible giant is squeezing his massive hands around my temples. I haven't properly slept in days.

"I still think Arno is cheating on me."

Dr. Abelson sighs, and I immediately regret being honest with her.

"And why do you think that, Liz?"

"Well, he lied to me," I admit. "I caught him in a lie. A . . . a big one."

Dr. Abelson looks up from her pad, surprised but still skeptical. I can see it in one of her eyebrows, half-cocked. "Oh, really?"

I launch into the entire barbecue story, describing how Cynthia took me aside and thanked me for letting her husband Brian have some coveted New York position that Arno had turned down without ever telling me about it, let alone discussing it with me. I mention how surprised he seemed that I found out about the job offer, how irritated he acted to even be discussing the possibility of us leaving the state of Massachusetts.

Which had me wondering, what was so important to him in Boston? Was it really just the proximity to his childhood friends and family, or was it something—or someone—else?

I describe what it felt like walking in on Arno and Viv sensuously slurping down pineapple slices by Cynthia's kitchen table. How it felt like I had walked in on them having sex. Her tender squeeze on his arm as we left the party. The way he told her he'd see her Tuesday morning with a wink and a kiss on the cheek, right in front of me, the bearer of his firstborn.

I leave out the fact that I got hammered and drove home. I also leave out that every day since, I've spent approximately four hours per day stalking Viv's social media accounts for any new activity. I just don't see how either of those facts are relevant to the larger point; they're more like contextual icing on the "my husband is cheating on me" cake.

When I finish rehashing the whole ordeal, I take a deep breath. Steady my hands on the tops of my knees like a cross country runner who's just finished a four-by-eight-hundred-meter relay. I'm practically gasping.

Dr. Abelson is notably silent.

"What are you thinking?" I ask, peevish. Sometimes she really plays up the whole brooding-intellectual thing.

Dr. Abelson steeples her pointer fingers together and draws them to her forehead in contemplation, while my foot starts tapping a restless thump on a gold-tasseled throw rug.

"What do you think I'm thinking?"

"Oh, don't do that!" I exclaim, exasperated. "Just tell me what you think is actually going on. What do you think I should *do*?"

She laughs.

"Liz," she says softly, "knowing what a client believes others are thinking about their circumstances often sheds a lot of light on their state of mind. So, what do you think I think of your situation?"

I fight the urge to stand, pick up Dr. Abelson's shiny purple pen, and hurl it at her metal table gong.

"If I had to guess? You think I'm catastrophizing again."

"Why?"

I glare at her. "Well, you thought I was catastrophizing the last time I told you I thought my husband was cheating on me. And I still don't have concrete proof, like a dirty text message or a nude photo or—or a burner phone," I stammer.

Dr. Abelson blinks at me. "Liz, you have every right to be upset with Arno."

"I do?" I'm aghast, and a little scared. Part of me, I realize, needs Dr. Abelson to say I'm being crazy. That this is all just a side effect of lack of sleep or mom brain or something.

"Yes, Liz. Arno shouldn't have omitted telling you about the job offer. He made a serious decision that affects both of your lives without getting your input. I can understand how upset that would make you feel. And when you're already feeling concerned about honesty in your relationship . . . well, this omission could naturally feel like a major betrayal."

I nod, puddle-eyed, like a toddler who stubbed her toe and is shocked to find a parent crouched at her side, comforting her with lollipops and kisses.

"Well, thanks, Dr. Abelson. That affirmation does a lot for my . . . my sanity."

"However."

I knew this was bloody coming.

"That does not mean Arno is being unfaithful with his coworker, Liz."

I let out a swift gust of breath. "I know."

"If anything, it seems Arno is taking steps to ensure you start feeling better."

"What do you mean?"

"Well, the nanny, Liz. From what you've told me, hiring a nanny was entirely Arno's idea, and she's been really lovely for both you and Emma."

"She has. Kyle's the best. Honestly, she makes a better mom than I'll ever be."

"Is there any possibility that Arno didn't tell you about New York to protect you?"

"Protect me? From what?"

"From change, Elizabeth."

Normally Dr. Abelson doesn't use my full name, so now I know she means business.

"Moving to New York would be an entire uprooting of the rich life you and Arno have cultivated in Boston. You have a beautiful home, a growing family, a nanny you trust and love. A therapist you're working with. Arno's family is nearby. Plus, he loves his job and his colleagues."

I narrow my eyes, and Dr. Abelson bats a hand at me like she's shooing away a horsefly. "Oh, you know what I mean, Liz. Maybe he thought New York would just be too much for you both right now. Maybe he wants to focus on improving your current life together."

I ponder this for a moment, thinking of all the small acts of kindness Arno's bestowed upon me of late. Outside of Kyle, I mean. His support of me spending time doing what I love: writing, reading, gardening, cooking. His excitement over my burgeoning friendship with Tracy next door. The new pair of running shoes he ordered for me when I mentioned the soles of mine were wearing out. The email he sent me from work yesterday: a link to a novel-writing workshop for struggling second-time authors.

He really is trying, in his way.

"I guess you could be right," I admit.

"Also, Liz . . ." Dr. Abelson clears her throat. "I'm thinking some of your current insecurities as a wife could stem from your childhood. The narcissistic, emotionally absent mother; the unreliable father figure. All of that discord could impact you in ways we're only just now beginning to understand."

Narcissist.

The double "s" rolls off the tongue like a snake in the grass.

When I first came to Dr. Abelson and shared my background, she quickly diagnosed my mother as someone suffering from narcissistic personality disorder. Though she couldn't make an official diagnosis, having never met my mother.

"The self-centered, arrogant thinking and behavior. The lack of empathy or consideration for anyone, especially her children. The idealized, grandiose vision she has of herself. It all points to NPD," Dr. Abelson had said. At the time, it was like a lightbulb went off in my brain.

And ever since, I've been having flashbacks.

Me, at twelve years old, asking to go to a sleepover, only to be told that I'll be babysitting my mom's boyfriend's five-year-old until they get back from dinner. Me, getting screamed at in our kitchen because I hadn't been polite enough to a new suitor who stopped by for lunch. Me, waiting and waiting for my mom to show up at my piano recital until I finally realized that she hadn't been listening when I reminded her of the event multiple times that week.

Dr. Abelson was almost certainly right about my mom, but that didn't mean her disorder had any bearing on my husband's fidelity. Right?

I decide to ignore her. "Do you think I should just ask him, though? Whether he's cheating on me?"

I don't look at Dr. Abelson's face as I say this, just my palm lines. They look deeper than I remember.

"Liz, what you and Arno talk about is entirely up to your discretion. I will say, however, that infidelity is a huge accusation to throw at someone, and I would think very long and hard about whether you think such a conversation would help—or hurt—your relationship with your husband right now."

I glance out a small, half-moon-shaped window to my left. It looks out over Brookline Avenue, tree-lined and impossibly long. People so small they look like beetles crisscross the asphalt road on their way to classes, lunch dates, writing workshops, their own therapy sessions. Their futures.

"And, Liz, I'm wondering if some of your current anxieties are related to postpart—"

I cut her off: "Yeah, you're probably right. I shouldn't bring it up."

Dr. Abelson coughs. Shuffles some papers around her desk. "Like I said, that's your decision, and I'm afraid we're at time, dear."

"Okay."

"Same time next week?"

CHAPTER 20

Three days after my visit with Dr. Abelson, my suspicions are aroused again, thanks to a near-transparent white scrap of paper. Square-shaped and light as a feather, with tiny black numbers and letters on it, smeared and blurry from water and grease and other mysterious liquids in the trash.

A receipt.

I first notice it when I'm bagging up the kitchen garbage to haul outside, a chore I rarely do. But it's Thursday morning, trash day, and Arno got in so late last night, he forgot to take it out. I myself nearly forgot till I heard the unmistakable crunch of the massive yellow truck rolling down our street. I hustle from my office to the kitchen and press my foot on the pedal of our gleaming mechanical trash can, fighting the urge to cough as the smell of decomposing eggplant Parmesan and day-old broccoli smacks me in the face. I'm reaching my hands along the mouth of the trash can, loosening the plastic bag from the lid, when I see the small white crumple of paper beneath half of a maple-syrup-soaked banana pancake.

Just the corner of a word was visible—*STON*—but something about the font jogs my memory.

My hand instinctively reaches out for the scrap of paper, then hesitates. It's wet, slightly sticky. *Gross.* Finally, I snatch it out with the tip of my thumb and forefinger and drop it on the countertop.

I take the trash out in the nick of time. Javier, the trash truck driver, and I are on good terms. He tips his forest-green trucker hat at me and asks how I'm doing. I hold my breath against the trash smell as he tells me about his son's dinosaur-themed first birthday party. I try to pay attention to what he's saying, but my mind is stuck on the scrap of paper on my countertop.

When I jog back inside, sweaty from my brief jaunt outdoors—it's already in the high 80s, a freakishly hot June day—I put a new liner in the trash can and wash my hands with extra-strong lavender soap. I eye the little white paper on the countertop like a mouse you're sure is stalking your kitchen at night; you just need the proof of droppings.

Kyle took Emma to the library for story time this morning, so I'm blessedly alone. But at this moment, the house's silence feels as loud as a train going by.

Finally, I pick the paper up with my fingertips and smooth it out till it's crinkly but flattened. It's hard to read in its condition, but I make out that it's a receipt from Thurston Flowers, a well-known family-owned florist in Back Bay. They were the florists we worked with for our wedding, I register with some shock.

The receipt looks old-fashioned, printed from one of those block-like black thermal printers from the eighties. I remember how smitten I'd been with Thurston Flowers' old-school charm and vintage way of running things. That was what had sold me on using them for our big day.

"Fri 06/02/2019 9:16 AM," it reads.

Last Friday morning.

The merchant ID, terminal ID, and transaction ID mean nothing to me, just a jumble of numbers and capitalized letters.

```
   Type:                           CASH
   Subtotal:                       $200.


 'Thank you for supporting local business!'
               'THANK YOU!'
```

Two hundred dollars is a fairly expensive bouquet, I think. But then again, Thurston Flowers is pretty pricey.

There is no other visible information regarding the arrangement that was purchased—whether it was a summery combination of lavender-hued hydrangea with curving stems of lysimachia, or two dozen long-stemmed red roses.

Were they a birthday present? A new baby gift? A "congratulations on your recent promotion" bouquet?

When you think your husband might be cheating on you, details matter. Context is everything.

I bite my lip. How could I figure out what this purchase was for?

Cash payment made it impossible to track through our bank statement, and I couldn't very well ask Arno. He'd want to know why I was snooping through the trash like some sort of dumpster-diving rat.

Could I call Thurston's? Ask one of the managers if someone named Arno Bennett purchased a flower arrangement last week, and if so, what it was?

I shudder.

No, that wouldn't work either, for a number of reasons. Number one, they might ask for my name and remember me. We purchased nearly fifteen thousand dollars in flowers from them for our seaside wedding: sculptural rose displays on every table; monstera fronds and elephant ear centerpieces; a full-on canopy of greenery above the hors d'oeuvres; take-home succulents and terrariums for every guest. We'd even been featured on their website: Arno and I, entwined beneath hanging branches of flowering cherry blossoms, rosy-cheeked and tipsy, as the Atlantic Ocean thundered its raucous applause on the shoreline.

Secondly, if Arno just walked in, waited for his flowers, and paid in cash, it's unlikely that whoever rang him up caught his name.

I scratch at my hairline, still unused to my newly short locks. It's frustrating not being able to throw my hair into a ponytail or messy bun when feeling overwhelmed: a small act of control I now lack. I settle on the next-best form of sleuthing: I run back into my office, where my laptop sits, patiently waiting for my return like an old friend. I Google Thurston Flowers and peruse all of their current products arranged by occasion: *Anniversary, Birthday, Congratulations, Get Well, Housewarming, Love and Romance, New Baby, Thank You,* and *Sympathy.*

It takes a long time to scroll through all of the "Over $100" options, which have ambiguous names like "Dahlia Daydream," "Berry Blush," and "Violet Enchantment." Many of the arrangements appear in multiple categories. It doesn't seem right that you can purchase "White Rose Hedge" for both the birth of a child and the death of a friend's parent.

After an hour of looking at dizzying arrays of baby's breath and sunflower sculptures, I come up empty-handed. I have no better idea of what Arno might have purchased than before I logged on. If anything, I feel even more flummoxed. Even if I call the florist, and he says Arno purchased the design of the month, it could mean any number of things. I only know that whatever it was wasn't for me.

A flash of pain at my temples signals an impending migraine. I've had them since childhood and usually can prepare for them with an extra-strength Excedrin and a dark room, but this time I hadn't noticed the aura—blurry vision, wavy lines, and flashing dots—in my periphery. I'd been too busy searching for hidden meaning in the rich textures of acacia pine, the hot-pink spray of a perfect summer rose.

Still, I persevere.

Rather than immediately lying down in bed, as I know I very well should, I perform a quick search of Viv's social media accounts that quiets my thumping heart: no new activity, and certainly no sneaky flower arrangements dotting her timeline.

I send Arno a quick text: Arroz con pollo tonight? Rent a new movie?

He replies almost immediately: I'll be home around 9, so maybe. Love you!

My breathing slows to a steady in and out that helps stymie the throbbing pain that pulses at the base of my skull. I close my laptop with a bang and stumble to the bathroom, whipping open the medicine cabinet so viciously, I nearly crack the mirror. But it's fine. Everything is fine. I take three or maybe four Excedrin and swallow them down with tepid tap water I scoop into my hands by the fistful.

Clamoring into bed fully dressed, I ask Alexa in my sweetest voice to turn off every single light in our house and close the bedroom's electric curtains. I am then enshrouded in pitch-black perfection. I turn on the silly sound machine to "midsummer's night," which is really just a weird combination of crickets and simulated thunder, and put on a plush eye mask.

As I drift in and out of steamy oblivion, my last thought is a hallucination. A nightmare.

Viv and Arno, dazzling in a white skintight lace dress and slim-cut tweed suit, respectively. Arms wrapped around one another like they're the last two passengers on the *Titanic*. Behind them, a never-ending wall that drips flowers from the sky to the floor: crimson dahlias and scabiosa pods and green summer grasses that undulate in an unseen breeze.

They're getting married, that much is clear. And though I can't see their faces, I detect a crowd just behind me, shrieking and screaming in excitement, as if they're attending a rock concert. Faceless people jostle and elbow me for a better view. Somehow, I know they are all Stonebridge employees, elated that finally Arno has made the right choice by keeping it in the Stonebridge family.

I begin to scream, but either no one hears me or no one cares.

Viv turns to the crowd, glowing in an ethereal light that comes from within. She smiles her megawatt grin. It's tough to look at her directly.

She begins counting.

"One . . .

"Two . . .

"Three!"

She throws a bouquet as big and black as a dozen crows into the crowd.

A number of women, all blond Stonebridgers, surge forward in a crushing wave, falling upon the flowers, scrabbling like vultures for a tiny portion. Shreds of black dahlias and hellebore, torn to pieces, surround my bare feet.

I sink into the grass-laced floor and cry.

CHAPTER 21

T he evening after the flower receipt discovery, I gather the courage to ask Arno what it was for via three glasses of wine on an empty stomach before he gets home from work. I should just bring up the root of my anxiety—the text—but for some reason, I'm too scared of what his answer would be. Addressing the flowers seems like an easier, less direct way of getting the answers I need.

We're sitting on our back patio, each of us nursing a glass of Malbec. The edges of Arno's mouth are stained purple. My socked feet are tucked into his lap, where he rubs them with one hand, absentmindedly. He's talking about some birthday party we have coming up, for his niece. I'm just enjoying the sound of his voice, so rich and deep, like church bells on Christmas Day, or raw honey—the good kind that's a deep shade of umber, imported from the rolling hills of Tuscany.

For the first time in a week, he got home before 8:00 p.m., and I am giddy with gratitude. The joy of sharing an unhurried meal with your spouse as your child sleeps soundly in her crib, exhausted from a jam-packed day of nature walks and sing-alongs with her perfect nanny, Kyle.

As if they can intuit our good moods, crickets chirp softly in the grass nearby, adding an unexpected backup chorus to the Otis Redding that plays from the speakers in the kitchen. The French doors that lead inside are only cracked open, so as not to let in the first of the season's mosquitoes.

When there's a pause in conversation, Arno refilling my glass, I dip one toe in the water. My hands tremble slightly, so I hastily set my glass down. Wine dribbles down the side.

"Hey, so guess who I was catching up with the other day?"

"Who?" Arno asks good-naturedly.

"David Thurston," I say, mimicking his casualness. "Remember him?"

Arno scratches his facial hair. "The flower guy?"

"Yes."

"Sure, of course I remember him. He and his brother Ted did the flowers for our wedding."

I wait for a beat, hoping Arno will fill me in on his own, unprompted. *Say, I spoke with him the other day, too. I was buying flowers for our secretary's birthday. No one ever remembers to thank her for all her hard work, poor old gal.*

But he doesn't.

"Yup, that's the one," I say finally. "I was sending flowers to my brother," I lie. "For his promotion."

"Oh, he got promoted? That's great! I didn't know that."

My brother works in sales at a tech start-up that sells warehouse management software. As far as I know, he has never received a raise, let alone a promotion, and talks about quitting every time we catch up.

"Yeah, nothing big. Just like, added responsibilities," I hear myself say, anxious that Arno might text him "congrats." "And a very small pay bump."

"Hey, better than nothing!" Arno says chipperly.

Arno has been sending my brother a monthly allowance ever since we got married. I asked him to. I knew that at the time, my brother was working two jobs, bartending in the evening in addition to his sales gig, just to afford his rent and pay off his student loans. Every time I spoke with him, he sounded frazzled, and I couldn't bear it. Besides, we had plenty of extra money. Arno agreed to the arrangement immediately and never brings it up, one of his many annoyingly wonderful qualities.

"Yeah, for sure." I take a long, even sip of wine. "Anyway, David mentioned that you'd been in recently, too!" I try to keep my voice upbeat. Carefree as a Sunday afternoon, nothing shady here.

I watch Arno's face for shock, alarm, concern—anything—but it remains placid, the surface of a pond.

"Oh yeah, I guess I did stop by there a week ago." He runs his hand through his hair, tossing this comment out like he's mentioned picking up a gallon of milk from the supermarket, rather than a mysterious two-hundred-dollar bouquet.

"Oh yeah?" I ask, nonchalant. "What for?"

"Well, you remember Mack, right?"

"Mack . . . with the dead dog? Cookie?"

"Right, that's the one," Arno says, sighing. "Well, you'll never believe the spate of bad luck the poor guy is having. His cousin died in some sort of freak boating accident."

"Oh my god, really? That's so terrible!"

"Yeah, it's truly awful," Arno says. "Anyway, I took the liberty of buying him some flowers on behalf of the Stonebridge fam. He's still been making it into the office, but it's clear he's really torn up over it. I guess he and his cousin were really close, more like brothers."

"Wow," I say, rendered speechless. *I wonder why Arno paid with cash, though, and not his black AmEx company card.* "I'm so sorry to hear that. Please give him my condolences. Maybe I should send a gift basket . . ."

"Are you going to bake him more cookies?" Arno cuts in.

I look up, surprised, and see that he's smirking.

"Fuck you!" I squeal, fake-kicking him with my foot.

We dissolve into laughter, clutching our stomachs as wine threatens to spill over the sides of our cups. Arno leans over and brushes a tear from the edge of my bottom lashes.

"Honey, I appreciate your bottomless wells of empathy, but you don't have to pretend to give a fuck about Mack."

He kisses me on the lips as I dissolve into laughter once more.

Later that evening, after the last dregs of wine settle into our limbs and we crawl into our bed, Arno passes out into one of his infamously deep slumbers. He only snores when he drinks, and tonight, he's positively roaring with each intake of breath.

Lately, it's near impossible for me to sleep, but this is ridiculous.

After pushing him gently, to no avail, I crawl out of bed into the pale blue gloom of night and creep into the hallway, pulling the door firmly shut behind me with a click. I wander upstairs to my office, where my laptop sits plugged into the outlet as I left it, the small white apple in its center pulsing its hello.

I open it and stare at my virtually untouched novel for a few moments, till the words blur together like a smudge of ink, and I close out of the Word document. I've never been very productive past 10:00 p.m., anyway.

Instead, I type "Stonebridge Partners" into Google Chrome and go to the company's home page. I'm merely curious about what happened to Mack's cousin, that's all.

Typically, when someone from the firm loses a loved one, someone from human resources is obligated to write a little statement on the company blog or newsletter. Something like, "Stonebridge Partners is deeply saddened to note the passing of So-and-So's mother, a retired elementary school teacher who lived in a cabin in Maine with her husband and two toy poodles. She will be remembered by her husband of forty-five years, Ted, as well as her three sons, who all went to Harvard." And then there will be a link to the obituary and, sometimes, details on the impending memorial or funeral.

I scroll and scroll, but there's nothing about Mack's cousin. The most recent company announcement was a reminder about a food drive for tropical storm victims in Haiti. I remember Arno mentioning it and us donating a few hundred bucks. Another recent obit-adjacent message is about the passing of Brian's grandmother, a ninety-five-year-old named Edna who had dementia and lived in a nursing home in Newton. We also sent something for that, though I can't remember what.

Frustrated, I dig a little deeper, locating Mack on Facebook. His profile is blessedly public—a common thing for dudes, I've noticed. I scroll through inane, jokey posts, mostly about the Patriots and how handsome Tom Brady is. Other than a few obviously conservative political remarks that garnered some heat, Mack's page is pretty sparse. He only got fifteen "happy birthday" messages this March.

Mack is handsome in a deteriorating-quarterback kind of way, with a Cary Grant jawline and a thickening midsection. He has swooping black hair, thick eyebrows, and the largest hands I've ever seen, like they've been blown up with helium. I wonder whether his reddish undertones are hereditary or alcohol-related as I click through profile pictures, mostly on different types of boats, with a bunch of other guys and lots of fish.

There are no mentions of a dead cousin in his most recent posts, though that's not unusual. I don't think many guys take to social media to grieve for their loved ones, but I'm surprised that there are no unsolicited messages from friends and colleagues. I've noticed that when people know someone who's just suffered a huge loss, they often forgo a card or flowers and head straight to the acquaintance's Facebook page. Particularly the older generation, baby boomers, but young people do it, too. They love to make unoriginal remarks on public forums like, *So sorry for your loss!* or, *Thinking of you! xoxo!* or the absolute worst, *Heaven gained another angel yesterday . . .* Even if they've never met the person who died, and aren't that close to the bereaved.

But on Mack's page, there is nothing. Zip. Zero.

White noise, like an indeterminable buzz, fills my ears. Anxiety, threatening to undo a perfectly wonderful evening with my husband. I cannot allow myself to spiral out of control like this.

I try to find Mack on Instagram, but either he doesn't have an account or I can't find it. Twitter either.

Flummoxed, I go back to Facebook and try searching for possible cousins among Mack's friends, but he has 567 of them, and without a definitive last name, it proves too difficult. I find one guy who appears to be Mack's actual brother—Mack is in his profile picture, and the caption is *"brother"*—but his page is private, so I can't check for condolences there either.

In a last-ditch effort, I search Mack's last name plus "obituary," "freak accident," and then "boating accident," but all that comes up is a three-year-old obituary for a Dave O'Leary, who was a father, brother, and beloved grandfather who died of pancreatic cancer. It's not even clear whether he's related to Mack's family or is part of an entirely different O'Leary clan. There are quite a few of those in Boston, I'd imagine.

I close my laptop around 3:00 a.m., bleary-eyed and defeated.

My anxiety attack has taken on a thick, grayish hue, the feeling in which I'm still a bundle of nerves, but my exhaustion has dimmed the attack's most pronounced effects: speeding heart rate, sweat-drenched armpits, trembling, shallow breathing. Time to head for bed, again.

I take a sleeping aid from Tracy that I haven't told Arno or Dr. Abelson about, because it's not really any of their business what exactly I put into my body, now is it? Soon I drift into a tumultuous slumber punctuated by nightmares I won't remember come morning.

Around 6:00 a.m., Arno turns over on his side and ruffles my short hair, like a puppy. The sleeping aid has slightly worn off, providing me with the disorienting effect of a brain that's wide awake and a body that's heavy and slow.

"Morning, baby," he says, stretching his arms overhead.

Luxurious, I think, *to be able to sleep like a king and wake up as handsome as one, too.*

"How'd you sleep?"

Three words that threaten to unravel me.

"Perfect. Just perfect."

CHAPTER 22

On a deliriously beautiful Saturday in mid-June, Arno and I attend his niece's third birthday party.

Beatrix is her name, and she and her parents, Arno's brother, Harry, and sister-in-law, Rose, live in a sprawling Georgian home in historic Newburyport. The drive takes about an hour and a half. They tend to host holidays, Harry and Rose, so we've spent many a Thanksgiving and Christmas crammed into one of their guest rooms, which still have the low eighteenth-century ceilings that Arno never fails to bump his forehead on. But today is just a day trip, thank god. My good manners and helpful nature tend to deteriorate after twenty-four hours around Arno's mother, Adrienne.

"Be-ah! Be-ah! Be-ah!" Emma babbles from her car seat, clapping her sticky hands together for emphasis.

"Yes, darling," Arno replies. "It's Bea's birthday today! We're going to give her the present you picked out for her, Timmy the talking pony."

In the rearview mirror, Emma frowns. She didn't understand giving Timmy away was a part of the bargain. She twists around in her seat, trying to spy where I've put the shiny silver gift bag, but I covered it with a throw blanket this morning, anticipating a meltdown at some point or another.

We sail past the south bank of the Merrimack River, coasting by historic redbrick steam mills and tanneries, a picturesque cobblestone shopping district, and hundreds of stunning Victorian and colonial homes that look straight out of *Little Women*.

I'd never admit it to her face, but I'm terribly envious of where Rose lives.

Newburyport looks and feels exactly how New England should, no matter the season. In fall, its winding cobblestone streets are covered in maple and oak leaves so orange and bright, they look like pools of fire. Come winter, homeowners fully embrace the histories of their storied homes, embellishing their eaves with fresh boughs of holly and red velvet ribbons. White candles flame in every glass windowpane.

Once spring dries up the mounds of powdered-sugar snow, the city remembers its shipbuilding roots. Visitors clamor for a few photos of its old wharfs and many lighthouses, crowd into the retro seafood joints for lobster rolls drenched in butter. Aesthetically, one could walk for miles and basically feel as if they were living inside a Louisa May Alcott novel. It's glorious.

Truth be told, Newburyport feels far more "authentic" than Wellesley ever could, but I'd never say this out loud to Arno. What would be the point? It's too far from Boston, too far from Stonebridge. And way too close to Rose and Adrienne—for me, at least.

"We're here!" Arno sings as we pull into Rose and Harry's circular driveway. Shells crunch beneath our tires, and I grit my teeth. The house looms over us, three stories with a fresh coat of white paint, black shutters. Stately and imperious as ever.

Before I can even open my car door, Adrienne appears at my cracked window, beaming.

"Where's my girl?!" she squeals.

Arno's mother wears a white, gauzy shirt and stone-colored khakis. Her long, gray hair is knotted into an impressive French braid that speaks to her youthful years as a star equestrian.

For a second, I almost reply, "I'm right here!" But she's talking to Emma, of course.

Emma screams, shaking her arms like one of those inflatable air dancers you see at auto dealerships. She kicks her chunky thighs against her seat, keening.

Adrienne opens the back door and unbuckles Emma with a practiced flourish, scooping her youngest grandchild into her strong arms.

"There you go, baby girl. Grandma's got you."

Emma presses her face into her grandmother's ample bosom, immediately grabbing at her chunky amber necklace and tugging with all her might. Adrienne seems not to notice and begins bouncing Emma up and down as if she's still a newborn trying to digest milk.

"What took you so long?"

"Ugh, sorry, Mom," Arno replies, lifting Beatrix's present, still secure under its blanket, out of the trunk. "Someone threw a bit of a tantrum when we told her Kyle wasn't coming today."

Adrienne's mouth presses into a firm, disapproving line. "I see. Well, that's to be expected when your child spends that much time with someone . . . not from the family," she says with a sniff.

Side note: Adrienne thinks Arno and I should have moved closer after Emma was born so that we could use the same nanny as Beatrix and the girls could grow up the best of friends. Not to mention grandma Adrienne would be a mere five minutes' drive away. She's deeply offended that we pay a young, hip stranger she's never met to care for our child. Our relationship, already tenuous, will likely never come back from this betrayal.

I'm okay with that.

"Where's the birthday girl?" I ask, steering the conversation back into friendly territory.

"Oh, she's riding the pony out back," Adrienne says, waving her hand dismissively. She scrunches up her nose. "It smells terrible. Clearly didn't get hosed off before they loaded him into the trailer."

"Wait, there's a real pony here?" I ask, shaking my head in disbelief. "She's only three years old."

"I learned to ride when I was two," Adrienne replies. "It's character building."

"Wow, Mom," Arno exclaims. "How cool!"

If any partygoers had doubts about which house was hosting a three-year-old's *Frozen*-themed birthday, all uncertainty would be cast aside by the time they reached Harry and Rose's mailbox. Weighted clusters of white, silver, and blue balloons are scattered hither and thither, with a single giant "3" foil balloon smack-dab in the center of the lawn. Glittering silver streamers bedazzled with white snowflakes hang from the home's windows, and fake clumps of snow line the brick walkway and spill from window boxes.

A six-foot inflatable Olaf sways in the morning breeze beneath an oak tree, his eyes black and unseeing.

"Damn," I mutter. "It's a shame the kid wasn't born in December, huh?"

"What's that?" Adrienne asks.

"Nothing."

We walk around the front lawn to the back of the house, where Beatrix's birthday party is in full swing. I check my watch and am disappointed to discover it's barely noon.

Harry and Rose's backyard looks like a winter wonderland, even more so than the front of their house. Fake snow and tinsel "icicles" drip from the oak and evergreen trees that line the property, and incredibly realistic looking snow drifts are artfully fluffed around the yard. A wintry balloon sculpture creates a rainbow over a table laden with mostly blue food. Toddlers jump, shriek, and pummel an inflatable *Frozen* castle bounce house. And Beatrix, resplendent in a shimmery blue Elsa costume and fake blond wig, sits atop a white pony being led by someone dressed up as the protagonist hunk, Kristoff.

"Well, this is really . . . something," I breathe.

"Rose never misses an opportunity to one-up the neighborhood moms, does she?" Arno whispers against my earlobe, giving my arm a little squeeze. I laugh out loud, quickly covering my mouth. At least we have each other.

"Arno! Liz!" Arno's brother Harry shouts. He's standing beside the bounce house, supposedly to "monitor things," but we can tell the mimosa in his hand isn't his first of the morning. He smiles widely, arms outstretched.

"There you are," Arno mumbles, giving his brother a huge, clapping hug. He ruffles Harry's thick head of hair. "Looks like you need to replenish your Rogaine supply, bro."

"Fuck you," Harry says good-naturedly.

Rose glares at the three of us from the nearby food table, where she seems to be fiddling with a cake-pop stand.

"Language, Harry. Language," she mutters, eyes flashing.

I've always liked Harry. Six foot four and burly as the Brawny paper towel guy, Harry reminds me of a kindly lumberjack or something. His beard is as bushy as though he's been living in the Alaskan wilderness for years on end, and he almost exclusively wears holey old flannel shirts, even in the summer. You'd never know that he was a multimillionaire app developer who sold his last company to a major California tech firm.

He's been "taking a sabbatical" since the acquisition, but Arno and I both know he probably already has his next business underway. Behind the good-natured, easygoing disposition, Harry possesses a machine-like brain that never sleeps, in anticipation of whatever tech trend will upend society next.

"So, how have you two lovebirds been?" Harry asks, ignoring his wife.

"We've been pretty good, dude, can't complain," Arno answers for the both of us.

"Are you bored of working for corporate America yet?" Harry asks, elbowing Arno in the ribs. "Ready to throw in the towel and come work for your big brother?"

"Never, man," Arno says, smiling. "Better health care, and you piss me off too much."

"Harry, can you please help me set up the blueberry lemonade dispenser?" Rose cuts in. "It's too heavy for me." Rose puts a hand to the small of her back and grimaces dramatically.

I desperately want to roll my eyes but do not, if only because Harry genuinely loves his wife.

"Sure, baby. I'll be right back," he says to Arno and me.

Rose and Harry met on one of the apps Harry developed in college as a joke, some stupid matchmaking platform called Meet Cute. It never got off the ground, but before Harry shuttered it, he made personal use of it for a few dates and happened to meet Rose, a fellow third-year student at Yale. They fell in love over a shared affinity for Impressionism—specifically Manet and Degas—and the plays of Anton Chekhov. They were married within a few months of graduating.

Pinch-nosed and slight, Rose reminds me of an expensive porcelain doll, with shiny blond hair and a waist so small I've wondered if I could fit both my hands around it to form a circle. She studied art history and theater at Yale, and as far as I'm concerned, she's been performing ever since. I've never voiced my true feelings for Rose to Arno because I can tell she holds a soft spot in his heart as the mother of Beatrix and the sister he never had. Besides, if she makes his brother happy, he'd never hear an ill word about her.

While Harry goes inside to retrieve the drink dispenser, I sidle up to Rose, determined to play nice.

"Hey, Rose. This looks absolutely unreal." I gesture around at the silver and blue balloons and a miniature gold throne that's appeared out of nowhere.

Rose glances at me and gives a small, tentative smile. "I've been up since four a.m."

"I'll bet."

She sighs in her signature put-upon way. "I just wanted everything to be perfect for her, you know?"

I frown.

"What could be more perfect than this, Rose? You got the kid a pony."

"Well, it's been a really tough year for B," Rose says. "Ever since she was diagnosed with Lyme disease, it's just been an uphill battle for us."

Again, I struggle to keep my eyes focused on Rose's wide ice-blue ones without rolling them. "Wasn't it never confirmed as Lyme disease, Rose?" I look out at the crowd, where little Beatrix is doing somersaults for an audience of rapt children. "Seems like she's doing great, actually," I point out, watching Beatrix stand and clap for herself. "Seems like she's just your average, healthy three-year-old."

Beatrix had a small pink rash on her arm last summer, which I saw in a photo that circulated in the family message threads. In it, a smiling Beatrix sat on a swing in a pink princess dress, proudly thrusting her forearm forward for the camera. A touch of pink, no bigger than a nickel. Probably rug burn, Arno and I had agreed. Maybe an infected mosquito bite, at the very worst.

According to Harry, there were absolutely no side effects aside from the rash. But if you asked Rose, Beatrix has been irrevocably altered, experiencing joint pain, exhaustion, muscle aches, neck stiffness, mood changes, and "brain fog." As a two-year-old. Rose took her to every physician, specialty doctor, and herbalist on the East Coast until she found someone who would confirm what she claimed to already know: something was wrong with Beatrix.

Rose is a hypochondriac to the nth degree. It's just one of her many dramatic tendencies I can't stomach.

"We'll see, I guess." She shrugs. "We'll just have to see."

We look out at the parents milling about, holding mimosas and mysterious glasses of blue punch, and Rose brightens momentarily.

"It really seems like everyone's having a nice time, don't you think?" Rose murmurs. "This is the most tasteful birthday party I've been to this year, certainly." She lowers her voice. "I went to Mimi Spears's daughter's birthday last weekend, and it could not have been more *tacky*. It was cowboy and Indian–themed; can you imagine? In this day and age? I almost didn't let Beatrix go, but that would have caused so much *drama*. So instead, we went, but she wasn't allowed to dress up like the other kids, and I wrote a private letter to the mother afterward."

"Good for you, Rose," I say, and I mean it, though it's tempting to point out that *Frozen* appropriated numerous indigenous Scandinavian elements. I look around for my husband.

He and Emma look on as another child, a wisp of a ginger-haired boy, gets a ride on the pony. The little boy looks absolutely terrified and keeps his hands hitched high on the reins, hovering jerkily above the horse's ears. That poor creature. Emma stares with her mouth hanging open and spit dribbling down her chin, entirely entranced. Adrienne hovers beside them, tousling Emma's curls and cooing.

I walk over to what I assume is the "parents' table," only because there is food that isn't blue on it, and pour myself a mimosa, taking a few swift gulps before refilling my flute to the rim. Being around the other women in Arno's life has always put me on edge, making me feel not quite good enough. It's not just the lavish birthday party—so expensive and outrageous; I'd never agree to throw something similar for Emma. It's the obvious *obsession* these two women have with Beatrix and Emma, as if every good moment in our collective future hinges on the two girls' total and unwavering happiness.

It's exhausting.

"Liz?"

I turn around.

It's Adrienne, alone. She's holding a glass of iced tea and has a glint in her eyes.

"Hey, Adrienne. How's it going?"

"Well, I'd ask you the same, but your haircut says it all." Adrienne laughs loudly. "You know, usually, women chop all their hair off when they're too busy to maintain it. But I understand you did this *after* hiring a full-time nanny."

I take a pointed sip of mimosa. "I just wanted a change."

"Mmm," Adrienne murmurs. "Don't we all, now and then." She looks me up and down. "It seems you've lost weight."

"I've taken up running."

"That's terrible for your joints. You should really consider something low impact, like swimming."

"Chlorine gives me headaches."

"I bet that does, too," Adrienne says, nodding toward my drink.

I take another swig.

"So, how are things going with the nanny? I hear that she dresses like a man. I hope that sort of behavior doesn't rub off on my granddaughter."

I nearly spit out my drink. Stare at Adrienne for a beat, blinking.

"You know what I hope doesn't rub off on my daughter? Homophobia."

Adrienne's face flushes red. "I didn't—I wasn't—"

"I don't care what you *meant*. Kyle is absolutely lovely. She's well educated and kind and cares about Emma deeply."

"Well, not as deeply as her family could, surely. I mean, that's just science."

I stare at my cuticles, and Adrienne shakes her head as if I'm a lost cause. Then, she brightens. "Did you hear the news? Beatrix got into Nightingale for pre-K."

"I had not. That's great."

"Most Nightingales end up going to Ivy League schools, you know."

"Do they now."

Nightingale is one of the New Age, free-range preschools Arno and

I laugh about behind closed doors: no grades, meditation instead of recess, curriculum designed *by the children*. A year's tuition costs about as much as a brand-new Mercedes.

"Mm-hmm. You and Arnie should really look into getting on their radar. I'm sure Rose could put in a good word . . ."

This is how my conversations with Adrienne go: criticism, concern over the well-being of my child, followed by more criticism. Like a tennis match in which I'm the ball.

Finally, in the distance, George shouts, "Cake time!"

I've never been so delighted to sing happy birthday to a toddler.

George is Arno and Harry's father, a portly man of middling height with a shiny bald head and ruddy cheeks, like an Irish rugby player who's had one too many pints of Guinness. It's unclear how he landed Adrienne, a graceful and poised beauty even in her older years, but I'm sure she had a nose for success. After all, George is stupidly wealthy, coming from old money and bringing in new. His parents hailed from England, where they owned dozens of properties and apartment buildings around London. George took his tidy little trust fund and copied their success in Boston, scooping up brownstones in the Back Bay and tottering old Victorians in Brighton-Allston and then flipping them. For Emma's first birthday, he wrote us a check for fifty thousand dollars.

All the revelers walk slowly to the center of the yard, where a white table's been dragged. I find Arno and Emma and stand beside them as Harry lights the candles on an ice-cream cake shaped like a gigantic reindeer.

The woman of the hour, Beatrix, has pink cheeks from too much sun and seems spectacularly grumpy for someone who's spent the last three hours alternating among pony rides, a bounce house, and sugary glasses of lemonade. She pouts and crosses her arms over her chest, refusing to blow out the candles. "Too many people," she mutters to Harry.

"C'mon, darling, we're all here to celebrate you!"

Rose looks frantically around at the guests, tittering nervously. "C'mon, B! Give it one good blow!"

"*No!*" Beatrix shouts in Rose's flushed face. "No cake!"

"Beatrix!" Rose yells. "No shouting at Mommy!"

Some of the partygoers laugh nervously. Others exchange empathetic glances.

Arno steps forward and leans down to Beatrix's height.

"Okay, well, then I guess I'm going to have to blow out all these cool candles by myself, huh?" He takes a big, exaggerated breath in, puffing up his cheeks.

"*No!* Uncle Arnie, no!" Beatrix yells, but she's giggling now. She claps her hands on either side of Arno's face and he releases the air exaggeratedly, so that it sounds like a loud fart. Beatrix dissolves into a fit of laughter, and Rose smiles gratefully.

"Okay, then let's do it together, on the count of three," Arno says, holding on to Beatrix's sweaty little hand.

"One . . . ! Two . . . . !"

On "three," Beatrix dutifully blows out her candles, and Arno picks her up with one arm, tickling her under her armpits. She squeals and demands that he take her to the bounce castle, and Arno promises to as soon as she tries a bite of her delicious reindeer cake.

As I watch them together, it occurs to me how much Arno truly loves children. He isn't putting on a show for the partygoers' benefit, or trying to save the day in front of his family. He loves Beatrix and wants her to have a great birthday—it's as simple as that. You can see it in his eyes, full of wonder, as Beatrix babbles on and on about how one day she'd like to have her own pony, and would name him Onion.

I hug Emma to my chest, inhaling her slightly poopy essence, and remember how lucky I am to have a child that's one half the wonderful man in front of me. In return, Emma looks deep into my eyes and utters one word: "Kyle."

I sigh. "We'll see her in two days, my sweet."

Emma screws up her face and looks to be on the verge of tears when Arno swoops back to my side, his radar for tantrums much more finely tuned than mine.

"Time to go home, girls?"

"Yes!" I say gratefully, nearly collapsing into his arms.

"I'll drive, so you can sleep on the way home."

"I love you so much." I kiss his bristly cheek, and he grins.

We say our goodbyes and strap ourselves into the car, Emma falling asleep almost instantaneously. I relax into the buttery leather seats, allowing my eyelids to droop, too.

"Wait, I want to show you something before you're lights-out," Arno says, reaching over to squeeze my arm.

"Oh, okay," I say, yawning. "What is it?"

"You'll see."

Arno drives about a mile and a half down the tree-lined street and throws on the blinker, turning right into the driveway of a large, historic Cape-style home. It's painted a gorgeous shade of deep, stormy gray and has navy shutters with red trim. A willow tree with a tire swing attached sways gently in the breeze, as if an invisible child is pushing it. It's a beautiful scene.

I glance over at Arno expectantly and am surprised to see him grinning mischievously.

"What's all this?" I ask, glancing around. "Whose home is this?"

It's just then that I notice a white sign stuck into a garden bed laden with purple and white petunias. In bright red letters: *For Sale.*

"Arno? What's going on?"

"Come on. Let's go inside."

Before I can say anything, Arno has turned the car off and hopped out. He walks around to the back door and opens it, pulling a dozing Emma from her car seat.

"Arno, you're going to wake her!"

But he just waves me off. "Follow me."

I unbuckle my seat belt and get out of the car, wary as a stray dog. What the hell is going on? I follow Arno up a brick walkway lined with more purple, red, and white petunias.

At the door, he turns.

"I just called the real estate agent from the bathroom at Rose and Harry's," Arno says, fighting to contain a smile. His eyes sparkle iceberg blue in the summer afternoon light. "Open house was this morning, but we can still put an offer in on it."

"What?" I look around me wildly, expecting another prankster to peek out from behind the home's bushes. "Arno, what the hell are you talking about?"

"Liz!" Arno remonstrates me in a loud whisper, nodding toward Emma's head, which lolls onto his shoulder. "Keep it down!"

More quietly, I repeat myself. *"What the hell are you talking about, Arno?"*

"Just come inside."

Arno turns the front door's brass handle and steps into the foyer. I follow, not having much of a choice.

The inside of the house is even more gorgeous than I imagined. Surprisingly modern, the home has an open floor plan with high ceilings, white oak flooring, and walls painted the color of freshly clotted cream. A large, unadorned plaster fireplace is flanked by floor-to-ceiling bookshelves crammed with dozens of novels. Brass chandeliers glimmer over a long, farm-style wooden table painted black. At its center is a wooden bowl filled with red apples.

Rendered speechless, I turn to Arno, gaping.

He grins, a cat that's caught the mouse. "Let me introduce you to Linda."

"Linda?"

I trail Arno into a spacious farmhouse kitchen. Reclaimed white oak beams cut across the high ceilings. The floors, dark slate tiles, feel worn with time beneath my ballet flats. The countertops are Carrara marble, cradling a deep white sink at their center with vintage-looking bronze faucets.

It's the perfect blend of old and new, exactly my aesthetic if I had a knack for decorating, which I don't. I ignore Arno's shit-eating grin and focus on a middle-aged woman with a bad perm standing in front of a series of windows, half open to let in the late-afternoon breeze.

"I assume you're Linda." I know I sound rude, but I'm unable to keep the sharpness from my tone. Arno glares at me.

Linda looks momentarily confused, but the worry passes over her face like a storm cloud. In a moment, it's gone. She must be used to ill-mannered clients.

"Yes, I'm Linda, a Realtor with Intrepid Realty Group. Arno and I spoke on the phone about an hour ago." She nods toward my husband, smiles. "He mentioned a keen interest in this one-of-a-kind property. You must be Liz?"

Her unruffled manner impresses me, and I relent. "Yes," I say, feeling very weary.

"Would you like me to show you around?"

I sigh. "Sure."

Linda walks us patiently through the first floor, outlining the history of the home and its series of impressive owners, dating back to the mid-1800s: mostly ship captains and lawyers, doctors, and a couple of professors. She brags about the reclaimed wooden beams, the spacious half-acre backyard with its very own apple tree, and the carefully tended herb garden. She points out the custom bookshelves, a redesigned fireplace.

"The windows are new. The roof is new. New heating system and septic, washer, and dryer." She drones on and on, her voice never wavering from its chipper cadence. We follow her up refurbished oak stairs, where she points to a large wooden door that looks straight off a barn.

"Let me guess," I deadpan. "Reclaimed?"

"Yes!" Linda beams.

Arno cuts a glare at me.

"So, you've got four bedrooms upstairs—perfect for when you two decide to grow your family—and there's even a mother-in-law suite in the newly renovated walk-out basement. It has its own kitchen!"

I wince. "How lovely."

"Isn't it, though?" Linda doesn't catch my sarcasm.

By the end of our tour, my head spins from looking at beautiful architecture. Linda seems invigorated. Arno won't stop grinning.

Linda clears her throat. "So, I want to make it clear that this home isn't going to last on the market very long. It's at a much higher price point than its neighbors because everything has been entirely redone in the last year, but you're never going to lose your value in a neighborhood as nice as this. If you're serious about buying it, and"—Linda pauses, looking from Arno to me and smiling—"I think you are, you should really get an offer in by tomorrow morning."

Arno nods vigorously. "Thank you, Linda. Makes perfect sense." He looks at me. "Liz? Any final questions for Linda, or are we ready to move forward?"

I stare at him and expect laser beams to shoot from my eye sockets, vaporizing my husband into dust. "No, Arno," I manage, "I'm not ready to *move forward*. Seeing as I didn't even know we were considering moving, I think we have a *lot* to talk about."

Linda winces and backs up slightly, her ample bottom nearly knocking over a ceramic vase filled with dried pampas reeds.

Arno's eyes widen, but then I see the shock transform to irritation. His face is hard, mouth a thin, pressed line. "Fine, Liz. Let's go 'talk' in the car." He turns to Linda, his entire manner softening. "Thanks so much for squeezing us in, Linda. I hope it wasn't too much trouble." He reaches out a hand and clasps Linda's.

She blushes. "Oh, of course not, Arno. No problem at all. Send your mother my regards."

My eyebrows lift, and Linda rushes to explain: "I found Adrienne and George's last home."

Oh, great, so the whole family is in on it.

I roll my eyes, turn, and exit the most charming Cape I've ever laid eyes on, letting the front door slam shut behind me.

Arno follows me, his body rigid as an arrow. He straps Emma into her seat and slides into the driver's seat. Turns on the car. Soft jazz plays from the speakers, a joke.

"Why were you so rude to that woman, Liz? What's going on with you?"

My mouth hangs agape, as though Arno's slapped me. "How, in this situation, am *I* the rude one, Arno? You just tried to buy a brand-new house without even asking me if I wanted to move from our current one!"

Arno shakes his head. "You don't even like Wellesley, Liz! You love Newburyport, always have. And this house just so happens to be right down the street from my brother, sister-in-law, *and* mom. How nice would that be, for you to have support nearby? For Emma and Beatrix to grow close?"

I stare at Arno, nearly speechless. "But—but—" I splutter. "Your *job*! How would you get to Stonebridge every day? You'd be on the train for ages!"

"Well, I could get a little apartment downtown," Arno says evenly. "Nothing fancy, just a bare-bones place for late nights at the office."

I stare at him in abject horror.

"I'd spend *most* of my time here with you and Emma, obviously," he adds in a flurry.

"But what about Kyle?"

"Maybe she'd be able to stay on! We could put her up in the mother-in-law suite. Or you could just use the same nanny as Rose. My mom would be thrilled."

I have the distinct feeling of free falling, like the moment after you trip, when you're suspended in time but acutely aware of how bad the damage is going to be when you make contact with earth.

"But I *like* our home, Arno. I don't want you to stick me out here in the boondocks while you live your own life in the city." I can feel my blood pressure rising along with my voice, shrill as a seagull's.

"Whoa, whoa, whoa. Liz, I'm not suggesting we 'stick you out in the boondocks.' This would be a new home for *all three of us*. A nice escape from city life, and a great way to be closer to family. Isn't that what you want?"

I shake my head frantically. "We're already close enough to your family! We're in the same state!"

And then I see it—the wall rising up over Arno's demeanor, sealing him off from me.

"My family *is* your family, Elizabeth. Or is that *not* how marriage works for you?"

I'm too stunned to respond. Finally, I sigh. "It's a beautiful house, Arno. Really, it is." I gesture to the weeping willow, the tire swing. "But this feels sprung on me, and I need time to think . . ."

"Well, it was supposed to be a nice surprise. I didn't realize the idea of living closer to my family was so horrid to you."

"Oh, c'mon," I say, tugging on the cuff of his shirt like a petulant child as he reverses down the driveway, eyes planted firmly on the rear-view mirror. "You know I don't think they're horrid. I just don't know that I want to be in Adrienne and Rose's back pocket, that's all."

Arno shakes his head, disgusted. "You really do like sequestering yourself off from people who love you, don't you, Liz?"

"What are you talking about?"

"You've found a way to be entirely alone despite my very best efforts, and even though you complain about it, you're determined to keep it that way."

"What on earth are you talking about? That's ridiculous."

"Is it?"

Arno slams on the brakes, jamming his hands onto the steering wheel, and I jump. "I think about you—alone in that house all day, frustrated and bored—and I just . . . I don't know. I thought a change of scenery might be nice for you. I thought you'd enjoy some adult company, in the form of people who know and love you, right down the street. That's all." Arno runs a hand through his chestnut curls, which always seem curlier when he's upset.

I take his hands in my own. "Arno, I really appreciate the thought. Really, I do. And maybe at some point that will be a great idea. But I'm just not ready for that kind of change right now, okay? I like our home in Wellesley. Seriously, I do."

"You don't feel alone all the time?"

"No."

"Even when I work late?"

"Even when you work late."

Arno shrugs. "Okay, well, don't say I didn't try."

We drive back to Wellesley in silence.

CHAPTER 23

∽

The week following Beatrix's birthday party is one of the worst in recent memory.

Arno's distance from me feels so great, he might as well live in Newburyport. He leaves the house first thing in the morning, before I've even risen to go running, and comes home well after dinner, looking haggard and stressed. Two days in a row, he leaves the packed lunch I've prepared for him in the refrigerator, untouched. It's unclear whether he's trying to make a point or he truly forgot. I let the Pyrex containers of rice pilaf, grilled chicken, and garden salad sit on the fridge shelf so that he'll see them when he gets home and feel something.

When Friday finally rolls around, I text him at 3:00 p.m. to see what he wants to do that evening. Trying to make amends, I suggest we keep Kyle on later and go see the new Edward Norton film at Coolidge Corner Theatre.

Mob noir flick and burritos? I text him, knowing he rarely passes up an opportunity to go to Burro Bar. Their guacamole is second to none.

An hour later, he replies, Sorry, can't. Huge M&A went through today. Team dinner + drinks tonight to celebrate.

I fight the urge to ask where they're getting dinner and drinks and play it cool. That's great, baby! Congrats on the deal. Love you!

I briefly see the flashing ellipsis that signifies typing, but it disappears so fast, I'm unsure if I imagined it. I wait a few more minutes, but he doesn't respond.

Kyle, who's been reading Emma a book about a family of disenfranchised elephants in Kenya, seems to sense my despondency as I walk into the family room. Or maybe it was me throwing my phone onto the couch and groaning that clued her in.

"Are you and Arno doing anything fun tonight, Liz?" she asks tentatively, her eyes tracking my movement over the tops of the pages.

"No," I reply crankily. "Arno's getting drinks with his coworkers."

"Couldn't you go?" Kyle asks. "I don't mind watching the little one." She smiles, tousling Emma's fluffy goose-down hair.

I look up from my phone screen in shock. Could I go? The thought hadn't crossed my mind, but now that Kyle's posed the question, I wonder why Arno didn't invite me. Why he never seems to invite me anywhere since I became a mother.

"I think it's just a work thing," I say slowly. "They closed some big deal today and they're celebrating tonight."

Kyle shrugs. "I don't see why you can't join them."

I smile at her gratefully. "I suppose I could, but I don't want to intrude. I don't think other spouses are going. If they were, I'm sure Arno would have mentioned it."

"Oh. Yeah, I guess . . ." Kyle says, but she's still watching me with her round owl eyes, magnified behind her grandma frames.

"What?" I ask, finally.

"Well, it's clear you were hoping to get out of the house tonight, so I think you should," Kyle says. "You could text Tracy and plan something?"

"I suppose I could . . ."

"You should! Right now! Make it a girls' night." Kyle throws a pillow at me, and I chuck it right back at her. She ducks just in time. Even Emma's giggling.

"Oh, Kyle, what would I do without you?"

"Probably have a lot less fun."

"You've got that right."

I shoot Tracy a text, and she responds so fast it makes me wonder if she's been cradling her phone on the off chance of this very occurrence.

YES GIRL OMG! Tracy replies, followed by a host of emojis. Pink and purple hearts. Twin girls in bunny ears. Dancing woman in the red dress. Foaming glasses of beer.

Jesus, Trace, I text back, but I'm smiling. Be cool.

We decide to go into downtown Boston, which I never do anymore. Some hip little Mexican joint called Lola that's decorated in all black and red, with waitresses who wear ripped fishnet stockings and lots of sugar-skull wall art. I went there once during grad school and left shortly after Mariana puked up jalapeño margarita in the bathroom. A part of me hopes we'll serendipitously run into Arno and his crew, but I know the odds are slim. He's never mentioned which bars they frequent.

It takes me over an hour to get ready, even with my newly short hair. I blast the top-100 pop over our speakers as I try on approximately thirty-five different outfits, finally settling on an army-green romper and wedges that show off my toned legs. I chug vodka and lemon soda water until I no longer give a fuck about Arno's plans.

Well, for the most part.

As I head out the front door, Kyle tells me how great I look. I wonder if I'll ever feel like the adult in our relationship.

Tracy meets me outside, as if we're two teenagers attending a middle-school dance, only she's wearing an outrageously skimpy black dress and actual Louboutin booties.

"Dude, are those necessary?" I gesture to the red-bottomed shoes.

Tracy giggles. "Yes! I never go out anymore. This is a big night for me."

Depressing. I ignore her and book an Uber, which arrives in three minutes. We climb into the back of a battered red Honda Civic, ignoring the overwhelming synthetic smell of the pine-tree air freshener that's failing to cover up the skunk stench of weed.

"You ladies like Drake?"

"Who doesn't?" Tracy shouts. "Turn it up!"

The man, a baby-faced brunet named Sean, laughs and turns up the bass so that I can feel its thump deep in my chest. Tracy rolls the windows down and dances like we're on our way to a club, which, who knows? Maybe we'll end up at one.

Despite my best efforts, Tracy's excitement rubs off on me, and by the time we arrive at Lola, I'm grinding to a Cardi B song I didn't realize I knew. I even let Tracy take a selfie of us together—just one.

A surly bouncer checks our IDs at the door, which makes me feel about a hundred years old, but once we get inside and I see how dim the lights are, I relax.

"Ugh, this place is *so fab!*" Tracy squeals, dragging me toward the packed bar. "I'm going to drink a thousand margaritas."

I roll my eyes but can't deny the pulse of anticipation in my chest, as if the whole world stands before me, an inviting red carpet. I used to feel similarly when Mariana and I hit the town in grad school. We'd try on different personalities, assuming fake names and accents to experiment with various strangers we met. Sometimes, men would figure it out almost immediately and get really mad at us, cursing us out or asking what was wrong with us. We never cared. We'd just look for the next set of guys to pretend to be interested in so that we could get free drinks.

Tracy miraculously finds us two empty seats at the bar, and we climb up, feeling the eyes of strangers dance across our backs. Tracy has to sit in a weird side-saddle position to avoid her crotch being on full display, but it doesn't seem to bother her. We order two spicy margs and a shot of tequila each.

I throw mine back and relish the gasoline-like burn. The sour bite of lime on my lips. Salt pressed against my teeth. Tracy and I exchange full-mouthed smiles, and I realize that it's the happiest moment I've had in months.

"So, what is Terry up to tonight?" I ask Tracy once I've comfortably settled into my second margarita.

"Poker night," Tracy replies without looking up from her drink, some hibiscus-flavored cocktail that smells like a rain forest. I wonder if she believes the words as they leave her mouth, or whether she even cares if they're true.

"Oh," I reply, waiting for her to elaborate. When she doesn't, I ask what the boys are doing.

"They're at their grandparents', thank fucking god," Tracy says. "Terry's parents take them one weekend per month. They live in the Berkshires and take the twins hiking and camping and stuff like that. It's really good for them." She pauses. "And me." She winks.

"So . . . how are you and Arno?" she asks tentatively.

I don't know if it's the booze or the relief of getting out of the house, but I feel more inclined to be honest with Tracy than usual.

"Honestly? I don't know. Every time I convince myself he's cheating on me, he does something so sweet or thoughtful, I feel like an asshole for having doubts. Plus, my therapist thinks I'm making it up in my head." I rattle the ice in my glass, enjoying the pebble-like clatter.

Tracy's eyes narrow. She's never met a therapist she liked. "Well, I don't know your therapist, but she shouldn't make you feel like you're crazy. That's not her job."

I'd imagine that Tracy's therapist, if she still has one, has told her countless times that she's insane for staying with Terry. But who am I to judge? Weirdly, I feel compelled to defend Dr. Abelson, who probably only wants what's best for me. "She doesn't say I'm *crazy*, per se. She just says that I have a history of assuming the worst. Catastrophizing. And she's not wrong. Besides, it's not like I have much proof. Just a slightly suggestive text message and a receipt for flowers that I can't place."

"A receipt?" Tracy looks up, interested.

"Yeah, for a two-hundred-dollar bouquet. But I asked Arno about it. He said it was for a work friend whose cousin died." I shrug.

One of Tracy's perfectly manicured eyebrows lifts. "And he didn't seem guilty? When you asked him about it?"

I reflect on Arno and me sitting out on our back patio as the sun set behind the trees, his warm hands rubbing my feet. A glass of red wine in each of our hands.

"No," I say definitively. "Not at all."

"Well," Tracy says, nodding, "that settles it, then. He isn't cheating on you. I mean, when I confronted Terry for the first time with that hotel receipt, his face turned absolutely gray. Like he'd just gotten a testicular cancer diagnosis or something." Tracy giggles. "Guys can't lie on the spot."

This logic makes sense to me. And yet. "Well, there were a couple other things that bothered me recently."

Tracy frowns. "Yeah?"

"Mm-hmm." I finish my second margarita and order a vodka soda. Tomorrow promises to be absolutely terrible, but I don't care right now. "So, first I found out he got a job offer in New York. He turned it down but never told me about it."

"Really?" Tracy says thoughtfully. "That's kind of weird, I guess. Why not?"

"Well, when I asked him that, he said he never considered taking it, so why would he bother telling me? He said he didn't want to 'uproot' our family and our life in Boston. But what bothers me is that he never told me about it in the first place. Isn't that technically a lie by omission?"

"I don't know," Tracy says skeptically. "I'm not saying he shouldn't have told you. But I can see how if he wasn't even considering taking the position, he wouldn't find it necessary to discuss."

"I just feel like, if you're not telling me about potentially life-altering stuff like that, what else aren't you telling me?" My cheeks feel warm, like overused lightbulbs. I lift my hands off my sweating glass and press them to my face to cool it down.

"I guess," Tracy says unconvincingly. "What was the other thing?"

"He's been looking at houses. In Newburyport. For us to move closer to his family there. Another thing he failed to share until he'd already found a house he wanted and had called a Realtor."

"What? Why?"

"I don't know, he claimed he wanted to surprise me. But it just pissed me off, you know? You can't just make decisions like that for the family without including me. Like, if he'd just spoken to me about it first, who knows, maybe I would have been on board with it. But the way he went about it only made me angry."

Tracy's brow furrows as though she's deep in thought. It's a funny look on her. "Well, *would* you really have considered it? If he had told you about the idea of moving from the get-go?"

I pause, chewing ice. "No," I admit. "Probably not. I couldn't bear living that close to his sister-in-law. Or his mother."

Tracy nods empathetically. "I hear that, sister. Terry's mom is fucking crazy. Every time I see her, she pressures me to have more kids. Like I'm a farm animal or something. Alive purely for the sake of reproduction." She scowls. "Like the boys aren't enough."

"That isn't right."

"No, it isn't."

Tracy squeezes my hand, then releases it. Then she grabs both of my shoulders and turns me toward her, forcing eye contact. "But, honey?"

I look into her eyes, rimmed with thick black eyeliner.

"That doesn't make him a cheater."

"I know."

"Seriously."

"I know."

Tracy nods, satisfied, and starts gyrating in her seat to Dua Lipa. The bartender, a man who looks like he spends all of his waking hours outside of Lola at CrossFit, grins at her appreciatively.

Suddenly, it dawns on me. "Tracy?"

"Yeah?"

"Do you cheat on Terry, too?"

Tracy pauses mid–booty pop to consider. Looks me up and down. "Does it matter?"

It's as good as an answer. Still, I can't help but wonder where Tracy even meets guys to cheat on Terry with. She doesn't have a job and, as far as I can tell, this is her first night out in ages. Maybe she uses apps, or meets guys in spin classes and coffee shops.

I don't know whether to be impressed or horrified.

Tracy lifts her arms overhead and does some type of belly dance, swaying her head back and forth so that a curtain of blond hair covers half her face. She looks ridiculous, but in the dim light, that doesn't seem to matter. As I glance around, no fewer than eight strangers are watching her move as though in a collective trance. I can feel them waiting for someone to make a move.

"Do you want to go dance?" I ask finally.

Lola has an actual dance floor in the back, and somehow that seems like the adult thing to do right now: take the married, grown-ass mother of two who's threatening to overturn her bar seat to the dance floor.

Tracy looks at me like I'm insane. "But here, everyone can see us."

I shake my head in disbelief, grab my drink from the sweaty bar top. As my eyes refocus, it hits me like a slap in the face. There's an absence in the bar tonight.

I look down at Tracy's manicured hands. Her long red nails are shiny and plastic-like. She isn't wearing her platinum wedding band or her emerald-cut diamond engagement ring. I had a feeling something about her looked wrong.

"Tracy, what the—"

But I'm cut off by a high-pitched beeping sound, a mechanical scream. Tracy scrabbles for her leather purse, which is hanging off the back of her bar seat. She pulls out her iPhone and looks at the screen.

"Fuck," she mutters. "Fuck!"

"What is it? What's wrong?"

"It's Ashton. He's had an allergic reaction. Fucking peanuts."

"Oh my god. Is he okay?"

"Yeah, they think so. They used his EpiPen, but his grandparents took him to the ER just in case. I've gotta go."

"Of course! Do you . . . want me to come with you?"

The words leave my mouth before I've had time to properly think them through. I guess this act of kindness would place Tracy and me in legitimate-friend territory.

"Oh, honey, thank you, but that's okay," Tracy says, patting my arm. She suddenly seems incredibly sober for someone who was, just moments ago, gyrating after a fourth drink. "This isn't my first rodeo. Ashton constantly ignores our warnings that he has to check *every single label* for a risk of peanut traces. He never does it. Feels fucking invincible, I guess. Terry's going to be so pissed." Tracy gathers up her purse and hands me a few twenties. "I have no idea what our tab is."

"Oh my god, don't worry about it!" I try to force the cash back into Tracy's hands, but she's already turned away, moving through a sea of men as though they're blades of grass. Inconsequential as ants.

Tracy is a good person beneath it all, I think, before wondering what my inner monologue says about me: my relief that she didn't want me to accompany her to an emergency room in the Berkshires. I reach over and finish what's left of Tracy's cocktail so that I don't have to dwell on this particularly grim musing for too long.

I should really go home.

The thought flitters in and out, erased as a stunningly handsome stranger occupies the seat that Tracy just left.

"Can I get an old-fashioned? Knob Creek, if you have it."

I dart a glance over at the man as he pats his leather jacket for his wallet. He looks to be in his early thirties, if I had to guess, and strikes me as an adjunct-professor type: tortoiseshell glasses, dark wild hair, a slight five-o'clock shadow peppering his jaw. Distressed leather jacket that looks legitimately old, like something he either thrifted or spent an entire month's paycheck on. Too young to be tenured, unless he's some kind of wunderkind.

The man finally locates his wallet and opens it, pulling out a Visa. He reaches forward to hand the bartender his card, and I get a whiff of his scent: dusty, like someone who spends all his time in a library or among basement archives. His credit card looks so flimsy—white and plastic, the exact opposite of Arno's heavy platinum AmEx.

I check my phone. Still no text from my husband.

I imagine him and Vivienne sitting side by side in a bar, clinking the rims of their dirty martinis together as they celebrate a deal. I put my phone away and steal another glance at the stranger beside me.

He notices me noticing, or maybe I'm imagining it.

"Hey," he says, breaking the invisible barrier between us.

I turn in my seat, pretending to be surprised. I try to look as though I'm placing him from somewhere: brow furrowed, lips pursed. His eyes are dark brown.

"Hey . . . do I know you?"

"I don't think so," he says. "I think I'd remember you."

I scoff. "Does that line usually work for you?"

"Usually. I'm Oliver."

"You look like an Oliver."

"Should that offend me?"

"I don't think so."

"What do Olivers look like, in your experience?"

"They wear tortoiseshell glasses."

"Ouch."

"Oh, c'mon. Don't wear them if you can't take the heat."

Some guys can't handle any kind of banter that assaults their fragile male egos, but Oliver can, and I appreciate this.

"That's fair. You know, some ladies find them sexy."

"Your English lit students? I was one of those once." I take a pointed suck of my vodka soda. It has reached its dregs, and I frown.

Oliver laughs, but looks shocked. "How did you guess?"

"You're a professor?"

"Yeah, working on my PhD at BU."

"No shit. That's where I went to grad school. What are you studying? Don't tell me English lit."

"Close," Oliver admits, laughing. "Anthropology." He sneezes into his elbow somewhat awkwardly. "Medical anthropology, to be exact."

"Should I know what that is?"

"Most people don't. But if you're interested, I could try very hard not to mansplain it to you."

Oliver's old-fashioned arrives, and he asks me if I'd like another drink. I really shouldn't—I'm very drunk, lightheaded and buzzy—but I like his attention, so I say, "Yes please," and he buys me what might be my fourth margarita of the night.

The bar thrums around us as Oliver talks about the suffering and sickness of strangers.

"Human experiences of affliction are deeply influenced by the historical and cultural contexts in which they arise," Oliver says, and I just stare at his handsome face, thinking he sounds as earnest as a child describing Santa Claus. Classic grad student. "And that's what drew me to the field."

"That's beautiful, I think."

The young and the slightly less young shriek and ogle each other and dance and make out in the background. Beyoncé is singing about single ladies. The bar lights dim even more somehow, casting us all in near pitch-blackness. Someone plugs in barely-there red fairy lights that track the ceiling, giving a weird, devilish aura to Oliver's skin.

Darkness is necessary for the bar's patrons, I think to myself. It allows us to lose our identities as mothers, fathers, students, teachers, whatever, and transform into something shinier. I look around, slightly disgusted. All these adults wearing glittery clothing, with their bodies mashed up together. We'd all be rendered obscene in the harsh light of day.

Then I wonder if the bartenders keep it this dark at night so they can stop looking at us. We all must appear so embarrassing to them, acting this needy and desperate.

I can barely make out Oliver's face, so I try very hard to focus on the movement of his thick glasses. Then our fingertips graze on the sticky countertop, and I'm excited to be there again.

The haze my drunken state casts over what happens next makes me question reality. Suddenly, Oliver's hand is on my knee. Or maybe my wrist, or my hip. He tells me how beautiful I am, and I lean into him suggestively. He's smaller than my husband, more wiry.

I vaguely wonder if he's noticed my engagement ring. Either he hasn't in the darkness, or he has and doesn't care.

After all, I am a woman alone at a bar.

Oliver asks if I want to "get out of here," and I do, I really do.

"Yes," I hear myself say breathlessly, against his bristly cheek that smells nothing like my husband's. Is it all really this easy? The whole adultery thing?

I close out my tab from earlier, and Oliver throws some crumpled bills down on the counter. He has a determined, set look in his eyes that makes me think he's no stranger to this.

As though guiding a blind elderly woman, Oliver places his right hand on the small of my back and gently pushes me forward. Tenderly, we move through throngs of people, Oliver's touch as light as a feather but persistent as a toothache. We bump into many strangers on our way out, and none of them say sorry, but neither do we.

Finally, we emerge into the humid night. Navy blue and sweaty. Bats swoop in and out of church spires across the street. Oliver swims in front of me, saying words about his apartment being close enough to walk to, but if I want to call a cab, we can do that, too.

Evidently, I'm the one who's supposed to make this transportational decision. I shrug and hand Oliver my phone after typing in my passcode.

Oliver is tapping at my screen, getting us an Uber I suppose, when I notice a woman pushing a black stroller across the street, in front of the Methodist church. She's in gray sweatpants and looks completely bedraggled, like it's taken her the entire day just to accomplish this nighttime walk. Her brown hair is tied into a messy bun that looks like a bird's nest, and her baggy sweatshirt has large, complicated stains on it. She glances over at the entrance of Lola, where Oliver and I stand and sway, and at first I think she looks wistful, but then I blink a few times and realize that she's disgusted.

Twentysomethings in variations of black sequins and leather stand in a queue that wraps halfway down the block, waiting for their chance at Lola's sultry interior. Their voices are *so loud*. The bouncer granting their admission looks like he's done a line of cocaine, his eyes bloodshot and pupils dilated.

I feel nauseous, and not from the alcohol swimming through my bloodstream.

"Give me that!" I shout, and Oliver is so startled he drops my phone. The screen shatters into a thousand glittering glass bits on the pavement.

"Oh my god, I'm so sorry. You scared me," Oliver says, bending down to retrieve the glass shards. They fall through his fingers like sand. "Fuck," he says, evidently getting cut. I feel glad for his pain.

"Look what you've done," I say with satisfaction. "It's ruined."

"I'm sorry. I can Venmo you . . ."

"I don't want your *Venmo*," I spit. "Can't you see I'm married?" I wave my left hand in his face, and my diamond solitaire sparkles angrily. "What's the matter with you?"

"I, I didn't . . ." Oliver splutters, but he looks like a caged wild beast. Equal measures confused and enraged. He abandons what's left of my phone on the sidewalk and begins to take quick steps backward. "You were coming on to me . . ."

"No I wasn't!" I shout, although of course he's right. "Get away from me."

Oliver's eyes widen. He looks as though I've stabbed him. Finally he mutters, "You're crazy, lady," and turns away from me.

Oliver jogs down the street with a lopsided gait that suggests some type of knee injury, and I want to throw up with the realization of how little I know of him.

I wait till he turns right at the end of the block, disappearing from my line of vision, to bend down and pick up my shattered phone. My hands shake violently as I manage to dial an Uber and put in my home address. My fingertips prick and bleed from invisible glass dust. The injury feels well deserved.

A driver named Emmanuel arrives seconds later, flashing his lights at me from across the street, and I stumble into his silver Jetta with relief. I lean back into the car seat and close my eyes, but I can still see the world spinning.

"You're not gonna puke, right?" he says, eyeing me warily in the rearview mirror. He has beady little black eyes and a unibrow that looks drawn on.

"No." I have no idea whether this is true or not.

I slip into a deep, immediate slumber that is only punctuated by the jerky turns Emmanuel makes onto and off the highway, like he's some kind of racecar driver. I yell at him to slow down if he wants to protect his back seat, and he threatens to kick me out of the car.

The rest of the ride passes in silence, save for the Christian-rock station he seems to enjoy, tapping his fingers to the beat on his steering wheel.

As Emmanuel pulls up in front of our home in Wellesley, I notice that the front porch lights have been turned on. I glance at what's left of my phone and realize with a sharp pain in my stomach that Arno hasn't texted me all night. It's nearly 1:00 a.m., so he probably got home hours ago.

I scramble out of the Jetta and walk unsteadily up our driveway, tottering in my wedges like a baby giraffe. Crickets chirp peevishly from the black lawn that looks ominously wide beneath the full moon. At some point in the night, I must have spilled margarita on me. A sticky circle on my chest is illuminated in the starlight.

He's probably just been lying in bed, waiting for me to come home safely.

I want to cry as I stick my key in the door and it turns so perfectly, with its satisfying little mechanical click that lets me know I belong here. Our security system gives a few beeps of welcome as I step over the threshold into utter stillness.

I creep down the hallway as best I can, pausing to smell my armpits. Do I smell like a man? Is almost-betrayal pungent? But all I can detect are sweat and tequila, body odor, and grease.

I am a disgusting monster.

I peek into Emma's room and exhale relief at her sleeping form, flat on her back with her tiny arms raised over her head like she's doing the wave at a ball game.

Ten more steps and I'm at our bedroom door, my unsteady hand on the firm, cool handle.

Poor thing; he's had such a long week, I reprimand myself as I turn it.

CHAPTER 24

W e're going on a little road trip, Emma and I.

Nothing serious, just satisfying our curiosity, that's all. I told Kyle she could knock off early today but paid her in full, a special treat.

We're parked in front of one of those chain cafés that sells very average prepackaged meat sandwiches and salads for fifteen dollars a pop. It has a French-sounding name, so it can get away with that kind of thing. Across the street is the parking garage adjacent to Stonebridge. It's nearly 6:00 p.m. on a blazing hot Friday in July, and, any minute now, Stonebridge employees' fancy vehicles will start to stream out of the garage as surely as sockeye salmon migrating upstream. On weekdays, they stay later, but Fridays past 6:00 p.m. are a rarity even in finance.

Emma is watching *Barney and Friends* reruns on my iPad in the back seat, babbling along to songs about washing hands and avoiding strangers. All of these children's tunes seem vaguely sinister now that I'm an adult.

I tune her out and focus on the exit lane.

Thankfully, I know what type of car I'm looking for today. It wasn't hard to find on Instagram. Viv posted a photo of the white Range Rover the day she bought it, with the caption, *Treat yo self*. It has a vanity plate that says *OMMMM*.

How fitting.

I blink, over and over, trying to stay vigilant as gleaming BMWs, Mercedes-Benzes, and Lexuses leave the garage, their owners nearly

Arno just wanted to celebrate a big deal with his coworkers, and I had to react by throwing an adult tantrum, getting hammered with my nit-wit neighbor, and nearly going home with a perfect stranger. *Nice work, Liz. You've really outdone yourself this time.*

I thrust open the door and step into the bedroom.

"Arno, I'm sorr—"

But there's no point. He isn't there. The words die in my throat.

Our king-sized bed with its butter-yellow sheets is perfectly made, as though it's never been slept in at all.

"Liz, you home?" Kyle whispers down the hall.

invisible behind expensive tint jobs. I'm starting to grow tired, my eyelids heavy, and I'm wondering if I have time to grab a coffee from the sandwich shop when I finally see it. First the license plate—*OMMMM*—then the rest of the white Range Rover as it glides into view. Viv is a faceless blob inside. She makes a quick left out of the garage, and I'm so frazzled, it takes me an inordinate amount of time to shift my vehicle from "Park" to "Drive" and peel out of my parking spot.

The days have just reached their apex for length, and the sun feels too high in the sky for 6:15 p.m. The cornflower blue above me feels oppressive. Forcefully happy. This feeling is only compounded by the singsong chorus accompanying each new *Barney* episode.

"Emma?"

She doesn't reply.

"Maybe we could take a break from *Barney* for a little bit? Roll the windows down and get some fresh air?"

"*No!*" she shrieks.

At least she's consistent.

"Okay, then," I acquiesce, but roll the windows down to show her who's really boss.

I stay at least one or two cars behind Viv as we flee west from the Financial District, crossing the Longfellow Bridge into Cambridge. It's where I guessed she lived, based on the high number of Instagram posts at Cambridge juice bars and feminist art galleries and, of course, her beloved yoga studio, Healing Lotus, in West Cambridge. We pass Kendall Square, the neoclassical campus of MIT, the redbrick buildings and wrought iron fences of Harvard University.

I point it all out to Emma, who ignores me and continues mumbling along with *Barney*.

Hordes of crimson-clad students spill into and out of bars and restaurants, T stations and coffee shops, and I feel lousy with jealousy, then sadness. They have no idea what's coming for them.

Real life's a bitch.

Viv sticks to the speed limit, and I envy this about her. It hints at an evenness of temper, a certain moderation I've always lacked.

We cruise down freshly paved roads with pleasant names like Garden Street and Concord Avenue, and I almost lose myself in the moment, pretending I'm visiting a girlfriend who lives in the city. Someone fun and slightly younger than me who finds the idea of having kids exciting and adventurous. Someone who's simply dying to meet Emma. A godmother, perhaps.

Finally, Viv makes a right into a little tree-lined community called Huron Village, and there aren't any cars between us, so I'm forced to slow down to a five-mile-per-hour crawl to give her car sufficient berth. The neighborhood is mostly renovated townhomes that possess an understated elegance: vinyl siding in calming shades of blue and pale green, with chipper red doors and lots of hanging plants. New money.

Viv pulls into the gravel driveway of a modest four-story townhome that's yellow with a green door and a wide, white porch. Two rocking chairs move gently in the early evening breeze, and wind chimes tinkle a greeting. An abundance of maple trees and thick green bushes shield the home's front windows on the first floor, but I have a clear angle at the second-story windows, which are cracked to let the breeze in.

Who leaves their windows open when they leave for work? I think, but then I remember that this is Viv, to whom nothing bad has probably ever happened. Carefree, yoga-loving Viv, who finds wind chimes beautiful rather than annoying, and who follows the speed limit because she's never had to rush anywhere. Of course she leaves her windows open when she isn't home.

I'm parked across the street and a few houses down with my engine running. I don't think she's noticed me. Why would she ever look at the vehicle a few cars behind her on her way home from work on a perfectly average Friday evening?

I thought my anxiety would be spiraling by now, but I'm weirdly calm, like an ancient warrior heading into battle. I take a swig of seltzer water with the *tiniest* splash of vodka in my thermos that's been my trusted copilot this afternoon. Emma is getting bored of *Barney* and starts asking for "Da-da." I assure her we will see him soon, which we will, once I've made sure Da-da isn't headed to Viv's house tonight.

It takes Viv a long time to get out of her car, and I picture her receiving dozens of texts from friends and coworkers, all clamoring to hang out with her.

When she finally emerges from the Range Rover, Viv seems tired, her hair slightly askew from driving home with her windows down. She carries a large briefcase under one arm and has a black gym bag slung over the other. In one hand, she clutches a coffee thermos. On her way up her driveway, she pauses to inspect some flowers that are blooming; calla lilies, I think. She drops her head and takes a deep sniff, smiling to herself.

My cheeks blush with guilt, as it feels like an intimate moment. But I keep watching.

She does not look behind her as she steps onto her porch and raises her free hand to tap the wind chime, which jangles its hello. Then she checks her mailbox. Nothing today. She closes the box with a metallic clang. She has remarkably long, slender fingers.

Viv fumbles with her keys for a moment before locating the right one, then slips into her house. I can't see anything beyond an entryway with hardwood floors and an end table with some sort of fern on it. She closes the door behind her, disappearing. No dog came to greet her, so I assume she doesn't have one. That's good. Arno loves dogs.

"Hung-gee," Emma says from the back seat, breaking my trancelike voyeurism.

"Oh. Erm . . ."

I peek into the diaper bag on the seat beside me, hoping I threw something edible in there before leaving the house. I honestly can't remember.

Sun Chips. An old packet of airport peanuts. A smooshed fig bar. That should work.

I peel back the wrapper of the bar and break off a small piece for Emma.

"Here, honey."

Emma scowls, crossing her small arms over her chest with exaggerated annoyance. "No. Feesh?"

"We don't have any Goldfish, Em," I say. "But this fig bar is delicious, see?" I bite off a huge chunk, grinning as I chew. "Mmmmm . . ."

It's quite bad. Stale, dry, and sort of hard where it should be gummy.

Emma sees straight through my act and shakes her head violently. "No no no no no no . . ."

Her chunky thighs slap against her car seat as she kicks hard as she can.

"Okay, fine. Have it your way."

I toss the rest of the fig bar onto the floor, pissed off. Emma starts crying in a hiccup-y, dramatic fashion usually employed by soap opera stars. She could win an Emmy.

"Christ. Fine, we'll go home and get some Goldfish. Just give me five more minutes, will you?"

Emma stops crying now that Goldfish are on the table and resumes her *Barney* marathon. Well, that was easy. I'll need to teach her better negotiation skills.

I check my phone and see that Arno still hasn't responded to my latest text from 4:00 p.m. As a test, I'd asked him if he wanted to order a pizza tonight and watch an Emma-friendly movie together. As a family. I even suggested he invite *his mother* over. Talk about playing wife of the year.

Arno would look like a bad husband if he shot me down when I'm clearly making an effort to atone for what happened after Beatrix's birthday. So, I've given him a mental ultimatum. If he says yes, I'll accept that Tracy and Dr. Abelson are probably right and Arno isn't cheating on me. But if he says no, Arno's thrown in the towel on our relationship and is meeting up with Viv tonight to have wild tantric sex at her modest Cambridge townhome. It could go either way.

If only he'd answer . . .

I'm snapped out of my reverie as a car door slams nearby. I look up in surprise to see Viv walking around the front of her Range Rover to the driver's side, wearing silver leggings that shimmer like liquid metal and a matching sports bra that looks great against her olive skin. Her hair is in a sleek, tight bun. I wonder where she's off to now—a barre class? Ashtanga yoga? Rock climbing? Or maybe Viv just wears yoga attire to go out to dinner, so she can show off her perfectly chiseled abs.

Athleisure *has* been making a big comeback.

I follow her, just to be sure she isn't meeting up with my husband at the nearest DoubleTree. I noticed at least two on the route from Stonebridge to Viv's house, and I know Arno prefers staying there for business trips.

Emma mutters about Goldfish from the back seat, like a tiny drunk sailor, as I drive ten miles per hour below the speed limit to avoid Viv's detection. We leave Huron Village and hang a right, going back the way we came. I can't keep track of the twists and turns through the leafy, sun-soaked streets, past small wine shops, juiceries, and vintage book stores. Cambridge seems like quite a nice place to live.

We're in West Cambridge now: lots of well-kept parks and green spaces, walking trails and placid ponds. Mom-and-pop grocery stores with old-timey fonts and bushels of flowers out front. Art galleries and ample bike lanes and artisanal donut shops that are only open three days a week. I'm just thinking to myself, *This is* so *Viv*, when Viv abruptly makes an illegal U-turn on a two-lane street, narrowly missing a Jeep Cherokee, in order to slide into the last open parking space on the street. I slam on my brakes, almost causing a pileup, to see where she's gone and spy purple curlicue font on a green sign shaped like a flower. The Healing Lotus.

Ah. Of course.

"Ouchie!" Emma cries from the back seat.

Oops. I guess I did slam the brakes pretty hard.

"Sorry, my sweet," I gush. "Now we can go get Goldfish."

Once we've arrived home safely, and Emma is strapped into her high chair with a plastic tray full of those blasted cheese crackers, I do something silly. I buy a five-class pack at the Healing Lotus, a yoga studio that's farther away from where I live than approximately fifty other yoga studios, and sign up for a class first thing tomorrow morning.

CHAPTER 25

It's easy to find a parking spot in Cambridge at 6:30 a.m. on a Saturday, and since meters don't start till 8:00 a.m., I take the spot directly in front of the yoga studio. I'm slightly worried that my vehicle will stand out somehow, and Viv will know it's me, but that's ridiculous, because she doesn't know what I drive, and there is a chance that she might not even be taking this class.

It's going to be a steamy day. Cloudy and muggy. The kind of morning where you imagine a fly buzzing incessantly from the other side of a window pane. I blasted my air-conditioning for the entire half-hour drive over while listening to a podcast on yoga for dummies.

I've taken yoga classes before, but I'm out of practice and anxious about standing out, as I've signed up for an advanced vinyasa class called "Empowering Flow for Powerful Women." All I can picture is some kind of device that makes your period heavier, yet it sounds exactly like the type of shit someone like Viv would wake up at 6:00 a.m. on a Saturday for.

I told Arno I was going to yoga, but didn't tell him where, obviously. Half asleep, he murmured happily that he was "thrilled I was getting back to the things I love."

Last night felt nice, normal.

Shortly after I'd spontaneously bought a yoga class pack at Viv's studio, Arno texted me back and said pizza and a movie sounded "fabulous," but his mom already had dinner plans and couldn't make it. This made me feel a little bit shitty, but not shitty enough to drop all of my suspicions cold turkey. Sure, he'd said and done the right thing in this instance, but where had he been so late last Friday, when I'd come home drunk and nearly unfaithful at 1:00 a.m.? How could he have not intuited how close I'd come to the edge of treachery?

As we watched *Ratatouille*, Emma sat on Arno's lap and fell asleep within thirty minutes, snoring like a French bulldog. Spit dripped from her open mouth onto Arno's waffle-knit pajamas, and he simply smiled down at her adoringly. We ate pepperoni pizza from our favorite Italian joint in Wellesley and drank ice cold sauvignon blanc. I glanced at my husband and wondered if he still loved me, really.

That evening, dozing to the sound of cartoonish French music and little rats talking, I'd slept deeply for the first time in months, knowing I had a plan.

I'm a little bit early for the class, which starts at 6:45 a.m., but I want to get a good spot near the back of the classroom. I grab my Alo yoga mat from the back of my car and scrunch my nose up at its rubbery, never-used scent. I sling its case over my shoulder and head into the Healing Lotus, trailing behind a tall woman with the most impressive posture I've ever seen.

The studio is small and cozy, like the closet of an eccentric aunt, and smells like an ashram. Well, what I'd imagine an ashram smells like, anyway, as I've never actually been to one. Incense and notes of dried sage, honey, and sweat.

Inside, it feels like late afternoon, or nighttime, even. There's only one small window that faces the street, and it's enshrouded in a purple tapestry embroidered with different phases of the moon. Multicolored Buddhist prayer flags hug the walls, and gold statues of Hindu gods and goddesses watch as I approach the front desk, where a small woman with a closely shaved head sits.

I clear my throat.

"Hello, I'm new here. I registered online for the 6:45 a.m. class with, er"—I glance down at my Google calendar, where I've saved the event—"Mandolin Moonchild?"

"Ah, yes, Mandolin is the best," says the woman in a slow and syrupy voice, looking at me in that specifically yogic way that never fails to irritate me. "Your name?"

"Liz," I reply. "But I registered as Elizabeth."

"Surname?"

"Bennett." I glance behind me nervously, but there's no Viv. Yet.

"Ah, yes, Elizabeth Bennett. I've found you!"

"Great. Is there a place for me to store my stuff?" I hold up my phone and car keys and jangle them.

"Of course, of course."

The woman points to a large wooden cubby system, like the type they have in day cares and preschools. "You can store any personal belongings there."

"Oh . . ." I falter. "There aren't any, like, lockers? That lock?"

The woman frowns quickly but fights her inner nature, immediately replacing it with a serene smile. It's clear this placid facade is something she's worked hard at.

"No, we do not. At the Healing Lotus, we focus on seeing the best in people and trusting our community. We would never lock each other out like that."

I somehow keep my face entirely impassive. "Of course; makes sense," I say seriously. "But"—I can't help myself—"has anyone ever had anything stolen?"

The woman glares. "We've never had anyone report anything as stolen for as long as I've worked here."

"And how long have you worked here?"

She looks really irritated now. "Two months. I'm doing yoga teacher training now."

"I see."

As though I've made a great point, I leave the front desk woman and her stupid "trust in the good of others" philosophy behind me and look around for the classroom. After a quick survey down a short hallway, it's evident there's only one classroom and a bathroom in the entire studio.

I forgo the ridiculous cubbies and carry my shoes and belongings into the classroom, which has oily wooden floors and navy-blue walls.

Large potted ficuses sit beside an old-fashioned boom box. White tapered candles flicker from bronze sconces around the walls. Wax threatens to drip onto the floor below.

"Seems unsafe," I mutter, looking for a means of egress, should one of these candles decide to fall onto the floor and light up the Healing Lotus like the Rockefeller Center Christmas tree.

No one else seems concerned. In fact, the women who have already arrived for the 6:45 a.m. class look as though they've rekindled their sleep from earlier, and lie as still as corpses on their mats, scattered around the room. Only their breathing, modulated in a slow and even manner that seems forced, reveals them as living.

The room is so small that what appears to be the back row isn't that far from the front, but I take the back right corner anyway, lining up my phone, keys, purse, and sneakers in a neat and organized line beside my mat. *No one is going to steal* my *personal belongings*, I think with satisfaction.

I look for Viv's dark bun among the fetal forms around me, but it's too dim for me to make out faces. I grab a yoga strap and a couple of blocks from two canvas bins near the front of the room and make my way back to my mat, where I attempt to look at ease in the sticky, cloistered space. The sound of women's collective breathing reminds me of the ocean tide receding. I close my eyes.

Inhale.

Exhale.

"Is this spot taken?"

No fucking way.

"No!" I whisper.

It's her. It's really her.

Viv nods her thanks and unrolls her mat beside mine, just inches away from me. It's clear she hasn't recognized me in the dark room. *Or maybe she doesn't remember meeting me at all*, I think with a pang.

She's wearing all black. Black leggings, a black sports bra with interesting asymmetrical shapes cut out of it, and black flip-flops. She looks like a sexy ninja warrior as she moves stealthily around the room, grabbing a bolster and a blanket from a little nook I hadn't seen when I first came in. Her hair is, once again, in a tight bun.

"Here," she says, setting the bolster and blanket at the front of my mat. "I noticed you didn't have these, but you'll need them for this class."

"Oh . . . thanks," I stammer. So she *can* see me.

"No problem. First timer?"

"Not to yoga, but this is my first time at this studio."

"Awesome. You're going to love Mandolin. Her energy is really special."

When most people say things like this, I roll my eyes, but Viv says it so earnestly, I find myself nodding in agreement. "I'm sure I will," I murmur, still wondering whether Viv knows who I am.

Viv retrieves the necessary yoga accessories for herself and places them beside her mat, then folds into child's pose. I try very hard not to stare at the taut muscles of her back, which ripple in the flickering candlelight with every breath she takes.

I wonder if I should take child's pose, too, but don't want to look like I'm copying her, so instead I sit on my heels and try to keep my back very, very straight and my gaze very, very focused on the front of the room. If she's going to pretend she doesn't know me, then I'll pretend not to know her, too.

After what feels like a million hours, a woman strides into the room with the poised energy of a class leader. Her hair—which appears to be dyed gray, because she can't be more than twenty-five years old—hangs in two long braids down her back. Silver bangles jingle on her wrists as she claps her hands together. "Welcome."

Her voice is rich mahogany, hot apple cider. All of the students in the room rise from their various sprawls to sit on their heels or cross-legged. Everyone's posture immediately improves, as if we just collectively remembered we're Russian Olympic gymnasts.

"I'm Mandolin."

There's no way this is her real name, but I can't deny it suits her. Mandolin tells the class that today's theme is women's empowerment and the sacred female form. She says that she will be turning the heaters on. I hadn't noticed them, but sure enough, there is one for every corner of the room, clinging to the ceiling. As though she's conjured a spell, they hum to life in unison. The room is instantly 15 degrees hotter.

I try not to panic. I *hate* hot yoga.

Mandolin guides us through some complicated bolster stretching before hitting us with three rounds of Surya Namaskar, sun salutations. After the final Chaturanga, I'm fully saturated in my own sweat and possibly that of others. All the while, Mandolin tells us about the goddess Kali, the fierce representation of Shakti. Mandolin says Kali is also known as "the destroyer," and that she's a woman capable of granting enlightenment. She talks about all the demons Kali's defeated and how she's depicted in Indian art with a crown of skulls and a knife in her hand. It's hard to follow what the point of the story is exactly, but I think Kali sounds pretty cool nonetheless. Besides, Mandolin's soothing voice is the only thing keeping me from running out of this inferno screaming.

The class does not disappoint in its description as "advanced," featuring a number of backbends and one-legged standing poses I don't even bother attempting. I take numerous child's poses on my mat, which now has the consistency of a Slip 'N Slide. Out of the corner of my eye, I watch Viv as she glides seamlessly in and out of half-moons, king pigeons, and something called "lord of the dance." Having adjusted to the darkness, my eyes can better make out her face, which is stunning and blemishless, even without makeup. In fact, the sweat makes her even prettier somehow, like the yoga goddess of dew.

I close my eyes and pretend I'm on a white, sandy beach in the Maldives, turquoise water lapping just out of sight.

I must have dozed off, because the next thing I know, someone's shaking my arm gently and asking if I'm all right.

I open my eyes and blink rapidly, thinking for a moment that I must still be dreaming.

"Viv?"

The words escape my mouth before I've remembered where I am and why I'm here.

Her eyes narrow, struggling to remember. "Oh my gosh—Liz?" She claps a hand to her face, embarrassed. "Sorry, I didn't recognize you at first!"

"Oh, that's okay," I say, scrambling to rise from my mat, but it's so slick, I slip and fall onto my butt. Viv sticks out her hand and pulls me up, strong and sure. Her palms are cool and dry.

I'm positive that my mat has made an impression on my face and that sleep crust dots my eyes. I run a hand through my hair nervously.

"I would never have expected to see you here!" Viv says, graciously ignoring my fall. "Don't you and Arno live out in Wellesley?"

As if you don't know.

"How did you find this special little studio?"

Her smile is wide, friendly. The lights have been turned on in the classroom, and I can see flecks of violet in the amber pools of her eyes, like cracked amethyst. Most of the other students have left. God, this is embarrassing.

"Um, my friend Tracy," I lie, saying the first name that pops into my head. "She swears by this place."

"Hmmm . . . Tracy." Viv frowns in concentration. "I've been coming here almost every day for three years, but I don't think I've ever met a Tracy."

My cheeks flame but I remain cool. "Oh, really? I mean, she doesn't come here, like, every day. But when she's looking for a *really* good flow, the Healing Lotus is her jam."

"Huh. Well, that's great! I'm so glad she introduced you to it."

Oh, I bet you are.

"It's like a hidden oasis!" I say, spreading my arms out wide for emphasis, and Viv beams in agreement.

"Have you been practicing for a long time?" Viv asks, rather generously if you ask me. If she even watched me for two seconds during class, she would know that wasn't the case.

"Eh, well, I've done it on and off for years, but I've never developed a consistent practice," I say, feeling horribly inadequate.

Viv nods empathetically. "It can be so hard to find the time for it," she says. "Especially with a baby!"

Something in me crackles like lightning. I bristle at the subtext: *You shouldn't have time for a yoga practice because your daughter should take up all of your time.*

"Well, it's not that I don't have time. I have plenty of time, more than enough, actually," I stammer. "We have a nanny, so."

I don't know what I'm saying or why I'm saying it. But I do want to yank Viv's perfect bun from her perfect head.

"Oh, that's lovely!" Viv says. "I grew up with a nanny, Louisa. She was the absolute best, made such an impact on my life."

I nod blankly.

"Well, it was so great seeing you!" Viv says, squeezing my arm. "Make sure you hydrate. These heated flow classes are no joke." She turns to leave the room.

I'm going to lose my chance.

"Hey, Viv?"

She does a half turn in the doorway.

"Would you want to grab coffee?"

CHAPTER 26

We head to a little artisanal roaster right next door to the studio, which I noticed when I parked that morning. I feed the meter enough coins for two hours, which should be more than enough time to suss out whether my coffee date is my husband's secret mistress.

As we approach the wooden door of the coffee shop, I wonder how many coins Viv put in hers.

"This place has the absolute best macchiatos," Viv says in front of me, waving to the barista behind the counter as though he's an old friend.

"Hey, Alex!" she says cheerfully.

"Hey, Viv," Alex, a strapping young man in a brown flannel shirt, replies. Golden wavy hair like a lion and a thick hipster mustache. "You bringing new business with you?" he adds playfully, waggling an eyebrow.

"Hi!" I give a small wave. "My name's Liz, and yes, I am new business."

"Well, we're glad to have you, Liz! Do you know what you'd like to drink?"

"A vanilla latte with oat milk would be great."

Viv orders a macchiato and a white chocolate lavender scone. I'm both surprised and impressed that she eats carbs. I'm too nervy to eat, but I order a toasted blueberry muffin anyway.

We grab a small table by the window overlooking the street and sit down across from one another. Soft indie music plays in the background. It feels very surreal.

"Thanks for grabbing coffee," I say, taking a sip of my latte. It's absolutely delicious, and clearly made with real vanilla—not that fake, cloyingly sweet syrup they use at large coffee chains.

"Wow," I murmur.

"I told you their stuff is the best!" Viv exclaims. "You have great taste, both in yoga studios and coffee shops." She winks.

And husbands.

"Yeah, well, it's just nice to get out of the house and spend time with other adult women," I say honestly.

"I'm sure," Viv says kindly. "Being a mom can't be easy. And Arno's mentioned that you didn't grow up around here, which I would imagine makes it hard to find connections. Honestly, most of my adult friends are the girls who lived on my street in Newton growing up. And my coworkers, of course."

Of course.

I bristle further, imagining Viv and Arno discussing me together.

"Yeah, it's definitely been a bit lonely at times, but I've made a few really close friends, and I think a few good ones are worth a dozen okay ones, right?"

This isn't even remotely true. I barely have a *Tracy*. But I can't stand the thought of Viv picturing me as some miserable, solitary old maid.

"Oh, totally," Viv says, nodding. "Really, all you need is one ride-or-die."

"Right," I murmur, thinking how much younger than me she seems.

I need to steer the conversation toward Viv's personal life, and fast. I don't have all day.

"So, how long have you lived in Cambridge?"

"Oh, for over a decade now, at least. I went to undergrad and grad school there. And business school. And I've stayed in the area since starting at Stonebridge."

Why won't she just say she went to Harvard? The faux humbleness grates on me.

"Very cool. I love Cambridge. And where did you go to school?"

"Harvard."

"Wow. *Impressive.*"

Viv feigns embarrassment, as I knew she would. "And how long have you been at Stonebridge?"

"Not too long. About a year?"

And how long after joining Stonebridge did you start having an affair with my husband?

"Do you like it there?"

"Where?"

"Stonebridge."

Viv pauses, considering. She takes a thoughtful sip of her macchiato, which leaves an adorable milk-foam upper lip. If I were a man, I'd reach across the table and gently wipe it off for her with the pad of my thumb. Then I'd lick it.

"Honestly? It's fine . . . I guess."

This wasn't the answer I expected. I lean forward with interest. "What do you mean?" I know I'm prying, but I don't care.

"Well, truth be told, when I first joined it had a very sexist, homogenous culture," Viv says seriously. She breaks off a chunk of scone and chews thoughtfully. "Like, *really* sexist. I'm talking 'women were made to be secretaries' sexist. Offensive jokes. Lewd looks. Drunken parties where senior men would make passes at the few women present, women who were often of a lower station than them. The whole nine yards."

She pauses, reading my expression to glean whether I want to hear more. I do.

Viv continues, "I don't want to toot my own horn, but I really turned it around in the last year. I worked with HR to create mandatory sexual harassment training and safer procedures for women to report harassment in the workplace. I demanded that women have better representation in executive leadership and asked for transparent pay scales. I expanded maternity leave and benefits for new moms . . ." She ticks the accomplishments off on her fingers. "And I'm currently working on programming to support Stonebridge women as they return to the workplace after motherhood."

"Wow, Viv. That's seriously incredible."

She smiles shyly.

"I'm really proud of it. I think it's my life's calling—supporting women, and especially new moms. To be honest, my day job I could take or leave. It pays the bills. But it's the side work that I'm truly invested in."

Her honesty and candor shouldn't surprise me, but they do. It's not hard to see why Arno would be infatuated with her. He's always loved passionate people. *Like the old me.*

"Besides the creepy old white guys, what do you think of your other colleagues at Stonebridge? How are they?"

Viv laughs, rubs her adorable little ski-jump nose. "Surely you know all about the people, Liz. You've been an honorary Stonebridger for much longer than I've worked there."

I flush crimson and take a pointed bite of muffin. "Yes, but you know how it is. As a spouse on the outside, one never really knows what it's like. And Arno's no gossip."

"That he's not," Viv agrees. "Well, some of the people are great. And some of the people are not so great. As is the case in every workplace in America, I'd imagine."

I nod. I can tell Viv is one of those annoying people who doesn't believe in gossip. "Yeah, there are certainly some Stonebridgers I could take or leave, but Arno seems to genuinely love everyone who works there." I pause and bite my lip. "It's a bit annoying, really."

Viv laughs. "That sounds like Arno, all right."

The insinuated familiarity irks me. "And you and Arno . . . you're close?"

Viv looks up, surprised. "Well, yeah, I suppose. He's been a good friend throughout all the ups and downs of my efforts to get equal treatment for the women at Stonebridge. Honestly, it was his support that really convinced Brian that we needed a nursing room for new mothers. He helped me draft a petition and was the first one to sign it and everything. And that was just the tip of the iceberg."

My husband, the activist.

I feel like Viv is talking about a complete stranger and can do nothing to hide my surprised expression. "Did he now? Well, that's great."

"He didn't tell you about it?"

"No."

Viv frowns. "Huh."

"So anyway," I say, trying to refocus the conversation. "You must work really long hours, like Arno."

"Sometimes," Viv admits. "But I try to set boundaries between work and home."

"That must be hard for dating and whatnot." I look down at my muffin as I say this, crumbling a bit of buttery topping beneath my fingers as though I'm not in the least bit interested in her response to this particular line of questioning. "The long hours, I mean."

Viv looks thoughtful. "In the past, it has been . . . I guess."

She seems distracted, or disinterested. Her eyes track a woman and toddler walking just outside the coffee shop's window.

"So *do you* still find time to date?" I press on. "I mean, how old are you, thirty? I got married at that age."

"I'm twenty-nine. And my romantic life just isn't my top priority right now," Viv snaps irritably, her gaze returning to me. "No offense—I mean, getting married is the focus for plenty of my friends right now, but it's just not for me."

I don't believe her. "Sorry, it's just . . . you're so gorgeous. I'd imagine you constantly have guys trying to date you."

Viv shrugs, as if to say, *Yeah, but so what?*

"Well, if I looked like you, I'd be dating all the hot Stonebridge guys. I mean, c'mon. You've really never had a fling with anybody at the office? Not even a one-night stand?" I waggle my eyebrows conspiratorially, but beneath it all I'm on a knife's edge. Everything hinges on her reaction.

Viv's eyes widen, then narrow.

As soon as I register her expression, I know I've gone too far. It's like a garage door has slammed shut over Viv's true self, leaving behind a blank, impassive mask. "I don't mix business with pleasure," Viv says coldly.

The atmosphere has shifted. The coffee shop no longer feels bustling, but overly hot and crowded. I fan myself with a pamphlet for a local farmers' market.

"Oh, I wasn't insinuating that—"

"Right," Viv cuts me off.

We drink from our ceramic mugs in silence. I realize that hers is shaped like a pear-shaped butt, the feminine form.

"Well, I should be—" we both say at the same time. "Going."

CHAPTER 27

On the Tuesday morning following my coffee date with Viv, I'm going for a run around our neighborhood, pushing Emma in her pram, when my brand-new iPhone buzzes in my legging pocket. When Arno asked how the last one broke, I panicked and said one of Tracy's sons ran it over with a scooter.

I pull the device out, wiping a thin veil of sweat from the display, and am surprised to see my husband's name light up the screen. He never calls while he's at work.

"Arno?" I answer in surprise. "Are you okay?"

There's silence at the other end, and I move the phone away from my ear, peering into the screen and wondering whether I'm imagining things. The sun refracts off its surface, and all I can make out is the reflection of my shiny, frazzled face.

"Arno? Is this a butt dial?"

When he finally speaks, his voice is as cold as Arctic tundra. "I feel like I'm the one who should be asking you whether *you're* okay."

"Um . . . what do you mean?"

I rack my brain trying to remember whether I've left any of Viv's social media accounts open on my computer. I can tell that Arno is walking outside because I hear the honks of cars and the faint rustle of wind.

"I just had an interesting conversation with my coworker Vivienne."

My stomach falls into my shoes, and I contemplate throwing my phone into a hedge of forsythia. "Oh, really? What about?"

"Viv said she ran into you at her yoga studio on Saturday morning. And that you two went out for coffee afterward and had an interesting conversation."

I gulp, feeling mild irritation at Arno's lack of variety in syntax. What does the adjective "interesting" even mean anyway?

"Yeah, so what?" I reply, pushing the pram back and forth so Emma doesn't fuss. "I ran into Viv after yoga class and thought it would be a good idea to grab coffee with her. She seems like a nice person, and you work with her. Why is that weird?"

"It's *weird* because you went to a studio that's nowhere near where we live. It's *weird* that you didn't mention your little coffee date when you got home. It's *weird* because you insinuated that Vivienne has had romantic flings with her male coworkers. You made her feel very uncomfortable, you know."

That tattle-taling bitch.

"Tracy recommended Healing Lotus to me," I lie for the second time. "I just wanted to try out a new yoga studio, to get back into the swing of things, explore some of the city outside of our tiny Wellesley bubble. How is it my fault that Viv just happened to be there?"

"It's just an interesting coincidence, that's all," Arno says in a way that makes it clear he doesn't find the serendipitous occurrence interesting at all.

"Okay, well, *sorry* your coworker was there. *Sorry* for reaching out to her and trying to make an adult friend." I sound pathetic and bratty, but that's exactly what I'm going for right now.

"Jesus, Liz. I'm not trying to make you feel bad for being friendly; it's just very unlike you to suggest coffee with someone you hardly know."

"Isn't that exactly what you've been telling me I need to do for the last year to get out of my funk?" I shout into the phone. "Haven't you been harping on me making new friends and putting myself out there?!"

Arno sighs loudly, and I imagine the grim set of his lips, how he'll run his hand through his hair in frustration the moment he hangs up. The aggravated slaps of his oxfords hitting the pavement.

"You're right," Arno says finally. "I have been encouraging you to get out of your comfort zone."

"Why do you have a problem with me doing that with Viv?"

The question escapes my lips like vomit. Hot-magma word diarrhea. I press my fist against my mouth and wait.

"I don't have a problem with it being Viv, Liz. But you have to remember that she works with me. She isn't some gal pal like Tracy who you can say whatever you want to. You have to maintain some semblance of professionalism, for my sake."

"I don't understand what I did wrong."

"You asked her if she's slept with any Stonebridge guys," Arno shout-whispers.

And she never answered me.

I can picture him now, striding purposefully past the towering glass offices of the Financial District, his reflection that of a Calvin Klein–handsome, prosperous businessman in an expensive blue suit. A cooling Au Bon Pain coffee in one hand, his iPhone clutched to his ear in the other. Anyone passing him by would assume he was in the throes of a tricky business discussion, not reprimanding his stay-at-home wife for being crazy and inappropriate.

"I'm sorry. I thought we were just having girl talk," I reply, my voice small and meek.

Arno sighs again, a hot gust of breath vibrating tinnily. "I know," he says finally. Exasperated. "I know."

I picture him biting his bottom lip, agitated. "Where are you right now?"

"Just walking to the waterfront for a moment."

"Oh. That's nice," I say, feeling weirdly jealous of Arno's proximity to Boston Harbor. On the other end of the line, I hear the laughter of strangers.

In grad school, on mornings when I didn't have class till the afternoon, I used to love walking through the Public Garden and Boston Common at midmorning, when all the businesspeople were already at work but the tourists and historical reenactment guides had yet to descend upon Beacon Hill. Past the gold-domed State House building, up the winding red cobblestone streets that bisect the Freedom Trail, finally reaching the jarring contrast of the glass-and-concrete Financial District.

Sometimes, on days when I didn't feel like going to class, I'd walk all day, till I reached the end of a random fishing wharf in the seaport. I'd sit beside a flock of seagulls pecking at day-old bread and watch the water lap at cargo ships in Boston Harbor, my mind as empty as a vase. Everything was easier then.

But I didn't have Arno.

"I'm sorry for overreacting," Arno says, breaking the silence.

"It's okay. I'm sorry for making Viv feel uncomfortable. Will you tell her I'm sorry?"

"Sure," Arno says. "It's just . . . she's very sensitive about her standing at Stonebridge. I'm not sure how much I've mentioned about her work, but Viv's taken a very active role in changing the culture toward women here. She's started a new maternity leave policy, a sexual harassment training, a nursing room, the whole nine yards. So for you to insinuate that female empowerment isn't her prerogative . . . well, it really offended her."

"I said I'm sorry," I spit, annoyed at having to hear how incredible Viv is for the second time in a week.

"I know."

I bite my lip. It feels cracked and raw. "It's not like you've ever mentioned her to me before. How am I supposed to know she's this great women's rights crusader?" I feel my cheeks grow warm with anger and shame. When have I ever had a cause worth fighting for?

"I know, honey. I guess I just never found any reason to tell you about her. You know I don't like bringing work home."

"But I *want* to know what's going on with your work life, Arno. I don't want to only talk about diapers and sippy cups and whatever cool new thing Kyle's taught Emma today. I want to be a part of your world, every piece of it."

Arno promises to clue me in more and apologizes once again for jumping down my throat. He assures me that he'll smooth things over with Viv and is positive we'll be able to be friends one day.

On my end, I swear to find a different yoga studio in order to give Viv some space. I vow to "keep things professional" and not interrogate her about her sex life ever again.

We exchange "I love you"s and Arno says he has to get back to work.

As I press "End Call," my fingers are shaking, and the sweat on my back has turned cold. I clench and unclench my fists. Grind my jaw.

Sprinting home, I nearly knock into Doreen Edwards with the stroller. She is out for a walk in oversized gray men's sweatpants, deep bags beneath her eyes. Pregnancy is no longer treating her well. She nods a hello, and I ignore her and the growing swell of her stomach. I don't have time for fake pleasantries today.

I am a woman cut loose. Unhinged.

And I've never been more certain of one thing. Vivienne Wood, little Miss Perfect, is out to steal my husband.

CHAPTER 28

The week after Viv rats me out to my husband, I am resolved to be good.

No more rifling through our trash bin for hidden clues. No more sniffing all of Arno's shirts, one by one, to see if I can detect any scents that seem womanly or "other." No more stalking Viv both digitally and IRL. No more drunken nights of bacchanalia with Tracy.

This week, I will be the best version of Liz, the one Arno met more than five years ago at a crowded bar in Cambridge. I will work out for the endorphins, not the calorie blast. I will cook meals that I enjoy, regardless of how much butter a recipe calls for. I will say hello to Doreen Edwards when I see her puttering around her garden and I will ask how she's doing and wait for her reply. I will call my brother and maybe even my mother. I will actually listen to them when they talk. I will let Kyle take off early a couple days this week so that I can get some one-on-one time with my child. We'll read *The Very Hungry Caterpillar* and *Where the Wild Things Are*. I'll work on my novel. I'll return my agent's calls. I'll remove Instagram on my phone. I will sleep at night without a sleeping aid or three glasses of wine or both.

It's a seemingly easy plan, at first.

My conversation with Arno left me so rattled that the next morning, I felt something like determination settle into my gut, hard and firm. My marriage *would* be fine, even if Viv would rather it blow up. There would be no more warning signals, like when your phone flashes red to let you know it's overheating. We were fine. *Everything* was fine.

I just needed to do the work, just like Dr. Abelson always said, and Arno would remember why he married me in the first place, why he trusted me to be the mother of his child. Vivienne would be forgotten; it was simply a matter of me trying harder.

Thursday, I leap out of bed at 6:30 a.m. with the willpower of a decathlete. Yesterday, I made a schedule mapping out my day from start to finish, and I'm eager to get going.

First, I prepare Arno's lunch for the day: homemade curried chicken salad on a croissant I picked up yesterday from the French bakery we like. I box up a little cucumber salad into Tupperware as a side and toss in a ziplock bag of purple grapes. Everything goes into a nylon lunch bag, and I slap a Post-it Note on the side at the last second.

It reads, *I love you, have a grape day!*

Then, I power walk around our neighborhood with Emma in her stroller, on the lookout for Doreen to make progress on our friendship. My knees have been bothering me lately, but I'm determined not to lose the athletic progress I've made running.

It's nearly 85 degrees by 7:30 a.m., and sweat drips down my crotch in rivulets. The birds seem particularly active this morning, or maybe I usually just blast my AirPods too loud to notice their chatter. After three long loops around the entire community, I admit defeat and wonder if Doreen is still going into the hospital for work. Maybe I should send her and William a fruit basket. Maybe Arno and I could even host them for dinner.

I start brainstorming potential meals that would be Doreen-worthy— prime rib with garlic-and-herb mashed potatoes? Is puff-pastry salmon too gauche?—as I stride up our driveway just in time to see Kyle arrive, backpack slung over one shoulder. Today, she's wearing a tan jumpsuit that reminds me of *Top Gun*, and I tell her she looks incredibly fashionable. She blushes down to her collarbone.

"How was your walk?"

"Oh, it was wonderful, Kyle. Thanks for asking."

"Kyle!" Emma shrieks from her pram.

"Looks like it's going to be pretty hot today. I'm thinking of taking

Emma down to the Charles to feed some ducks, then get ice cream. Wanna come?"

"Not today, Kyle. Big plans. But I'd love to do that another time."

I make a mental note to plan a day trip into the city with Arno and Emma before the end of the summer. We could rent kayaks with Kyle and paddle along the river, stuff Emma into one of those bright-orange life jackets. Arno would love that, and Kyle could see what a great dad he is.

"What are you up to today—writing?"

"Yes," I say forcefully, then smile. "I signed up for a workshop through a local writing group called Jump-Start Your Second Novel. It's for writers who've sort of gotten . . . off track with their second book and need help finding their rhythm again. I registered for it last night."

"Oh, Liz, that's so great!" Kyle exclaims, bouncing up and down.

"Yeah, I'm really looking forward to it," I beam, exuding confidence and calm. I grab a green juice from the fridge and gulp it down while doing some stretches I found online. They're supposed to be "heart openers."

"Well, I'm proud of you," Kyle says, sounding very therapist-y. "It's not easy admitting you need a little help with something."

I'm slightly irritated by her assumption that I *need* help, but this version of Liz doesn't let it get to her. Her comment slides right off my back, like water slipping off a duck, and I pop in my earbuds to do a ten-minute guided meditation through Headspace.

If only Dr. Abelson could see me now.

Kyle mouths that she's going to leave with Emma and mimes driving. I toss Arno's keys, since he took the train today, before turning away to show that I'm serious about my meditation.

The writing workshop is in Cambridge, which I can't help, obviously. It's not my fault that our instructor is having us meet at a mixed-use center ten minutes away from Vivenne's stupid yoga studio. If I bump into her, that's Mistress Fate at work.

I miraculously find street parking in front of the center, which is a square, modern building made of concrete, like a bunker. A little black plaque out front says that the building was donated to the city of Cambridge by a couple of dead rich people, for the arts. The doors are unlocked, so I push my way inside, feeling as nervous as a kindergartener on her first day of school. I hope that my white linen dress and leather ballet flats give off a serious but artsy vibe.

The classroom isn't hard to find. The instructor, whose photo I saw on the website, is standing at the end of the hall, smiling wildly. She has gray, frizzled hair and turquoise glasses, and I quickly Google her name to see if I recognize any of her work. Her bio online simply says that she's contributed to the *Paris Review* and an obscure literary journal, and then lists a couple of books of short stories that were published.

As she gives me a nerdy mom wave, I wonder if she self-published them and hope that I didn't just waste a whole day to sit in some amateur writer's presence.

I find a seat between two fellow students, a husky young woman with jet-black nails and a septum piercing, and a balding, middle-aged man with an impressive snake tattoo down his biceps. He's wearing a baseball cap that lets me know he's a military veteran.

A quick scan of the room reveals a hodgepodge group whose constituents couldn't be more different. It looks like the attendees of Taylor Swift, Paramore, and Bruce Springsteen concerts got mixed up and landed at the same wrong venue.

I nod hello at the students on either side of me. Septum gives a smile that's more like a grimace and scribbles something inside a composition book that she shields from my line of vision. Serpent Tattoo tells me he's working on his *third* memoir, which he expects to be published sometime next year. I ask him how the first and second ones did, and he frowns.

The instructor, a woman named Leila White, shuts the door to signal the start of the workshop. Side conversations die in whispers, and everyone sits up straighter. Leila lets us know that she studied at Oxford and the University of Edinburgh, and despite my first impression, I'm intrigued.

"I've been teaching English literature ever since, but writing short stories has always been the great passion of my life," Leila says, smiling benignly. "I'm so grateful to take this journey with all of you."

I look around the room, wondering how many other students Leila has taught and, out of all of them, how many have been successfully published. Something in my bones tells me not that many.

Leila makes us go around the room and say our name and favorite author. After introducing myself as Elizabeth Bennett, I get a few chuckles and realize the other students might think I'm joking and that I can't say Jane Austen is my favorite author, though she is. "Charlotte Brontë," I say. Then, worried that this makes me seem dated, I quickly recant my answer and choose Zadie Smith.

This get-to-know-you exercise takes a good thirty minutes, and I'm fidgety with irritation over the time we're wasting on pleasantries. Who cares that Dominic from Somerville was "altered" by Maggie Nelson? I'm here to finish my second book.

After the last person has gone, we have a bathroom break. I openly groan but text Arno that I'm finding the workshop "super enlightening." I buy a Coke from the vending machine outside and return to my seat to jiggle my leg and tap my pencil.

Leila hands out copies of a passage that she wants us to read in silence. It's an excerpt from *In Cold Blood* by Truman Capote. I've read the entire book at least five times as an English major; I suspect everyone here has.

"Please take the next fifteen to twenty minutes to read this excerpt, and then we'll have a discussion on how Capote uses syntax to allude to the hidden relationship between Dick and Perry," Leila says serenely. She glides by my seat, and I'm enveloped in the scent of ginger mixed with cat hair.

I look at my iPhone. By the time we're done reading, there will only be thirty minutes left of this class today, and I will have gotten nothing out of it. Nothing.

I clear my throat.

"Excuse me, Leila?"

"Yes . . . Liz?" Leila asks, glancing at my name tag. The clunky silver fishbone earrings dangling from her ears jangle even when she's standing still.

"Um, I don't want to seem rude, but how is this exercise supposed to help us, you know, 'jump-start' our second novels?" I look around the room for support, but no one meets my eyes. The guy to my left seems to have noticed something particularly compelling in the wood grain of his desk. "Online, it said this class would help us develop our writing, critique our peers, and finish our book, all in three months' time."

Leila smiles daggers at me.

"Truman Capote is a master wordsmith, Liz. Reading and analyzing his work will highlight the various ways in which you all can elicit tension in your own novels. Surely that's not a waste of time."

"Um . . . it's just that . . . I thought we were going to get to read each other's work and offer feedback by now."

The room is mute as a mausoleum.

If Leila is ruffled, it's indetectable. "As Stephen King once said, a writer should *finish* their novel before showing it to anyone else, lest they risk receiving so much negative feedback, they lose all motivation to carry on. Have you finished your second novel?"

"Well, no, but—"

"And you want to finish your novel, correct?"

"Yes . . ."

"Then I suggest you take this time to read the work of an accomplished author and learn something. We wouldn't want you to become a one-hit wonder, now would we?"

I press my lips firmly together so that I don't say anything else offensive. I try to read the words of Truman Capote, but they swarm in and out of focus like gnats. I rub my eyes and sneeze into my elbow. I watch the minutes tick by on my iPhone, which I'm fairly certain Leila told us to put on airplane mode and out of sight. I wonder what Viv is doing at this very moment. Probably closing another big deal, or hobnobbing with my husband by the sparkling-water machines.

When everyone is finished reading, I tell Leila I need to use the restroom, but I gather my phone, notebook, and pencil into my purse and leave the building without looking back. What a joke. Clearly, if I'm going to get any work done, it won't be through *Leila.*

As I pull out of my parking spot, my phone dings. It's Arno. How was the rest of class, babe?

It was awesome! The teacher is great. I really think this is going to help my writing get back on track, I reply. Cheers to book No. 2!

Of course, I could be honest with him, but as Dr. Abelson says, it's wise to ask oneself, "Would this information be helpful or hurtful to my relationship?" Arno wants me to get something out of this workshop. So what harm is there in letting him think that I have?

Arno responds with a dozen heart emojis followed by fifteen stacks of books. I'm proud of u, babe, he writes. I smile as I drive home with the windows down, a soft breeze rustling my hair.

CHAPTER 29

Friday morning, I'm making homemade maple-nut granola when my phone dings from the bookshelf where I've laid it to rest while charging.

I hustle over to the small device as if it's a fussy child, hoping that the message is from Arno, saying his last meeting of the day was canceled and he'll finally be home in time for dinner on a Friday night.

I imagine making something light and lemony that pairs well with white wine—shrimp scampi? Pan-seared scallops? We'll eat on the patio and play Etta James and listen to the crickets chirp as we plot out our Saturday. There's a hike I've been dying to try in Blue Hills Reservation called the Skyline Trail that promises stunning views of the Boston skyline. We could bring Emma, and Arno can finally use the three-hundred-dollar Osprey child carrier I got him for Christmas.

It's just Tracy, asking if I'm free this evening to go on a shopping trip. Tomorrow, Cooper and Ashton are getting dropped off at a sports camp, and she wants to surprise them with a present that conveys the gravity of their willingness to go a whole week without access to their cell phones.

Matching monster trucks? I suggest.

OMG they would LOVE that!!!! Tracy replies instantaneously.

I was kidding.

OH!!! Hahaha they would still LOVE that!

I roll my eyes but smile in spite of myself. I've missed Tracy. I haven't seen her since the night we went to Lola, and I've been semiconsciously avoiding her. Part of me thinks she's been doing the same to me, and this text is her extending the olive branch to say, "Hey, I know both of us are a little fucked up, and maybe we don't have the perfect lives we've pretended to, but I'd still like to get wine drunk with you from time to time."

I have to meet her in the middle.

Yeah, I'm free tonight, I text back. I'll ask Kyle to stay a little later, and we can go to Central Street?

PERFFFFF, Tracy replies, followed by a scary-clown emoji and the sly-face emoji that looks up to no good. Someone really needs to teach her how to use these.

CENTRAL STREET IS where the most prestigious and affluent residents of Wellesley go for their Paper Source birthday cards, Cocobeet acai bowls, post B/SPOKE spin classes, two-hundred-dollar blowouts, and other purchases one makes when attempting to stave off existential dread for an hour or two. There's usually the thrill of finding parking, which is scarce, followed by the sheer rage of being cut off by pedestrians looking at their phones. It's an emotional roller coaster each and every time, but tonight, Tracy seems completely unfazed.

We're in her Lexus SUV, and she's whipping in and out between packs of teenage girls wearing leggings and Air Jordans and holding matching black bags from Beauty and Main.

Tracy is talking about her latest neighborhood frenemy, Frederica Ducksworth, the second wife of an actuary whose first wife died of a suspicious fall down their staircase last year. Tracy's long been on the husband's side, calling him "misunderstood" and his first wife's death "tragic," and she can't get over the age difference between Frederica and Ted, the widower.

"Like, *someone* needs to tell him she's a gold digger," Tracy says, as we swerve out of the way of a Mercedes traveling in reverse. "She looks like she could still be in boarding school." Tracy smacks some cherry-flavored gum against her teeth. "Ted told me they met on one of those new dating apps, and I bet it was one that targets unsuspecting widowers like him."

"Do you think maybe he's okay with that?" I counter, biting my nails and watching the street for small children or toy-breed dogs.

"No way!!!!" Tracy screeches in order to be heard over the radio. "Ted is a sweetheart, Liz; you just haven't properly gotten to know him. We became *so* close after he lost Gretchen, and I honestly think his fragility is how Frederica roped him in. She's, like, *never* home; have you noticed that?"

"Honestly, no. I didn't even know she existed till . . . just now."

"Exactly," Tracy says, nodding furiously. "You've proved my point."

"Proven."

"*Aha!*" she yells, fist-pumping the air.

A mustard-yellow Hummer with an offensive bumper sticker about rodeos pulls out in front of our destination, the Wellesley Toy Shop. It's sandwiched between O'Neil Jewelers and a gourmet cheese shop, and its candy-striped awning and adorable redbrick exterior make me think of Santa's workshop. I feel a surge of gratitude to live in such a nice neighborhood and think maybe I'll buy Emma something educational but fun, like one of those Melissa and Doug wooden puzzles that makes farm-animal noises.

Tracy's struggling to fix a contact that's fallen out, muttering about how she still can't believe she doesn't qualify for LASIK surgery, as I watch young families on their way to J.P. Licks, for ice cream cones, or La Toscana's for a Friday pizza night.

I miss Arno and Emma. A warm rush of love wraps tightly around my heart and squeezes like a fist. I check my phone to see if Arno's made it home to relieve Kyle, but he hasn't messaged me yet. As expected, he wasn't able to leave the office early today because of some international client call.

"Do you need me to do that for you?" I ask Tracy. She hands me the contact.

"Hold still," I say, feeling more like a mom than I usually do.

Tracy holds her breath as I slip the clear piece of plastic onto the surface of her eye. It attaches. Tracy exhales.

"God, you're brilliant," Tracy says.

I shove her away, laughing. "For my sake, I hope you're reconsidered for LASIK surgery. Eyeballs are so gross."

We leave the car's cool interior and step outside into the warm dusk. The hum of people talking and laughing envelops me. Tracy points to the toy store and beckons for me to follow her.

Inside, we're blasted with air-conditioning so strong, goose pimples appear on my arms. I rub my hands together and breathe into them to generate heat, to no avail.

"Hey, Trace, I'm gonna run out to the car and grab my jacket."

I'm grateful I thought to bring anything at all on this muggy night; you just never know how cold the shops will be.

Tracy tosses me the keys to the Lexus and nods, already mesmerized by a life-sized castle with a drawbridge and a fake moat.

I beep her car to unlock it and grab my oversized denim jacket and Tracy's cashmere wrap, just in case she needs it. I lock the car back up and have just turned to head back inside the toy store when I see him.

Arno, emerging from O'Neil Jewelers with its small signature navy-blue bag dangling from his fingertips.

I gasp and duck beside Tracy's car, praying he doesn't see me.

I expect to hear him say, "Liz?" but the question doesn't come. I wait five breaths, then peer around the hood of the car to see him approaching his Audi, which is parked just four cars away. He barely looks up as he unlocks his car and tosses the bag into the back seat with a careless flick of the wrist, like he's throwing out an apple core. He checks his phone absentmindedly before sliding into the driver's seat and backing out quickly.

When I'm sure he's out of sight, I stand up to full height, feeling my lower back protest with a painful cracking sound. "So much for yoga," I mutter, breathing heavily.

I make my way back inside the shop and catch a glimpse of my reflection in a mobile made of tiny, glimmering mirrors. A ghostly white Liz greets me, as if I've just foreseen how I'll die.

"Liz? What do you think of this?" Tracy calls loudly from somewhere near the back of the shop.

I squeeze by mothers accompanied by little boys and girls looking at dinosaur figurines, dollhouses that look like real Victorians, and miniature plastic kitchens and ironing boards. I almost trip over a stuffed porcupine as I walk mechanically to where Tracy hovers before a $250 stunt kite.

"Huh," I say, admiring its streamlined edges and bright metallic colors of blood red and iron gray. "Well, it certainly doesn't look like the kite I flew when I was a little girl," I manage.

"Isn't it so *cool*?" Tracy gasps, watching a video play on loop on a television overhead. It shows the kite in action, as a tanned and shirtless guy below jerks black plastic handlebars with his wrists and digs his heels into the sand. Overhead, the kite spins and wheels, performing acrobatic feints and loop-the-loops that make me feel slightly nauseous.

"Um, yeah, sure," I admit, glancing at Tracy to see if it's really the kite she's swooning over. "It's just, aren't Ashton and Cooper into toys that are a little more . . . high-tech?"

I think back to my recent run-ins with the twin terrors and am certain that every time, there was a mechanical car, scooter, or bike involved. I'm even pretty sure they each have their own drone—there'd been a hotly contested neighborhood association meeting over it.

"Well yeah, but that's the point. I want to get them something that focuses their attention away from all that. Something . . . quiet," Tracy says, staring trancelike at the video till I cough into my elbow.

"Okay, well, then maybe it's a great present for them. Do you think they'd have the, er, patience to learn how to use these? They look kind of complicated to manage." I gesture vaguely at the muscular beach guy. "A full-grown man can barely do it."

"I'll buy them lessons for that," Tracy says, waving my concern away with a swat of her hand. Her jaw is set, eyes firm. The boys will have stunt kites and they will like them, goddammit.

Tracy grabs two packages from the rack, making sure the colors are different, but similar enough that the boys won't fight over them. I follow her to the register, dawdling by the puzzles, but too morose to really consider buying one. Does Emma really need another toy? If I'm soon to be a single mother, how will I even afford fancy wooden blocks?

We exit the store into the cooling summer night, the sky a vast purply blanket overhead. I can almost see the stars through the light pollution from Boston.

"Do you want to go to Eileen Fisher? Victoria's Secret? The makeup shop?" Tracy asks, peppering me with possible ways to spend money that I might not have access to soon.

"No," I snap. "Let's just go home."

Tracy glances at me, surprised at the bite in my tone. "Are you okay?"

"Can we just—" I point toward her car with my index finger and feel my lower lip start to tremble.

"Oh, honey, sure!" Tracy opens my door for me and helps me get inside. She throws five hundred dollars' worth of kites into the trunk and slams the rear door shut with a bang I feel in my teeth. When she starts the car, Justin Bieber comes on and I groan, covering my face with my hands. She turns the volume down to the lowest setting, so that Bieber's voice is a mere whisper.

"What's going on, Liz?" she asks, squeezing my arm with her freshly manicured hand, her hot-pink nails that make me think of a Barbie mannequin I used to have as a kid.

"I saw Arno while you were inside. Coming out of the jeweler's. He had a bag."

Tracy's face screws up in a frown. "Arno? But you said he had to work late."

"He must have lied to me."

"Are you positive it was him?"

"He's my husband. He's pretty familiar looking."

Tracy presses her lips together, deep in thought. "But . . . couldn't it just be a present for you?"

"Jewelry?" I scoff. "Arno's sweet, sure, but he doesn't just go around buying me diamond earrings and necklaces for the hell of it."

I can feel the panic rising in my throat, threatening to turn into regurgitated salad on Tracy's dashboard.

"You don't have any special occasions coming up? Or maybe it's for his mother!"

I shake my head, and she pauses, scratching a mole on her chin. "Your birthday was back in February, right?"

"February eleventh. And then there was Valentine's Day, and Mother's Day . . ." I tick the jewelry-worthy occasions off on my fingers. "Oh shit! Oh my god, Tracy, you're right!"

"I'm right?!"

"Yes." I exhale and sink into the smooth leather seat. "Our wedding anniversary is July twenty-fourth. Just a couple weeks away."

"Oh, thank goodness!" Tracy cries, squeezing my hand. "That's wonderful. That's definitely what he was buying—something special for your wedding anniversary. Not that I really had any doubts."

Tracy throws the car in reverse and barely glances in her rearview mirror before backing out. I close my eyes tight and take deep, cleansing breaths to reassure myself that I'm right, Tracy's right. Of course we're right.

"I'm such an idiot," I murmur.

"No you're not," Tracy reassures me. "We all have our doubts and suspicions now and then. It's just a part of life!"

I don't have the energy to point out that *for her* they aren't just "suspicions."

"Want to get froyo?"

CHAPTER 30

July 24 dawns clean and bright, and I awake to the smell of pancakes and bacon. Birdsong trickles in through our half-open window. The curtain moves gently against the glass pane, tickling the windowsill like a whisper. Emma's tiny babble emanates from down the hall as she says as many words as possible for daddy.

I smile and burrow deeper beneath the velvety sheets, luxuriating in a full night's slumber, my body and mind finally at peace, knowing I won't have to wait much longer to know for certain that my husband still loves me.

I doze into a kind of half sleep that feels golden and clean. I dream of a meadow somewhere in Europe. My skin is tawny and warm against the sun. A bottle of wine sits beneath a tree on the edge of a forest, on a picnic blanket with ants marching across its checkerboard pattern. Arno's sun-kissed curls are the exact color of an amber stone. There's a straw basket filled with ripe green pears. We're celebrating something.

My second novel's completion, could it be?

"Sweetheart?"

A kiss on the cheek, a faint trace of tobacco and musk and fig.

I open my eyes, and he's there, like he always is, ringing in each Saturday with his blazing smile. Would an unfaithful husband make his wife breakfast in bed?

"I made pancakes," he whispers in my ear, tickling my waist.

I giggle and move his warm hands. Press my fingers to his rosebud lips. "These should be illegal," I murmur, as he kisses each individual fingertip.

We eat breakfast outside, not on the patio but on the lawn because that's where Emma wanted to toddle around, pulling up weeds and prodding at the dirt with a tiny stick. She takes approximately two bites of pancake, which she's grown sick of, but devours strips of bacon by the fistful.

We laugh at the small carnivore we've created.

"If she ever becomes a vegan, let's remind her of this moment," Arno says, stretching his arms overhead. His shoulder muscles ripple beneath his thin white cotton T-shirt, and I feel a little guilty wishing we were completely alone. I snap a photo of him with Emma in the background.

"Kyle would be appalled," I reply, and we giggle. Emma rolls around in the dirt like a piglet, smearing her greasy hands up and down her pink onesie, laughing to herself. She can always tell which behaviors get the biggest reactions, and it's slightly alarming to see the wheels turn in her head, the lengths she'll go to for Arno's attention.

"So, tonight, for dinner, I was thinking about Sarma?" Arno asks, looking up mischievously.

"Wait, really?!"

"I made a reservation there a month ago, but if you'd rather go somewhere else . . ." Arno teases.

"No! That sounds absolutely perfect." I set my mimosa down so fast, orange juice and champagne splash over the rim. I crawl over to where Arno sits and wrap my arms around him.

"Thank you," I murmur into his hair.

I've been dying to go to Sarma ever since it opened, but it's run and owned by a James Beard Award nominee, so we've never been able to snag a reservation, as it books up months in advance. It's four-star Mediterranean food, my absolute favorite, and served tapas style by candlelight. Optimal for romantic, late-night celebratory dinners that last five courses and end with the happy couple tumbling into bed together.

"Anything for you, my love," Arno replies, tracing a finger along my jawline.

∽

SARMA IS BUSTLING on this humid summer night, but Arno assures me he asked for a quiet table in the back, near a window. He knows me too well. I hate sitting near the front door and getting distracted with who's coming and going.

The inside of the restaurant is beautiful and eclectic, with bright turquoise walls covered in assorted ceramic plates in gorgeous shades of geranium red, canary yellow, and tangerine orange. The dining chairs are dressed in crushed gold velvet, and green Moroccan throw rugs dot the hardwood floors. Industrial chandeliers that look like metal spiders crawl across the high-beam ceiling. It feels as though we're inside the body of a very fashionable piñata.

"Wow," I gasp, taking it all in, and Arno beams in response, knowing he's done well.

He looks absurdly handsome tonight in slim-fitted black jeans and a cream henley with artfully distressed leather boots, like a foreign biker just passing through this part of the US for a stint before returning to somewhere far sexier, like Spain or Italy. His summer tan gives him a relaxed, well-slept aura that he sometimes lacks in colder months. The overhead lights cut an impressive shadow on his jawline, and I assume every single woman in the restaurant is jealous of me.

I think I've cleaned up well. I chose a pale blue wraparound dress from Anthropologie that reveals the most flattering amount of cleavage, and paired it with the pearls Arno got me for our wedding day. My hair has surpassed the Twiggy phase and has moved on to a slightly tousled Michelle Williams moment, which I feel, on the whole, good about.

As promised, our table is at the right-hand back corner of Sarma where our only companions are a large ficus plant and a window, which is blessedly open. The flames of small white votive candles flutter in the evening breeze.

Arno and I have eaten out with each other enough times to know immediately what the other will want. Him: the quail and Turkish cornbread. Me: pumpkin fritters and cauliflower tagine. When our waiter stops by, we go back and forth playing ordering tennis, waiting to see who will stop ordering first, making a game of it. We end up selecting eight tapas, which is exactly twice as many as our waiter recommended for a party of two.

"What do you think will be the best, and what do you think will be the most surprising?" Arno asks as soon as our waiter leaves.

"Hmmm." I place my chin on my knuckles, pretending to be deep in thought. "I think the quail will surprise me and be one of my favorite dishes, even though I don't want it to be because I think Kyle's vegetarianism is rubbing off on me."

Arno laughs. "And?"

"I think the cauliflower could be a potential miss. The pumpkin fritter we'll ask for seconds of."

Arno nods seriously at my bets, like a veteran sports reporter. "Those are pretty solid guesses, Liz. My vote is falafel as crowd favorite, but delicata squash as the dark horse."

Our cocktails arrive. Arno ordered something rye based, with raspberry, mint, and cocoa, and I got a mixed gin drink with lemon, soda water, and orange bitters. We guzzle them down thirstily, and the liquor goes straight to my head. I haven't eaten since my pancake this morning.

Arno tells me how beautiful I look, and I tell him, "Likewise," which makes him laugh. He pretends to swat me away, but he knows I'm right. He's without a doubt the most attractive guy at the restaurant tonight.

We look around and guess the stories of our fellow diners. It's one of our favorite date-night games that we haven't played in . . . god, months? A year? I feel flushed with love. Young, happy, and so grateful to be chosen by the man across from me.

He asks about my writing workshop, and I tell him most of it—the hodgepodge student body, the Truman Capote reading, the instructor who went to Oxford—but leave out the part where I thought the whole thing was garbage and left early, never to return. Arno listens with rapt attention, laughing at all the right parts, especially when I tell him how ridiculous some of the fellow writers were.

"They all think they're going to be the next Sally Rooney."

Arno laughs. "Well, maybe one of them will. Who's to say?"

"I say."

"Well, I'm sure their work doesn't hold a candle to yours, love," Arno says. "I'm so proud to be your husband." When he says this, our eyes meet, and I try to discern any hint of untruth, any glimmer of regret in his features. But it's just Arno. Smiling, charming, charismatic Arno.

We polish off three cocktails each, along with Turkish red-pepper soup, salt-and-pepper shrimp and grits, delicata squash with whipped lentils, and mushroom falafel with crisp apples and creamy goat cheese. By the time we receive our last two tapas, we are engorged versions of ourselves, patting our stomachs and shielding our eyes from the quail.

"I'm so sorry; we'll have to take that to go," Arno tells the waiter bashfully. "And the fritters."

"Of course, sir," our waiter replies. "The check, then?"

"No!" Arno and I shout in unison, causing the waiter to jump back.

"Sorry," I say, laughing. "It's just, we have to try the baked Alaska. We've been looking at pictures of it on Yelp for about a year now."

"Yeah, we have to know if it's worth the hype," Arno adds. "Which I'm sure it will be, if everything else we've just had serves as a good barometer."

The waiter laughs and reassures us it's the best dessert on the menu, and certainly the most popular. He hurries away to the wait station and punches it in on the computer.

I lean back in my velvet chair, feeling like a queen, albeit a very full one. But it's worth it, I think, smiling at Arno as he takes a long pull from his highball.

I'm so relaxed and happy, I nearly forget about the jewelry box he should be producing any moment now. When I reach across the table to cup his chin with my hand, I surreptitiously glance to the floor to see if there are any gift bags lurking, but the tablecloth blocks my vision.

"There's another reason we have to stay for dessert," Arno says, as if reading my thoughts. He brushes a stray hair out of my eye. My heart thumps a rat-a-tat-tat in my chest.

"Yeah? Why's that?"

"Well, I have a little present for you, to celebrate our wedding anniversary."

The moment I've been waiting for.

Arno extracts a thick box from beneath the table, wrapped in silvery paper with a bow on it. I feel a chunk of falafel deep in my throat and suck down some cold water till I feel capable of speech.

"Wow! How did you manage to get that in here? I didn't even see it," I exclaim.

"Eh. I tipped the valet to bring it in through the back when we got here," Arno says, smirking. "He ran it over when you were in the bathroom."

"You are so sneaky."

"I try."

Arno places the box on the table and gives it a gentle push. I pick it up and am surprised by its weight. Heavy as a brick, almost. Perhaps he got me more than just a piece of jewelry . . .

I unwrap the silver ribbon and let it fall to the side, gently pulling the perfectly taped edges away from the box. Inside, a nondescript black box. I glance up at Arno, nervous with apprehension.

"Open it!" he exclaims.

I'm vaguely aware of other couples watching us in the dim candlelight and try to regulate my facial expression accordingly.

I gently lift up the lid and gasp. "Oh my god!"

"Do you like it?"

"I. . . . I . . ."

Inside is a thick book with a worn but clearly restored red leather jacket and gilt title. I trace a finger along its spine. It's a first-edition (or very early) copy of *Pride and Prejudice*.

"How in the world did you get this?" I ask, lowering my voice, too stunned by the presence of the book to grasp the meaning of the jewelry's absence.

"Don't you worry about that," Arno says, squeezing my hand in his. "Do you like it?"

I am momentarily rendered speechless. Tears prick my eyes, and my throat feels tight. "Do I *like* it? I—I love it, Arno," I manage. "Of course I love it. This is the most incredible gift anyone has ever gotten me, or will ever get me. Thank you so much."

"Of course, sweetheart. Happy anniversary. Now, don't go leaving that around where Emma can get her grubby little mitts on it."

"Oh my god, no. Honestly, this should be kept in a safe. I can't believe you even brought it here!" I look around anxiously, wondering who might have overheard our conversation.

"Oh, honey, don't worry," Arno reassures me, glancing at our fellow diners. "These people just see an old book. They don't know its worth. Not like you do."

I think someone with even a basic knowledge of English literature would have some understanding of the value of a first-edition Jane Austen, but I don't say this. I just stare at the book in silence, flipping through its pages, which feel like the velvety nose of a horse. I have no idea what it cost him.

I shut the book. The title on the spine sparkles and shimmers like melted gold, but inside me, despair weighs damp and heavy on my heart.

I look up to see if Arno's watching me, but he's staring at the bottom of his highball.

CHAPTER 31

Over coffee one morning, as if he's mentioning the score of last night's baseball game, Arno shares news of an impending work trip to Las Vegas, two weeks from now. To me, it feels as though he's just said a meteor is headed straight for Boston.

"Oh really? What for?" I ask, struggling to keep my voice even.

"It's a huge conference called Money, Meet Tech. The whole team is going for a week, to stay on top of the latest tech trends in financial services. There will be a lot of boring talks about mobile and retail and data protection . . ." Arno's voice trails off. "*But* it's also the perfect place to meet new clients, which is why Thomas is so keen on me going."

Arno's voice lifts in excitement at the end. Anything to please Cynthia's father, Thomas Stone.

"Well, that's exciting, honey. And . . . you said 'the whole team' is going? What does that mean, exactly?"

Arno glances at me as he tops off his thermos with a splash of cream. "It means exactly what it sounds like. The *whole* team is going. Or, everyone that matters, anyway. It will be me, Ryan, Dirk, Jack, Brentley, Spencer, Viv, Diane, Wesley, Steve—" He ticks the names off on his fingers. "The Boston branch basically shuts down."

I wince when he says her name, but Arno doesn't seem to notice. He's looking down at his phone, firing off a message. "And . . . and, where will you be staying?"

"The Cosmopolitan, I think? Hey, they've got one of those Egg-sluts."

I nearly choke on my coffee. "Sluts?!"

"Eggslut," Arno says slowly, as if I'm stupid. "That breakfast chain we went to when we were in LA? You loved their bacon, egg, and cheese sandwich."

"Ohhhhh," I murmur. "Haha! Eggslut, right. I—"

"All right, I gotta run," Arno cuts me off.

Arno kisses me on the top of the head and tells me to let Kyle know that he *did* watch that new Netflix documentary on prison reform and found it "profoundly moving." "And give our girl a big kiss from her dad!"

"Will do."

"Oh, and Liz?"

"Yeah?"

"Eat something today, will you? You're looking a little . . . peaky."

Then he's out the door.

He's gone on work trips before, to New York, California, Dublin, London, and yes, Vegas. But those times were different. They were back when I felt beautiful and safe and cherished, encased in a loving cocoon of familial bliss. In the three weeks since our wedding anniversary and the missing jewelry box, I've felt a rising panic—premonition-like in its doom—that threatens to undo me each and every day.

My constant Instagram and Facebook stalking has returned with a vengeance, but now I've grown careless, leaving the search tabs for "Vivienne Wood" open on my laptop as a dare, not so much as bothering to erase my search history. I've called Arno's office and pretended I can't reach his cell, just to get a confirmation from the secretary that he's there and not, say, gallivanting with his colleague at the Mandarin Oriental.

I've left my thermos of vodka—watered down from melted ice cubes—among the innocent dishes in our sink, unwashed, so that the acidic smell, slightly like potatoes, commingles with Emma's mashed carrots and butternut squash.

I feel as though I am watching the swell of a very large wave, too big and crushing to survive, start to crest above me.

I am daring it to crash. I want to deal with the detritus, rather than live in this terrible limbo.

Once I hear Arno's car drive away, I dump the rest of my coffee into the sink and watch it swirl, tepid and milky, down the drain. I fill the cup with water, which I use to chase down a Xanax Tracy gave me.

I force myself to get dressed for the day, but showering seems beyond me. I've lost all energy for running, though it doesn't matter because in my new state, I have no desire for food. My hip bones jut out from my sides, and I poke them in the mirror like they're someone else's. My hair clumps in greasy patches to my skull, so I pour some water from the sink over my head and ruffle the tips up like a bird in a birdbath.

Wearing a shapeless, gauzy peasant dress with no bra, I answer the door when Kyle arrives feeling slightly more lucid from an Adderall.

"Hey, Liz," Kyle says as I beckon her to come inside. "Are you doing okay?"

Her concerned tone—a higher pitch than usual—needles me, as every concerned person who came before her has.

"I'm fine. Why wouldn't I be? Are you okay?" I snap, irritable.

"I'm great," Kyle says quietly.

"Emma's on the floor in the family room with her blocks. She just started fussing over something." I motion aimlessly with my hands.

Kyle pauses, seeming unsure of whether to move on from this conversation or press forward. She takes a deep breath and juts her chin out, steeling herself.

"I'm a little worried about you, Liz. You've seemed really tired the last few weeks, and . . . are you eating?"

I sigh. "Kyle, with all due respect, you are our nanny. Not my therapist or nutritionist, all right? I'd appreciate it if you stuck to your job description."

Kyle lets her shoulders slump, defeated. I feel bad but allow the silence to hang between us. Eventually, she retreats to the family room, where Emma's fussing immediately ceases and turns into burbling giggles.

I need a new game plan.

"I'll be writing!" I shout toward the family room as I shuffle to my office and slam the door shut behind me. I don't wait to hear Kyle's response.

I go through my usual search routine for Viv's whereabouts: Instagram, Twitter, LinkedIn—and find what I've been looking for on Facebook.

"Vivienne Wood is looking for hotel and restaurant recommendations in Las Vegas."

Aha.

I scroll through responses to her post to get an idea of where Viv—and potentially, my husband—might be eating and sleeping together in Sin City. It reassures me slightly that she's still looking for a place to stay. If she and Arno were having a romantic tryst, wouldn't she have already booked her room at the Cosmopolitan?

Or maybe, my brain cries, this is a ruse. She's probably going to book a room on her work account at a different hotel across town to throw colleagues (and myself) off her traitorous scent.

Most of the recommendations come from overzealous friends of Viv's clamoring for her attention, desperate to show her and the rest of Facebook how worldly and cultured they are.

"OH MY GOD, you *have* to go to Sapphire by Juan Andrés. Five-star dining at its finest!" wrote someone named Tilly Crenshaw.

"The Palazzo is a pretty iconic place to stay," Billy Tan posted.

"The Bellagio has a state-of-the-art fitness center that is very clean," Barbara Bobbin adds.

VIV LIKES EVERY single recommendation without fail but does not make any commitments. Because, obviously, she's already booked a secret location where she'll be meeting my husband.

My mind struggles to formulate a plan of attack, as I haven't been sleeping most nights. I grab an hour here, thirty minutes there, but never enough to feel truly rested. The wiring in my head feels faulty, prone to catching fire.

I haven't told anyone about the Jane Austen first edition. I've kept it in its black box, shoved under our bed like a dirty secret. Sometimes, when I lie in bed at night, not sleeping, I can almost feel it humming, electrical and evil, beneath us.

Not even Tracy knows about the missing jewelry, and I fear she's the only person who would understand its significance. I haven't felt capable of telling her for fear the words will get jumbled in my mouth and come out in a hot stream of nonsensical vitriol.

My unhinged state might scare her too much. She'd stop calling me, and the invitations to shop and drink pink wine in her basement would cease.

Arno would notice the death of our friendship and worry.

I think about telling Dr. Abelson, but I'm not ready to give up and admit defeat just yet. Besides, the jewelry box could still be tucked away somewhere as a future present to me, though that's seeming less and less likely, as I've ransacked our house from top to bottom four times since our wedding anniversary. I went so far as to slash open a couple of our throw pillows with a kitchen knife. Pulling out the stuffing onto the floor, I reached my hand around inside their linings.

Nothing.

Emma had watched me with wide eyes before pointing to the fluffy piles drifting around the floor as the ceiling fan rotated on its axis.

"Snow?" she'd asked.

"Yes, honey, just some snow."

I had to throw the empty pillows away like they were animal carcasses, stuffing a bunch of tattered magazines, unopened mail, and old food on top of them in our trash bin to hide the evidence, then ordered new ones from Pottery Barn and paid extra for expedited shipping.

I GO FOR a walk to clear my head and get out of the house, which I fear is closing in on me. The smell of my armpits is like that of a feral kitten, so I breathe with my head turned away from myself.

The neighborhood is still as glass.

The drone of a lawn mower somewhere in the distance. Pavement hot beneath my house slippers. The sky feels too big and bright and oppressive. I'm unable to look up, even with large sunglasses shielding my fragile eyes from the sun.

I wander over to the clubhouse by the community swimming pool, where a listless teen lifeguard texts on her phone. An old, wrinkled man floats on his back in aviators. Inside the fitness center, I receive a shock: Doreen Edwards doing crunches on the tile floor. Her bulbous stomach prevents her from fully sitting up with each crunch.

The door is unlocked, so I push my way inside. Doreen startles, looking around her stomach at me in the doorway.

"Oh. It's you," she says listlessly, falling back on the floor with a thump.

"Just me," I confirm.

Doreen is silent.

"Should you be doing those?"

"Doing what?"

"Crunches. When you're this far along, I mean."

"Are you a doctor?"

"No," I admit.

"A midwife? Doula?"

"Nope."

"Then I will continue exercising as I please," Doreen says.

She stands up and starts doing lunges. Sweat dots her brow.

The fitness center is filled with a dozen treadmills, a couple Stairmasters, three bikes, and a rowing machine. A black weight rack with shiny metal dumbbells sits beneath a large high-def television. But I've never seen anyone here before. Why would I? Everyone in our community can afford a luxurious home gym. Or at the very least a Peloton.

"My husband is cheating on me, I think."

I rub my hands over my flat, nearly concave, stomach beneath the peasant dress, trying to remember what it felt like to have a person in there. Doreen stops lunging and puts her hands on her hips, leaning back into her heels, the universal stance of tired pregnant women. Her ankles are swollen and purple.

"Why?"

"Why do I think he's cheating on me, or why would someone cheat on me?" I say, with a laugh.

Doreen thinks for a second. "Both."

I pause.

"I think he's cheating on me because he's purchased flowers and jewelry that he never gave me. He works late all the time and keeps big secrets, like promotions he's declined and houses he wants us to buy." I tick the transgressions off on my fingers. "He gets flirty texts from coworkers who are more beautiful and smarter than me."

Doreen nods in a way that conveys this is unsurprising.

"And I think he *would* cheat on me because I'm not who I was when we met."

Doreen's eyes narrow. This seems to interest her. "How so?"

"I used to be fun and independent and have interests. I used to enjoy things . . . writing, reading, cooking, and traveling. I published a novel, you know." I tug at a hangnail, savoring the prick of pain as it detaches from my thumb's cuticle.

"Now, everything feels pointless, and my future is predetermined. I exist to be a mom and make sure our child doesn't die, but now I pay a nanny to do that. I spend most of my days obsessing over the life my husband has outside our home, without me. The exciting people he gets to meet and work with. I don't know how to get back to the person I was before Emma. It seems like she exists in another dimension."

The air conditioner is unbearably loud, and I have to yell over it for Doreen to really hear me. My voice does not sound like my own, more like that of a witch from a fairy tale—screechy, bitter, alone. Still, the exorcism of honesty feels good, cathartic, like screaming at the top of your lungs in a forest, or taking a massive shit after Thanksgiving.

Doreen sways back and forth on her feet, shifting her weight. "Well, maybe you shouldn't have gotten married or had a baby," she says finally, biting her lower lip. A little apologetic. "You should have stuck to your original plan. The one you had before Mr. Handsome came along."

"Mr. Handsome?" Is that what people call Arno around here? I shiver, thinking about what they call me.

Doreen waves her hand like his nickname is beside the point.

"I didn't really have a plan before Arno came along," I admit. "I was enjoying grad school, for the most part. Hanging out with my girlfriends, taking long walks, and writing a lot. I was broke all the time, dated some questionable assholes, but somehow I made it work. That was pretty much it."

"That sounds nice," Doreen says wistfully. "God, I miss school."

I laugh in agreement. "Yeah, who doesn't?"

Doreen sighs, then pauses.

"You love him?" she asks.

"Yes," I say firmly. My mouth feels dry as bone.

"Then I guess you've got to fight for him," Doreen says. She looks me up and down. "But to do that, you need to fight for yourself first." She points at my dress, my hair and face. "You're a mess. You don't care about yourself. That's a problem."

I could point out that Doreen doesn't look so hot herself, but I don't.

"It's just that . . . I put *him* first, that's all. And Emma," I add, though this feels like a lie.

"You can't keep doing that," Doreen says, shaking her head firmly. "If you keep behaving this way, like he's the center of the universe and you're just orbiting him, then you will lose him." She pauses, scratching her chin. "You know who the other woman is?"

Having a stranger confirm Vivienne's existence in my husband's life feels unbearable, but I nod. "Yes. Her name is Vivienne. She works with him. She went to Harvard and does yoga. They're going on a business trip together in a couple weeks. To Las Vegas. She has really dewy skin . . ." My eyes start to well up.

Doreen looks perplexed.

"Her skin," I explain. "It's like it's got a permanent layer of dew. Poreless."

Doreen sucks on her teeth.

"That's no good."

"No," I agree, nearly sobbing. I wipe my sniveling nose with the back of my hand. "It's not."

"You need to go," she says, taking a step toward me.

"Huh?"

"Las Vegas," Doreen says, throwing her hands up in exasperation. "Surprise him."

"What?!" Perhaps Doreen is even crazier than me. I want to fix this mess more than anyone, but showing up unannounced at my husband's work conference would be crossing a line. "He wouldn't like that," I say firmly.

"Maybe not," Doreen agrees. "But at least you'd be able to spy on him. Figure out the truth. That's what I'd do."

My eyebrows lift in shock, and I give a small, hiccupping laugh through my tears. There's more to Doreen than meets the eye.

Suddenly, my stomach roils as though I might vomit. But that would require eating, right? I take a deep gulp of air instead, close my eyes for a moment. The room spins. Doreen takes another step forward and gives a hesitant pat on my arm.

"It might be a bit risky," Doreen admits. "But if you follow him to Las Vegas, then you'll find out for sure, right?" She looks me up and down, considering me. I can tell from her raised eyebrow that she does not think I'll be able to handle this assignment.

"That plan is completely nuts."

Doreen laughs, crowlike. "You don't think you're already nuts?"

She has a point.

Doreen turns away from me and looks out the half-moon window facing the clear blue swimming pool. The old man still floats on his back, and I wonder if he's dead and, if so, how long it will take the life-guard to notice.

She rubs her shoulders like she's caught a sudden chill, then looks down at her hands in the sunlight. Flexes her fingers like she's putting on surgical gloves.

"Hey, Doreen?"

She turns.

"Are you feeling any better about that?" I point to her stomach. It peeks out from beneath her sweaty T-shirt, white and veiny.

"Not really, no," she admits, looking defeated. "I still don't know how I'll balance my job with a baby. Maternity leave starts next month, and I just can't imagine being alone in that big house all day . . ."

She shivers.

Then brightens.

"William is happy, though. He says he's never been more in love with me."

I sigh, reminiscing.

"Arno said that, too."

CHAPTER 32

Planning a secret getaway to Las Vegas is laughably easy. So much so, I wonder whether legions of suspicious married women book flights to Sin City every week to tail their husbands on work trips.

I have Tracy book the plane ticket on her credit card, so that Arno won't see evidence on our bank statement, and pay her in cash. I tell her that I'm planning a surprise getaway for Arno and me.

"Oh, how fun!" she says. "Terry and I did that once, after I found out about the old nanny. He wanted to make it up to me. We stayed at Caesars Palace and didn't leave our room for the first seventy-two hours . . ." She gives a dirty little chuckle.

"That's great, Tracy. Just great."

I decide to stay in Vegas for three days, so that I arrive after Arno gets there and return to Boston before his departure.

Using an ancient credit card in my name, I book a room at a place called Barney's Inn, because it's the cheesiest hotel on the Strip and there is no way in hell anyone from Stonebridge would stay there. It boasts free circus acts, and rooms start at fifty dollars per night. I make a mental note to pack my own linen.

It's strange to have a secret from my husband.

I realize I'd be very bad at hiding a long-term affair, as I jump in my seat every time my phone buzzes or beeps in the days between booking my ticket and leaving for the trip, as if *I'm* the one with a hidden lover.

Once I have a plane ticket, I purchase a wig of medium length in chestnut brown at an upscale store in Somerville that exclusively sells slutty costumes: nurse's uniforms in starched cotton, black latex cat-suits, pink Playboy-bunny corsets and fuzzy ears.

"I need something as normal as possible," I tell the saleswoman, who raises her eyebrows but says nothing.

I also purchase some clothing to match my new persona, whom I've started thinking of as "Meadow" in my mind. She's the type of free-spirited gal who *would* book a solo trip to Vegas, just to push her own boundaries and get outside her comfort zone. She's someone with an extensive crystal collection and a penchant for colorful wigs. Her favor-ite place in the world? Sedona, Arizona.

I buy Meadow a few long, shapeless maxi dresses in desert colors of rust, sand, and azure blue. She also gets two new hats: a floppy, wide-brimmed straw hat for lounging at the pool, and a brown felt western number that looks like something an Australian sheep farmer would wear in the Outback. All of the bags and boxes get crammed into the back of our walk-in closet, beneath plastic bins filled with Christmas decorations.

The only tricky part is Kyle. I need her to stay with Emma, but I can't have her know where I'm really going, and I can't have her mention any trip to Arno.

Ultimately, I have to lie to her.

One morning, exactly five days before I'm scheduled to leave, Kyle's making some sort of roasted vegetable sandwich in a panini press that must have been a wedding present she found tucked away in a kitchen drawer when I take a deep breath and burst into tears.

Kyle's so startled she drops a red pepper she was scraping mold off of into the sink. She turns in horror.

"Liz? What's wrong?!" she shouts, dashing to my side.

"I . . . I need help . . ." I sob, holding my shoulders and rocking back and forth, just like I practiced.

"Help with what?" Kyle asks, so concerned, the wrinkles in her fore-head grow wrinkles. She darts a glance at my thermos filled with gin, lemon sparkling water, and ice, and I wonder whether she knows at least a few of my secrets after all.

"I have an anxiety disorder," I say quietly, shoulders hunched, head down. "I was diagnosed in my early twenties, and I thought I'd gotten ahold of it, but it's gotten a lot worse since having Emma."

All of this is true, by the way. The crocodile tears, however, are for good measure.

Kyle nods sweetly and rubs my back with her hand. "I can tell, Liz. I can tell you're really struggling right now."

I grit my teeth and manage not to roll my eyes. Instead, I nod. "Anyway, I'm trying to manage my disorder so that I can be a better wife and mother, but it's really hard. I think I need a reset button, Kyle."

"A reset button?"

"Your panini's burning."

"Shit!" Kyle claps a hand over her mouth as though she's said the c-word and darts back to the metal contraption, which is spewing gray smoke. She hastily unplugs its cord from the wall and opens the panini maker to reveal a charred sandwich with black clumps of burnt broccoli and cauliflower spilling from its sides. Gingerly, she picks up the sandwich with her fingertips and tosses it onto a ceramic plate. "I'm so sorry about that," she mutters. "Please continue."

I realize I've forgotten to continue crying, so I rub my eyes with my fists to hide them. "I was saying . . ."

"A reset?"

"Yes, Kyle, a reset." I sigh. "Something to get me back on track and feeling calm again. But I need your help."

"Sure, of course, Liz. Anything." Kyle leans in so close I can smell a mixture of coffee and eggs on her breath. Today's button-down shirt is robin's-egg blue with little white clouds. She is such a good person it hurts.

"I want to go on a silent retreat. By myself. In the Berkshires. It starts Monday and lasts three days. There will be lots of, er, meditation. And yoga. Maybe some inner chanting."

"That sounds awesome!"

"Right?"

"Yes. I think that will be *so* good for you." Kyle pauses, realizing the issue at hand. "Oh, wait—that's when Arno's away on business, right?"

"Unfortunately, yeah." I let my shoulders sag, eyes cast downward. "Arno's mom and sister-in-law are busy. I've already checked." Then, as if it just occurred to me, I brighten. "Well . . . I mean, surely you wouldn't be able to, you know, watch Emma for us?"

Kyle frowns, racking her brain for next week's schedule. "You know, I think I actually could. There's a protest Tuesday night I'm supposed to attend about that recent oil spill in Alaska, but—"

"Thanks, Kyle, you're the best."

Kyle smiles, squeezes my hand. "Of course, Liz. Any time. And honestly, I think this is brilliant. It will be so good for you." She turns back to her sandwich, shoulders relaxed.

"There's one more thing."

Kyle turns. "Yeah?"

"Would you mind . . . not telling Arno about it?"

Kyle frowns. Good people don't like keeping secrets from half of their employers. "You mean, you want me to lie to him?"

"No, no, of course not!" I shout, waving my arms to dispel the ridiculous notion. "Not *lie*. Just omit from conversation."

"But why? Wouldn't he support something like that?"

I feign a world-weary sigh. "The thing is, Kyle . . . Arno thinks generalized anxiety disorder is . . . well, a bunch of hooey."

Kyle's cheeks turn pink with anger. "What?"

I nod sadly. "Yeah. He's a wonderful man, Kyle, but he was raised to think that any mental disorder is a sign of weakness. A tragic flaw, if you will. It's not his fault."

Kyle shakes her head in disbelief. "But that's, like, *so* toxically masculine. And so unfair to you!"

"Sure. But I need to work on myself before I can work on us," I say, a tired smile playing across my lips. "You get what I mean?"

"I think Arno should support you no matter what, and accept you for who you are!" Kyle says, crossing her arms over her chest, her cheeks still two rosy splotches. "I mean, it's the twenty-first century. Mental health issues should be normalized."

"I agree with you, Kyle. But I really need this right now, and I'm not ready to talk about what I'm going through with him just yet. Do you think you could honor this request for me, and let me tell him in my own time?"

Kyle takes a deep breath. "Of course, Liz. You can count on me."

AND JUST LIKE that, I'm on a JetBlue flight across the country, seated in Blue Basic because I'm too nervous there could be Stonebridge stragglers in Mint, the airline's version of business class.

I'm seated beside a potbellied man with ruddy skin and a long gray ponytail, secured with a turquoise brooch. He takes large gulps from a thirty-two-ounce plastic bottle of cranberry juice and flips through a book about Las Vegas.

"Are you enjoying that?" I ask, pointing to the cover, which seems to depict a couple getting hitched at Graceland Chapel.

"Oh yes, it's quite fascinating," he replies, his voice carrying the scratch of a corn husk. "Did you know with its millions of lights, it's considered one of the brightest cities on Earth?" He edges the book onto the armrest between us. "You can read along with me if you'd like."

He chuckles, but then his laughter turns to a deep-throated cough, phlegmy and wet. He spits into a brown paper napkin, balls it up, and sticks it into the netting of the seat compartment in front of him.

I stifle a grimace and say thanks, but I've brought my own reading material: a classic by George Eliot. Unfortunately, my mind is like frenetic birds cartwheeling across the sky. The words, which used to bring me pleasure and a quiet, cozy feeling, seem meaningless, overly contrived.

Instead, I scroll through Instagram and refresh Vivienne's Facebook profile fourteen times. I try to limit the number of times I watch her latest TikTok videos—not because she can see me viewing them, but for my own sanity. Today, however, I'm out of control. I watch a video of her shimmying beside a scale model of the Eiffel Tower at Paris Las Vegas five times in a row. Her dark hair is tousled in loose waves and shines in the afternoon sun.

I can't stop wondering who took the TikTok.

My seatmate uses the bathroom no fewer than five times over the course of the next five hours, and I'm tempted to hide his Big Gulp cran

while he's away. Every time he gets up, he asks me to "watch his stuff," as if someone would want to lift his Las Vegas guidebook.

I somehow resist making a joke about urinary tract infections.

Eventually, popping in my ears lets me know we're dropping altitude. As we approach the grim Vegas landing strip, I alternate between watching a romantic comedy with Kate Hudson from the early 2000s and refreshing Vivienne's various social media pages. By this point, I'm sleuth-y enough that I also follow Viv and Arno's colleagues on Instagram and Facebook under pseudonyms, which gives me a bird's-eye view of the Stonebridgers' Sin City whereabouts.

Today is day two of Money, Meet Tech, which, according to the conference's website, means that as I descend into Nevada, thousands of businessmen and -women are crammed inside various event rooms at the Venetian, pretending to listen to the "movers and shakers" of the fintech world.

At this very moment, Viv and Arno could be sitting side by side beneath gaudy purple overhead lights as leaders from IBM and American Express tell attendees how their companies are *industry disruptors*. I shudder, imagining their knees grazing as the lights dim before one of the conference hosts switches to PowerPoint slides on the projector, Viv pretending to drop a cocktail napkin and bending down to . . .

"Hey, do you want to grab a drink tonight?"

It's my seatmate.

The lights flicker, and the plane's walls begin vibrating, the captain telling everyone to remain seated, we are landing. White-knuckled, I grab onto my armrests without thinking. My forearm grazes my neighbor's. It's scratchy, covered in thick gray corkscrew hairs.

He looks at our arms. Smiles.

"Sorry, what's that?" I ask through gritted teeth.

"I was hoping you'd like to get a drink with me tonight," he says calmly, the now-empty plastic cranberry juice jug balancing on his kneecap as though he's a magician.

"*Haven't you had enough to drink?*" I mutter under my breath.

"You're going to have to speak up, little lady." He points to his ear, where thick tufts of gray hair spill out.

"SORRY, I'M BUSY TONIGHT."

The landing has reached its crescendo; we are careening down the tan concrete strip, the airplane's wings shuddering outside my window like those of some large, dying bird. I close my eyes and hold my breath. Wait for the delicious slam of the brakes.

"Well, if you change your mind . . ." He slides a little white scrap of looseleaf onto my book's cover.

Henry B., it says. *Co-manager of the Starlight Bar.* An address follows.

I slide the paper inside my book's jacket. Pat the cover to show Henry it's secure. "Thanks."

"Take it easy."

CHAPTER 33

Las Vegas greets me like a smack in the face with a frying pan. The temperature, according to my iPhone, is 107 degrees Fahrenheit.

You know those people who say dry heat is better than humid heat? Those people have never been in the Nevada desert on a late August afternoon.

My armpits are slick with sweat mere minutes after stepping out of the taxi that drops me off at Barney's Inn, my white blouse sticking to random parts of my bra. I readjust my wig, which has gone all lopsided over the course of my journey, and set off to check in and find my room.

Though it's just after 2:00 p.m. Pacific Daylight Time, Barney's is lit up like the opening night of Disney World. Thousands, possibly millions, of tiny red and white lights flash overhead, creating a canopy-like awning you'd find at a circus. I glance around at the other people getting out of taxis and rideshares: mostly hassled-looking families with little kids and college-aged couples who clearly went for the cheapest deal they could find.

A pamphlet I printed out from the hotel's website informs me that Barney's is primarily known for its "Adventuredome," a six-acre amusement park with twenty-five rides and attractions, including a free clown show, a bowling alley, and indoor bungee jumping. Tonight, according to the hotel calendar, is SpongeBob night. *Hold on to your bikini!* it warns.

At a hulking faux-marble front desk, a serious-looking young man who can't be out of high school reads *Crime and Punishment* by Fyodor Dostoevsky. A filmy gold name tag on his chest lets me know his name is Teddy. A half-eaten bag of sunflower seeds sits at his elbow.

"Damn," I say lightly, sidling up. "Quite the heavy read for such a fun place." I nod toward a middle-aged man dressed up as Patrick Star, waving his bubblegum pink arms at a crowd of sweaty children. One of the brave ones prods Patrick with a stick.

Teddy blinks at me. "Are you checking in?"

"Sure am!"

"Name?"

"Meadow." I cough into my elbow. "Meadow . . . Lark."

"Do you have a photo ID or driver's license, Meadow *Lark*?" Teddy enunciates my fake last name.

Shit! I forgot they'd need that. "Sorry, I lost it. My driver's license, I mean. In a sauna. Just last week."

Teddy frowns, the corners of his lips drooping into an impressive show of displeasure. He jabs at the keys of a large boxlike computer, like the one my parents had when I was in middle school. I almost expect to hear the sound of dial-up.

"I already paid to be here," I explain gently. "In full, up front. It saved me ten percent."

"It says here the reservation was paid for by an Eliza—"

To shut him up, I grab his skinny arm—a chicken wing poking through his starched white button-down—and peer around, wild-eyed and fearful. I know the odds of someone from Stonebridge being here are probably one in a thousand, but I can't risk it. "Keep it down!"

He glares at me quizzically, then down at my fingers wrapped tightly around his arm.

I release the young man and try a different route: pleading. "Sorry, it's just . . . I need to keep my presence here on the down-low. It's a matter of . . . national security." Sweat drips from my cleavage down to my stomach, where I can feel a warm pool forming in my belly button.

Teddy looks from side to side, the way the bad guys in movies always do. "Okay, I don't believe that for a second, but you're lucky you look way older than eighteen, lady. Don't cause me any trouble, you hear?"

"I assure you, I am over eighteen and I will not cause you any trouble, Teddy. Thank you for your understanding."

Teddy presses his lips together, probably immediately regretting this random act of kindness toward an insane person. He pushes a white key card across the counter. "Don't lose this, or I'll have to get Sid involved, and then it will be a whole thing, okay?"

"Okay."

A thrum of anticipation courses through my body like an electrical current. I won't have to wait much longer.

Twenty floors up the SkyBeam Tower, I arrive at my room. It is not much to look at, as far as hotels go: an extremely flat queen-sized bed covered in a thick gold quilt. A small oak side table with a Bible on top, likely never opened. A flickering lamp from a low-budget horror film. Heavy gold-and-purple paisley curtains shielding me from the razzle and dazzle of Las Vegas's most infamous stretch of land.

I check that my minibar is fully stocked. It is, with neat little bottles of Smirnoff peach vodka and Bacardi watermelon rum. In the bathroom is a basket of soaps and lotions all in the same scent, mysteriously dubbed "A Trillion Wishes." I squirt the pale-pink lotion into my palms and smooth it all over my legs and ankles, swollen from the flight. It smells like warm prosecco.

"This will do just fine," I say to the air.

I take a long, scalding shower, cleansing myself with brown-sugar body scrub and yellowish oils that leave my skin shiny and pliable as rubber. I blow-dry my hair with a bright yellow mini Dyson I packed and put on far more makeup than usual, in an attempt to make myself look like someone else.

With my brown wig securely fastened in place, a long floral maxi dress, and a pair of oversized seventies sunglasses, I am transformed into Meadow. I contemplate a suede fringe vest in the floor-length mirror but decide it would be overkill.

I then try on a different voice for size, one with syrupy Texan undertones. Maybe a sordid past with a religious cult? A priest daddy from the Bible Belt?

"Howdy, stranger. Fancy seeing you here." I lower my sunglasses, flirt with myself. Pour some chilled Bacardi into a plastic cup and throw it back all at once.

"Who's ready for some Cirque du Soleil?"

CHAPTER 34

It wasn't hard to figure out that the Stonebridge crew was going to see the Beatles LOVE show at the Mirage this evening. Dirk, Ryan, and Diane all posted about it on Twitter. Even Arno texted me about it, in his once-per-day check-in text.

The hard part is getting in. According to Cirque du Soleil's website, the show is sold out. Has been for days. I suppose I could try and get a hawked ticket outside, but that seems risky—potentially exposing myself to Stonebridgers as they arrive for the show.

I decide that I'll wait until the show is over to tail them; that's when things will get interesting, anyway. I mean, it's not like Viv and Arno would have a quick shag during intermission in some Mirage bathroom stall, would they?

Oh my god, would they?

Calm down, Liz. Deep breaths.

I drain the last of a raspberry Smirnoff nip and check the length of the show: ninety minutes with no intermission.

Oh, thank god.

I check the time. It's only 7:00 p.m., and the show starts at 8:00, so I've got a full two and a half hours to kill. I peer out my window at a spectacular sunset, the sky the exact shade of a daylily: yellow-bellied and crimson at the edges, streaks of orange running through. I wish Arno, Emma, and I were on a proper vacation, watching the sunset together right now.

Below the sky, the Strip comes to life. The gamblers, tourists, and bachelor and bachelorette parties emerge from their hotel rooms, blinking and hungry. The heat has cooled to a mere 95 degrees, and the tiny people below walk *slowly*, physically recoiling from the fever dream of the day.

I open my George Eliot book and am startled to see the scrap of looseleaf, the loopy blue writing of Henry B. of the Starlight Bar. It occurs to me how it might look to Arno if he were to shake loose this scrap of paper. Would it rattle him? Shake cracks into the foundation of our marriage? Would it cause him to distrust me, stalk me, hate me?

Fight for me?

I'm not sure, so I tuck the snippet back inside the book jacket as insurance.

Like every other hotel in Las Vegas, the Mirage has a bar. Multiple, in fact. I figure they're about as good as any of the other Strip bars and as close to the action as possible, so that's where I will go to wait.

Tonight, the megaresort is bumping, with throngs of people loitering around its enormous pool and giant volcano, where there will be a fire-and-water show later this evening.

A man-made rock waterfall gushes warm, clear water from some unseen source. Verdant palm trees shoot upward into the twilight sky, stiff in the brittle heat.

I've been to Vegas once, for a college friend's birthday that I barely remember. Yet I feel it in my bones that the Mirage played a starring role in that weekend's bacchanalia, and as I walk into the lobby of the resort, déjà vu—no, *a memory*—plagues me.

Me, in a red sequined minidress, hunched over a slot machine based on *Willy Wonka and the Chocolate Factory*. Chocolate riverboats and orange Oompa-Loompas and golden tickets and giant jewel-toned Everlasting Gobstoppers rained down as I fed the machine penny after penny, all I could afford from my tutoring gig at the university's writing center. Every time I lost, I checked my cell phone, a clunky old Samsung with two missing buttons, frantic to hear from my ex-boyfriend, who'd been ignoring me all day. While the rest of the girls club-hopped into the wee hours, I'd gone back to our room at the Wyndham, ate a carton of ice cream, and watched *The Office* on my laptop till I cried myself to sleep.

Ha! And to think I thought I had problems then.

I mosey into Central Bar, mere steps away from the Mirage's iconic glass atrium, and am glad to see it's not too busy yet. Most people are probably still having dinner at some of the less dated Strip establishments, eating overpriced burgers in preparation for a wild night out.

The adjoining restaurant feels very "corporate business retreat" inside, with movie-theater carpeting in some unidentifiable mauve paisley print, overhead glamour lights, and stiff, economical furniture that doesn't give when you sit down.

The bar itself is square-shaped, with a cage in the center where two bartenders hold court beneath four big-screen TVs showing various sports events. I take a seat across from the entrance so that I can watch people come and go through the open-air bullpen.

I've grown more comfortable as Meadow. This is partially thanks to alcohol, which I've been steadily dribbling into my bloodstream since this morning, and partially because no one seems to be looking at me— like, *really* looking at me. When I first put the wig on, I felt terribly self-conscious that it looked fake and that people would stare. But once I realized I'd gotten through security at Logan Airport, flown five hours across the country, and had a complete stranger try to pick me up without addressing the twelve inches of synthetic chestnut framing my face, I relaxed a bit.

I was even starting to enjoy it.

The bartender who catches my eye is a petite brunette with a button nose and a no-nonsense manner. She finishes pouring a glass of wine for an elderly man in a white suit, then approaches.

"Hi, ma'am, how are you doing this evening?"

"I'm doing all right, thank you."

"Would you like something to drink?"

"Just a cranberry juice, please."

Now that the witching hour fast approaches, I realize I need to ease up on my alcohol intake, lest I risk doing or saying something that blows my cover.

Besides, Henry got me hankering for it.

The bartender slides a small glass tumbler of juice across the bar top, where it moves forward an inch before getting stuck on some viscous left-behind substance. I reach out to grab it at the same time the woman pushes it forward, and our fingers touch—mine hot, hers cool from the glass.

She smiles, removes her hand. "So, what brings you to Vegas?"

I take a swig of cranberry juice, swish it around in my mouth. Pondering.

"Business, I guess."

"You *guess*?" She laughs, a clipped little bark. "What kind of business are you in?"

I wipe my mouth with the back of my hand, like Meadow from Texas would. "Bounty hunting."

She bursts out laughing and I join in, because what else is there to do. She slaps the sticky counter with the palm of her small white hand.

"You're a funny one."

I tip Meadow's felt hat. "Thanks."

I LEAVE THE bar with a sugar-coated mouth and a buzzy feeling in my hands. No wonder Henry had to use the bathroom so many times midflight.

I check my phone. Ten minutes till hundreds of Beatles LOVE show attendees flood the atrium and the casino floor, the bar where I just spent two hours chugging cranberry juice and watching Clippers highlights.

I position myself near the entrance of a women's restroom, because if there's one thing I feel certain of, it's that Vivenne will have to pee after enduring ninety minutes of John, Paul, George, and Ringo. She might look like a goddess, but she's still mortal.

I find a discarded *Cosmopolitan* magazine on a metal bench and hold it loosely in my hands in case I need to hide my face. I try to look natural, but natural for Meadow is hard to discern. Is she someone who fans her face when hot and bored? Or would she just stare down at her phone like a zombie? I end up doing a little bit of both, fanning then scrolling, scrolling then fanning, till I work out a nice rhythm.

Eventually, a timid-looking Cirque du Soleil employee in a purple shirt jacket begins opening the sets of shiny gold double doors that lead to the theater, wincing with each kickstand employed.

Poor guy must have been trampled at some point.

Here they come, a positive downpour of humans surging forth from the belly of the theater like a colony of ants. Large packs of laughing men in suits and ties. Multigenerational families speaking loudly in foreign languages. Elderly couples clutching one another close as though they might be robbed, knocked over, or lost in the crowd. People jostle and push one another to get out of the theater faster, faster.

Where are they all in such a rush to get to? They're already in Vegas!

I struggle to track everyone who comes out, peering up and around the throngs for a glimpse of Vivienne's silky dark hair, Arno's tall, easy gait. But it's impossible. There are simply too many people.

My heart races with the possibility that they could stroll right by me, arm in arm, and I'd miss it. I try taking deep breaths but my chest burns as though I've run a great distance. Maybe I should just call it a night, try again tomorrow when I'm more alert and less jet-lagged, and there are fewer people to parse.

I heft my purse onto my shoulder, readjust my felt hat. Might as well use the bathroom while I'm here. I shove an elbow into the swinging wooden door, and *bam!* The door connects with a body on the other side, a body that yelps, "Ouch, watch it!" A body that, upon opening said door, looks eerily familiar.

A body that belongs to my husband's mistress.

It is almost too much to handle.

Vivienne glares at me, at Meadow, with a withering scowl. Tosses her Pantene Pro-V–ad hair over her shoulder.

"You should really knock when it's this crowded."

I nod because I am incapable of speaking. I stare down at a puddle of water on the tiled floor. Vivienne turns away from me and begins speaking to another woman, whom I recognize as Diane, a senior analyst at Stonebridge.

"Well, that was unnecessary," Vivienne sneers, and it takes me a moment to realize she's talking about the Beatles show and not me.

Diane laughs, in a mean-girl way. "So unnecessary. Why does Ryan have to try to turn every business trip into, like, a family vacation?"

Vivienne chuckles. "I know. Like, we're all adults. Just get us a nice meal and a few drinks and let's call it a night."

"Well, I'd take *more* than a few drinks after today," Diane admits. "Jesus, how many dudes can explain the future of e-commerce to me in a five-hour workshop? Fifteen? Twenty-five? A hundred? I'll wait."

"*Seriously,*" Vivienne agrees.

They pause for a moment, checking their phones in unison.

"Oh, did you get Arno's text?"

"No, what'd he say?"

My heart pounds a funereal thump.

"He said they're waiting outside for us, then we'll all head over to the Umbrella Lounge for drinks."

Two stalls open up at the same time, and the women disappear inside, commiserating over the lack of toilet paper left. Viv tosses some scraps over the top of her stall to Diane, and I feel an unfamiliar surge of affection for her. For their sisterhood. For the only two women deemed worthy enough to attend this Stonebridge field trip. It must be hard for them.

I stare at my cuticles till they emerge, then dare a glance at Viv as she checks herself out in the mirror. She looks smoking hot, as usual, in a creamy pantsuit that accentuates her toned ass and tan skin. Diane tosses her a tube of lipstick, saying it looks "like shit" with her Irish complexion, but that she thinks it will look amazing on Viv.

Shocker of shockers, Diane's right. The coral shade makes Viv's large brown eyes pop, plumps up her pillowy pout to offensive levels of sultriness.

"I hate you," Diane says for all of us.

Viv laughs.

They leave the bathroom together, and I realize that multiple stalls have opened up and there is an impressive queue forming behind me, women irritated and confused as to why I'm immobile. "Does she not *see* that there's an open stall?" one of them mutters.

"Sorry, ladies," I murmur, turning abruptly on my heel and pushing past my weak-bladdered compadres. I follow Vivienne and Diane out into the night.

The Umbrella Lounge looks like something out of a Disney movie. Tucked in between a bustling casino and a glass atrium bedazzled with fake cherry blossoms, a lounge room and bar sit beneath hundreds of upside-down umbrellas, suspended in midair.

Despite the seriousness of my mission, I forget myself for a moment, looking upward as I enter the lounge. Amid the rainbow of umbrellas, huge orange cutouts of monarch butterflies and red paper lanterns dance back and forth in the air-conditioned breeze. There's the rush of a waterfall somewhere in the distance. Goose pimples ripple down my arms.

The Stonebridgers have commandeered a couple of red leather couches adjacent to the old-fashioned bar: tiers and tiers of top-shelf liquor in front of an antique mirror, heavy oak paneling. Two handsome male bartenders wearing white button-downs with black pressed vests and matching bow ties bustle behind the bar, taking drink orders and shaking cocktails.

I find an open seat at the bar so that my back is to the group. My pulse is racing so quickly, I briefly wonder whether I'm having a heart attack.

Seated, I can just make out the top halves of their bodies when I slightly turn my head. Arno's chestnut curls gleam beneath the glow of the paper lanterns. Vivienne is seated beside him, leaning in as he tells her a story. Diane checks her phone, looking bored. Ryan holds court for Dirk and a couple of Stonebridgers I've never seen before. I glance at the group a few times, furtively, but no one notices.

My stomach feels as though it's lined with sharp knives, and my throat constricts with each breath. I'm so close.

"Can I get you a drink?"

The stentorian voice of the taller bartender nearly unseats me. I fight the urge not to quiet him with a hiss.

"Um, sure. Whiskey sour?"

"Of course. We've got Maker's Mark, Wild Turkey, Four Roses, Stranahan's . . ." He ticks their various bourbons off on his fingers, his voice as loud as a radio host's.

"Whatever you recommend. You're the expert," I whisper.

I turn away from the bartender and reposition myself on the barstool so that I'm angled toward the restaurant. People watching, that's all. I focus my attention back to the Stonebridge group.

The men look like they've gussied themselves up for a night of fun, wearing dark slim-fit jeans that probably cost hundreds of dollars and tailored button-down shirts. Expensive platinum watches gleam as they all pause for a toast led by Ryan. I can't hear exactly what he's saying, but I catch "to the future leaders of Stonebridge Boston" and an overly eager "Let's *go!*" from Dirk.

They clink their tumblers and champagne flutes together, Diane looking slightly embarrassed. Their server rushes over to take another round of orders.

"Whiskey sour for you, ma'am, shaken and stirred." The bartender sets an old-fashioned glass on a black napkin and slides it over. "Would you like to open a tab?"

"No!" I say too sternly, pushing a twenty-dollar bill across the bar top. "I mean, no *thank you*. Keep the change."

Glancing back at Arno, I study the glow of candlelight casting shadows across his chiseled face. He runs a hand through his tousled curls somewhat self-consciously, looking a little tired and on edge.

His colleagues don't seem to notice because they don't know Arno like I do. They hover around him, making it clear he's their leader, their decision maker.

I train my eyes on Viv's face, which appears carved by some renowned ancient sculptor. They skim her high cheekbones to her slender, ski-jump nose. Her graceful swan neck and Cupid's-bow lips.

Her perfection's disgusting; it really is.

She chats a little with the people across from her, a hefty redheaded guy I've never met before and Diane, of course. But most of her conversation is directed at Arno, that much is clear.

She whispers something in his ear, and his head bobs forward and back as he responds animatedly, tilting backward once or twice in a full-body laugh.

I *hate* that she makes him laugh so hard.

I don't even notice when my next drink arrives, just reach for it behind me like a robot preprogrammed for self-destruction. I take a gulp of the smoky brown whiskey, then another, and another.

So much for staying sober tonight.

Around 10:30 p.m., Arno stands from his spot on the couch, stretches his arms overhead. Yawns somewhat dramatically, making a show of it. I glance away, paranoid that he'll notice me, but the urge to keep watching is too strong. I look back.

Everyone stands to give him a clap on the back. Fist bumps from the douchier Stonebridge guys. And from Viv, a kiss on the cheek. A light squeeze on his arm. Their faces remain close. *Why are their faces so damn close?*

My stomach roils like open water, my chest tight as a drum.

Why did she kiss his cheek? Diane didn't do that.

Finally, Viv turns away. Sits back down and resumes talking with Diane, empty wineglass clutched in her hand. Smiling and laughing, tossing her dark, wavy hair around.

Arno gives one more wave to the group as he saunters out of the bar, headed for the atrium, where the exit is.

Is he going back to the Cosmopolitan to sleep, or is he going to another bar, where Vivienne will join him later? Or maybe Viv will just meet him *at* the Cosmopolitan and they'll fall into his bed together, laughing at how stupid their coworkers are for not knowing what is right in front of them. Or perhaps Viv ended up booking a different hotel, and Arno has to kill time till she can surreptitiously make her exit and meet up with him?

Ryan and Dirk deflate a little without Arno there to impress, like day-old birthday balloons. Their voices get quieter. Fewer rounds of shots are ordered.

The overhead lights have dimmed, and there's a pleasant buzz to the air, the voices of strangers playing a drunken serenade. Looking at the various couples scattered around the lounge, I can tell who will be going home with whom from a single glance. I wonder when Viv is going to make her move.

Another hour ticks by.

I drink two more whiskey sours and hope I'll be able to find my way back to Barney's later. I've fended off at least three older gentlemen who all said they were here on business. Two wore wedding bands.

I order another drink, but the taller bartender just makes a frowny face and turns his back to me, cutting me off. I contemplate asking one of my former suitors to buy me one, but decide it's too risky. I can't call attention to myself.

A sudden titter of goodbyes.

I turn in my seat.

Viv is standing now, pointing to her purse slung over a side chair. Ryan hands it to her, pretending to hold on to it so that she can't leave. She swats at his hand, playing along, but her face looks pissed.

Only Diane stands to give her a hug, and then Viv disappears from the lounge, headed toward the glass atrium.

I stand up too quickly, and the room spins like a top. I grasp at the bar, steadying myself. Ignore the looks from the bartenders.

"I'm fine," I say to them, or perhaps myself, a weird steely sensation spreading throughout my limbs. "I can do this."

I make my way toward the exit, trying not to walk too quickly or too drunkenly, which is more difficult than I anticipated. Lucky for me, Viv is wearing four-inch heels and hasn't gotten very far. I catch her making a right out of the atrium and follow close behind, tilting my felt hat low on my brow like Carmen Sandiego.

I expect her to stop and hail a taxi or call an Uber, but she keeps walking, occasionally looking down at her phone and firing off a text. It's a weird sensation, walking a mere ten feet behind Viv; I almost get to feel what it would be like to *be* Viv. That is, every man turning to stare at me as I walk by, a few of the brave or stupid ones trying to slow my pace in order to talk to me. Women glaring, as though it's *my fault* I'm so genetically blessed.

Viv ignores everyone, an island unto herself. She must be so used to the attention. To her, beauty is much like breathing, something to be ignored and taken for granted.

After two blocks, she crosses the street, approaching a nondescript black bar with no sign, just a large pink octopus painted on its door. She barely looks up as she wrenches the front door open and disappears inside. The bouncer doesn't even blink.

I approach warily, trying to hide my drunkenness with a huge smile. "Hello!"

The bouncer, a three-hundred-pound man in a black Thrasher T-shirt, just stares. *No Mercy* is tattooed across his knuckles.

"Do you need to see an ID, or . . . ?"

The man shakes his head no and nods toward the door. I've passed a mysterious test.

Inside, the bar is disorienting, like the inside of a tanning bed. Pink neon lights cast a sunset hue on the patrons and interior furniture of white Mod chairs that look like marshmallows. Low black tables house dozens of untended drinks, abandoned by their owners.

The octopus theme carries over, with huge silver sculptures of the sea creatures placed artfully around and murals of more octopi in various colors and designs spackling the walls.

What the hell is this place?

The crush of people is completely overwhelming, and for a moment, I feel like turning around and making a break for it. But then I spot Viv, weaving her way toward a hot-pink bar, and my resolve returns.

I'm on a mission.

I stick to the side of the bar, shoving my way through hordes of women in miniskirts and jeans and ripped tanks and Doc Martens. Lots of short, edgy haircuts and eyebrow piercings. Low-slung jeans revealing belly buttons. It's weird how many women there are.

I bump into a short woman riddled with tattoos, one of which is a naked mermaid with long hair and massive tits, floating on a sea of toned biceps. She tells me to "watch it," and I realize this is the second time I've been told to do that tonight.

Self-consciously, I scan the room for Arno. No dice.

Perhaps he's one of the backs turned toward the bar, ordering drinks for Viv and himself beneath the tentacles of yet another hanging octopus, this one covered in mirrorlike sequins.

I stumble forward, trying to avoid knocking into any more strangers.

Viv veers away from the bar and approaches a booth I hadn't noticed, built into the wall. It's dark and intimate inside its confines, and I can't make out if there's anyone inside.

Surely there is.

Heart pounding in my ears, stomach in my toes, I walk forward. Something primal drives me.

A tall figure wearing a blazer emerges from the booth, opens their arms wide as Viv comes near. They embrace, their faces mashed together, a hand clasped tight to Viv's ass.

Then, someone pushes me from behind, and I'm sent flying. An accident, but still. My arms cartwheel as if I'm in a *Tom and Jerry* comic strip, my mouth frozen open in surprise.

I land on my hands and knees, tabletop position. The laminate floor is wet and sticky beneath my palms. Two women help me up, asking if I'm okay.

"Just embarrassed," I say, and they laugh. One offers to buy me a drink, but I decline. I acknowledge the sweet gesture with a slight smile.

When the women turn back to their friends, I'm granted a clear shot of Viv and her mysterious suitor. They're still entwined at first, their lips suctioning frantically off one another. Finally, they part.

And it's—it's a woman?

Viv's making out with a woman.

I blink once, twice, three times, and the person standing opposite Viv is still a woman. A six-foot-tall, blazer-wearing absolute *stunner* of a woman.

The pair climb into the booth, Viv's girlfriend helping her step inside in her heels. Before she joins Viv, I get a good look: short hair, dyed platinum blond and swooped attractively to one side. Pale skin, like ice, glimmering beneath the weird pink lighting. Tailored navy suit and shiny oxfords, making her look like a total boss.

She's exactly as impressive as Vivienne herself.

Every part of my body is shaking. With what, I'm not sure. Relief? Exhaustion? Stupidity?

I take a deep breath and turn, pushing through the sea of people with my arms wrapped around myself. As I approach the door to leave, something occurs to me. I turn toward the nearest person, a woman in tight checkered pants and a crop top that shows off her toned midsection. "What is this place?"

She looks momentarily confused, but smiles anyway.

"Octopussy. Best lesbian bar in Vegas."

CHAPTER 35

Dawn breaks outside my window at Barney's Inn, throwing fire onto the Las Vegas Strip.

My head pounds like someone's jackhammering it into submission. I lurch out of bed, nauseous and unsteady, and fill a plastic cup with ice. I pour the cubes into my mouth, sucking on them till they melt. Drinking actual water seems too hard.

I wonder if last night was a dream, something my frayed brain conjured up out of pure desperation. But when I pull out my iPhone from my purse and type in "Octopussy" on Google Search, an image of the bar comes up: its nondescript exterior, the pink octopus painted on a black door. I remember everything with crystalline clarity: the blond woman in the blazer, biting at Viv's earlobe, kissing her mouth, grabbing her ass.

I toss my phone aside on the bed, feeling sick.

How could I have been so stupid? How could I have been so wrong? I get back into bed.

My phone buzzes, and I jump, fingers trembling as I retrieve it from my bedcovers and read the new message. It's from Arno. Hey baby! Hope my two best girls have a great day. Can't wait to come home. Xoxo.

I groan, run my hands over my face in despair. How could I have done this to Arno? To Emma?

After a long, sobering shower during which I deny myself hot water,

I reply, telling Arno that I miss him, too, and can't wait to give him a big hug. When I hit send, I feel physically repulsed by myself. All the stalking, all the lies, and for what?

Arno's not cheating on me, never has, and never will. And I've risked our entire relationship to try to prove otherwise.

Why?

My phone pings. I look down and see that Kyle has sent me a video of Emma with the message: I know you probably have your phone turned off for the retreat, but I couldn't resist sending you a video of your munchkin for when you do turn it on!

I press "Play."

Emma is sitting in her high chair with mashed banana all over her face, bib, and hands. Some of the brownish-yellow globs even cling to her eyelashes. She's sucking at her fingers and giggling, beaming at the camera. Then she looks around Kyle, like she's waiting for someone.

"Ma-ma?" she asks.

The fleeting joy on her face is written over with confusion.

"Ma-ma?" she repeats.

Mama.

Somehow, this is the most sobering moment yet of my trip.

How could I have risked ruining this little girl's life?

You were always going to ruin her life, a voice in the back of my head sneers.

I hurl my phone across the room, and it skitters beneath an armchair. I sigh and quickly drop to the floor, crawling on hands and knees and sticking my head under the chair to retrieve the device, which now has a fresh crack across its screen and is covered in dust. I save the video.

Why can't I just be grateful for what I have? Why can't I just be *happy*?

Maybe Dr. Abelson is right. Maybe all of this craziness has less to do with Arno and more to do with Emma. More to do with motherhood. Maybe this isn't just anxiety; maybe I *do* have postpartum depression.

She'd broached the topic in one of our more recent sessions, asking if I'd had any trouble bonding with Emma after birth. I'd felt as though I'd been slapped and responded with signature defensiveness. "Of course not!" I'd stammered. "I love Emma! She's the best. We're incredibly close."

Dr. Abelson had just looked at me, blinking.

Eventually, she'd gently added that some of her patients who suffer from postpartum depression have symptoms similar to what I'd been experiencing: insomnia, loss of appetite, an inability to concentrate, intense irritability, and a deep sense of vulnerability. Sometimes, they have frightening thoughts or fantasies. Dr. Abelson said it affected up to 20 percent of all new mothers and, like prescribed medication, it was nothing to be ashamed of.

I'd simply told her that she was mistaken.

Over the course of the next hour, I pack my bags, stowing away Meadow's stupid brown wig and hats, her dumb gauzy maxi dresses. I throw in a couple of sample body lotions at the last second—a tangible reminder of my foolishness.

I take the elevator down to the lobby, where Teddy eyes me suspiciously over the top of a new novel. Today, it's *The Bell Jar*.

"Wow, another zinger," I say drily, tilting my head toward the book. "Don't read that all in one sitting, you might have *too* much fun."

"What do you need, *Meadow*?"

"I think the more polite phrasing would be, 'How can I help you?'"

Teddy ignores me, but he sets the book down. "Where's your wig?"

I touch my short, natural hair, shocked that Teddy of all people saw through my facade. It feels dry from the weird hotel shampoo.

"I changed up my look, Teddy. You got a problem with that?"

Teddy smiles, suddenly shy. "It looks nice like this. Better."

"I need to check out early."

"Oh." Teddy looks somewhat crestfallen. His thick brows furrow so that they almost meet in the middle. "You didn't enjoy your stay with us?"

"No, no. It's not that!" I sweep my arm around, gesturing toward the antique popcorn machine, the tacky red and white balloons everywhere. "This place? It's great. This is a *me* problem." I slide over the key card, and Teddy thanks me for not losing it or causing any trouble. He was sure I would, on both accounts.

I tell him to stay in school and think about life after Barney's. If his taste in literature is any indication of his academic prowess, Teddy could really go places.

He thanks me for the advice, and I leave Barney's behind me, stepping out into the stifling Vegas heat a new woman, with a much clearer head on her shoulders.

CHAPTER 36

Back home in Boston, sitting snug on Dr. Abelson's brown leather couch, I nurse a mug of chamomile tea with extra honey. The mug is shaped like a sloth, its arms the handle. A kitschy touch that's incongruous with the severe woman sitting across from me.

It's my first time visiting her since the Vegas expedition seven days ago, and I wonder if my newfound familial security and ease is evident in my skin, which is smooth and hydrated from a week of full nights of sleep, yoga, and plenty of green food. Not a drop of alcohol.

Well, for the most part. You can't fault a woman for a glass of red wine with dinner.

Today, Dr. Abelson wears a pink swirly shawl and lime-green glasses that make her look like a kooky music teacher. Her fingers drum a rhythm across the edge of her table.

She smiles at me.

"So, Liz, what would you like to talk about today?" She pauses. "How have things been at home?"

"Honestly, Dr. Abelson, things have never been better. I've been making some progress on my book . . ." Not entirely true, but I'm sure I'll get to work on it soon in my new unencumbered state. "And things with Arno have been, well, perfect."

"Perfect," Dr. Abelson repeats, her eyes widening.

My mind flashes back to the night he returned from Vegas. I was already in bed, as planned, freshly showered and dressed in the over-sized button-down he likes.

"We've never been closer."

Dr. Abelson looks surprised. Almost suspicious.

"Really, Liz? Well, I'm so happy to hear that . . . Quite a one-eighty from our conversations just a few weeks ago. What's brought about this change?"

I blush, unsure, as always, how much of myself I want to reveal. *What the hell.* I offer a confident closed-mouth smile. "Well, truth be told, I went on a bit of a reconnaissance mission, Doctor Abelson."

"A recon . . . what now?"

"I went to Las Vegas. To spy on my husband. But not like *spy* spy, just, sort of keep tabs on him and see what he was doing on his business trip."

Dr. Abelson takes a deep breath and repeats what I said, her shoulders sinking ever so slightly beneath her gauzy shawl.

"You went to Las Vegas to spy on your husband while he was on a business trip."

"Yes, but you're making it sound really serious. It wasn't *that* serious." I laugh to show how lighthearted the whole endeavor was.

"And what happened, Liz?"

"Well, nothing, I suppose. Nothing happened. He went to a boring conference, saw a show at Cirque du Soleil, got drinks with his coworkers, and that was it. No evidence of infidelity. In fact, the woman in question turned out to be a lesbian, which is great."

"The woman in question?" Dr. Abelson parrots.

"Yes. Vivienne. Remember her? Gorgeous yoga teacher–slash–Stonebridge VP, just like Arno. Seemed awfully close to him at a Memorial Day party? She's gay. So, everything's fine now."

Dr. Abelson's lips are a thin line.

"Anyway," I continue. "You were right. My friends were right. Arno is faithful. It was all in my head. I was catastrophizing, as usual."

I give a little chuckle, smoothing over any lingering doubts about the flower receipt and the missing jewelry. His coworker's cousin probably *did* die. And as for the jewelry, well, I'm sure a mysterious gift box will appear come Christmastime. Arno has always planned so far in advance.

Dr. Abelson looks concerned, her eyes narrowed. She wrings her hands. "Liz, what you've just described is very concerning behavior—"

"I just needed assurance that everyone else was right," I say, feeling somewhat defensive. "Anyway, it was my neighbor Doreen's idea."

"Doreen?"

"My neighbor."

"I thought you two weren't friends," Dr. Abelson says, confused. "I remember you describing her as *an icy bitch* in a former appointment."

"Did I?"

She nods.

I wave my hand. Irrelevant, irrelevant. "Well, turns out, she's pretty cool. Cool enough that she helped save my sanity, anyway. Or my marriage, at the very least!"

Dr. Abelson is quiet, evaluating me with her owlish eyes, her long, thin fingers steepled together.

"Does Arno know?"

"Does Arno know what?"

"That you followed him to Las Vegas and *spied* on him?"

"Of course not. Why would I tell him that? You're the one who said I should think about how certain conversations would impact our relationship. And telling him that I followed him to Las Vegas would definitely be a negative conversation."

"Liz, I strongly, strongly recommend that you and Arno come in to see me together for couples therapy."

"Couples therapy?" I shake my head, perplexed. "But Arno's fine."

"Perhaps." Dr. Abelson nods. "But I think you and Arno are on some very shaky . . . even treacherous . . . ground, maritally speaking. Spying and lies and secrets? None of these things lead to a healthy, honest, and open marriage. You two need to *communicate*. I think it would be highly beneficial to have an unbiased third party present, to hold you both accountable for having these tough conversations."

Unbiased, my ass.

"Um . . . I'll think about it? Arno isn't really into therapy," I admit.

"He's never been. And I think me suggesting *couples therapy* would really freak him out and make him think something's actually wrong with us."

"Liz, dear, something *is* wrong with you two. Something is very, very wrong."

Well, this certainly isn't what I signed up for today.

"I thought you'd be happy for me," I whisper. "I even had a break-through, while I was in my hotel room. I think you were right, and that I might have . . . I think I might . . ." My eyes prick, a warning of ugly tears to come. I pick up my mug for something to do with my hands and take a sip, but the tea has cooled to tepid broth.

"Liz," Dr. Abelson cuts in, "I want you to be happy. You know that. Everyone in your life wants you to be happy. But the behavior you're describing is . . . well, it's delusional." I wince as though Dr. Abelson has raised a fist to hit me. "And I don't use that word lightly," she scrambles to say, as though reading my thoughts. "If you're unwilling to consider couples therapy, I think you need more help than I can provide, if I'm being perfectly honest."

I'm gobsmacked. Is she breaking up with me?

"But there are certainly many other practitioners who can help fig-ure out a solution," Dr. Abelson says quickly.

"But . . . I'm fine!" I gasp, nearly screeching. I slam the stupid sloth mug down on the table. Dr. Abelson jumps in her seat, then regains her composure.

"Liz, I fear we've come to the end of our journey. As I said, I'm more than happy to provide couples therapy for you and Arno, but I think you'll need to solicit someone else's services for this level of erratic behavior."

"Are you saying that I'm *beyond help*?"

"I just want you to get the help you *need*."

She reaches out her hand, as if to squeeze mine, but I snatch it away and look out the window, down toward the bustling street below.

My therapist just dumped me.

"Is this even . . . can you do this? Is this legal?"

"Yes," Dr. Abelson replies crisply, clearly offended by my shredding of her thin olive branch. "There is something called a 'license to deny.' Perfectly legal. Google it, if you want."

Dr. Abelson stands, picking up my discarded mug of tea and pouring out the urine-colored dregs into a nearby trash can. She then busies herself, shuffling some papers on her desk and rearranging her rock collection.

It appears our meeting has ended.

CHAPTER 37

When I get home from my unnerving meeting with Dr. Abelson, I can't relax. Everything in our house looks wrong. The white walls, the white kitchen countertops, even the vase of white tulips. They all needle me. Why is everything so . . . austere?

Kyle appears from the family room, Emma trailing her like an obedient dog.

"Hey, Liz. How was therapy?"

"Terr-a-pee," Emma echoes, sucking on her thumb.

"It was fine."

I pace circles around the kitchen island, wringing my hands.

Kyle looks worried. "You sure?"

She was shocked when I came home from my fictitious silent retreat in the Berkshires early. I'd called her from the airport and told her I'd decided to leave, that I missed Emma too much.

At least my explanation was half true.

"Yeah, I'm sure."

I ask Kyle if she can stay a couple hours late so I can have an important conversation with Arno. Our eyes meet, and she nods meaningfully, expecting that I'm ready to come clean about my generalized anxiety disorder. But that's not the case; there are other lies I need to atone for first.

Hours later, I'm seated on a picnic blanket in our backyard when

Arno emerges from the sliding glass doors, his easy smile breaking open his face and slicing through my heart like it's sashimi.

"Hey, baby, is everything okay? Kyle mentioned you wanted to talk to me about something." He checks his wristwatch. "A little late for her to still be here."

"Can you sit down?" My voice cracks ever so slightly, betraying me.

Arno frowns, concern seeding his brow. He makes his way over to me on the grass, sits down cross-legged, his long limbs too big for the tiny blanket. I almost want to laugh.

"What's going on?"

Deep breaths, Liz. Deep breaths.

"Arno, I have to tell you something."

He takes my hands in his. They are warm and slightly rough, how they've always felt. "What is it?"

"For the last few months, I've . . . I've been convinced that you were cheating on me."

Arno's eyes widen, two blue saucers.

"With Viv."

"Liz, I—"

"I'm not finished."

Arno shuts his mouth, presses his lips together.

"I know you aren't. Cheating on me, I mean. Vivienne's a lesbian. I saw her with a woman, and it was clear they were together."

I pause to catch my breath. Close my eyes and I'm back in that depressing Vegas hotel room.

Does he really need *all* the details?

"Anyway, that's why I've been acting so strange lately, so erratic. I saw some stupid text she sent you, and it had a flirty emoji, and I just . . . I spiraled, Arno. It wasn't pretty. And I'm really ashamed of the lengths I went to before I figured it out . . . bringing those stupid cookies to your office, following Viv to yoga class."

I can't mention Vegas. I just can't.

"But that's all over now. I hope you can forgive me for not trusting you. I think I've just really struggled with figuring out who I am as a mother. I feel so far away from myself . . . and I've let that get in the way of our relationship. I'm so sorry, Arno."

I don't realize I'm crying till drops of water drip off my chin and land on my thighs. My vision is blurry, and mucus hangs from my nose in thick green strings. Arno reaches out with the cuff of one of his nicest button-downs, a gift from his mother.

"Arno, don't!"

"I don't care about it, Liz. It's just a shirt." He carefully cleans the snot from my upper lip, my chin, and wipes it gently onto the grass. He smiles.

"It's okay, Liz. Everything is going to be okay."

"What?" I stare at him, open-mouthed. "You don't hate me?"

"Of *course* not," Arno says, appalled. "How could I hate you?"

"Because I'm . . . I'm . . . crazy? That's what Dr. Abelson said, at least." Remembering the look on the older woman's face as she said she could no longer counsel me causes me to shudder. I gasp, tears coursing down my face anew.

Arno reaches out and pulls me into his warm, sturdy chest. Presses my head into his body. Envelopes me.

"Forget that old bat," he says. "I never liked the sound of her, anyway."

I laugh, thinking about how Dr. Abelson *does* sort of look like a bat. I could almost imagine her hanging upside down from the ceiling of her creepy, old office building.

"She said she didn't want to be my therapist anymore."

"Good riddance!" Arno rubs my back in rhythmic circles, the way I do for Emma when she's upset or scared.

"Don't you worry what anyone thinks of you, Liz," Arno says. "I love you and I forgive you, and that's all that matters."

I hold on to him even tighter, thanking whatever deity that might exist for sending this wonderful creature my way.

LATER THAT EVENING, after Kyle's left, Arno and I are cuddled up on the couch with Emma in between us, watching *Frozen* for maybe the hundredth time, when Arno turns to me and whispers, "Hey."

"Hey."

"I know you didn't like the idea of it at first, but have you given any more thought to that house in Newburyport? That Realtor emailed me today. It's somehow still on the market."

To be honest, I hadn't. I've been so consumed with stalking Viv that it never even occurred to me that it was still on Arno's mind.

"Not really, no."

Arno looks away, disappointment etched on his face.

"But I'd consider it."

"Wait, really?"

"Yeah. If you think it would be good for our family. I trust you."

"I think it would be good for *you*, Liz. You'd have female family members right down the street, a built-in support system! Plus, the Realtor said the family next door has a kid around Emma's age. Apparently, the mom is an English teacher. How cool is that? You could have a friend who actually shares your interests. No offense to Tracy," Arno adds, laughing. "But you know what I mean."

"That sounds like it could be really nice."

Arno beams and leans over Emma's head to give me a kiss.

"Thank you, Liz. Thank you for being open to change."

CHAPTER 38

When we pull up, the Cape is exactly how I remembered it: A modern charcoal gray with navy shutters, red trim. A weeping willow tree on the front lawn that looks prehistoric, its green, drooping branches like tears falling to the ground. White and purple petunias scattered across the flower beds.

Linda, the Realtor, stands somewhat awkwardly by the front door, unsure of whether to smile or not. She runs her fingers through her stiff blond perm.

My stomach turns, a stab of guilt. I shouldn't have been so rude to her. I'll make it up to her today.

Arno and I get out of the car, unstrap Emma from her car seat. She's squirmy today—grabbing fingers and lots of squealing—and I get the sense she's feeding off Arno's mood. He's been grinning since we pulled out of our Wellesley neighborhood and got on the highway, blasting old Willie Nelson songs and singing along. He wants this for us so much, I realize.

"Gram-ma?" Emma asks, clapping her pink little hands together. "Bea?"

She's realized where we are, knows how close her family is. My cheeks grow warm with shame. *Of* course *it would be good for Emma to live here.*

"Hi, Linda!" I call in a voice higher than normal. As we approach the front door, I go in for a hug, which startles the woman greatly.

"Oh, er, hi, Liz! Hi, Arno and Emma!"

As we pull apart, she readjusts her wire-framed glasses. Gives a big smile. "I'm so glad you all decided to give this special place another look."

"Yes, well, a lot can change in a couple months," I reply, giving Arno a tentative smile. He reaches out and squeezes my arm.

Emma makes a break for the tire swing, toddling on unsteady legs, but he snatches her up.

"Not yet, little missy, but maybe later, if we make this our home," he says, lifting her T-shirt and giving her a flurry of raspberry kisses on her tummy. She laughs hysterically, screaming, "Dada!"

Linda leads us inside, and once again, we admire the high ceilings and open floor plan, the gleaming white oak floors and creamy, unblemished walls. I imagine the three of us tucked into our green velvet couch, a fire in the plaster fireplace roaring as the snow falls outside.

I envision me, filling the floor-to-ceiling bookshelves with all of my favorite novels, alphabetized and segmented by genre. Fiction to the left of the fireplace, nonfiction to the right. The perfect nesting place for my first edition of *Pride and Prejudice*.

I picture inviting my mom and dad and brother for a Thanksgiving dinner here at the long, farm-style wooden table, white tapered candles in the brass chandeliers sparkling overhead. Maybe we could be something like a family again.

This could work, I think to myself. *This could work quite well.*

Out one of the kitchen windows, Linda and I watch Arno and Emma out back as he shows her the apple tree, the herb garden. She crawls on her belly in the bright green grass, yanking at dandelions, and Arno clutches his stomach, laughing.

I run my hands over the Carrara marble countertops. Imagine fixing a bouquet of hydrangea in the deep white sink.

"We'll take it, Linda."

The woman jumps, turning to me in disbelief.

"Really? Are you sure?"

I look out the window once more. Arno swings Emma back and forth by her chubby hands as if she's a small monkey, and Emma squeals with delight, kicking her plump legs. He sets her down, and she reaches out her arms, and he lifts her up, spinning her around and around in the sunshine.

"Yes. I'm certain."

I join them in the backyard and whisper the news to Arno. Tears prick his eyes, and he yanks me to his chest, then kisses me.

Emma ambles over to the apple tree to run her palms over its smooth bark. Arno says her name, and she looks back with a gummy smile.

"This is the best day ever," Arno confirms.

Linda emerges from the house rosy-cheeked and sweaty with anticipation; she can't believe her turn in fortune. I suspect she's still a bit apprehensive of me, but she approaches with a shy smile.

"Liz, I hope this isn't too forward, but would you want me to introduce you to the neighbor? I just have a feeling you two would really hit it off."

"Sure, Linda, that would be really nice of you."

Linda beams.

I hadn't really noticed the house to the left of ours the first time we visited, but now that I'm standing in front of it, I can't believe I didn't.

It's a stately Greek Revival home, red brick with forest-green shutters and two chimneys. The front lawn is freshly mowed, and a line of trimmed green bushes stand sentry around the yard.

There aren't any blooming flowers, no kitschy lawn adornments. A small white sign by the front door says *1855* in curling black font.

As Linda presses the doorbell, my heart beats a peg faster. *What if I don't like my new neighbors? What if they're stuffy and uptight? What if—*

The door swings open, and a woman emerges, blinking into the midday sun. She looks about my age, with slightly unkempt, curly hair in a loose bun. No makeup, jeans, and a faded T-shirt that says, *Oink for Porkies pot roast sandwiches.* Dangly silver earrings, hammered metal rings on most of her fingers.

She looks back and forth between me and Linda, a smile playing across her lips.

"Are you going to be my neighbor?"

∽

ZOE SHOWS US around her home, apologizing halfheartedly for the mess.

"The front yard is all Tim," she says, pointing to her husband, who's making caprese sandwiches in the kitchen. "I tend to be a bit of a slob indoors."

She's not kidding. There are piles of stuff everywhere.

Books, magazines, and newspapers with large sections clipped out are fanned out on the living-room floor. Beads and costume jewelry fill ceramic bowls on the kitchen table, and a large plastic bag crammed with feathers sits in the center of the foyer.

"I'm sort of a part-time artist," she explains, pointing to clusters of paintings that take up virtually every wall. Most are portraits of people in rococo or Victorian garb, but modernized. One that catches my eye is of a Marie Antoinette–type woman in a pale-pink corseted dress with a floor-length silk train. She's texting on an iPhone, mid–eye roll.

"These are incredible," I say honestly. "I'd love to buy one, if any are for sale."

Zoe laughs self-deprecatingly. "Oh, I don't know that they're worth anything, but thanks for saying that. Just a fun side hobby I've picked up to take the edge off teaching asshole high schoolers all day."

Zoe pushes aside a stack of books on one of their couches, making room for me and Linda. She has an impressive contemporary literature collection, and I'm excited to discover we share more than a few favorite authors. We sit down, and she tells me a little more about her and Tim: how they never anticipated they'd end up in Newburyport, where Zoe grew up, but her mom had to go and die and leave Zoe with her childhood home that she couldn't bear to part with.

"If she could see how messy I've made it, she'd turn over in her grave."

They've lived here for ten years now, Zoe says, with her teaching English at the local high school and Tim doing software development from home. They have a daughter who is one year older than Emma, named Robin.

"She's currently sleeping off a big sleepover hangover," Zoe explains. "Went and stayed at Tim's parents' house last night, and they let her rage till ten p.m. with her older cousins. She comes home exhausted; it's freaking amazing."

Zoe is nothing like I imagined, and I like her immediately. She's so . . . real. So down-to-earth and comfortable in her own skin. She's relaxing to be around, and I find myself not wanting to leave.

"Newburyport can be a little uppity," she shares. "Like my mother, may she rest in peace. But there are still plenty of good people here."

Linda nods in agreement.

"It seems that way," I reply, smiling.

"So, when do you all move in?"

I look at Linda, who grins like an old-fashioned matchmaker.

"As soon as we can."

CHAPTER 39

Two months later, Kyle and I are hard at work in our new backyard, and I am beginning to regret my decision to buy an outdoor playhouse.

"There are just so many . . . parts," I say, wiping the back of my hand across my brow. "When I read the review, there was no mention of a built-in kitchenette, or a working mailbox."

Kyle laughs, throwing her head back. The sun catches on her large plastic eyeglass frames.

"That's what you get for buying something sight unseen off the Newburyport Facebook Marketplace, Liz," she says wryly, but she's not mad. In fact, I think Kyle's more excited for the playhouse than the girls. They're too young to really enjoy it now, but in a year or two, they'll use it constantly. Besides, I think Beatrix will enjoy using it immediately, whenever she comes for a visit with Rose. Kyle and I have been putting it together since seven o'clock this morning.

"We're almost there," she reassures me when I groan.

Emma and Robin sit on a blanket in the shade of a maple tree, playing with stacking blocks. Robin is doing most of the stacking, while Emma watches with rapt attention. She's clearly obsessed with the older child, follows her around like a shadow, constantly asking for "Rob-rob" the second the two-and-a-half-year-old leaves our house. Normally, Robin would be at a day care right now, but there was a lice outbreak, so we've been watching her this week.

Zoe can't thank us enough, but I honestly don't mind, and I don't think Kyle does either.

Much to Adrienne's chagrin, Kyle moved into the mother-in-law suite once we'd settled in, and I wouldn't have it any other way. I know Kyle won't stay with us forever, but she's already made such a huge impact on Emma's life, and mine. I know she's not technically family, but I've come to think of her as a little sister, albeit a very wise one. Sometimes, when Arno's watching Emma, we sneak out for a glass of wine at a local restaurant with Zoe or, yes, a yoga class. I'm even becoming a part-time vegetarian—Kyle's taught me all about the versatility of beets—and I think I'm okay with that.

As for Arno and me, we really never have been better. Admitting my anxieties and fears about our marriage and motherhood was purifying, like a juice cleanse for my soul. It brought us closer together. We've instituted a formal date night, every other Friday, where we get dressed up and try a new local dinner spot. Sometimes, when we're really tired, we cheat and just wear sweats to go pick up takeout, and those are some of the best date nights of all.

Sure, he still has to work a lot of late nights, and go on the occasional business trip, but I feel like he's never been more present. More ... mine. He's renting an apartment that I jokingly refer to as his "bachelor pad" in the waterfront district, just minutes away from Stonebridge, for the *really* late nights when it's easier for him to stay by the office. I've only been there once, when he first moved in, and Emma's been twice—when migraines got the best of me and Kyle was out of town for a much-deserved vacation. It's sparse and depressing: a queen-sized bed, a big-screen TV hanging opposite a black leather couch that Harry gave him for free. No art on the walls, no plants, no literature.

I shuddered when we left, as Arno locked the deadbolt. "That place gives me the heebie-jeebies," I'd said half jokingly.

"Well, good thing my girls never have to spend any time there!" he'd replied.

As I screw in one of the white plastic window frames to the playhouse, I smile, thinking of the writing progress I've made since we moved.

I abandoned the novel about a woman who loses her memory and can't remember how she ended up in her supposedly "perfect" life. Too depressing. Instead, I'm working on a thriller about a woman who goes to untold lengths to find out if her husband, a handsome and enigmatic day trader, is cheating on her. But of course he isn't.

The subject matter is a little on the nose, I know, but it's easiest to write from experience. Freja is enthused that I'm "headed in a new direction."

I've worked out a pleasant, reasonable schedule in which I write for three hours in the morning, and then spend the rest of the day hanging out with Emma and Kyle. In the past month, we've gone hiking (Emma tucked securely into our Osprey backpack), gone to a local petting zoo, and done face painting, which even Arno joined in on when he got home. Watching Emma smear bright blue glitter paint all over my husband's face while he sat with his eyes shut, smiling patiently, made me feel the deepest-rooted sense of love for him yet.

I hang the delicate red curtains on their delicate plastic rods. Position them over the windows I've just assembled from scratch, feeling incredibly proud of myself.

Kyle stands back to appraise our work. "Damn, Liz. We did good."

Kyle never curses, so this makes me laugh out loud. I can't believe we built this! I flex my biceps, slick with sweat, and Kyle drops and does a push-up to make me laugh. Women *are* strong as hell.

"Hey, Kyle?" I ask, an idea forming.

"Yeah?"

"I think I might surprise Arno today, take Emma into the city for lunch."

We haven't been in so long, and I think it might be fun for Emma to see Daddy in his fancy office with its glass windows and gleaming coffee machine. All of his coworkers would freak out to see Emma in the miniature gingham overalls she's wearing today.

"Aww," Kyle says. "That sounds like a great idea!"

"Think you and Robin will be okay without us for a few hours?"

"Of course! Kid is probably exhausted from stacking blocks for the past three hours. I bet she'll fall asleep in no time."

I go inside to shower and freshen up, imagining the look of adoration on Arno's face when he sees his two best girls.

CHAPTER 40

With traffic, it takes Emma and me more than an hour to drive into the city, and by the time I turn onto Purchase Street downtown, she's getting cranky—kicking the back seat, asking about Robin and Kyle over and over.

"Emma, sweetie, we're going to see *Daddy*," I keep reminding her, which works for about five minutes at a time before she seems to forget, like an amnesiac.

We pull into the massive concrete parking garage for Stonebridgers, and I'm pleased to see Zeke, a familiar face.

"Hey, Zeke," I say, flashing a broad smile. "Just here to visit my husband with the little one."

Zeke pulls out his white earbuds and peeks into the back window, giving Emma a big smile. He pulls on his ears and sticks out his tongue, making her giggle and shriek.

Then, he surprises me. "You're Arno's wife, right?"

"Yes," I reply, flushed and pleased that he somehow knows this, and remembers my face.

"He actually just left, like, five minutes ago."

"Oh!" I say, surprised. "Huh. I guess he ran back to the apartment for something."

Zeke shrugs. "Maybe. I'm not sure, ma'am."

"Hm, well, thank you, Zeke! I guess we won't be needing a spot today. I'll just drive over and try to catch him there."

We peel out of the parking garage, and I fire off a text to Arno, "Hey, babe, are you at the apartment? I've got a little surprise for you . . ."

Emma and I cruise down Atlantic Avenue and get lucky. A Mercedes-Benz SUV has just pulled out from a metered spot just up the street from the apartment building, One Atlantic Wharf. We pull into the open spot, and I give a little fist bump to the air.

"It's our lucky day, Emma! There's *never* any parking around here."

"Da-da," she says, in between thumb sucks.

I get Emma out of her car seat and smooth out her overalls. Brush her soft, downy hair from her eyes. She chews on her fist.

"No sticking our hands in our mouths today. Let's show Daddy what a big girl you are." I gently pull Emma's slobbery fist from her mouth and her eyes widen, threatening tears. I look away while she crams her hand back inside.

Oh well. Tomorrow's another day.

I scoop her into my arms and am astonished at how heavy she's gotten, how long her legs are suddenly.

"When did you get so big?" I ask her.

Emma drools in response.

It's a gorgeous October day, when Boston's at its very best: temperatures in the mid-60s, clear blue skies with fluffy cumulus clouds drifting across. A breeze coming up from the harbor, keeping everyone cool in the last few weeks when they can get away without heavy jackets.

We walk by food trucks hawking grilled cheese sandwiches and smoothies, gourmet french fries and fresh lobster rolls. The smell of melted cheese and buttery lobster flesh mingle in the air, and my stomach rumbles.

"Maybe Daddy will want to do a food-truck lunch with us, Em. We could take it down to the water and watch the ships roll by. Would you like that, sweetie?"

Emma ignores me, watching a woman with long red hair. She's walking parallel to us, headed in the same direction. Huge aviators shield her eyes, but she pauses midstep, looking over.

"Liz?"

"Cynthia?"

She's wearing a tight denim jumpsuit and five-inch snakeskin booties.

A gleaming diamond choker wraps around her throat. Always just a tad overdressed for any normal-person situation.

"What are you doing here?" she asks, just as Emma shrieks, "Cyn-see-uh!"

"Hi, Emma." Cynthia nods primly, as if Emma is just a very small adult. Then she turns back to me.

I tug at my sweater self-consciously to cover my gingham shirt. It matches Emma's overalls, and I suddenly feel slightly ridiculous.

"Oh, we just wanted to surprise Arno for lunch. I went to the Stonebridge office, but he wasn't there, so I just assumed he's grabbing something from our apartment . . . What about you, what are you doing here?"

She looks me up and down, as she always does. Runs her talonlike nails through her long red hair. "Oh, I was just in the neighborhood. Daddy actually has a condo near here." She pauses, cocks her head. "That's a very farmer-girl look you two have going today."

"Um, thanks. I think."

She fingers her diamond necklace, which catches the light and sparkles maddeningly.

I get the sense that we're being watched and scan the people milling about the food trucks. Then, I see it—Arno moving toward us with long, determined strides.

Cynthia's fingers fly from her necklace, and she gives a little wave. "Oh, hello, Arno!" She perches her aviators atop her head like a crown. "Fancy seeing you here! I just ran into your lovely wife and daughter. And how are you doing on this beautiful afternoon?"

"Hey, Cynthia," Arno says evenly, just as Emma screams, "*Da-da*!"

She reaches out her chubby arms, hands opening and closing, closing and opening. Arno scoops her up, plants a kiss on her nose.

"Hi, princess!"

Arno leans over to give me a kiss on the cheek. He looks a little worn-down and tired, but handsome as ever in slim-fit khakis and a white button-down. A navy blazer is tossed over his arm.

"How did you find us here?" I ask.

"I saw your text, sweetie. Figured you were probably parking nearby." He smiles, ruffles my hair.

"Well, I better get going . . ." Cynthia says, looking back and forth between us. "I'm meeting Daddy for lunch, and he does *not* like to wait." She pauses a second, as though considering saying something else.

"Good seeing you," I say without heart.

Emma gives something like a tiny wave.

"See you around the office," Arno says.

Cynthia turns and walks in the opposite direction, teetering ever so slightly in her ridiculous booties.

It's that feeling again, like a tickle in my throat I can't clear, a thought that darts across my mind like a mouse but is too quick for me to catch. A nagging.

I steal glances at Arno as we make our way across the warm pavement to a food truck selling creative iterations of grilled cheese: pizza grilled cheese, macaroni grilled cheese, maple-bacon grilled cheese.

Arno orders one of each and three ice-cold lemonades, and we sit on a wrought iron bench overlooking the harbor, just as I'd wanted.

Seagulls laugh overhead, swooping and diving at discarded french fries by a pier. Arno points out a huge tugboat and tries to explain to Emma that even though it looks small, it's strong, strong, strong and can pull the massive cargo ship in its wake. Emma's mouth hangs open, spit dripping onto her chin. Somehow, pizza sauce and dried mozzarella are already all over her gingham overalls.

When we're finished with our meal, the wind has picked up. I wrap Emma in my sweater. Arno says he has to get back to the office; that he's already been gone far too long, but he's so glad we visited him.

Twenty minutes later, Emma and I stop for gas at a grim little Sunoco off I-93 North. I'm holding my credit card in one hand, a filthy gas pump in the other, when it hits me.

Emma has never met Cynthia.

ACKNOWLEDGMENTS

I would like to first acknowledge the astounding amount of debt I owe to my agent extraordinaire, Helen Heller, who treated this book (and myself) with a level of warmth, care, and precision I wish for all debut authors.

I would also like to express my sincere gratitude to my editor, Shannon Criss, for her continual support, vision, and guidance, as well as to Henry Holt president and publisher Amy Einhorn for believing in this story. Many thanks to Molly Pisani for her eagle-eyed copyedits, Julia Ortiz for her editorial assistance, and Chris Sergio and the creative team at Holt for their beautiful cover art.

My life would be a lot less joyous without my friends, and I'd be entirely lost without the love and friendship of my siblings, Tara, Megan and Ryan, and honorary sibs, Kevin and Joe.

Thank you, Mom and Dad, for always encouraging me to bring the largest L.L.Bean tote bag to the library and thank you for cheering me on.

Can you shout-out your dogs here? I don't care, I'm going for it. Fig and Ziggy, my sweet, terrible, funny, wonderful companions. Thank you for adding levity to the darkest days. I could watch you two snuggle till the end of time.

To Heath, the peanut inside of me. You've already turned my world upside down, little one. I can't wait to tell you all of the best stories.

And, finally, to Nick, my most steadfast supporter and loving partner in this ridiculous adventure called life. Your calming presence is the only thing that settles this brain of mine long enough to put pen to page. I love you.

ABOUT THE AUTHOR

JUSTINE SULLIVAN was born and raised just outside of Baltimore, Maryland, where she failed to learn how to shuck a crab and never attended a single Orioles game. She did, however, discover a passion for reading at her local Harford County library. She went on to study English literature at the University of Delaware and then earned her master's in journalism from Boston University and has since spent a number of years working in both newsrooms and the world of branded content.

Justine lives outside of Boston with her husband and two terribly behaved dogs. *He Said He Would Be Late* is her debut novel.